Laurie Graham

A Humble Companion

A CIP catalogue record for this book is available
from the British Library.

Quercus

First published in Great Britain 2012 by Quercus Editions Ltd
This paperback edition published in 2013 by Quercus Editions Ltd

55 Baker Street
7th Floor, South Block
London W1U 8EW

PB ISBN 978 0 85738 783 7
EBOOK ISBN 978 0 85738 782 0

10 9 8 7 6 5 4 3 2 1

Printed and bound in Great Britain by Clays Ltd, St Ives plc

Typeset by Ellipsis Digital Limited, Glasgow

To Mr F. purveyor of tea and encouragement

PROLOGUE

We buried Sofy last week. I would have wished to be with her at the end but when a person takes such an age to die it's easy enough to be caught off guard. The message came that it was feared she could not last the day, and by the time I got to Kensington there was black crêpe on the bell knob and the chamber nurse was burning vinegar in a coal scuttle. I really had no place there. I wasn't family and I wasn't a servant. There was only one useful thing I could do and that was to make sure her last wishes were respected.

They turned out drawers and cupboards looking for her will while I sat at the door of her room like a grizzled old hound. If I'd allowed them to take her to Windsor she'd surely have haunted me the rest of my days. It was Mr Drummond who settled the matter. He came all the way from Charing Cross bearing a letter from his bank vault with Sofy's seal upon it. She wished to be laid to rest in the new garden cemetery at Kensal Green, exactly as I'd told them.

It was a modest funeral procession for the daughter of a king. There were no mutes, no plume bearers, just a hearse and six and a plain velvet pall. The Prince Consort was represented by an equerry, the King of Hanover and Lord Melbourne both sent their empty coaches, and I rode in the last mourning carriage with Dr Snow, who had attended her at the end, Mrs Martin, her French reader, and her dresser, Mrs Corcoran.

By the plainness of my costume and the limberness that speaks of an active life Dr Snow took me to be an elderly servant of some kind. He was an observant young man, which may be the best any of us can hope for in a physician. I corrected him gently. My position in Sofy's life was an unusual one, the result of a royal experiment: a radical notion dreamed up by the most unradical of kings, old George, that his daughter should have a playfellow, a humble companion plucked from the ranks of ordinary people so that she might have a better understanding of the world. I know very little of science but I believe the custom is never to dismiss an experiment as a failure but rather to salvage from it whatever lessons can be learned. In Sofy's case the lesson was that the world can only be understood by living in it. Nevertheless, a girl kept cloistered behind palace walls can certainly be happier for knowing she has a friend.

I was plucked carefully, of course, not from any random harvest of draymen's daughters or chimney-sweeping girls. There are degrees of humbleness, and Sofy was a Princess of the House of Hanover. Let's just say that when the search for a suitable girl began I was in a position to be noticed, and for that I had to thank a steward in the household of Sofy's brother George, Prince of Wales. I owed it all to the Comptroller and Clerk of His Royal Highness's Kitchens and Cellars — a hatcher, broker, deviser and contriver, a man of business, ever alert to ways in which he might assist his royal master and his royal connections might repay him at an attractive rate of interest — my father, Louis Welche.

My career as humble companion began in 1788, when I was thirteen and Sofy was eleven. I cannot say I excelled at it but I never did so badly that I was dismissed. The gulf between us, the fact of her royal birth, didn't go away. I suppose it never can, but somehow we reached across it. I was an only child, alone but not lonely; she suffered the loneliness of living in a vast family where everyone talked and no one listened. It's easy enough to see what I gave Sofy. I seasoned her dull daily fare with news of where I'd been and what I'd seen, and in return, she gave me her secrets, so you might say her friendship was more generous than mine.

My title of Humble Companion was never officially dispensed with. From time to time it was brought out and dusted off, usually when some Royal Highness thought I had forgotten my place, but Sofy and I became true friends very quickly and so we remained, except for a few quarrels, until we were both grey old ladies.

A pen can do a great deal of hurt. Miss Fanny Burney gave me that warning a lifetime ago, though she did allow that some people are too puffed up to feel the point of even the sharpest quill, or to recognize themselves, no matter how skilfully they're drawn. But Royalties are a particular case. They

3

have few hiding places and if they are wronged they must choose between having redress or licking their wounds in dignified silence. I believe Miss Burney was a naturally kinder person than I am, and perhaps the prospect of a royal pension influenced her. A hundred pounds a year for life might keep anyone discreet. In any event I always remembered her words. I have waited to tell what I know until most of those it concerns are in a better place and those that aren't . . . ? The Devil take them.

I am now in my seventy-fourth year. I've seen out three kings and a multitude of royal highnesses, and lived to see Victoria upon the throne, long life to her. But Sofy is gone. Now she's where gossip can't wound her and secrets can't stifle her. And so I shall tell her story.

1

My father wasn't always Louis Welche. He was born Ludwig Weltje, the son of a Utrecht gingerbread maker. My grandfather Weltje heard there was a better living to be made in Brunswick, so he walked to Hanover and married a girl from the Luneberg Heath. A willingness to move on in the interests of business was in the Weltje blood. Papi and his brother Christoff both left Hanover when they were hardly more than boys and made their way to London. Uncle Christoff was employed in the kitchens of the old Duke of Gloucester; Papi sold Jew biscuits and ginger cakes from a cart, and they saved every penny they earned until they had enough to open a pastry shop.

Weltje's became known for its good, plain fare: steak puddings with mustard gravy, mutton pies with caper relish, apple turnovers with cloves, and of course gingerbread – and as no Weltje money ever lay idle for a minute the profits were put to work in their next enterprise. They took over the lease of a chocolate house in St James's Street. The Coconut Tree had always catered to young men about town, and under my father's management it became quite the place to go.

The gaming tables were open until breakfast was served and a set of retiring rooms was kept for those who had drunk too deeply or gambled too rashly. That was how Papi gained the patronage of the Prince of Wales, and the friends who followed wherever he led. The Prince loved good food and a game of faro, and he appreciated the fatherly friendship of a discreet host: someone who turned a blind eye to a young man's follies and was willing to help him out of his financial embarrassments without any fuss. When the Prince attained his majority in 1783 and was given his own establishment in Pall Mall he didn't need to look far for a steward.

Uncle Christoff always said it was as well Papi was the one who'd been asked because he wouldn't have had the patience for it himself. It was one thing to be a cook, to stay below stairs and quietly, invisibly go about your business. A steward was a very different animal. He could be envied and resented by those under him and blamed and bullied by those above him, and when all was said and done he was still a servant, no matter how grand his title. But servitude didn't bother my father. He wore it lightly and used it cannily. All the butchers and vintners and grocers were eager to show their gratitude for a royal warrant, and the perquisites were substantial. The royal cinders and meat bones and oyster shells were Papi's to dispose of to the road menders, and we were kept very comfortable on the sale of once-used tea, and pork and beef drippings from the royal kitchens, and beeswax candles, sometimes less than half consumed. The Prince of Wales demanded fresh tapers every night.

My father liked comfort and plenty himself, but only according to what he could afford. I see now how carefully he covered his disdain for the Prince's wastefulness. He would never have permitted it in his own house. No son of his would have been allowed to grow up so extravagant, but my father had no son. There had been two boys, both stillborn, then my sister Eliza, then me. My parents' marriage bed was hardly blessed, and in the spring of 1788 it was dealt another blow. Eliza went to Uncle Christoff's house in the country to help Aunt Hanne with her sewing, and while she was there she caught the measles and died. Papi went alone to Hammersmith to bury her. My mother took to her bed.

Though Eliza was older than me by five years and was tall and rosy cheeked and gifted with a needle, her mind was trapped in perpetual childhood. It was a puzzle to know what to do with her and Mother hated the exertion of puzzles. Still, she loved Eliza very deeply so after she died it was ordained that she must never be spoken of again so as to spare Mother's nerves. That was when my terrible hunger began. I ate and ate but nothing filled me, and our neighbour Miss Tod, who made it her business to call on Mother every day and cheer her up with reports of murder and mayhem, remarked that I looked like something the mudlarks had dragged out of the river, bloated and ghastly.

'Don't take it amiss, Nellie,' she said. 'I only mention it out of concern. We don't want to lose you.'

From my earliest years I'd been warned against peering in mirrors. I'd formed the idea that it was as inadvisable as putting my hand in the fire, so I didn't look to see if what Miss Tod had said was true. But the next evening Papi announced that as it was time for him to go to Brighton to prepare the Prince of Wales's house for the season, he intended to take me with him to see if the sea air would do anything for me. I surmised that I must be looking very bad indeed.

First Mother feared it was madness to expose me unnecessarily to the dangers of travel. Then, after she had discussed it with her friends, she questioned whether Brighton was a suitable destination for any female who cared to keep their good name. As I recall, the strongest argument she could marshal was that an exceptionally high number of Brighton's lady residents offered French lessons. The significance of this piece of intelligence sailed straight over my twelve-year-old head. It seemed a feeble objection and, anyway, Papi always had the last word. I went to Brighton.

The furthest I had ever gone out of London was to Hammersmith, to my uncle's house. The idea of going to Brighton made me feel quite the intrepid traveller. I decided I must keep a journal, and what I began that summer I have kept up, more or less, ever since. From my first entry, June 22nd 1788, it seems I was impressed more by the variety of cakes available in the Brighton tea gardens and the number of novels stocked by the libraries than I was by my first sight of the sea. The sea shore was certainly a noisy place. The dippers shouted, their customers screamed, the horses whinnied to one another and the wheels of the bathing machines crunched over the pebbles. Still, the sea itself disappointed me. I had expected it to roar but all it did was sigh.

Brighton's salty waters were recommended as a remedy for a great number of ailments. Some people bathed in them, some drank them too. The waters were what had brought the Prince of Wales there in the first place. He had what Papi called 'the family complaint': inflammation of the glands, eruptions of the skin. Whether the Brighton waters did anything for him, I cannot say, but Mrs Fitzherbert had an establishment there too so, as I eventually came to realize, that was one royal itch that could be scratched.

When the Prince decided he would like to visit Brighton often and must therefore have a place of his own where he could stay, Papi went as harbinger, inspected various properties and leased a house he believed would be suitable. On one side, convenient for its principal entrance, was the London Road, on the other the pleasant meadows of the Steine sloped down to the sea. The house was plain but substantial, a kind of villa, private enough for a Royal Highness but close to the Castle Inn where the Prince's friends could put up. The Prince, who approved of Papi's choice but could never bear to leave any lily ungilded, set about enlarging and improving it at once. It was nothing then to what it became, but to my young eyes it seemed like a delicious house. It was wide and low, cream on the outside, with some pillars and balconies, and on the inside, oh the inside … My journal records my impressions:

June 25th 1788

Today I saw the Prince of Wales's rooms. His library is the colour of butter, his cabinet has a sky-blue ceiling and he sleeps under a sea-green tent made of silk. I suppose a prince may have any colours he pleases. His Royal Highness was expected today and I was afraid he would come and catch us looking at his ac-commodations but Papi said the Prince never arrives when he says he will.

We were lodged in a little cottage across the stable yard and my instructions were that if by chance I should ever find my-self in the Royal Presence I should curtsey, lower my eyes and speak only if spoken to. I was also to remember that my given name is Cornelia. All very well, my father explained, to be called Nellie in the bosom of my family, but in higher circles it might be regarded as a name more suitable for a carthorse. As it happened I was in the kitchens, trailing behind Papi and dipping my finger in anything he stopped to taste, when the Prince appeared.

The very idea of a prince in a kitchen was so extraordinary and he came upon us so suddenly and billowed over me, tall and portly and smelling of oil of jessamine, that I quite for-got everything I'd been told. He asked my name. I said, 'Nel-lie'. And I heard Papi sigh through his great purple nose.

I see that the Prince's waistcoat was pink, worked with

flowers in gold thread. Strange, if you had asked me to recall it I would have said it was sapphire blue, so thank heavens for journals. I also noted that he had several chins which spilled out over his neckcloth, and soft curls, like a baby's hair. What I remember with great clarity is how I was emboldened by the gentleness of him. His eyes did dart away of course, before they settled back on me. It's always the way when people look at me for the first time. I wasn't offended by it. Even at that young age I understood that people couldn't help themselves.

He said, 'Did your father make a pastry cook of you yet, Nellie?'

I said, 'No sir. Papi says I have baker's hands. Too warm for pastry.'

Papi pinched my arm. When Royalties address you, you're supposed to reply succinctly and then shut up, but I suppose I thought I should never meet the Prince of Wales again so I might as well say all I wanted.

I said, 'I can balance a ledger though, and write stories.'

'Can you, by Jupiter! What kind of stories? Do they have battles in them and adventures?'

'Only adventures, sir, not battles, because I don't really know how a battle goes.'

'Well,' he said, 'never mind. An adventure story can be a jolly fine thing.'

He looked at me directly and steadily then. It takes most people longer. Some never manage it.

So I said, 'I was born this way, sir.'

Better to say it and be done. I was in trouble anyway.

'Splendid girl,' he said, very, very quietly. Which fills me up just to think of it. I believe I could count on the fingers of one hand the number of times I was ever called 'splendid'.

He had begun to walk away when he asked my age and Papi rushed in, trying to save me from myself.

'Only tvelf, Highness. Still a child.'

But I sensed I didn't need saving. I spoke up and said I was nearly thirteen. And the Prince said the King wished Princess Sofia to have a playfellow, an ordinary girl with good sense and a cheerful spirit. Papi read his master very well. He saw the Prince was taken with me and seized the moment. He assured him I had cheerfulness and good sense in buckets, that I knew my place – which was wishful thinking – and sang tolerably well, which was a downright lie. Also, that I had been inoculated against the smallpox.

The Prince said, 'Then she might do very well. I shall propose her to their Majesties. She might go to Kew. Now sir, I have a great longing for a smoked herring.'

I had no idea what or where Kew was but Papi, suddenly rather delighted with me, explained. Kew was a village, across the river from Chiswick and more remote even than Hammersmith. Their Majesties had a palace there with gardens and a menagerie of animals from Africa and India, and the younger princesses lived there in the summer with their governesses. Princess Sofia was one of the Prince of Wales's very many sisters and she was, as near as Papi could remember, a year or two younger than me. He was excited, I could tell. He drummed his fingers, the way he did when he was about to make a good bargain, and he told an under-cook to coddle me two fresh eggs. The matter of my forgetting to be Cornelia was never mentioned and after a week of sea air he escorted me back to London like a trophy. I was a splendid girl, endowed with good sense and a cheerful spirit. The Prince of Wales had as good as said so.

Weeks passed and no word came from Kew. It had evidently been decided that a girl named like a carthorse was unsuitable company for a princess and I had no one to blame but myself. I'd looked forward to seeing a real tiger, not to say a real princess too, and I'd looked forward to eating my fill at royal banquets, but my disappointment faded. I'd been warned often enough not to expect too much of life. Mother set me the task of sorting her button box and reading to her from *Belmont und Constanza*. Then, at the end of August, I was summoned. I was to attend a garden tea party and stay one night at Kew Palace.

It was as though a great emergency had been declared. Everyone went to their post. Mother summoned her war cabinet of Miss Tod, Mrs Romilly and Mrs Lavelle, and it was decided that as I was to be the guest of Princess Sofia I must wear watered silk at the very least. Papi said I was not a *guest* but a possible future *companion*, and that the princesses lived very simply so I must in no wise outshine them. Guest or companion, for a whole week I was the household's best darling. Twyvil fed me the top of the milk, Susan our Necessary Maid did the best she could with sugar water and coaxed my hair into half-hearted curls, and Mother denounced Papi as the meanest old *geizhals* that ever came out of Brunswick. But Papi was our Commander-in-Chief because there was no gainsaying he knew the best way to go on around the Royalties. I went to Kew dressed in plain cotton lawn.

2

When the great day came Mother had a watery flux brought on by the strain of the preparations and Papi was called away urgently to Carlton House where a hog, bought for roasting, had turned green. I travelled to Kew in the gig with only Morphew for company. Morphew was our general outdoors man, trusted to lock the street door when Papi was away at night. He was also our footman, coachman, and the only member of the household who could master the Beast, our sly, biting, kicking grey. There was a cantankerous streak to Morphew too – I suppose the Beast recognized it had met its match – but he was honest, he worked hard, and he seemed to have no one in the world except us so employing him gave Mother an agreeable flush of benevolence with very little effort on her part.

I remember feeling relieved about the arrangements for my journey to Kew. Travel terrified Mother and I was glad to be spared two hours of her vapours. I had my own reasons to be nervous but I was distracted from them by two of Morphew's peculiarities. First, there was the yellow horsehair wig he insisted on wearing no matter how many times he was offered a superior substitute. Morphew's wig appeared to have a life of its own. It was always on the move, one minute on the back of his head, the next sunk down low over one eyebrow. I would sometimes play a little game, closing my eyes for a count of one hundred and guessing where the wig would be when I looked again. Better yet, Morphew could read tolerably well, and he provided a continuous narration of our journey.

'William Wilking, supplier of anchors. I knew a Bill Wilking years back, worked for a maltster in Southwark but I heard he drownded, so that won't be him. Fresh Mackerel. Ha! Fresh when they put the notice out. I wouldn't trust a mackerel if I harn't seen it caught. Merritt's Wholesale Spermaceti. That worn't there last time I come along this way. That used to be Joan Badger's. Hams and Tongues Cured. I love a good pickled tongue. Wholesale spermaceti, though, they say that's a profitable line to be in. Now Miss Nellie, do you look to your left you'll observe the Turk's Head alehouse, as used to be the Greyhound and afore that it was the Two Magpies ...'

A blind man could have travelled with Morphew and missed very little of the passing sights.

They were building a new bridge across the Thames at Chiswick. It ran close alongside the old one and by the time we got to the Surrey side I was all dust from the stone-cutting. Morphew kindly stopped the gig at the pump on Kew Green and wetted a handkerchief to wipe my face. He tried to put my mind at rest too, that I shouldn't be nervous about meeting Princess Sofia or any other royal person. His argument ran something like this:

'They only chance to be royals, see? On account of their hangcestors. If you was to follow it back, all they did was help theirselves to a passel of land. Worn't theirn to start with, was it? Third day God made the dry land but He didn't say "this passel is for Hanover and this one's for Stuart", did He? No. They just come along and took it. Then this one married that one, or they might start a bit of a war. And all the time they're clambering higher and setting up as kings because they've got the land. As was made for all of us. In the Beginning. But they're hoomans, same as me and you. They might have thrones under them but they're still sitting on their rumps, if you'll pardon my language. And that's all you need to remember.'

I felt much better after that. Papi had reassured me too, though he had been more specific about why I had no reason to be anxious. Only the three youngest princesses were in residence at Kew: Mary, Sophia and Amelia. The King and Queen were gone into Worcestershire to take the Malvern waters and the elder princesses with them. Nevertheless I had committed to memory all the names of that enormous family, even the brothers, though at the time it seemed unlikely I ever should meet any of them. Their lives were like chalk and cheese, for the princes were never at home and the princesses rarely left it.

17

The eldest I had already seen. George, Prince of Wales, with the pretty curls and the perfumed handkerchief. After him came Frederick, Duke of York, who was a soldier, and Prince William that they called 'Billy'. He was on the high seas, commander of a frigate in the King's Navy. Next came the eldest of the princesses, whose name was Charlotte but never was called anything but 'Royal', and after her Augusta and Elizabeth, but with Prince Edward somewhere in between. I never was quite sure where he fitted in but as he was away in foreign parts I didn't trouble myself to find it out. Prince Ernest was the next, then Augustus and Adolphus, who was called Dolly and still is. Then there was Mary that was called Minny, and Sophia that was called Sofy. There had been two more princes born after Sofy: Octavius and Alfred, but they had both died. Princess Amelia was the last, the youngest of fifteen children.

A king needs an heir or two, certainly, and some daughters to be his consolation, but why so many? Miss Tod had a theory which she shared with me in later years. The King's stubborn fidelity was to blame. If only he had taken lovers like any normal monarch, the poor Queen might have been spared twenty years of relentless childbed.

Morphew set me down outside a square red house. Two unsmiling little faces watched me from a downstairs window and a plain, brisk young woman came out to meet me. She was Miss Gouldsworthy, an under-governess. For two pins

I'd have jumped back into the gig and begged Morphew to drive me home. At the time it didn't occur to me that Princess Sofy might be as apprehensive as I was. The King had said she should have a Humble Companion and one had been chosen for her, but she had no idea what she might be getting. And as she told me, long after, Amelia had played on her nerves all morning, predicting I would be barefoot and not know my letters. So Sofy was beside herself with joy when she saw I wore shoes. There was, though, the no small matter of the mark on my face. But princesses are trained from the cradle to master themselves, to appear serene and resolute no matter what they are thinking. After the first shocked flicker of her eyes Sofy was warm and welcoming.

I remember saying, 'Didn't they tell you?'

And she just took my hand.

There was a difference of six years between Sofy and Amelia, and for several days they had been reduced to each other's company because Princess Minny was confined to bed with an abscess of the shoulder. Little wonder Sofy was so glad to see me.

My diary entry, made on my return to London, makes me blush now at its priggishness:

September 10th 1788

P. Sofy has light brown hair and big grey eyes like the P. of Wales. She has hardly any books & plays with a doll's cradle v. inferior to the one I had. I suggested we dress in bed sheets and act

out scenes but Sofy is qte cowed by the governesses and said she
was sure we were not permitted to unmake beds. P. Amelia is a
brattish child but v. pretty.

In those days I imagined princesses had to be pretty, that if they weren't they'd be locked away in a dungeon. Amelia was horribly fascinated by me, following us around. Sofy told her not to stare.

I said, 'I don't mind stares. I'm accustomed to it.'

Amelia said, 'Then I'm very sorry for you. I'm sure I couldn't bear it. I suppose you're very, very poor too?'

And bearing in mind Morphew's revelation that Royalties were merely 'hooman' and I shouldn't be intimidated by them I told her I was certainly not very, very poor. We had two drawing rooms at home and my father kept his own berlin.

'Well,' she said, 'I think you *are* poor but you don't know it. You're the daughter of a cook and we have to treat you kindly. Gouly said so.'

Gouly was their name for Miss Gouldsworthy. She was spinsterish, and as blank a page as any royal servant does well to be. I see now that her rank was uncomfortably middling. She had some authority − over music tutors and drawing masters and dressers and housemaids − but she was overseen by Peggy Planta, the principal governess, and by Lady Finch, whose word was law whenever the Queen was absent and sometimes even when she wasn't.

Before I left home I'd received any amount of direction

concerning my comportment at Kew, in particular not to plunge in with every remark that came into my head, but rather to watch and learn. Fine counsel indeed from my mother, who was rarely so selfish as to keep a thought to herself and it was, anyway, advice I hardly needed. My natural preference has always been to listen. But Amelia's error was so great it had to be corrected.

I said, 'My father isn't a cook. He's Comptroller to the Prince of Wales.'

Sofy said, 'Don't mind Amelia. She's a very little girl.'

And Amelia declared that she would be five next week and she hoped that if she was ever obliged to have a Humble Companion it would be someone more agreeable than me.

Several questions troubled me during me those first few hours at Kew. I wondered what house I was in and when the coach would come to take us to Kew Palace. There was also the promised tea party. My stomach was growling in anticipation of royal cakes, but I saw no sign of any preparations. Then the rain began.

I said, 'What about the garden party? It'll be ruined.'

Sofy said, 'Not at all. We can have it in the schoolroom,' and she set about arranging cups of water and plates of torn paper for their dolls. We had nothing to eat till dinner was served at five o'clock: plain broth, cold meats and soft, year-old Worcester apples. Then we were obliged to be usefully occupied until bedtime. Amelia threaded beads and Sofy embroidered a tray cloth while Mademoiselle Montmollin read to them in French, and Gouly asked them questions to see that they had paid attention and understood what they'd heard. I had no sewing and I understood no French, though I knew the sound of it well. On Dean Street you were as likely to hear it as you were to hear English. Amelia seized on my lack of French as further evidence of my poverty.

I said, 'I know German.'

'Oh, so do we,' she said. '*Everyone* knows German.'

Sofy said, 'I expect Nellie forgot to bring her sewing.'

The truth was, Nellie wasn't gifted with a needle, for no matter how much Nellie was rapped across her knuckles she still favoured her left hand, which as every sensible person knows is the Devil's hand. So Nellie spoke up, before something was found for her from the mending bag. I said that I preferred not to sew because it reminded me of my dead sister and Miss Gouly replied that industry was a better cure for grief than sentimental moping and it was a terrible thing if I was allowed to sit idle at home.

I said, 'I don't sit idle. I run important errands and help my Papi with his receipt books and I read to my mother every night.'

I might have added that I was only obliged to read to Mother till her head drooped, and if it was a book I didn't care for I'd read it in a slow, droning fashion so that sleep would overtake her quickly. As soon as she began to snuffle I was free to creep away to the morning room and hide there, writing my own stories until my candle was spent.

The hours passed and no carriage came to take us away. The sky was still light when Gouly instructed us to wash our

22

faces and put on our nightgowns. Sofy and I shared a bed in Amelia's room so that Princess Minny shouldn't be disturbed. The news from the sickroom was that she was still in much pain in spite of being cupped but bore it as bravely as ever. By all accounts Princess Minny was a saint as well as a great beauty.

I waited until Amelia was asleep before I dared to ask Sofy my most urgent question: was this really a royal palace?

She said, 'I think so. It's called Kew Palace. Why do you ask?'

I said, 'Because it's just a house. I think it should be bigger, don't you, to be called a palace?'

'I don't know,' she said. 'It's quite big enough for us, don't you think?'

I tried a different approach and suggested it didn't seem quite *royal* enough for a king.

'Oh I *see*,' she said. 'But the King and Queen don't live here. When they come to Kew they stay in the white house, across the lawn. Royal and Augusta and Elizabeth stay there too. Then Lady Finch has a place on Ferry Lane, and there are plenty of houses on the green for the princes to live in if they ever come, so we really manage very well.'

I didn't want to appear boastful but I could have told her that my family's house was much better appointed than Kew. Our windows didn't rattle. We had well-stuffed chairs and a new flushing water closet, and fruit tarts at teatime every day if we wanted them. I tried to let her down lightly.

I said, 'I suppose there may be different kinds of palace. I saw the Prince of Wales's house at Brighton and it was nothing like this.'

'Oh, tell about it,' she begged. 'Only whisper, because if Amelia hears you she's sure to blabber and the King dislikes talk about the Prince's houses. They cost a very great deal of money.'

'Yes, and some of it borrowed from my father,' I might have said.

Sofy was enthralled by my account of the Marine Pavilion, especially the card room with its scarlet walls and the maraschino cherries that were dipped in chocolate and set in little dishes here and there. She said she'd like to see it for herself but would never be allowed.

I said, 'When you're of age you can. Then you may go anywhere you please.'

'No, Nellie,' she said, 'you're mistaken. Not if the King doesn't wish it.'

That was my first lesson regarding Sofy's lot. She could only do what the King permitted. She had to live in bleak houses, eat yesterday's mutton, and wait for a German cousin to offer her marriage, but only after four of her sisters had been suited before her.

She said, 'What games shall we play tomorrow?'

I asked if we might go to the menagerie, to see the tiger, but there was no tiger at Kew. It had died.

'Royal says it was because they didn't find it a husband, so it grew sad and pined away.'

The Princess Royal might have been speaking from her

heart: twenty-two and still not established. She'd a long while yet to wait too, thwarted and kept a maid because this one didn't suit the King and that one didn't suit the Queen. A lonely tiger had at least had the option of refusing its food.

I couldn't sleep that night, for the silence. In Soho Square there was always some comforting racket to lull you. When the sound of carriage wheels began to subside the night watch started up, and when the night watch had called his last hour the milk maid and the night-soil men began clattering about. Kew was like a graveyard.

We did visit the menagerie the next morning. Miss Gouly allowed it on condition we went equipped with paper and pencils and the guidance of Mr Wuppert the drawing master. There were few moments of idleness for Sofy, or even for Amelia who was really still a very little girl. The hours were filled, the day's activities were preordained, the year portioned out; this month at Kew, that month at Windsor. Time was killed before it could give birth to any dangerous whimsies.

I'd had some schooling myself – Papi had taught me to add a column of figures, Mother had done her best with me on the spinet and the rest I'd learned from Miss Barbauld's *Lessons for Children* – but my education had been administered quickly, like a draught of senna, not dragged out for the sake of keeping me occupied. There was no need. I wasn't the kind of girl to get into mischief or to lollop on a couch, sighing with boredom. I could be helpful if needed, and when not required I had the gift of becoming invisible and entertaining myself.

25

The more I learned about the Royalties the more I thought my own family's way of doing things vastly superior.

Even the menagerie didn't impress me. I noted:

. . . pheasant and peafowl and an elk which is a mighty kind of deer sent from Canada. Also a striped horse from Africa, called a quagga. We were not allowed to stroke it in case it kicked. P. Sofy said she hoped it would soon have a baby. I think she is old enough to know a quagga cannot have a baby if she doesn't have a husband. A surgeon called Mr Hawkins attended Princess Minny and lanced her abscess. Mrs Chevely who is her nurse said she didn't cry out even once. Sofy gave me a fairing of a milkmaid and P. Amelia gave me a hair ribband because Sofy told her she had been unkind to me, refusing to kiss me goodbye. I don't know if I was found suitable as a Humble Companion. I should like to be Sofy's friend but I don't much care to go to Kew again. Mother told Miss Tod I came home with bites and now it's all around the square that the Royalties have bed bugs.

3

It was late October before I was summoned again, to be present at the celebration of Sofy's eleventh birthday at Windsor. Whatever test had been set me, I had apparently passed it. My trunk was prepared, this time with a silk gown as well as a woollen one, and Mother was triumphant. Nellie Welche, invited to a Royal Highness's birthday! Then the King was indisposed, the Royalties delayed their departure for Windsor and my gowns were taken out of the trunk. They were put back when he was reported to be a little improved, taken out again when he was sufficiently unwell to be taking laudanum and out they stayed – until it was confirmed that the Queen and the Princesses had finally shifted from St James's and the King had followed on after attending a levee. On the morning of All Hallow's Eve Morphew drove me out to Windsor in the berlin.

The news sheets said His Majesty was suffering from a bilious form of gout but Papi said more likely he had the marsh ague, for he'd heard the King had been seen wading in the river at Kew to talk to the basket weavers who lived on

Lot's Eyot. It was certainly true that when I got to Windsor the King was drinking cinchona in peppermint water and feeling much better.

There was a castle at Windsor, that much I knew, and I was thrilled to see that it had towers and battlements and arrow slits. Unlike Kew Palace, it conformed to my idea of what a castle should be. But the castle wasn't my destination. In those days only the Prince of Wales ever lodged there. Such other rooms as were habitable were occupied by tenants who had tenancies for life and therefore, disobligingly, lived to be a hundred. The rest of the castle was in a shocking state of disrepair. Papi said if it were his he'd have had it pulled to the ground and the land built upon, but the King loved Windsor for its hunting and its venerable history and so had begun a scheme to restore it, little by little.

Meanwhile the living arrangements were much like those at Kew, with the King and Queen and older Princesses in one house, just outside the castle walls, and the younger Royal Highnesses in another close by. Their numbers dictated it and Sofy welcomed it, for who would want to be under the eye of a Queen every minute of the day?

The Princesses were all present on that occasion. I know because I critiqued them:

November 1st 1788
    P. Royal is 22. She has a thick waist and never smiles.

Poor Royal. No Wonder. She wanted a husband and she

needed one, for until she was matched there were no prospects for her sisters, and there were certainly husbands enough to choose from. Mecklenburg and Brandenburg and Saxony had princes by the cartload. Royal's problem was that the King couldn't bear to part with her.

P. Augusta is jolly with v. red cheeks. She is a great taker of walks, whatever the weather. P. Elizabeth has dark hair and dimples. I think she is the prettiest. P. Minny is pretty too but v. thin.

I hadn't wanted to like Minny, praised as she'd been by Miss Gouly as a paragon of sweetness and accomplishment, but I found I did like her and I still do. The famous beauty of the family, with the voice of a nightingale. You'd never think it to see her now, more shrunk and lined even than I am and as tough as a bone button. Minny observes little things, though not unkindly. As we grew to know one another, if she was amused by something that had escaped everyone else's notice she would look to see if I had caught it too and raise a quizzical eyebrow. She's the last of the sisters left now, sitting in her merlin chair with her memories.

That Sunday we trooped up to the castle for morning prayers, with Her Majesty and Royal leading the way and all of them in enormous hooped skirts, quite out of fashion. It was my first sighting of the Queen and the Queen's first sighting of me.

'Ach!' she said, 'poor child. Vot a face! Ken nussink be done?'

I might have said the same of her. She still wore her hair high and was as ugly as a turbot, sallow and stooped, with no neck to speak of, which must have been a great disadvantage for a queen with so many fine necklaces at her disposal. I was tall for my age so we were able to inspect each other eye to eye and, though I learned to dread encounters with her, that first day I felt bold. If she didn't like me, I thought, let her send me back to Soho Square. It's common knowledge that companions are liable to be ill-used, but at least I wasn't one of those unfortunate creatures with no home to retreat to. Besides, I'd heard Sofy and Minny mimicking her, and if they had so little respect for her I saw no reason why I should care for her good opinion.

The King was a different matter. They all adored him and, well, he was the King. Even my father, who believed in progress and enterprise and was in the service of the Prince of Wales, even Papi esteemed King George. But that Sunday I was spared the ordeal of being inspected by the King because his legs were gouty and he was feverish again, so on the advice of his physician, he kept to his bedchamber.

After prayers we went to Upper Lodge for a breakfast of hot oatmeal and there I saw Miss Burney, the author of *Evelina* that Mother had once tried to read but had found too facetious. Miss Burney was a member of the Queen's household, an assistant Keeper of the Robes. I imagined some terrible reversal must have forced her to leave off authoring and become a servant. I longed to speak to her, but at the Queen's table conversation was by Her Majesty's invitation only. The Royalties were hemmed in by many silly rules but this was one of the most regrettable, for the Queen was no judge of wit. Quite the opposite. Unerringly she turned to dullards and left people with lively minds to stew in silence.

It became my great hope to see Miss Burney again, perhaps even to speak to her, because she had been a real authoress, even if her fortunes were shockingly reduced. On Sofy's birthday she appeared at Lower Lodge with the gift of a crewel-work heartsease pansy, framed in wood, and Sofy, dear soul, showed her the book that had been my gift to her: *The Queen's Quagga*, written and illustrated by Cornelia Welche. I had decided 'Cornelia' looked handsomer than 'Nellie' for a book cover.

Miss Burney looked it over most carefully. 'My compliments, Cornelia Welche,' she said. 'This is a fine piece of work.'

Which set my heart thumping and robbed me entirely of my voice and all the questions I had planned to ask her.

Sofy said, 'We call her Nellie.'

And Amelia said, 'She's Sofy's humble companion and there's nothing can be done about her face except to paint it with ceruse when she is growed a little older.'

Miss Burney said, 'I hope she will not. A young face should be left fresh and natural.'

Then Miss Gouly tried to hush Amelia but Amelia wouldn't be hushed.

'Oh, but Burney,' she said, 'the Queen says Nellie must paint it for if she don't she'll frighten the horses.'

My face was on fire but not because of Amelia. I was burning with happiness because Miss Fanny Burney had called my book 'a fine piece of work'.

Sofy stared at her slippers and Minny threw a ball of paper at Amelia. Miss Burney bobbed a curtsey and hurried away. She almost always was in a hurry. When you were a Keeper of the Robes you never knew when the Queen might require you for her toilette. How terrible, I remember thinking, to have no time to call your own.

Miss Burney had no sooner left when the Prince of Wales arrived, with gifts of a clockwork parakeet and a necklace of seashells. He was accompanied by Frederick, Duke of York, who wore a bob wig and a coat that was far too tight. He giggled like a girl, *and* he had forgotten to bring a birthday gift. Then at three o'clock Lady Finch came to escort the Royal Highnesses to Upper Lodge for Sofy's birthday dinner with the King and Queen, and I was left to dine with Miss Gouly, Mademoiselle Montmollin and Mrs Chevely, a poor widow, who had been the nursery nurse and was kept on out of charity, and against the day any of them should fall sick.

We ate in silence until I said, 'It seems very odd to me, to invite a friend to your birthday and then go to dinner without her.'

Gouly and Mrs Che looked at each other as though the cat

32

had coughed up a fur ball. Which of them should deal with it? It fell to Mrs Chevely, whose manner was less severe, perhaps because it was my first offence.

She said, 'You mistake your position, Nellie. You're a companion, not a friend. Do you understand the distinction?'

I said, 'I know I'm not paid.'

Another fur ball.

I was sent to the school room to consider whether I was suitably grateful for the great honour done me. My mind though ran on other things. I wanted Sofy to return, to tell me what they'd had for dessert and who had said what. I waited and waited but she and Minny and Amelia slipped back into the house without my hearing them and went straight to their beds. Miss Gouly sent a maid to tell me I should do likewise. I found Sofy weeping and when I asked her why, she wept all the more.

'I cannot tell you,' was all she'd say. 'I cannot.'

And I, fool that I was, couldn't leave it at that but had to start guessing what was troubling her.

I said, 'Is it the Illustrious Personage?'

That was what they called the Queen when they made fun of her.

'Don't be disrespectful, Nellie,' she said, and cried all the more. 'Poor, poor Mama.'

That was how I learned that though it was acceptable to laugh *with* Royalties it was not permitted to aim a solo barb *at* Royalties. I fled down the back stairs and out of the house. I thought I would run away from Windsor and never return, but in my haste I hadn't put on my warm joseph or taken my change purse which contained two shillings and six pence. It was dark and an icy wind was tossing the trees. I believe I should have frozen to death if Miss Burney hadn't come upon me.

'Cornelia Welche!' she said. 'What do you do out of doors without a coat?'

I told her I was quitting my position as Humble Companion and asked her which was the road for London. She said it would be the greatest pity for a promising author to have her throat cut by a footpad before she had begun to make her name in the world, and she wrapped her mantle around my shoulders and took me to her little chamber at Upper Lodge and gave me a dish of tea.

I learned then that Miss Burney had had published not one novel but *two*, and though she was presently unable to write a third, kept as she was in a permanent dither by the Queen – forgotten for hours, sent for with great urgency, dismissed, not needed after all – she still wrote a journal. When I asked her if she thought she would ever write more books she said, 'Oh yes. Writers, you know, never stop, no matter how many obstacles life throws in their path or how much publishers plead with them. I'm afraid it's an incurable vice. Now, tell me why you planned to run away.'

I recounted my unhappy day. I said, 'I thought I was going on quite well but now it seems I was mistaken. Well, better if they find someone else.'

She said she understood how difficult it was to judge

34

distance with the Royalties, that their lives were fixed and narrow in ways we couldn't begin to imagine, but whatever Mrs Chevely might say, Sofy had as much need of a friend as of a humble companion.

I said, 'I don't see why. I've never had a friend. I don't even have a sister any more and Sofy has five.'

She said, 'But you have an inner life that she does not. And if you knew what occurred this afternoon you would feel nothing but compassion for her.'

And I said, 'But I don't know. So how can I?'

Miss Burney had a long nose and a trembling watchfulness, like a little woodland creature. In later years, when I learned what became of her, I concluded that it must have been living with the Royalties that made her seem so timid because after she left the Queen's service she lived her life with the courage of a lion.

She thought for a while, considering how much to tell me. Then she related the afternoon's events in a very low voice. First, she said, the King, who was a stickler for punctuality, had come very late to the dinner table and in a state of great agitation. He wouldn't sit or eat or drink but wanted only to pace about and talk and talk and would not be calmed by anyone, even when his voice began to fail. Later I heard it whispered between housemaids that his breeches had been unbuttoned too and spittle had foamed from his mouth, but Miss Burney omitted that. She spoke only of his agitation. He had kissed the Prince of Wales and clasped him to his bosom, then, in the space of five minutes, thrown him roughly across the room and called him an idler and a glutton. The Queen had wept, the Prince of Wales had wept, then Fred York had joined in. It had taken the best efforts of Royal and Augusta to persuade the King to retire. Sir George Baker, the physician, had been sent for, and the King was to be blistered if he would only stand still long enough for the mustard plaster to be applied to his head.

I asked her what they called the King's affliction and she said it didn't have or need a name because it was not to be spoken of. And then I did feel for Sofy. Since my sister's death I understood what it was to live with sadness walled up.

An Assistant Keeper of the Robes only merited a tiny fire in her grate but I'd have sat by it happily for hours. Nellie Welche in conversation with Miss Fanny Burney.

She said, 'We must pray tomorrow brings happier news. And you know, there's a silver lining to the cloud. This evening you and I are both excused our duties. We should put our time to good use. Do you have a candle? Do you have paper? I can give you paper.'

It was her gentle way of getting rid of me before I took up any more of her precious free time. She insisted she must see me back to Lower Lodge but we hadn't taken two steps before we saw the flicker of storm lanterns and heard faint voices calling 'Nellie' over the roar of the gale. I had been missed, and two outdoorsmen had been sent out to bring back Sofy's humble companion, dead or alive.

4

Next morning the wind still howled along the passages and blew wet leaves against the window panes. This meant I was spared, yet again, the threat of being made to ride a horse. All the princesses rode, though neither Minny nor Elizabeth cared for the activity and gave it up at the first opportunity. Sofy was a great enthusiast though, and hoped to make one of me, but it had been left too late. I had seen enough of our own Beast and heard enough of broken necks to know that I could never trust a horse.

Lower Lodge was a comfortless house. The schoolroom chimney smoked, the windows let in draughts and the coals gave off no heat. Sofy had me read aloud to them again from the book I had written for her birthday. It concerned a quagga kept by a queen who thought it a very boring creature until she discovered, quite by chance, that it had the gift of speech. Being a well-bred quagga it knew that in the presence of a majesty it must speak only when spoken to. When the Queen realized how special her quagga was she wouldn't be parted from it, demanding that it entertain her night and day and only allowing it to sleep when she did. But quaggas require a great deal of sleep, in deep litter made from thistledown. They are not at all suited to chintz coverlets, and being prodded awake by a jewelled sceptre makes them very cross.

Eventually the Queen's quagga was so desperate for relief it told an untruth: that in its homeland of Muscadonia diamonds lay on the streets, as common as pebbles. The Queen, who was always eager for more diamonds, insisted on the quagga taking her there immediately. They travelled through the centre of the earth, which the quagga knew to be the fastest route, but when they popped up in Muscadonia the Queen discovered that the diamonds the quagga had spoken of were playing-card diamonds. Worse still, the only thing to eat in Muscadonia was liquorice, which was the Queen's least favourite thing. So she hurried home vowing that no quagga should ever set hoof in her kingdom again and the quagga was reunited with her brothers and sisters and slept for a year.

I read it in the voices I had imagined, wondering if I'd be accused again of mocking Her Majesty, but Sofy and Amelia seemed not to recognize anything treasonable in my sketching of a whimsical queen. Minny caught it, I'm sure, but she was preoccupied. The topic of the previous day's events hung in the air but no one spoke of it. Miss Gouly came in and had us name countries she pointed to on a globe, and when Miss Gomm, the other under-governess, came to the door to beg a quick word, she greeted her with forced cheerfulness. They whispered in the corridor.

Royal and Augusta, we heard, were with the Queen. Elizabeth came and went between Upper Lodge and the schoolroom. At eleven o'clock the word was that Thursday's Drawing Room at St James's Palace would not take place. But at noon the King was sufficiently restored to say he would like to go for an airing in the park and Princess Augusta might accompany him. Then Augusta was sent away because the King had changed his mind. It was the Princess Royal he most particularly wished to speak to.

This intelligence acted like a spark on dry tinder. If the King had something to say to Royal it must concern a prospective husband. Names were brought out, weighed and found wanting. Oldenburg was too ancient, Friedrich of Prussia looked like a bloodhound. Amelia said it had better not be the Duke of Bedford because she had chosen him for herself, which provoked the first laughter of the day, and the last. Soon after that we were drawn to the window by the sound of raised voices.

The Princess Royal was seated in the King's chaise but the King wouldn't keep his seat beside her. He walked about and conversed with the postillion, or perhaps he was talking to himself, for his gaze was directed always at the ground. He climbed into the carriage again and immediately climbed out. The Vice-Chamberlain came running with two pages, and then the physician, as fast as his spindly old legs would carry him, and they ushered the King back to Upper Lodge in a most unkingly fashion. His agitation of the brain had returned.

Hours passed without news. The little we did learn was told us by Miss Gouly and only after whispered consultations with Lady Finch, the arbiter of what was fit for our ears. Another physician had been sent for and a surgeon and the King was to be bled to reduce his racing pulse. At Upper Lodge all music and loud voices were forbidden and the celebrations for Princess Augusta's birthday next day were postponed. Straw was brought out to muffle the noise of carriage wheels in the street but then, on Royal's orders, it was taken away without being put down. She had stepped forward, quite out of her usual character, and ruled that it was enough for the house to be kept silent and that there was no need to draw the townspeople's attention to the King's indisposition. It was a private matter.

But a king is never a private matter. Whatever the King did, and even then I understood there was more to it than sitting on a throne with a crown on his head, clearly he could not do it if his mind was deranged. There were ministers to see and papers to be signed. The Queen couldn't take his place because the King would not wish it, and she was anyway greatly indisposed herself. This we had from Mrs Chevely who had it from Miss Planta, the senior governess, who had it from Mrs Schwellenberg, the Queen's Dresser. Her Majesty remained in her dressing room with her Ladies, and a guard at her door to prevent the King from entering because the sight of him distressed her. Furthermore, not even the senior princesses were to be admitted because the Queen's nerves could not endure any girlish fussing. Minny, Sofy and Amelia were to stay quietly in their own apartments. It was no deprivation for them to be kept from the Queen. It was their poor sick father they cried for.

The Prince of Wales was recalled from Brighton and in his wake came more physicians. Mrs Che said the Queen mistrusted anyone recommended by the Prince but as Sir George and old Dr Heberden were at a loss and the King's life was believed to be in danger something new had to be tried. At Lower Lodge we were in a state of frozen ignorance. We knew that across the park something terrible was happening but we were not to speak of it, except to God. We had Lady Finch's permission for that.

I did pray, of course, for the King's recovery but I prayed harder to be rescued from Windsor. It was Sofy's prison but I saw no reason why it should be mine. At home I could go about in the world. I could talk to the boys from Dr Barrow's academy or walk to Bond Street to buy a new accompt book – in fact I was *expected* to do it – but Sofy and her sisters lived in a high-walled maze, bustling aimlessly, bumping into each other and getting nowhere. On November 20th my prayer was answered. Amelia was looking out of the schoolroom window and suddenly cried out, 'Sofy, Nellie, come and see. Here's a man with a bird's nest on his head.'

There beneath us was Morphew's yellow thatch, and then I saw Papi. His breath hung in the cold air as he puffed and panted and eased himself out of the carriage.

Papi said he regretted any inconvenience to Her Royal Highness but he must take me back to London where my mother was unwell and could no longer spare me. Sofy clung to my arm and made Papi promise that as soon as Mother's health was restored I should be allowed to visit her again for she really didn't know what she'd do without me. Then I felt badly about wishing to escape. It's so much easier to feel sympathy for other prisoners after the turnkey has opened one's own cell door. I was careful not to smile too much until I'd kissed Sofy goodbye and Morphew had set the carriage for the Brentford road and home.

Papi had told a little untruth. Mother was no more indisposed than usual. He had only said it to rescue me from the gloom of Windsor. For all his calculating and scheming my father had a soft heart.

'Sree veeks, Nellie,' he said. 'Iss long enough. No?'

I said, 'Did you know the King is very sick?'

'All der vurld knows it,' he said. 'In London zey hat him dead already.'

I said, 'He has a great many doctors. Five at least.'

And Papi said heaven help them, they had better put their heads together and cure him, because now he was half dead everyone realized they loved him and wanted nothing so much as to be ruled by him for many a long year.

He said, 'Zey should send for Mayersbach.'

Dr Mayersbach was a water-caster and one of Papi's greatest friends. He could divine the cause of any ailment by looking at the patient's water. He had begun in Middlesex, living there very plain, and had treated Papi for kidney gravel with some success. It was on Papi's advice that he had moved his consulting rooms to Red Lion Yard, for as any fool knows, a doctor with an address in town must be vastly superior to one in Harrow. Thanks to Papi, Dr Mayersbach's list had grown long and grand, so Papi had felt able to recommend him for the King's case and the Prince of Wales had promised to keep the name in mind if the interpreter of pulses and the analyst of stools already attending His Majesty failed to hit upon a cure.

It had seemed to me that if the King couldn't reign and the Queen wouldn't reign the Prince of Wales must be called upon. Papi said I was right, but it wasn't a simple thing that could be agreed over their breakfast eggs. A Bill of Regency must be presented, an Act of Parliament must be passed and then the King must give it his Royal Assent. But how could he give his assent when he was too unhinged even to dress himself? It was a puzzle. And as Papi said, one that the Prince of Wales might be in no great hurry to have solved for, if he was declared Regent, his days of strolling on Brighton's Steine would be over. He would have to get up in the morning and listen to his ministers. He would be pestered by friends looking for preferments. The Queen would watch him like a hawk. And then, what if the King came back to his senses and discovered the furniture had, so to speak, been moved? To be Regent sounded like a thankless, dangerous profession.

From Windsor to Soho cannot be more than thirty miles

but it was another world, to be back where people were cheerful and food was served hot. I was the feather in Mother's bonnet too, for many days after my return, displayed before her friends like one of Sir Joseph Banks's rare botanical specimens. For hadn't I personally witnessed the King's condition? Wasn't I the bosom companion of the Princesses? Didn't I know the names of the physicians, the comings and goings of the Royal Princes and the innermost thoughts of the Queen? To hear my mother, I was only one step from being a member of the Privy Council. No one was impressed that I had met Miss Burney. Mrs Lavelle agreed with Mother that her stories had too vexing a number of characters and Mrs Romilly declared *Cecilia* had given her a three-day headache.

Snow fell on St Nicholas' Day. It was the start of a long, hard winter. I received a letter from Sofy to say that they were all removed from Windsor to Kew, quite out of their usual order of things but in the hope that the seclusion of country life would aid the King's recovery. She wrote:

We are in different apartments. The Prince of Wales has managed everything very well. He has had parts of the King's House closed up, for His Majesty's greater peace and privacy, so Kew Palace is needed for those who have been put out of their usual quarters. Minny and Amelia and I are lodged in a dear little house on the green but it is FEARFULLY COLD. I have chilblains on both feet and Amelia says she doesn't see how she

44

can be expected to write her lessons when she is obliged to keep her hands inside her muff.

At Soho Square we had German stoves in every room and were quite comfortable. I asked Mother if I might send Sofy some woollen stockings and an eiderdown quilt but Mother said the Royalties had money enough to buy their own quilts.

Sofy also wrote that the King got along quite well and the doctors were confident of a full recovery, but that wasn't what we heard from Miss Tod, who read all the news sheets and came every day to give us her digest of events. According to Miss Tod the King went from bad to worse and had been put on a lungeing rein, to be broken like a horse. According to Miss Tod, the Duke of York had been seen in Brooks's Club howling like a dog in imitation of the King, and the Prince of Wales was giving gay dinners and making promises of high office to all his friends in expectation of soon becoming Regent.

It was certainly true that dinners were being given. We hardly saw Papi through the month of December. Also, Miss Tod said, Mr Sheridan was determined to be Chancellor of the Exchequer and Lord Sandwich to be First Lord of the Admiralty but the Duke of Portland said he wouldn't sit down with either of them and, to add to the uproar, something that had formerly been hinted at was now being trumpeted everywhere: that the Prince of Wales was married to Mrs Fitzherbert.

There I had the advantage of Miss Tod and my mother

because I had seen Mrs Fitzherbert with my own eyes. She had smiled at me as I was crossing the stable yard in Brighton. She was just a neighbour, a stout, lonely widow the Prince kindly invited to his house. I didn't see how the news sheets could publish such a preposterous story.

Papi returned home at last on Christmas Eve, released to enjoy the comforts of his own hearth while the Prince of Wales did his duty and attended the King and Queen at Kew. Uncle Christoff came, all the way from Hammersmith, wrapped up against the cold, to deliver our Christmas goose and a spruce bough from his garden. It had always been Eliza's job to hang the bough with gilded nuts and lye pretzels and now, without anyone saying a word, it became mine. It was Morphew's privilege to stand guard with a pail of water and a sponge on a stick after Papi had lit the little candles.

However much we ate and chattered and pretended not to notice Eliza's empty seat, it was a hollow Christmas. Papi was also distracted by a matter of business. The Prince had asked him if he would very kindly buy a troublesome news sheet called the *Morning Post* and take it in hand, to silence its jibes about Mrs Fitzherbert. Mother thought this was beyond his call of duty and it did seem a strange commission for a victualler and quartermaster, but Papi said he didn't mind obliging the Prince because now he'd looked into it he could see there were easy profits to be made. The secret, he said, was to squeeze up the news which a person could anyway just as well hear in a coffee house and make more space for advertisements. When he and Uncle Christoff had had their pastry shop they had never felt the need to advertise — their ginger-bread and their meat pies recommended themselves by their smell and their reputation — but plenty of traders were willing to pay to advertise their wares and Papi had no objection to taking their money. All things considered, he said, he was looking forward to this new line of business.

I saw my opening.

I said, 'Papi, why does the *Morning Post* tell lies about the Prince being married to Mrs Fitzherbert?'

Mother passed the cabbage unasked and took the opportunity to bang the dish on the table and give Papi a warning look.

'Ven you are older, Herzchen', was all he would say.

It was the first time in my life I could remember being denied something on account of my age. I was shocked, but I took the blow meekly. My parents had no idea what pleasure it would give me to ferret out for myself whatever it was I was too young to know.

We were interrupted by a commotion below stairs. There were shouts and cries of alarm, followed by a smell of burning and then the appearance of Twyvil at the dining-room door. It was practically unheard of for Twyvil to come upstairs. When I was a very little girl I believed that our kitchen must have been built around her for she seemed too wide ever to get through its door.

Mother said, 'Vass? Iss der plom puttink?'

Twyvil said the plum pudding was quite unharmed but Morphew's wig had caught fire and in his haste to extinguish it he had hurled it into the pan of spiced wine which was consequently ruined. She regretted the inconvenience and deplored the stupidity of men who play the giddy goat next to a naked flame, but she believed the wig might be saved.

I didn't even attempt to return to the subject of trouble-some news sheets and Mrs Fitz. Mother took up the theme of What Was To Be Done With Morphew and examined it without a pause until our meal was finished. I understood her method. She was luring us away from a controversial topic and Morphew was merely the decoy. He was in no real danger of losing his position. In fact on St Stephen's Day he was deputed to take me and Susan our Necessary Maid to the Frost Fair. His wig had taken on an orange tinge from its Christmas Eve drowning and it gave off an agreeable smell of wine and cinnamon.

We skated from Hungerford Stairs as far as Temple, where there was a Punch and Judy puppet show set up on the ice, then we crossed to King's Reach. Morphew was an excellent skater. He was from the county of Norfolk where there were few roads, only water dykes that froze in winter and so gave people the opportunity to put on their skates and visit their aunts and uncles. Susan the Necessary Maid had never skated before, but she wore the blades I had outgrown and we pulled her along between us.

All of London seemed to be on the river that day. Some had walked from as far away as Fulham. There were whole sheep being roasted at Southwark and prizefighters, stripped to the waist in spite of the cold, and booths where you could drink hot salop for a penny. Morphew was in great good humour. He bought us baked apples and a tiny glass trinket to give to Twyvil. I believe he was affected more than a little by the fumes from his wig.

I said, 'I wonder what the Prince of Wales is doing today?'

Morphew said, 'Junketing. Feeding his fat face off the sweat of working men.'

I said, 'Or visiting Mrs Fitzherbert.'

Susan had never heard of Mrs Fitz.

'She's a lady he's not allowed to marry,' I explained, 'but some people say he already did. What do you think, Morphew?'

'That in't a case of thinking,' he said. 'That's a case of knowing. And I hope to God that don't come back to trouble Mr Welche. I hope he's never called to account.'

'But what did Papi do?'

'Only went to the Fleet hisself, to buy out a parson as was willing to do the marrying. I should know. I driv him there. Two hundred pounds, that cost. The parson was all a-tremble, poor beggar, and Mr Welche warn't happy neither but you know how it is, Miss Nellie. He dussen't disappoint his Royal Nibs. And then I took them to that certain lady's house in Park Street.'

'Did Papi actually see the marrying?'

'He did not. Soon as we'd delivered the cleric we come back to the Square. And that's as true as I stand here.'

I still couldn't make sense of it. Mrs Fitz wasn't the stuff of princesses. Her front curls were grey. Her waist was thick.

And at Marine Pavilion she always went home after dinner. Wives didn't do that. They embroidered screens and then went to bed to get babies. I didn't know then how unaccountable love's fancy can be.

5

On the last Sunday of February Mrs Lavelle called on her way home from church to tell us that, for the first time in many weeks, there had been no prayer for the restoration of the King's health. Instead, there had been a prayer of thanksgiving for his perfect recovery. The Royalties had left Kew and returned to Windsor to complete their customary winter residence. A week later I received a letter from Sofy:

> *The King is entirely recovered. You would hardly know us. We walk about with him on the terrace every afternoon and the townspeople come to see him and cheer him. All we need now is for the Queen to regain her spirits. She is GREATLY DIS-COMPOSED by our recent difficulties and finds she must live as quiet as possible but I hope I may VERY SOON be allowed to ask for you. Minny has a toothache. Amelia begs you will please write us another story and send it EXPRESS.*

I was usually happy to provide Amelia and Sofy with stories but suddenly I found I could not write. My sister was haunting me. As the anniversary of her death approached I smelled her everywhere. There was the scent of the dusting powder she loved, True Rose, and there was her own warm, milky odour, at the turn of the stair, in Papi's cabinet, and even on the street. No one else seemed to notice it but I knew she was there. On the anniversary itself Mother remained in bed, seeing no one, and Papi dined with Dr Mayersbach. I took my supper in the kitchen and we talked and talked of Eliza until there was nothing left unsaid. I wept into my gravy, and Twyvil and Susan the Necessary Maid did too, though Susan had only been with us six months and had never known my sister.

The tears exhausted me. I slept a dead sleep that night and the next morning I felt different. Sofy's cloud had lifted and so had mine. I could stop thinking 'this time last year'. I ceased gorging myself on cake, the strain on my buttons eased and I began to write again.

In June I was summoned to Windsor, and went with mixed feelings. I looked forward to seeing Sofy but the thought that the King might slip into his agitations again filled me with dread. Miss Tod had been several times to Moorfields and paid her penny to see the mad Bethlemites. She told Mother it was a great novelty and better value than the opera any day, but I never had any wish to see it. If madness could capture the mind of an anointed King, who was safe?

Morphew drove me to Windsor. 'Now, Miss Nellie,' he said, 'you keep your eyes and ears open. Some people say the King ain't recovered at all. Some people say he's six foot under, only they've got somebody dressed up to pass for him, to keep that perfeck fool off the throne.'

I said, 'I don't know that the Prince of Wales *is* a fool. I think people form their opinion of him from his dress but I'm sure a person can wear a yellow coat and still have his wits. And he was very agreeable to me, you know.'

'Don't signify,' he said. 'There's no call for princes to be agreeable. Main thing is they don't be too handy spending other folks's money, and that one'd beggar the Queen of Sheba.'

'Anyway, Princess Sofy says the King goes on very well. We must allow her to know the truth. And Papi. If the King had died Papi would have been one of the first to hear of it.'

But Morphew tapped the side of his nose and said, 'He might do. But that might suit him to pretend he don't. You see what I'm saying? Mr Welche, he's in clover now but that won't last, not when His Nibs is King. There'll be new people brought in, depend upon it.'

Windsor was in an uproar of packing trunks. The Majesties and the older Princesses were soon to leave for Weymouth in the county of Dorset, where the King's brother, the Duke of Gloucester, had a house. The doctors had recommended the King try sea-bathing, in aid of his continued recovery. In any normal family he might have gone very conveniently to Brighton and stayed in his son's well-appointed house but I

53

suppose Mrs Fitzherbert was the obstacle, invisible and unacknowledged but substantial enough to make the King drive for two days instead of one morning.

When the Royalties travelled they took their household goods with them, as though other people's houses had no basins or cloths or spoons. Also a great train of servants and attendants went with them too. The only items missing from the inventory were Sofy, Minny and Amelia. For some reason their presence wasn't reckoned to be essential to the King's recuperation. They were to remain at Lower Lodge. I saw the hand of the Queen in this strange decision, for what father wouldn't be comforted by the company of all his daughters? But the Queen found six girls to be too much of a good thing and preferred to torment them in twos or threes. Sofy accepted the ruling without complaint and I was quite the toast of the schoolroom, in part because of the stories I had written for them through their long, lonely winter, but principally because I had done something they had not. I had seen the sea and could describe it.

On my second morning at Windsor, Monsieur Hemet the dentist was expected. I asked Gouly if, while Sofy was having her teeth inspected, I might take a walk. My real intention was to go to Upper Lodge in search of Miss Burney but I was learning how to manage governesses. Walks were considered A Good Thing and permission for them was always granted.

Miss Gouly said, 'Only don't venture too far, Nellie. And don't speak to anyone.'

Well, I obeyed her first instruction. Upper Lodge was no

distance at all. But I did speak to someone. It was quite unavoidable.

June 28th 1789
Today I saw King George. I was in the park when he came along with P. Royal & Augusta. He walks with a cane. P. Augusta told him I was Sofy's HC and he asked me where I lived. I told him King Square.

King Square had been reborn as Soho Square many years before, but I doubted His Majesty would know that and I thought he would enjoy its old name. As a child I was clever at framing things to delight people or flatter them. I had the knack of it from very young and eventually I grew to dislike the trait. It took me many years to eradicate it. The reward of easy approval can be too tempting to resist. King George certainly rose to my fly that morning.

'King Square!' he said. 'Fine thing. And what king is your square named for, Nellie?'

'King Charles II, sir,' I crowed, and then tried to remember my history. Was Charles II a monarch King George would approve of or had I uttered an unmentionable name? Hadn't there been a great number of natural children born and no heir? But it seemed not to matter to His Majesty. He was more interested to know if we had trees in our square. I assured him we had lime trees.

'Excellent,' he said. 'Excellent. *Unter der Linden, an der*

Heide. Birdsong. Branches. Etcetera, etcetera. We should like everyone to have the benefit of trees.'

He wasn't at all as fearsome as the Queen, perhaps because he never quite looked at me. He seemed to be casting about, searching the horizon for something he couldn't find. Nevertheless, when Augusta asked me where I was going I found my voice came out like a mouse squeak.

I said, 'I hoped I might see Miss Burney before she goes away.'

The Princess Royal touched the King's elbow, as if to set him in motion again, but he didn't move.

Augusta said, 'Nellie is a writer of stories, sir. She keeps Sofy and Amelia greatly amused. I think our Miss Burney intends to bring her on.'

And the King said, 'Stories? Well there's a thing. Never saw the point of stories myself but Miss Burney is an excellent, sensible woman and the ladies find her diverting so who can argue against that. The ladies, the lovely ladies. Who can argue? Continue on.'

He pointed his cane ahead and they left me. My heart was pounding. Whatever Morphew believed, a king didn't feel like a mere hooman when you were standing so close to him you could see a dog hair on his cuff.

Finding Miss Burney proved impossible. A scullion referred me to a Page of the Backstairs who referred me to a maid of the Queen's Dresser. She said the Queen was presently at her second toilette and Miss Burney was not likely to be dismissed before the hour of three unless she was excused, and then only briefly, while Her Majesty was powdered. I took the street way back, and quickly. I didn't feel equal to another conversation with the King just yet. And as I made my way to the schoolroom I decided to say nothing about my encounter. If I did I would be quizzed on it and was sure to be found guilty of some disrespectful lapse. In the event, no one was interested in where I'd been or what I'd done. Caries had been found in two of Amelia's teeth and so the world was about to end.

The next morning the great caravan set off. First the baggage and boxes and a wagon filled with provisions, for the Majesties objected to the price of food in Weymouth. Next, the ladies of the household, followed by the Queen with Royal, Augusta and Elizabeth. The King was the last to leave. Then the clatter and shouting ended and Windsor fell quiet.

Sofy said, 'How dull we are now. I wish Ernie would come home, and Dolly and Gus.'

Prince Ernest and Prince Adolphus were in Göttingen, perfecting their German and being turned into good Hanoverian soldiers. Prince Augustus had been sent there too although he hadn't the constitution for soldiering. They should have let him stay in England with his books. He might have made a very happy country parson if he hadn't had the misfortune to be born a prince.

Sofy spoke often of her brothers. Years had passed without her seeing them and in their absence their virtues were magnified. She held them to be altogether more dashing and brilliant than I could believe possible if the Prince of Wales and the Duke of York were a fair sample of the male line, and she despaired of them ever coming home. There was no soldiering for them in England and they needed to appear honourably occupied. The public were in no mood to hear of any more Royalties sitting in the Kit-Kat Club drinking claret wine. People were watching what was unfolding in France.

King Louis had been warned by his Parliament that he and his lords ought not to live so high when the coffers were empty and the poor went hungry. Papi said the poor always go hungry. It was the natural order of things. And if France had no money she had only herself to blame, for hadn't it all been spent encouraging America to turn against her mother country?

The French King, I suppose, wasn't accustomed to being lectured on the price of bread and the need to pay taxes. He hesitated, then conceded a little ground, thinking perhaps that it would be easily enough regained. In July his militias were ordered to surround Paris to remind the people of his sovereign power, but he misjudged the tide. The people were already on the streets and two great arsenals were seized. At the Bastille, when the governor tried to prevent the mob from making off with gunpowder and muskets, he was cut to pieces in the street.

It was not the English way. If there was a march because barley was in short supply or oats had gone up in price, or if carters were discontented and a tollgate was pulled down, when the point had been made everyone went home to their beds. And if they found they couldn't sleep, they composed a pamphlet. In England the weapon was the pen not the pike. Nevertheless, a tremor of unrest was brought even into our peaceable house. Morphew, who had never been known to miss a meeting of the Haymarket Grumblers' Club, began instead to attend debates organized by the Friends of Liberty. He brought home a paper, *On the Grievances of the French People,* which he asked me to read aloud to Twyvil and Susan after Mother had retired for the night.

He said, 'You'll make a better job of it than me, Miss Nellie, for it gets me all choked up. And you may learn something from it, besides. Something as may be worth passing on to certain friends of yours.'

The pamphlet laid out the causes of France's ills. I have it here still. Every other Frenchman was a lord, it seemed, and all congregated at court, perfumed, pirouetting parasites who paid no taxes and left their estates to rot. 'The cupboard is bare,' the text runs, 'but it is a well-known fact that kings don't cut the coat according to the cloth they have but rather snap their fingers and order more cloth to be supplied. So the poor working man is squeezed to pay for it.'

Twyvil said she couldn't remember the last time she had a new coat and Morphew said, 'The touch-paper's lit, Sarah Twyvil. Mark my words. The touch-paper's lit.'

Susan the Necessary Maid had fallen asleep.

Above stairs, Miss Tod came every day to pass on the news sheets' warnings that the French contagion could easily spread to England. Eventually she reduced Mother to such a sleepless wreck she had to be asked to stay away. Papi was calm but watchful. I know he called in several loans he had advanced, and a quantity of gold was taken out to my uncle's house in Hammersmith to be stored in a secret closet. A new axe was purchased too, at Mother's insistence, and kept convenient to the street door, until I asked whether it was intended for us to use against the mob or the mob to use on us. Then it was concealed and forgotten.

At the end of July Papi set off for Brighton to prepare Marine Pavilion for the season. The Prince of Wales, nothing daunted by the stories from France, planned a great celebration for his birthday. There were to be seated dinners, and dances and bonfires and illuminations. My Aunt Hanne had an unshakeable affection for the Prince. When people criticized him she defended him as nothing worse than a high-spirited boy. The fact that he was rising twenty-seven and had already come within a mad King's whisker of sitting on the throne did nothing to change her view of him. And so she conceived the idea that she would like to see this Brighton that God-fearing people so deplored, and perhaps even catch a glimpse of the Prince himself. She also wished to try the sea bathing for relief from an abdominal derangement and, as I had already been there and returned unscathed, she claimed me as her companion. We travelled to Brighton in Uncle Christoff's sociable.

Our days in Brighton followed the pattern laid down by discerning lady visitors. On alternate mornings we went either to Dr Awziter's Consulting Rooms or to the shore to be dipped from Mrs Gunn's bathing machine. If it was a morning for Dr Awziter's, where my aunt would drink a vile, salty whey made from milk, sea water and cream of tartar, I could depend on her being confined for much of the day within easy reach of the close-stool. She swore it did her a power of good and it left me free to walk about and visit Crawford's Library. If it was a day for being dipped, Aunt Hanne would screech a great deal and declare the terror of it would kill her but she never failed to go back for more. I thought it the most wonderful sensation, to be held in a dipper's big, mottled arms and feel how the salt water lifted me.

In the afternoons, abdominal derangements permitting, there was shopping to be done and fashionable ladies to critique, and in the evenings there were theatricals. We saw *Love for Love* and a burlesque with pierrots. The houses on the Steine were filled with the Prince's friends, many of them famous reprobates, and sometimes in the early evening they could be seen playing a game of cricket, or at least their own version of it. Lord Skeffington, Colonel Hanger, Hellgate Barrymore, the Dukes of Norfolk and Orleans. There was always some onlooker who could put a name to them for us.

The day before the Prince's birthday Papi brought us into the kitchens to see the feast that was being prepared. An ox roast and free ale had been ordered for the people of Brighton but there was to be a far richer spread for the Prince and his friends. There were woodcock and snipe, and turkeys stuffed with pigeon and trussed into ballotines. There were pike ready to be stuffed with lobster meat and a *pièce montée* of Marine Pavilion made of pie crust, with lawns of chopped spinach and the little marchpane figures of sea birds. A fat, sweating man was spinning white sugar and fashioning it into diadems, one to be placed before each guest, and the table-decker was already at work in the dining room.

The heat and noise of the kitchens proved too much for Aunt Hanne who was fit to faint so Papi took us to one of the stillrooms for a glass of cordial. A man was at work there making ices, directing two boys in a quiet voice.

'Iss der best,' Papi whispered, as though we were in church. 'From Gunter's, you know? On Berkeley Square?'

There were to be two water ices served, one of brandy punch and one of muscadine with white currants, and two cream ices, one made of rye bread and one of toasted filberts. We were given a spoonful of each to taste. They were very good.

Aunt Hanne asked the man from Gunter's if he knew how to make a buttermilk ice.

He said, 'I can make anything.'

He had a funny flat way of speaking, and said to me, 'And what's your name, Tuppence?'

I was fourteen and not inclined to be called Tuppence by anyone. I stuck my chin out to show him 'Cornelia' was all he'd be getting from me.

Aunt Hanne said, 'But ve call her "Nellie". Nellie is companion to Princess Sofia, you know? She goes many times at Vindsor.'

'Does she now?' he said, and turned back to his freezing pots. 'Then we'd best mind our manners.'

And that was Jack Buzzard.

6

I was shocked the next time I saw the Queen. Her hair had turned entirely white and everything about her seemed reduced in size. Suddenly she was an old lady. Now I calculate it she was forty-five.

I thought she must be sick but Sofy said she was simply ravaged by the worry of what was to become of the poor French Queen, who had been harried from her country home, forced to lodge in Paris whether she liked it or no, and had her rooms ransacked. It seemed an excessive reaction to someone else's distant misfortunes but, as Morphew liked to remind me, Her Majesty was merely hooman and if Queen Marie Antoinette could suddenly be at the mercy of vicious, common people, what queen was safe? Of course, if our Queen Charlotte had only followed what the news sheets published she might have been reassured. Public opinion had never held her in greater affection. It was all on account of Lady Herbert, the Countess of Pembroke.

The King, it was said, had visited the Countess in his past delirium and forced himself upon her. At fourteen I was still not fully acquainted with the particulars of men's appetites, but if the King had truly gone to Sofy's birthday dinner with his breeches unbuttoned I guessed there might be some truth in the reports. Lady Herbert was certainly much handsomer than the Queen.

And whether it was true or not, my mother was convinced. 'Ach!' she'd say. 'Poor vooman. Fiftin children und now ziss.'

'Well,' Mrs Lavelle would reply, 'all men are beasts, even kings,' and Miss Tod would agree, although she had never married so I don't know how she'd formed this opinion.

The material point though was that the King, who had been the nation's treasured father while he was mad and kept in a strait weskit, had ceased to be the object of affection or interest now he was well again and all sympathy was with his Queen. That's the way it goes with the man in the street. He enjoys a good tragedy and is much more excited by what is done *to* a person than by what a person does.

At Lower Lodge no one seemed concerned about the Queen or Lady Herbert. All the talk was of husbands, or rather the want of them. Prince Ferdinand of Württemburg, a lieutenant general reckoned to be tolerably handsome, had paid court to Princess Augusta and Augusta would have been happy to have him, but the King said Ferdinand and all other suitors might save their boot leather because, as everyone very well knew, Royal must marry first.

Royal kept to her rooms at Upper Lodge. Sofy said it was because she had a summer cold but I believe it was because of her humiliating situation. The Duke of York was marrying,

65

Mademoiselle de Montmollin was marrying, but Royal was left to moulder, like a chop in a meat safe that everyone agrees had better soon be used but no one volunteers to taste.

Prince Billy was home that summer, retired from the Navy and newly created Duke of Clarence. He seemed not to have any occupation except rising late and apologizing for one drunken rout before embarking on another. I first saw him at Sunday prayers. He looked like a man who had dressed in a hurry. Sofy believed it was the Navy that had coarsened him.

'I'm sure Ernie would never behave so,' she said, 'nor Gus nor Dolly. Thank heavens Billy has come back to us before he grew too fixed in his ways. A season at St James's will soon refine him.'

The refining of the Duke of Clarence was a minor project that summer. The principal thing was the Queen's new plaything: a cottage in the castle park, called Little Frogmore. I suppose it was intended to distract her from the plight of the French Majesties. Royal and Augusta had assisted with the choice of furnishings and Elizabeth, who practised very hard at her drawing, had been called upon to decorate the walls with botanical paintings. On Midsummer's Eve we were invited to take tea there and admire the finished effect:

June 22nd 1791

HM's cottage parlour is all ribbands and swags. V. hectic. She wore a plain gown and cap and poured tea. She called me 'dear child' and made me stand closer so she could see if there had been any improvement to my face. There had not. She has snuff

66

stains around her nostrils. L. Herbert passed the cups so I think
it cannot be true abt. the King, unless HM means to keep Lady
H always in view to prevent further mischief. Miss Burney was
not present. P. Royal perspired and was v. glum. Her gown was
too heavy for the season. There is thunder and our room is
airless but Gouly says we must go to bed.

The storm we all longed for didn't come until the next day.
It rolled around all afternoon without reaching any great
conclusion, and then in the evening came a different kind
of thunderbolt. The King and Queen of France had been
arrested. Minny heard it from a footman and hurried to tell us
but she was soon silenced by Miss Gomm who said it would
give Amelia the night terrors and must on no account be
discussed. I had to wait until I was back in Soho Square to
hear the story in full.

King Louis and his queen had left Paris in disguise, playing
servants to their children's governess who was got up as a
grand Russian lady. Whether they had intended to flee the
country entirely or just wished to escape the angry mood of
Paris depended on who was telling the tale, but the sequence
of events that undid them was generally agreed.

They had stopped for refreshment and a change of horses
and the innkeeper had remarked to his wife how one face in
the party was quite the double of a certain profile on a coin in
his pocket. I imagine a great deal of whispering in the
scullery.

'Say something, Jacques.'

'No, *you* say something.'

'You're the one who noticed it.'

In fact no one said anything and the royal party might have got clear away if their coachman hadn't taken a bridge too fast and their carriage lost a wheel. Then, while they waited for a wheelwright to be found, news of the King and Queen's flight reached the little town. Who was dressed first, the innkeeper or his wife? Or did they both run out of the house in their nightgowns, hearts pounding, racing to waken a justice of the peace and charge him with the unhappy duty of arresting his king and queen. Wretched man. He must have wished himself far, far away as much as the King did.

Miss Tod said there had to have been a traitor in the King's household.

She said, 'Dressed as a butler? Then why was his face observed so close? In a country inn, and by candlelight? No, they were betrayed, poor dears.'

Perhaps she was right. But I could see another way it might have happened. I could picture King George got up in Morphew's greatcoat and periwig, and the Queen in Twyvil's apron and cap. No one would suspect them as long as they kept their mouths closed, but there lay the difficulty. Any fool knows how to play a king, but few kings bother to study how ordinary men behave. One word from a royal mouth would have been enough to make that innkeeper look again at his guests.

It had been a foolish plan from first to last and it lost King Louis such friends as he still had. Some said it wasn't his leaving Paris they disapproved of as much as his manner of going, sneaking away like a thief. Others said it was all of the Queen's doing, which was a greater condemnation for it showed she was the one who wore the breeches. Whatever the truth of that, it had been very badly conceived.

At the beginning of August I was called back to Windsor. I was to spend a week there, then go on to Kew with Sofy and Minny and Amelia while the Majesties and the senior Princesses travelled to Weymouth for the waters. Then the plans changed. Minny was deemed old enough to join the Weymouth party and Sofy and Amelia were to go with Lady Harcourt to her home in Oxfordshire. So Sofy envied Minny, and Princess Elizabeth said she envied Sofy because Weymouth was boring, with nothing to do but walk on the strand or be rowed about the harbour by handsome, untouchable young oarsmen.

Humble Companions are taken up and put down as easily as dust sheets. No longer required for Kew, I was to be driven back to London as soon as Morphew could be spared to fetch me, and as I very much wished to speak to Miss Burney before I left, I walked across to Upper Lodge one afternoon. I knew that on any fine day the Queen was likely to be at the Frogmore cottage, botanizing with her gardener and Miss Burney might be free. She seemed very pleased to see me.

'Cornelia Welche!' she said. 'You've come to say goodbye. How good you are.'

'I expect to leave on Friday.'

'Oh but I go tomorrow,' she said. 'Her Majesty has graciously released me.'

She was retiring from her court duties. One more day and I would have missed her.

I said, 'So now you can be a writer again.'

'Well,' she said, 'I believe I shall write another book but perhaps not yet. I'm going home to rest and be with my family. My health hasn't been good this past year. But I see you haven't been idle.'

I had with me a story I was working on for Amelia's eighth birthday. Amelia had requested a book about a beautiful golden-haired princess, beloved by everyone, but I found I made little progress.

I said, 'I wish I'd never agreed to write it. For two pins I'd throw it on the fire but Amelia never forgets a promise.'

'Not on the fire,' she said. 'When I was about your age, in a fit of discontent I burned a bundle of my papers, and I soon regretted it. The back of a cupboard is a better place, then it can be taken out at some future date and improved. Of course, it may still deserve to end in the fire, but first allow it to live a little longer.'

She was gayer than I could ever have imagined. There was no hurry about her, no feeling that at any moment Mrs Schwelly might burst in and she would have to jump to her duties. She took my pages.

'A beautiful, golden-haired princess beloved by everyone?' she said. 'I do see your difficulty. A disagreeable princess would have made a far more interesting study. But here are two useful lessons. Avoid being obliged to any patron, especially a royal one, and keep your writing close to your chest until you know you've done the best you can. Let anyone else read a word of it and it's sure to end in pieces.'

She handed back my story without reading it, and said, 'The world is full of editors and arbiters of literature. They'll tell you precisely what's wrong with your story and would write a far better one themselves if only they had the time. So the young Highnesses are going to Nuneham Courtenay instead of Kew. Are they pleased with the plan?'

'No. What they really want is to go to the seashore with the King and Queen and I don't understand why they're not allowed. I'm sure Lady Harcourt wouldn't mind. It must be a great inconvenience to receive royal visitors.'

But Miss Burney said it was a harness Lady Harcourt hardly felt, she'd worn it for so long, and that Sofy and Amelia might have a livelier time in Oxfordshire than they would at Weymouth because the Queen was quite out of sorts and was not to be fatigued.

I said, 'Sofy doesn't fatigue anyone. She's so good and obedient. If the Duke of Clarence can go to Weymouth she could certainly go. Mrs Chevely says Billy Clarence's language makes the Queen's ladies blush and they all wish he might be given another frigate and orders to sail immediately.'

'Ah,' she said, 'I think Mrs Chevely confuses the Duke's boyish exuberance with vulgarity. Fortunately for His Royal

Highness the Queen doesn't fall into the same error. I'm told it takes a mother to understand the distinction.'

Miss Burney only ever laughed with her eyes.

She said, 'But I must leave off gossiping. Her Majesty has been all consideration to me since I asked to leave my position. She's settled a half-pay allowance on me when I truly had no reason to expect anything. And I believe she's been thinking of you too, Cornelia. I hear you're to receive a gift.'

'A gift? From the Queen? What is it?'

She said, 'I won't say. But when you see it try to bear in mind it's kindly meant. And about your story, Nellie. Perhaps there could be a dog that bites?'

We said goodbye and I saw her only once after that day. I should have liked to have had a better acquaintance with her. I know she survived many adventures and tribulations. And she was right about the Queen's intention to make me a gift. On the morning of my departure Augusta and Elizabeth came from Upper Lodge and presented me with a bottle of Bloom de Ninon Guaranteed Complexion Whitener.

Mother would have had that bottle exhibited under a glass dome. It was brought out and showed to everyone who called on her, though they were not permitted to touch it. Tea parties were given and cake was made in its honour. I hadn't realized what a large acquaintance Mother had until Queen Charlotte made a project of the port-wine mark that covers half of my face.

I said, 'It can't be kept forever. I shall have to use it. When I go to Windsor I shall be expected to wear it.'

Mother said, 'But not ziss bottle, Nellie. Ziss is from der Qveen herself.'

And she gave me five shillings from her own pocket, to go to Harding Howell in Pall Mall and buy another bottle of ceruse.

7

Sofy's birthdays were often tinged with melancholy. Perhaps it was the season. The trees were bare, the days were short. But in truth I think we were stalked by the spectre of '88: the King's terrible episode that announced itself at her birthday dinner that year.

Her fourteenth though was a little gayer. All the Royal Highnesses were in a state of great excitement. They had gained a sister. Frederick, Duke of York, had made a desirable match and was expected to arrive at any moment with his bride, Princess Frederica of Prussia. In Soho Square Miss Tod had already informed us that the new Duchess of York had a tiny waist, delicate feet and a dowry of thirty thousand pounds. When she finally got to London she was discovered to suffer from *hauteur* and rotten teeth, but if the Duke was willing to overlook these imperfections what was it to us? Parliament had settled another eighteen thousand a year on him to assist in her upkeep so I suppose she could have been without a tooth in her head and still worth the price.

People predicted that the happy improvements to the Duke

of York's finances would encourage the Prince of Wales to unmarry Mrs Fitzherbert and take a more suitable wife himself. He was said to be over his ears in debt, with banks brought down by loans he could not or would not repay. This made me a little anxious for Papi, but he assured me he only ever lent what he was willing to lose.

'Viz Prince of Vales,' he said, 'der books iss balanced.'

By which he meant that the connection had brought him advantages worth more than the unpaid rent on Marine Pavilion. The lease was still Papi's and remained so for many years. Not everyone came out of it so well as Papi though. Mr Weston the tailor still had to pay his cutters and pressers. The hatter and the saddle-maker still had to eat. And the Prince showed no sign of giving up Mrs Fitz and making a regular marriage. Indeed he was more and more at Brighton, and so, in consequence, was Papi.

I raised the subject with Sofy one afternoon when we had the schoolroom to ourselves. I am generally most resistant to boredom but the torpor of Windsor did sometimes tempt me into mischief.

I said, 'I wonder who the Prince of Wales will marry?'

'Yes,' she said, 'I wonder. He has to choose very carefully, you know, for whoever he marries will be Queen some day.'

A queen, according to Sofy, needed a very particular constellation of traits. She must be noble, obviously, but not so elevated that she wouldn't willingly submit to her king. Also she must be moderate in her opinions, of a contented nature and not meddlesome, strong enough to bear children, and pleasant to look at but not overly beautiful. Great beauty was apparently a suspect quality.

I said, 'Of course first he must free himself of the wife he already has.'

'Nellie!' she said. 'You can't believe those silly stories.'

I said, 'I know he dines with Mrs Fitzherbert every day when he's in Brighton.'

'That's because he's good and kind and she has no family.'

'He can be good and kind *and* married to Mrs Fitz, and as a matter of fact I rather think he is. I suppose he did it without thinking of the consequences and now it must be very difficult to undo the muddle.'

'But you're wrong,' she cried. 'You're wrong, wrong, wrong.'

And she was so emphatic that the muffin fell off the end of her toasting fork and into the fire.

In those days Sofy wouldn't hear a word said against any of her brothers, not even Billy Clarence who had just credited a new scandal to his account: he had taken up residence with an actress.

Dora Jordan was the kind of woman not read about in decent houses so we had relied entirely on Miss Tod for our information. She hardly knew where to begin. Mrs Jordan, as the person styled herself, was Irish, and as if that wasn't crime enough, had two children living but no ring on her finger. Worse yet, she appeared in theatricals in roles that required her to wink at the public and strut about the stage in close-fitting breeches.

Mother said, 'Ach, der poor Qveen! How she must soffer. I senk Gott my boys did not liff to break mein heart. Nellie iss no trouble to me.'

My mother rarely paid me a compliment and when she did it was cleverly disguised.

Miss Tod said, 'But Mrs Welche, we can comfort ourselves that the Duke of Clarence is of no importance to the life of the nation. We have Wales and York who go before him when we need another king.'

And so it did seem at the time, though I've lived to see Billy Clarence on the throne and Dora Jordan in a pauper's grave in spite of the ten children she bore him. When the country begins to look for its next king an inconvenient wife may be cast off as easily as a pair of old stockings.

Sofy made her debut in the summer of 1792. She was given a very modest ball, befitting such a junior princess, but that did nothing to reduce her worries: could she delight society while keeping her gloves immaculate and balancing ostrich feathers on her head?

She said, 'It was hateful, Nellie. Everyone *looks* at you. Be glad you're excused such tortures.'

In fact my mother had had some fancy of bringing me out into society in a small way, but Papi had over-ruled her. He knew it would be money wasted. He knew that if they were ever to get me off their hands it would not be by means of a cotillion.

But Sofy's new status brought some advantages. It meant that she and her Humble Companion were included in the annual visit to Weymouth and so, in late July, our carriage rolled out of Windsor at the start of a journey that should have taken no more than two days but, on account of being a royal journey, took five. We stopped first at Winchester, where children danced and hurrah'd us and the Majesties and the Princess Royal honoured the High Sheriff by staying a night at his manor house. The rest of us were put up in accommodations on Jewry Street, Augusta and Elizabeth sharing one room, Minny, Sofy and myself squeezed in with Amelia, who was an unexpected beneficiary of Sofy's coming out. The King had said it would be too cruel to leave her alone at Windsor.

The next morning brought the first delay while the King's fitness to go hunting was debated. To my eyes he seemed full of vigour. He no longer used a walking cane and his manner was brisk and hearty. But when hunting was proposed, with long hours in the saddle, Her Majesty foresaw over-exertion, sweats, chills and – well, who dare say what else. The royal physician hesitated, wanting neither to thwart his King nor anger his queen, and the King, putting his own interpretation on the doctor's silence, turned south for Lyndhurst and his buckhounds. We turned west for Blandford Forum, which we reached at dusk after a teeth-rattling drive and fell into our beds.

Augusta came to us as we sat at breakfast. Her Majesty, who feared the jolting of the carriage had done her internal parts a great injury and so had need of perfect quiet and rest, wished the younger, *noisier* members of the party to proceed without her, but not directly to Weymouth. We were to go as far as Piddletown where she would join us, if she lived to see the day.

Sofy said, 'Where's Piddletown? Is it by the sea?'

Piddletown was not by the sea. But it did offer a suitable house where young girls might laugh and bang doors and talk all night without disturbing a more delicate person's health. Ilsington House was the home of Major Garth, one of the King's equerries. 'Old Garth', as Augusta called him, had recently returned from Jamaica, and it was evidently reckoned that his life as a soldier would have accustomed him to trials and discomforts far worse than the arrival of three Royal Highnesses, two governesses and a Humble Companion. A messenger had been dispatched at first light to advise the Major to expect us in time for dinner.

We arrived to find that Old Garth was away from home, attending His Majesty at Lyndhurst, but another message had been sent informing him of our taking over his house. Mrs Chaffey, his housekeeper, was beside herself with worry that we would find the beds insufficiently aired, the servants too countryfied and the river trout too meagre a supper. Minny, who was the senior Princess of our party, assured her we would be grateful to sleep on planks of wood and dine on bread and cheese. As for servants, we could perfectly well shift for ourselves, and to prove the point Miss Gomm said, 'Indeed Mrs Chaffey, don't trouble your man with the small portmanteaux. Nellie will bring them to us.'

Mrs Chaffey showed me the way through the back of the house. Its lawns were bathed in the last of the afternoon sun.

I said, 'What will the Major say if he comes and finds his home invaded?'

'I think he may like it,' she said. 'It's too big a place for a man on his own. And the Royal Highnesses are so amiable. If I'd only had more notice of their coming . . . The Major will want them to be comfortable, that's the thing. He does like things to be done properly.'

I said, 'Is he very elderly?'

'Lord no,' she said. 'In his forties yet. Now you'll find a lad in the tack room. His name's Heppenstall. Tell him to help you with the bags. Tell him Mrs Chaffey said so.'

The stables were very fine, as you would expect of a cavalry man. Enoch Heppenstall was cleaning stirrup leathers and whistling through his teeth, his broad back turned towards me. He didn't hear me come in and jumped when I spoke to him.

'Is it Miss Garth?' he asked.

'Miss Welche,' I told him. 'I'm with the Royal Highnesses. The housekeeper said you'd kindly help with the bags.'

He looked at me. He had a wind-weathered face.

He said, 'You a lady-in-waiting?'

'No, not a lady-in-waiting.'

'A maid then?'

'Not that either. I'm Princess Sofia's companion. There are four small valises. I can manage two.'

He wiped his hands and put down his cloth.

He said, 'How long you here for?'

'Until the Queen comes. Then we go on to Weymouth.'

He carried all four bags as though they were nothing.

He said, 'King were here, last back end. I seen him in the flesh. Major Garth were only just back from campaigning, gave me a start here. I were a groom at Owermoigne before that but the old gentleman passed away so I were out of a place.'

I said, 'Who's Miss Garth?'

'Master's sister's lass,' he said.

'Is she expected?'

'Couldn't say,' he said. 'I heard she might come. I just thought, when I seen you, I thought you might be family.'

Ilsington House was a proper country house, plain but comfortable. It had mullioned windows and worn flagstone floors and there was a green parrot who sat on a perch in the stairhall and called out 'Land o'Goshen!' and 'Bumpers all round!' and then chuckled in a deep, dark voice.

We stayed two nights at Piddletown, with Sofy so desperate to see the sea that she had no interest in anything else and, much as I liked the house and its park, I had my own reasons for wishing us gone. Wherever we walked the stable-hand, Heppenstall, happened to appear and give me a lazy smile.

Sofy said, 'I believe you have an admirer.'

I said, 'Then he must be blind or feeble-minded, or both.'

'Nellie,' she said, 'don't say that. I'm sure your figure is finer than any of ours. And your follower is very manly, don't you think?'

I said, 'I'm not looking for a follower. I know better than to set myself up for disappointment.'

'But why should you be disappointed? He's the one showing an interest. You might encourage him a little. Just think, all we need is for Old Garth to give him a testimonial, then he can be employed at the King's mews and you can marry him. It would be very convenient. I'd be able to see you almost every day.'

I said, 'I see a flaw in your plan. You'll be far away, married to some Hessian Grand Duke and having babies every year and I'll be stranded in St James's with Enoch Heppenstall and the smell of horses. Also, I think he may be a half-wit.'

'Aha!' she countered. 'But I see you've taken the trouble to discover his name.'

8

On our second morning, just before noon, relief arrived in a great rumbling swirl of dust, a cavalcade of carts and carriages and spare horses, maids, valets, dressers, ladies, Royal Highnesses, and finally both Majesties accompanied by Old Garth himself. Amelia let out a little scream when she saw the Major and hid behind Minny.

'Min!' she whispered. 'It's a hobgoblin.'

Tom Garth was a short, elfin man. His ears seemed slightly too big for his head, his head seemed too big for his body and the right side of his face was stained with a port-wine mark from his hairline to his chin, practically a mirror image of mine. Then I understood why Enoch Heppenstall had taken me for a relative. There are those who believe marks such as mine lurk in a family's blood, like ginger hair or an unfortunate nose, and are liable to break out unpredictably, to curse another generation.

The King and Queen took their dinner alone in the small parlour. The rest of us were seated in the dining hall, and Old Garth looked in on us to ask if there was anything we lacked.

Royal said, 'Won't you sit with us, Major? You must be hungry after your long drive.'

He thanked her and sat, though it must have been the last thing in the world he wished to do, a bachelor soldier thrown into a hen house. All he took was a glass of small ale, but there was an ease in his manner I liked immediately. Perhaps soldiers acquire it when they mess together. He was a good judge of subjects likely to appeal to young women: dance partners, for one thing. The Dorset militia were camped outside Weymouth so there would be no shortage of officers at the Assembly Rooms. Then, did we enjoy ghost stories? Had we heard about the phantom legion that marches along the old Roman road west of Dorchester? Or Athelhampton Hall where headless men had been seen walking through walls and gathered around the dining table? This so won over Amelia that she grew quite bold.

She said, 'Nellie, isn't it the oddest thing that you and Major Garth have the same mark on your face?'

Sofy was closest to her and dug her in the ribs but an eight-year-old isn't easily silenced.

'I wonder how such things come about?' she said. 'And there is no call for you to poke me so slyly, Sofy. I'm only developing a laudable spirit of enquiry, aren't I, Gouly?'

Miss Gouly paid close attention to a slice of ham.

I said, 'I've heard many theories about how I got my mark. Our cook blames herself, for feeding my mother too many roasted beets when she was carrying me. My mother's sure I'd have been born unblemished if she hadn't chanced to walk along Greek Street in her last month and see a boy with blood dripping down his face. But I subscribe to a more rational explanation. The moon was waning gibbous, the wind was from the south and a pink-eyed cat was seen on our doorstep the very day before I was born.'

I saw Garth bite the inside of his lip. I was playing to him, wanting to amuse him, though at the time I didn't fully understand why, and I'd succeeded.

Amelia said, 'You see, Sofy? Nellie doesn't at all mind discussing it and I'm sure the Major doesn't either.'

'Not at all,' he said. 'Though I confess I haven't looked into the science of it as thoroughly as Nellie has.'

A smile made all the difference to his face.

When dinner was finished the augmented royal procession formed up to drive the final ten miles to Weymouth and as the road dropped steeply from the ridgeway we saw, if not the sea itself, a haze that prefigured it. There were clusters of children along the turnpike throwing flowers and at the toll gate the mayor and aldermen met us, to lead us into the town. The crowds grew bigger, some people leaned out of their windows to cry 'God save the King', and as we swung towards the sea front the guns of the Nothe garrison fired a salute of twenty-one rounds. It was very exciting and quite different from the Prince of Wales's unremarked comings and goings at Brighton.

Gloucester Lodge was hardly adequate for our party. There were so few rooms that some of the servants had to lodge in other houses along the esplanade and Sofy, Minny, Amelia and myself were squashed into an attic barely big enough for two. There was also the disadvantage of living at close quarters to the Queen. I had little choice but to apply her beastly ceruse every day. I must have looked such an oddity, promenading in the sun with a painted face.

Weymouth was a much gentler shore than Brighton. The sands were soft and level and afforded us long, open spaces for our daily walks. We became creatures of routine, up at six, because the King's doctors had ordained that dipping, if it were to be beneficial, must be done as early in the day as possible. We all sea-bathed, except for the Queen who found the idea too alarming – she preferred to go to the Esplanade Hot Baths and pay three shillings to be boiled into good health – and also Royal, who refused to have anything to do with sea water, hot, cold or served in a cup. Royal wasn't in the mood for anything: another year gone and still no husband.

After breakfast, if there was no excursion planned, we'd begin our rounds of Harvey's Library and Mr Love's Reading Room to inspect the registers and see who was newly arrived in town. Except for Sundays, the King rode out every morning and, if the weather permitted it, in the afternoon he liked to go to sea. Sometimes we accompanied him, rowed about by Elizabeth's handsome, untouchable oarsmen, and once we visited a frigate, the *Southampton*, that was standing off the harbour. We were hoisted to the entry port one by one with nothing but the creaking cradle between us and the dark green water. The Royal Highnesses at least were in no danger of drowning. If they'd fallen into the sea I'm sure their silly skirts would have billowed up and kept them afloat.

It was a great adventure. We were showed everything, from the ship's wheel to the chicken coop, which the King looked into very closely and was pleased to receive a new-laid egg. Amelia was allowed to turn the sand glass before the ringing of six bells and then we went down to the captain's cabin and were given glasses of cordial. There was a deal of mad whispering and blushing in our attic that night. Minny admired the blue of a particular lieutenant's coat. Sofy preferred a marine in his scarlet. Elizabeth said if she had a beau she wouldn't care what colour he wore for she'd soon have him out of his shirt and Amelia, who was supposed to be asleep, asked why.

Minny said, 'What about you, Nellie? Surely someone caught your eye?'

'No. What's the point? We'll never see any of them again.'

'But we can *dream.*'

Sofy said, 'Oh but Nellie doesn't need a sailor to dream about. She already has an admirer.'

Amelia shot up in her bed.

She said, 'Nellie? An admirer? Great heavens!'

And there was an anxious pause until I said, 'Astonishing, isn't it? But I've had the great good fortune to meet a man who loves nothing so much as a girl with her head in a bag. I'm really very hopeful.'

It was the only way with Amelia. I couldn't bear her being made to kiss me to make amends for her rudeness.

I said, 'But if you insist I choose someone from the *Southampton*, I'll have one of those strapping side boys that brought us safe on board. In fact, I'll take them all. They say you can't have too much of a good thing.'

Which set them all squealing, even Amelia, though I'm sure she didn't understand the half of it.

On the afternoons when we weren't out on the water or driving about hoping to hear the tramp of ghostly legionnaires, we'd sketch or read or ride around the gardens in a little cart pulled by a jenny ass. Then, at five o'clock, we faced the greatest challenge of the day: turning ourselves into visions of loveliness ready for the evening's entertainment.

The Queen didn't care for going out and would happily have sat at the card table every night of the week, but the King loved to go to the theatre, and a king trumps a queen. It didn't matter that he'd already seen the play. He would laugh as loudly the sixth time he saw it as he had the first and I believe he would have found a joke even in *Macbeth*, but we were never fortunate enough to see it acted.

By September I was word perfect in *Mistress Warnock's Triumph* and *Barnaby Brittle*, but the theatre wasn't our only diversion. Twice a week there was a ball at Stacie's Assembly Rooms and this gave the Royal Highnesses what they really craved: a setting where they could see and be seen, where they could inspect young men at close quarters and even brush fingertips in the innocent name of dance.

One Tuesday evening the King put aside his own prejudices about dancing and looked in at the rooms for an hour. He was attended by two equerries, Major Garth and Major Manningham. Coote Manningham was reckoned gay enough to be recruited to the dance floor and he was showed no mercy, *Gathering Peascods* with Elizabeth, *Beating the Kettle Drum* with Sofy and *Climbing St Margaret's Hill* with Minny, and all with a cheerful smile. Garth stood with his back to the wall longing, I was sure, for His Majesty to signal that he'd seen enough and it was time to retire. As equerries and humble companions are mindful to speak only when spoken to I feared we might stand there all night in polite silence, so I opened the bidding.

I said, 'Major Garth, I should like to know about your parrot.'

'She's a yellow bill,' he said. 'Found her in Jamaica. No, that's not quite true. It was she who found me. I was close to death till she decided to nag me back to health.'

He had had a fever, he told me, contracted in the jungles of Nicaragua, and had not been expected to live. I had never heard of Nicaragua. He explained it very well. If North America was his hand and South America was his coat sleeve, Nicaragua was the pearl button on his shirt cuff.

'Bad business altogether,' he said. 'Plan was to break through to the Pacific, do you see? Doomed from the start. We went out on the *Hinchinbroke*. Young whippersnapper of

89

a captain, only just made post, took it into his head he'd lead the transports upriver. Never should have happened. No experience, you see? He paid for it though, by God, and so did I. They took us both back to the Jamaica garrison in cots, more dead than alive.'

'And is that when the parrot comes into the story?'

'It is. Flew into the infirmary one morning, fixed me with her eye, and we've been together ever since. Did you hear her talk?'

'I did. Her voice wasn't what I expected. She sounded more like a grand old lady than a bird, and I didn't understand everything she said.'

'Just as well,' he said. 'She has some Spanish curses, acquired I may say before she lived with me. I aim to make her fit for polite society but a parrot won't be hurried, you know? I teach her new words but weeks can pass before she condescends to say them. She seems to wait until I've given up hope.'

I said, 'I've heard Miss Gouly make the same complaint about Princess Amelia.'

He smiled. 'Nellie,' he said. He had remembered my name. 'There is something I should like to say to you.'

He studied his boots for what seemed an age.

'Your face,' he said, when he finally dragged it out. 'I mean to say, your mark. I observe you've painted it over.'

'I don't like to, but it's Her Majesty's wish.'

'Ah,' he said.

'And my mother agrees, although she never thought of it until the Queen did.'

90

He said, 'Then I find myself in some difficulty. Obedience to your Queen is laudable and to your parent is natural. Nevertheless ...'

'You disapprove.'

He said, 'I've seen its consequences. Countess Torrington. Have you ever seen the Countess? You'd remember if you had. She's as yellow as a Chinaman. Lady Thynne and Mrs Bly Lennox too. Teeth gone, hair gone. And all devoted users of ceruse. How old are you, Nellie?'

I said, 'I'm seventeen. Her Majesty said my face would frighten the horses if I didn't cover it, but you have the same mark and you're a cavalry man, so I suppose you disprove her theory.'

Another smile. Then we saw Princess Augusta approaching us.

He said, 'I believe I'm about to be drafted to the dance floor.'

But Augusta said, 'No more dancing for me. I made the mistake of wearing new slippers so I'm *hors de combat*, but I don't believe I've seen Nellie dance at all this evening, nor you, Major. It won't do, you know.'

I longed to dance of course, but not as a charity case.

I said, 'I don't think Major Garth is a dancer.'

'What rot,' she said. 'All soldiers are dancers. How else do you think they pass their winters?'

And so I had my moment. Tom Garth partnered me for *Mr Isaac's Maggot*. He was light and neat on his feet and as we led up he said, 'God save you, Nellie, from the interfering of well-intentioned fools.'

I wasn't sure if he meant the Illustrious Personage for insisting I paint my face or Augusta for making him dance with me, but I clung to my preferred interpretation, that he cared for my health. When it was time for the carriages I was only too happy to make more room for the Royalties' hooped skirts and go back to Gloucester Lodge by chair. I wanted to be alone, without anyone to enquire why I smiled so inanely. Major Garth was a man who had seen the world. He had battle honours, he was the King's most esteemed equerry and he was no fool. And yet he smiled at my quips and cared for my well-being. The thought caused me a pang of sheer pleasure, though later it turned to an ache, the hopeless longing that I could ever find a man like that to love me.

The summer of 1792 was the best I ever spent in Dorset. I saw Tom Garth almost every day and stored up every detail of him, to feed my little secret. The colour of his eyes: grey. His quiet attentiveness to the King. The little neck-scratch of thanks he always gave his horse before it was led away.

The mood at Gloucester Lodge was happy too. The King was in robust health therefore the Queen was in good spirits, and no Princes came visiting, to discompose the Majesties with petitions for more money or higher command. With six daughters around him the King was a picture of contentment. One afternoon, too wet and windy for outdoor pleasures, I came upon him playing spillikins with Amelia.

'Nellie Welche,' he said. 'How do you do? What do you think I did this morning?'

'Did you ride, sir?'

'I did,' he said. 'I rode to Portland with Garth, and do you know what I did there? I bought six ewes. Six. Yes. Fine breed, the Portland. I mean to cross them with one of my Merino rams, do you see? That way we shall have the tastiest mutton clothed in the warmest wool.'

To see him seated on the floor, in his shirt sleeves and a soft stocking cap, it was easy to forget he was my king. Later I realized he must have heard the news from France but he betrayed no sign of it and made sure it was kept from the Royal Highnesses. It was only after I returned to London that I learned all its horrid particulars from Morphew.

9

In August a machine had been set up in front of the Tuileries Palace where King Louis and his queen, Marie Antoinette, were confined. It was called a guillotine. Morphew said it was sharper than the Halifax Gibbet, faster than the Scotch Maiden, and could separate a head from a body faster than you could blink.

He said, 'They say they don't feel a thing.'

I said, 'How do they know?'

The machine was a great advancement, according to Morphew, because it granted its victim, no matter how lowly, no matter what his crime, the same privilege at his execution that a lord had always enjoyed: a swift end from a sharp edge instead of a slow death by rope or flames. I had never seen a burning or a hanging but Twyvil could remember when the Tyburn tree was still used. Indeed, in her locking box she had a scrap of the very rope that had been used to turn off John Rann, a highway robber. It had been bought for her by the late Mr Twyvil. Some people might think it a gruesome love token but Twyvil was a connoisseur of executions.

'That was a good hanging,' she said. 'Merry as a cricket he went up, and dressed like a real dasher. He wore a coat, Miss Nellie, the colour of sparrowgrass, and he sang and bowed to all the watchers. So I don't know as this new device is an advancement. A hanging gives you value for your waiting about and I wish they wouldn't of moved them. Newgate's too far for me to go now, with my legs.'

Morphew told her she had a fine pair of legs and I believe she blushed, although her face was always so red it was hard to say. I could only wonder that Twyvil had any legs, let alone that Morphew had seen them. She seemed to me to roll around the kitchen on some kind of ball-like base.

The guillotine machine was a novelty, put where it could remind King Louis that times were changing. And perhaps it might have served that purpose, made him consider, given him the chance to be a wiser King, but he was undone by the actions of a well-meaning friend. The Duke of Brunswick, who was married to our own King George's sister, had marched towards the French frontier with a great army and pledged to release Louis and his queen from their confinement and put them back on the throne.

Morphew said, 'Well, that done it. Heart alive, that put the cat in the pigeon loft. Them Frenchies worn't having no cabbage-head interfering in their affairs. Soon as they heard Brunswick was getting close they was out on the streets, beating to arms.'

Priests were snatched from their seminaries. Houses were searched and people were taken away: news-sheet writers sympathetic to the King and Queen, anyone who had been their friend or loyal servant or even looked the part. It seemed that in France it was enough to be seen wearing a good pair of boots to get yourself thrown into prison or run through with a sabre. Morphew said it was a start.

Twyvil said, 'A start of what?'

He said, 'Of certain people being made to understand the rightful order of things. Of lessons being larned.'

Some were tried, others were butchered where they stood in the street and some, it was said, were roasted and made into pies. If there was one fearful image that kept me awake it was the pies, for hadn't Papi been famous for his pies and wasn't he famous now for being the Prince of Wales's loyal steward? If the French fever spread to England I felt I knew what Papi's fate would be.

Morphew especially relished telling the story of the Princesse de Lamballe, who had been brought before a tribunal and given the chance to review her loyalties. If she'd refused to swear that she loved equality and liberty more than she loved her King and Queen had she anyone to blame for her fate but herself? She had been handed to the mob and her head carried on a pike beneath the royal lodging, so the Queen could look out and see her particular friend one last time.

Twyvil, who had heard the story several times already, said, 'But she didn't see it. She fainted away, poor soul.'

Morphew said, 'Poor soul, my eye. She's an unnatural beast what has fed off the life blood of innocent little children.'

'Well,' Twyvil said, 'you've changed your tune. All the years I've knowed you, Dick Morphew, you've never had a good word to say for the Frenchies. Not even the little innocent ones.'

Morphew blew his nose very thoroughly, a thing he always did when facts threatened to get in the way of his opinion.

I said, 'So will the killing stop, if King Louis sees the rightful order of things?'

But Morphew said it was late in the day and a nation's ills weren't so easily cured. He said, 'That in't only the King and Queen. That's all his nobs, all his lords and ladies. And I'll venture to say some of them won't never larn their lesson. They'll all have to go.'

'But then who will be left?'

He said, 'You're still a young 'un, Miss Nellie. You ain't seen enough of the world to understand. But I'll quote you a forhinstance. If I was to see a rat in my stable I wouldn't go just after him. I'd go after all his friends and relations too and make a thorough job of it. Because if you leave but two of them they'll soon make twenty. See?'

But as Twyvil pointed out, there *were* rats in our stables, always had been and always would be, so where did that leave the Revolution? Would it carry on till there was no one left but executioners, and babies still in their cradles? And Morphew, who knew when he had reached his limit, drew the discussion to a close with his usual, 'mark my words' and took out his handkerchief again.

Papi was circumspect. He had every hope that the first snap

of cold weather would clear the French mob from the streets, and if that failed that the Duke of Brunswick would soon be at the gates of Paris. He thought it unlikely the unrest would spread to England, for whatever else you might say about an English lord he didn't abandon his tenants and leave them to starve in the hedgerows. He sat with them at their harvest suppers and played cricket with them too if they asked him.

Papi said, 'Alvays I am prepared. Also your Onkel Christoff. Ve heff eggs in many bazgets. Vee kem easy to Enkland, vee can easy go avay.'

'But where would we go?' I asked him.

America, he said. There was always America.

'Does Mother know?'

'Nussing for her to know,' he said. 'Only zat I vill look after her. Nellie, you remember Jack Buzzard? At Brighton?'

He slipped the question in so smoothly.

I did remember Jack, or rather I remembered his name and the taste of the muscadine water ice he'd made for the Prince of Wales's birthday.

He said, 'Jack comes tonight to eat viz us.'

I said, 'Good. You're not often home for dinner.'

'Liebchen,' he said, 'listen to Papi. Do you like Jack?'

It was upon me before I saw what was coming.

'Like him?' I said. 'I only saw him once in my life.'

'But *could* you like him?'

'How can I say? I don't know him.'

'Miss,' he said, 'you are seffenteen. Soon Jack vill be surty. Is gut age for man to marry.'

He said Jack Buzzard was a skilled craftsman, that he planned to open his own establishment and it might be a profitable investment, a good way of providing for my future.

I said, 'So it's a question of business. He's coming to inspect the merchandise.'

Papi banged his hand on the table.

'Jesu Maria!' he said. 'Jack Buzzard is gut man. Vill you heff him or no?'

I didn't like to cross my father. He was a kind man and I knew he wanted the best for me. In the ordinary way of things it's reckoned to be no bad thing for a girl to show some flirtatious resistance when she first receives an offer, but my marked face deprived me of that privilege.

I said, 'How can I say? I haven't been in his company. I've never thought of him. I've never thought of anyone as a husband. Who would ever want me with this face?'

I saw a tear come to his eye.

'Mausi,' he whispered, and I knew I was forgiven. 'Miss' and 'Little Mouse' signified the ebb tide and the high water of my place in Papi's affections. So then it was my turn to say something conciliatory, to give him hope even though my true intention was to find myself a man like Tom Garth.

I said, 'Well, let me meet him, Papi. First let me know him a little.'

Which Papi took to be near enough my consent. He slapped the table again, but this time in joy.

'Nellie, Mauschen!' he cried. 'You sink he comes tomorrow viz horse und cart, takes you avay? *Nein, nein*. First he

vill make hiss bissness. Oh yes. He vill be most best convec-
tioner in all London.'

Mother had been listening outside the door. She had begun
the day with a headache but what she'd overheard had cured
her.

'Oh, Nellie,' she kept saying, over and over, 'vot a gut Papi
you heff, to find you husband. *Vass Glück, vass Segen.* Only
sink! Married!!'

But I couldn't think. I couldn't even recall Jack Buzzard's
face. And I was very anxious that Mother should say nothing
to Miss Tod, our Herald Extraordinary. I knew she would
parley my reluctant agreement to consider an offer of
marriage into a firm betrothal, then everyone would know
about it, from Charing Cross to Piccadilly and there'd be no
way out.

I hardly know how I got through the day. I'd woken that
morning without a worry in the world. Then suddenly I was
under an obligation. I was being offered something I had
no business refusing. And to make matters worse I wasn't
allowed even a minute of solitude, for Mother was in such a
girlish mood, pink-cheeked and simpering, trying my hair
this way and that. I kept her talking on any subject I could
think of. I feared that if I once fell silent she would start to
give me some womanly advice I would rather not hear.

At five o'clock sharp Jack Buzzard arrived and I understood
why I'd been unable to picture him. He wasn't handsome and

he wasn't ugly. He was just himself, with light brown hair and a square, serious face. Before dinner was served we were left alone in the best drawing room for fully ten minutes and it was clear he thought we were coming to a definite understanding. Papi had misrepresented me.

I told him I was too young to marry.

'You won't be,' he said. 'Give it a year or two, you'll be just right. And that suits me. I've business to attend to first. I'm going to be my own master, me.'

I suggested he could do better.

'No,' he said. 'You're from a solid family, sensible with money, well thought of. But you're not too tied to them and that's a good thing. I couldn't be doing with a wife who's always running home to her mother.'

'I meant my face.'

'Yes,' he said, 'I did think of that. But looks are soon gone and then what are you left with? No, you'll do very well.'

I didn't give him any encouragement, not even the faintest smile. But Jack had everything worked out.

'Now,' he said, 'I know it's usual to give a thimble but I hear you're not much of a needlewoman. I hear you can keep accounts and write a clear hand and that's a more useful thing. Sewing girls are ten a penny. So I picked this out instead.'

He brought a small package out of his coat pocket. It was a traveller's inkwell, with holes for two quills and a tiny castor for pounce powder hidden in its base. There was that side to Jack. He could surprise you. It was a very lovely gift.

I said, 'I write stories too and keep a journal. A writer likes to write something every day, you know?'

As well to get that on the table, I thought, but he showed no interest.

He just said, 'I thought it'd come in handy. I know you're up and down to Windsor a good deal. But you can tell those Royal Highnesses to enjoy your company while they may. Once we're wed I won't have you coming and going.'

I see Twyvil outdid herself:

October 15th 1792
Mushroom soup, roast pheasant and sherry wine syllabub. All like ashes in my mouth. Jack Buzzard is hard working and very ambitious. He doesn't drink, his fingernails are immaculate and he is a stranger to self-doubt. I cannot love him because I think I love TG. I am trapped.

10

I didn't tell Sofy about Jack, at least not immediately. It was my way of pretending nothing need come of it. He'd find a pleasanter face to look at across the table or a father-in-law with deeper pockets. The Royalties, anyway, were distracted by the turn of events in France: the King was to be tried for his crimes. But was there still a King of France? Some clever devils argued that the monarchy had been extinguished so how could charges be brought against it? Louis, they said, could only be indicted of crimes committed since he lost his crown and there were none, kept as he was under lock and key, unless playing shuttlecock and battledore had become an offence. Others argued that a trial was quite unnecessary. A man, they argued, need only be tried to establish his guilt or his innocence, but Louis had been king and all kings were tyrants whether they intended it or not, therefore Louis was guilty. *Quod erat demonstrandum.*

Amelia said, 'It's too absurd. How can a king be locked up in a prison? Why doesn't he tell the jailer to release him immediately?'

Minny said, 'Read your history, you silly baby.'

Sofy was gentler with her. She said, 'I expect he's kept there for his own well-being, until he can be given safe conduct. I expect he'll go to Vienna, to his queen's people.'

Sofy knew her royal houses and her geography. I always thought how strange it was that she could place all her cousins, in Mecklenburg and Saxony and Hesse, when her own world was so very small. There was the Queen's House at Buckingham Gate, there was Windsor, and the old red house at Kew. Then she might go to Lady Harcourt's in Oxfordshire once in a month of Sundays and to Weymouth in the summer, if the King decreed it. That was her orbit and she had no say in any of it. The Queen's spaniels had more freedom. They could at least run into a shrubbery and sniff around unchecked.

Beyond the walls of Lower Lodge everyone guessed that King Louis was doomed. People would have been disappointed if it had gone otherwise. His sorry situation cheered them up. They might be struggling through the mud and misery of winter but at least they weren't locked away, waiting for the footfall of a priest come to confess them for the last time.

Papi, who had found it sensible to subscribe to St George's, Hanover Square, when he became an Englishman, suddenly insisted on our attending services. He said we must pray that sanity would prevail and the French King be spared. But like our own first King Charles, King Louis was beyond saving. He wasn't a cruel man or a particularly avaricious one, but the times were against him. The French people were like a fire that had been banked and now began to burn bright. If he gave way too much to their demands, he was weak. If he resisted them too firmly, he was a tyrant. He was caught on a turning wheel that could not be stopped.

It was evening when we heard. Papi came home at an unusually early hour. The Prince of Wales had been giving a supper at Carlton House, but when the news was received his guests' appetites had failed them and the party had broken up. Papi said the theatres had closed and people were milling about in the streets in spite of the cold, telling and retelling the awful details of King Louis's fate.

He had been woken at five. No, he had been woken at four. Well, to tell the truth, he hadn't been woken at all for how could a man sleep when he knows what the dawn will bring? He had seen his queen one last time, but then again, he had not, and the Queen for her part had rent her garments, fallen in a dead faint, or conducted herself with quiet dignity, depending on who you listened to. On certain points there was unanimity. Paris had closed its gates before first light and ordered all windows shuttered, and when the long, slow carriage ride was over and the King arrived at the scaffold and had been shorn and bound, a loud drum roll was ordered so that his final words shouldn't be heard. At first it seemed a great novelty for a king to be treated with such insolence. Eventually I recognized it for what it was. Sheer malice, to the very end.

By morning the mood around Soho Square had changed.

What had shocked people at first hearing became less chilling and more thrilling. What a thing it would have been, people said, to have seen it, to have dipped a pocket handkerchief in the King's blood and taken it home for a memento.

January 22nd 1793

Twyvil says King Louis's execution doesn't sound to her like much of a spectacle if honest people weren't allowed to watch it from their own windows. Morphew says it's a mark of how well things are done now in France, that a king can be despatched with no more fuss than the sticking of a pig and the ordinary business of the day resumed before his body had even been laid in lime. Susan takes it all in. They make me sick to my heart with their talk. I should write to Sofy, but what can I say? They must all be quite terrified.

I needn't have worried about Sofy. She had decided to dispel any dreadful thoughts that might have kept her awake at night by treating King Louis's execution as a very distant affair, the outcome of a quarrel between people too foreign for us to judge. '*French ways are not at all our ways,*' she wrote, '*but I think he cannot have been a good king and father to his people as our Majesty is.*'

That was all she had to say on the subject. She was far more interested in the war now declared between France and England. To Sofy it held out the promise of battlefield glory for her beloved brothers. She certainly didn't seem to fear for their lives:

Dolly is promoted colonel in the Hanoverian Foot Guards and Ernie is in the Light Dragoons. Gusta wishes we had all been born boys then none of us would be left out of the campaigning, except the Prince of Wales of course. His health must be preserved AT ALL COSTS. Fred York is already on his way to Flanders. His wife encouraged him to go as quickly as possible.

It was whispered that the Duchess of York found her husband dull-witted, that she preferred the company of her dogs, and whenever possible remained in her apartments until she heard him leave for town. She really had no one to blame but herself. She'd been acquainted with York for several months before they were married and any person with a brain in their head needed only an hour in his company to know he was a perfect blend of tedium and foolishness.

War can be a bracing thing as long as it doesn't come too close to your own door. London was suddenly full of men parading about in their red coats and shakos, admiring themselves in shop windows. Indeed, I think it was the notion of wearing so splendid a hat that made Morphew threaten to join the Westminster Militia. He, who had so recently thought it an excellent idea for the French to kill each other, had changed his tune when they threatened to kill Englishmen. Twyvil told him they'd never take a man of fifty. Jack Buzzard, on the other hand, was just the age to enlist and he was worried for his position at Gunter's and any setback to his plans to go into business on his own account. Papi said I shouldn't fret, that there were always ways to ensure a man was spared from the levy, but of course it wasn't Jack I was concerned for.

My thoughts were all for Tom Garth. I guessed that any cavalry major would soon be sent to the battle front and I decided to prepare myself for the worst. Instead of a secret lover I imagined myself a secret war widow. That way, if ever I heard Garth had been killed practice would have made me strong.

I see from my journal that even Mother was roused to domestic war effort:

March 15th 1793

Twyvil has orders to buy only prime roasting meats so that there will be gravy beef enough for our soldiers. Mother also resolved to give our skim-milk to the poor French refugees who are lodged in Meard Street but Papi says better to sell it to them at a fair price because charity weakens the character. I'm sure I shall never see TG again.

I was supposed to join Sofy at Windsor after Easter but then I received word that she had chicken pox and I had better delay my departure until she went to Kew to recuperate. Jack was pleased. He'd paid to be excused the Army lists, and war or no war he'd begun his search for premises. He came to Sunday dinner at Soho Square every week to tell us what progress he'd made. Finding the right place for his shop was no easy matter. The address had to be good but the lease affordable, there had to be accommodations above for us to live in, and the place of business had to be of a particular conformation. He needed store rooms and cool rooms, a good-sized window to display his confections, and a private office that could be made comfortable for ladies to sit and peruse the catalogue.

He said, 'I'm not setting out to ape Gunter's – nobs lounging about all day for the price of a jelly – I'm going to be catering to households. High-quality confectionery, bespoke or ready-made, for delivery.'

I said, 'I wonder if there'll be enough demand for sweetmeats, now we're at war? Papi says the Prince thinks of closing up Carlton House.'

Since the French King had lost his head there had been no shortage of advice for the Prince of Wales. Some said displays of pomp and splendour were more important than ever, to reassure people that whatever abominations the French stooped to, there would always be an England, with processions and levees and a good King firmly on his throne. But louder voices said the Prince would do well to settle his debts and go quietly into the country to shoot birds until such time as he was required to fulfil his destiny.

Jack said, 'The Prince of Wales! I won't be looking to HIM for custom. I'd as soon build a house on sand. If he won't pay Coker for silver dishes he looks at every time he sits down to dine, what hope is there he'll pay for sugar plums, eaten and forgotten? No, Nellie, we'll do a steady kind of trade, with people who settle their accounts. There'll always be ball suppers.'

One day he showed me a sketch he'd done of how the shop sign would read.

At the Sign of the Green Pineapple
sole proprietor John Buzzard
Purveyor of wet and dry sweetmeats, ices, cordials
and ornamental table furnishings.

He said I might have my name on it too, once I'd learned the trade. I couldn't think what he meant.

He said, 'There's a good deal to know, Nellie. The sugar work alone takes years.'

I said I had no intention of being a confectioner. I was going to write books. Mother laughed nervously, Papi said 'Pfft', and Jack said books didn't fill bellies but no matter because I was young and would soon get over that silly fancy. I was in a fury:

June 17th 1793

*Sometimes I don't mind Jack Buzzard but today he was so condescending I quite hated him. He said there'll be no time for **scribbling** when we have a shop to run and children to raise. He said we'll have two boys and then a girl, as though you order babies like cream ices. Well I may be young but I don't see that writing stories is any more fanciful than making castles out of pastry. I wish Sofy would send for me.*

Sofy didn't but Mrs Chevely did. She was at Kew supervising Sofy's convalescence. She said Sofy was now clear of the chicken pox, though still weak and troubled with spasms of the throat, and I might attend her at my earliest convenience. Papi said it sounded like the family malady: swelling of the glands. He said Sofy should go to Brighton and try the waters.

I said, 'With Mrs Fitzherbert in town? Papi, you know she'd never be allowed.'

'Ach!' he said. 'But Miss Fitz iss finish! Now he doss not never see her. Only he plays cards viz his friends. Soon he vill make gut marriage viz gut German Princess. You see.'

Jack didn't want me to go to Kew. He said, 'How long will you be gone?'

With Royalties you never could say.

He said, 'Well that's not right, Nellie. They should say how long. They should make it clear. You're not a servant.'

I said, 'No, I'm a friend.'

'Do you reckon so? Friend to a princess? Can that be?'

'I don't know. I never had a friend before Sofy so I've no measure for it.'

He went away cross but he came back before I left for Kew and brought a bottle of walnut cordial for Sofy, highly recommended for debilitations of the throat.

Sofy's condition was much worse than Mrs Chevely had described it. She was very weak and could swallow nothing but clear soup. But the worst of it was the spasms that gripped her, sometimes twenty times in a day. She might be sitting comfortably at her work or listening to me read and suddenly be thrown about by terrible convulsions, gasping for air, sometimes to the point of fainting away. Then she'd revive and seem to have little recollection of the crisis. Mrs Chevely slept by her side every night and the physician came every day, scratched his head and went away again.

Gradually though, in the third week of my visit, she began to regain her strength. The spasms lessened, and there came an afternoon when she seemed so improved and was sleeping so peacefully beneath the horse chestnut that we crept away, Minny, Amelia and myself, to net butterflies. We hadn't been gone more than five minutes when we heard cries of alarm and ran back to find Sofy in the throes of another fit and Mrs Che fanning her with one hand and waving a bottle of hartshorn salts under her nose with the other. When she came to her senses she was in the very devil of a mood.

She said, 'Where were you? I couldn't swallow.'

Amelia said, 'But you were asleep. Why did you need to swallow?'

Sofy said, 'I wasn't asleep. I was resting. And when I looked up you'd all gone away and left me, and I couldn't swallow. I could have died.'

Mrs Chevely was quite put out. 'Royal Highness,' she said, 'I swear I was no more than two steps away.'

Minnie said, 'As Sofy very well knows.'

Then Sofy began to weep. She declared that no one cared for her except her brothers and they were all far away soldiering.

Amelia said, 'I might say the same.'

'No,' Sofy said, 'you know you're quite the favourite. Fred and Dolly write to you much oftener than they write to me and so does the King. You're their treasure and Minny is their beauty and I'm nothing.'

Minnie said, 'You're a goose, that much is certain.'

And Amelia said she didn't know that Minny was so very beautiful.

Two thoughts occurred to me sitting on the lawn at Kew that afternoon. One was that the Queen showed no concern for Sofy's health. To my knowledge three weeks had passed without Sofy receiving either a letter or any promise of a visit. Her Majesty remained stubbornly at Windsor, absorbed in her new venture. She had exchanged her Frogmore cottage for the larger house beside it and was attending to every detail of its refurbishment. My other thought was that it didn't matter if the Queen never came. There was nothing she or anyone else could do. Sofy had decided upon a profession. She would be an invalid.

Jack was no great correspondent but his letters arrived too often for me to keep Sofy entirely in the dark.

I said, 'It's from the gentleman who sent the walnut syrup. He asks how you get on with it.'

'Tell him I thank him but I get along very poorly. Who is he, did you say?'

'A confectioner. He makes ices sometimes for the Prince of Wales.'

She said, 'Is he old?'

I said, 'He's thirty-two.'

'Ah,' she said. 'I see. So I expect you'll marry him and I'll be left without a friend.'

I said, 'No husband will ever keep me from my friends.'

It was the best I could do. How could I explain to her what I could hardly explain to myself, that I prayed every day for deliverance from Jack's expectations. He was a careful, steady man and I wished him no injury, but if he had happened to fall for another girl it would have suited me very well. For in spite of my duty to my father and mother, to do what was prudent and be grateful for the chance of any husband, I could no longer deny that my heart belonged to someone else. I was in love with Tom Garth, a man widely regarded as old and ugly, not to say faithfully married to his regiment and oblivious to my feelings. No sensible person would ever believe it.

How we all tried to humour Sofy that summer. The Prince of Wales sent her a pair of slippers. Princess Augusta came from Windsor and gave us an impersonation of the Illustrious Personage, bustling about Frogmore, playing the *hausfrau*. And I wrote a little entertainment – an imagined conversation between Twyvil and Morphew in which Morphew tried to explain to Twyvil the newest animal in the Kew menagerie: a kangaroo. Minny and I acted it out, she playing Twyvil, padded fore and aft with pillows, and a bed sheet wrapped around her for an apron; I played Morphew, with my nose rouged and a nest of mop strings on my head.

Augusta said it was better than any of the theatricals she had seen at Weymouth.

When Sofy was strong enough to travel it was decided she should go into Kent, to drink the Chalybeate waters at Tunbridge Wells, and I was dismissed. I could remember a time when I was eager enough to go home and leave off being a Humble Companion, but that was before Jack Buzzard began laying out my life for me, like a recipe for candied ginger.

Some days I dreaded seeing him, some days I bore it better by provoking him. He rarely failed to prove to my satisfaction what a dullard he was and I lived in the hope that he might conclude I was too ungovernable to be his wife.

He said, 'I'm glad to see you back, Nellie, but you talk different when you've been with those Highnesses and I can't say I care for it.'

I said, 'Oh but an author must sometimes take on a different plumage, you know? To try a voice and see how it might be used?'

'Author!' he said. 'I wish you'd stop harping on that. There'll be no time for your scribbling when we're wed. Scribbling won't get the baby a new bonnet. You write a good letter, I'll give you that, but authoring's a different line altogether. For one thing you need an education for book writing.'

I said, 'Fanny Burney had no education.'

And he said, 'Fanny who?'

11

Sofy wrote to me in high excitement. Her brother Dolly was on his way to England, with sabre wounds to his cheek and his shoulder. His regiment had tried to capture a Flanders port called Dunkirk but they had been routed in a fierce battle at Hondeschoote and there were very many casualties. I scanned the list of dead and wounded in Papi's *Gentleman's Magazine,* fearing what name I might see but still unable to stop myself looking. Hondeschoote was a great reversal for our soldiers and a blot on Freddie York's command, but Sofy didn't dwell on that. All that mattered to her was that Prince Dolly was coming home. She wrote:

September 30th 1793

   I suppose I shall hardly know him. He was a boy of twelve when last I saw him and now he's a grown man. We hoped he would come straight to Kew but our Illustrious Personage means to keep him to herself first, at Windsor. Prinnie recommends sea bathing for his wounds and would have him go on to Brighton but the King says we cannot be seen GADDING ABOUT

when we are at war. I pray Dolly's wounds are not grave. A
scar can be very dashing as long as it doesn't run too deep. And
dear, dear Nellie, my spasms have quite subsided and I have no
further trouble with my swallow.

Her prayers concerning Dolly were answered. His cuts
were not life-threatening, but just enough to add an interesting feature to his rather empty face and to gain him a few
months' furlough. And to add to her joy another brother was
on his way back to England, though without the glory of a
battle scar. Prince Augustus, who had been settled in Italy for
the sake of his weak chest, had been ordered home by the
King. A rumour had reached the King's ears that instead of
sketching ancient ruins Augustus was courting an unsuitable
lover, Lord Dunmore's daughter, Lady Augusta Murray.

You might think love was a natural enough pastime for a
man with nothing else to do, but Augustus was only twenty
years old and Goosy Murray was fully thirty and merely the
daughter of an earl, so the Majesties wished to rein him in
before things went too far. But things had already gone too
far. Prince Gus and his Goosy had been secretly married in
Rome. I was at Windsor when he arrived, without his new
wife. He was a pale, willowy figure, almost girlish. There was
no sign of the corpulence the Hanovers ran to so easily. That
caught up with him much later in life.

As was usually the way with the Royalties, the facts of the
case emerged slowly and to a selected few. Princess Elizabeth
was Gus's first confidante. He and Lady Murray had not only

married in Rome, a foreign ceremony that surely counted for nothing, but the very instant they reached London Goosy's mother had made sure they compounded the crime by marrying again at St George's in Hanover Square. She was evidently determined to have a royal son-in-law. Perhaps she'd been too long away from England to understand that the statute books were piled against the marriage.

A king's son may not marry without the king's consent. And then, what was the second ceremony worth when Gus had made his vows under a false name? The vicar could hardly be held accountable but he apparently feared he could and so promptly passed the blame along to the curate, who handed it on to the parish clerk, and he no doubt found it was due to the negligence of his wife's cat. When all was said and done, Prince Augustus was well and truly married, and yet he was not. It was a puzzle.

Elizabeth came to Lower Lodge and told Minny and Sofy but not until Amelia was out of earshot. The Majesties and Princess Royal were still in the dark.

Minny said, 'Can it be annulled without the King knowing?'

Elizabeth said she thought it could not. 'And anyway,' she said, 'I'm not sure it would be the right thing to do. The situation is delicate.'

A child was on the way.

Sofy said, 'A baby! We shall be aunts! Well then, there's no need for Gus to fear telling the King. The King loves babies.'

But of course the King didn't love babies conceived

without his consent. He expected such babies to be put quietly away, with a small allowance paid for their upkeep, if absolutely necessary.

Goosy Murray was reputed to be plain and domineering but as she was never seen we were unable to verify the report. She was kept hidden in her father's house in Berkeley Street and her secret royal husband used the back stairs when he called on her. The Queen, in her ignorance of all this, was in the best of moods. She had two sons at home, two at the battle front, and the Prince of Wales had pledged to pay his creditors and lead a more sober life.

Her Majesty's great project that autumn was an afternoon party, to be held in her new Frogmore house and attended by the King himself, who never went to teas. Sofy said he was making an exception because Elizabeth had been so industrious in covering the walls of the new house with her botanical paintings and he wished to encourage her. The date was set, Elizabeth was at Frogmore every daylight hour perfecting her handiwork, and there was a good deal of discussion as to what cakes would be served. Then the news came from France. The French Queen was to be put on trial for acts of moral turpitude, for stealing from the Treasury and for conspiring to overthrow the Revolution.

At first Sofy chased away any dark thoughts. She decided Marie Antoinette would be allowed to go home to her own people.

'It's the only possible outcome,' she said. 'Poor dear. I'm sure she has no wish to stay where she's not wanted.'

But everyone else guessed what lay in store for the French Queen. She had been taken from the Temple Prison to a new place of confinement, the Conciergerie, and I had heard of that from Miss Tod.

'They say,' she once whispered to my mother, 'that Conshurgy is so terrible, death comes as a relief. They say...'

And Mother said, '*Nein, nein!* I kennot listen.'

But she did listen. Lice the size of fingernails, rats the size of dogs. Darkness and damp and the cries of its prisoners, day and night.

The Queen's tea party was cancelled, Frogmore was closed up for the winter, and the Illustrious Personage withdrew to her apartments. This would usually have led to an outbreak of gaiety at Lower Lodge, but the significance of what was happening in France outstripped the joy of being excused attendance on a demanding mother. Even Sofy grew pensive.

She said, 'It could not happen in England.'

It was more a prayer than a statement.

When I returned to London I learned in full what had happened to the French Queen: two days standing before her prosecutors, the sentence pronounced, then just three hours to make her confession and write her final letters.

Miss Tod said, 'They say you wouldn't have known her. Only thirty-eight but they say she looked like an old woman.'

Mother had already heard this several times but forced herself to listen again. 'Der poor soul,' she said. 'Taken like pig to market.'

When they took King Louis to be killed they'd allowed

120

him a closed carriage, but not his queen. She had been taken in an open cart, so everyone might enjoy her misery.

Mother said, 'Perhaps der vurst iss over,' but Papi said more likely it was just beginning. Next they would kill the Queen's friends, then the friends of her friends, and when that was done they would begin to kill each other. They had dispensed with God too. There was no need for Him now the Age of Reason had dawned. Anything was possible.

Mother said, 'Zen I sank Gott ve are English.'

So yet again Sofy's birthday was overshadowed. She lay awake at night wondering what had happened to the French Royal Highnesses now the King and Queen were both dead. Princess Marie-Therese was fifteen, just a year younger than Sofy, Prince Louis-Charles was only eight. Some said they had been killed, some said they were behind bars and the key thrown away, others said they were already gone from France, spirited away in coffins bored with air holes. It was all the stuff of nightmares.

In fact Marie-Therese was miles away in Kurland, and although she was safe from the spiteful mob she can't have found much joy there, hemmed in by exiled Bourbons. They dreamed of France with its throne restored and plotted how they could use her, how remorse might make the people take her to their hearts. It is possible for a pawn to become a queen, but in the meantime it does well to accept that it's merely a pawn. She married a cousin – well, she would have done that anyway – and they lodged in England for some years, though Sofy never met her. And she did become Queen of France, but only for five minutes. They were soon on the road again, she and her King, perpetual exiles.

Remorse or no, the French are done with Royalties. Perhaps Marie-Therese preferred it that way, for how could she sleep easy with that blood-stained crown on her head? I believe she lives yet, very quiet and retired, in a wing of some relative's castle. Her brother though was lost for ever. They say many stepped forward over the years to claim his name, but she rejected every one of them for the madmen and impostors they were. As if the sad creature didn't have enough to haunt her.

When Morphew came to drive me home from Windsor I found not only Papi seated in the berlin but Mother too, in her best bonnet and very gay considering how far she was from home. We were bound for Hammersmith, to see a house Papi thought of taking. It was called Seagreens and it had a number of features to recommend it: spacious, light rooms, parterres and orchards, a clear view to the water meadows at Barnes and, above all, the best possible neighbours: Uncle Christoff and Aunt Hanne lived in the house next door.

My uncle lived in the country to be as far away as possible from the smell of his business. After he and Papi gave up the Coconut Tree Uncle Christoff had gone into the night-soil trade. His men collected it and delivered it to the saltpetre factories where it was turned into money and, Uncle Christoff being the man he was, the money was spent on a bright, airy river-front house filled with pretty things. And now Papi had decided to be a country gentleman too. He and Mother were like sweethearts, planning a new life that took no account of my wishes, for wasn't I engaged to Jack Buzzard, wouldn't I very soon be off their hands? There was a bone-chilling wind blowing off the river that day and it seemed as though it was directed entirely at me. Even the excellent dinner at Uncle Christoff's house didn't comfort me. Mother was burbling like a merry brook.

'Oh Hanne,' she said, 'Ludwig says ve vill grow artishoke und epples, und ve vill heff ein milch cow but I sink Tvyvil vill not like it. In London, you know, der milch comes in ein kann.'

Papi said he had a mind to give Twyvil notice and be done with her airs and graces. Damned if he wouldn't milk the cow himself.

Aunt Hanne couldn't believe that Papi would truly be happy to leave, as she saw it, the splendour of working for a prince, but I'd seen enough of royal households to understand. The days were long, everything must be conducted according to a tangle of rules, and the principal occupation was waiting, always ready, never impatient. Papi had had enough. He could see anyway that before much longer there would be changes at Carlton House.

He said, 'Der time comes. Soon Prince of Vales vill marry.'

Aunt Hanne, who was from Marburg, said he couldn't do better than choose a good, strong Hessen princess. Mother was staunch for Brunswick.

If Papi knew anything he wasn't sharing it with us.

'I am steward,' he said. 'He doss not tell me. Only I know ziss, he vill do vat he moss do.'

I said, 'But there's still Mrs Fitzherbert. What's to be done about her?'

And after a long pause while he puffed and grunted and enjoyed a mouthful of beef he said the knot the Prince had tied with Mrs Fitz was a loose one and easily undone. Without the King's permission all the priests in Christendom couldn't make the contract stick. I thought of Prince Gus's secret wife, kept out of sight on Berkeley Street, and wondered whether she had yet understood the hopelessness of her position.

Papi went to the attorney, the papers for Seagreens were signed, and we rode back to London in the dark with Mother gripping my hand and begging Papi not to let Morphew take us through Hyde Park to have our purses taken and our throats cut. The further behind we left Hammersmith the more subdued she became, and when we were safely back in our warm parlour she burst into tears.

She said, 'Ludwig. If ve go to Hemmersmit, I vill neffer see my friends no more.'

I imagine Papi regarded a life free of Miss Tod and Mrs Lavelle's daily visits as a wonderful prospect but he kissed Mother's hand and promised to bring her to town once a month at least and regale her with a glass of ice cream at the sign of the Green Pineapple.

November 13th 1793

The world is busy rearranging itself without consulting my feelings. Soho Square is to be let. The only home I have ever known. Worse still, Jack has found premises. Now I have to choose: to be an old maid in Hammersmith and a reproach to my parents or to marry and never have a minute to call my own.

12

The shop Jack took was on Park Street, by the corner with the Oxford road. It had stillrooms and stores enough for his needs and an ice pit, and a yard where a cart could be kept. What it lacked was a place for us to live. The rooms above it were already occupied.

Jack said, 'It's a plum of a position and I'm loath to pass it up but I'm stretched as far as I dare go, Nellie. It's the shop or a house. I can't take both. We can't marry yet a while.'

I know how to play a part. I could have acted on a stage like Dora Jordan.

I said, 'You're right, Jack. The business must come first. I understand.'

He thought me a diamond for saying that. It would never have occurred to Jack that I was in no hurry to be chained to a shop counter. But there remained another difficulty. Even though Mother was nervous and Twyvil predicted nothing but misery and mud for her ten guineas a year, my family was removing to the country.

Jack said, 'Here's the thing, Nellie. You'll be out in

126

Hammersmith and I'll be working all hours. I'll never see you.'

Well, I thought, I'll bear that deprivation as bravely as I can. But in truth I didn't much care for the prospect of country life. I loved to walk about busy streets and listen to what people said, and so I concocted a plan that was more to my liking and, conveniently, to Jack's. It was agreed that when Papi and Mother shifted to Seagreens I should lodge with Miss Tod in Meard Street. She vowed to watch over me like a mother but I knew she wouldn't have time to do any such thing. Miss Tod was in a small way of business herself, trimming bonnets, but she was also an active, sociable person so she did what she had to do with speed and efficiency, the sooner to be paid and free to go out of her house. She kept current with the affairs of the nation and cultivated a very mixed acquaintance. Between Hog Lane and Wardour Street very little happened without Miss Tod being one of the first to know.

She was older than my mother, though she didn't seem it. She took Godfrey's Cordial night and morning as a preventative against headaches and, never having had a husband to accommodate and not affording to keep a cook who had to be pandered to, she made her own dinner and ate at whatever hour she pleased. I moved in with her in January 1794.

In February a letter came from Sofy:

Such MISERY! Our new sister has been delivered of a baby boy but we are not allowed to know him and Gus hasn't even

*seen him, his own little son. The Queen said he must go away
IMMEDIATELY, for the sake of his health. It's too cruel. We
saw him before he left for Harwich and he said his heart was
broken but he did not dare oppose the Majesties. Minny thinks
he should have showed more spine. How could he abandon his
wife at such a time? What do you say? Billy Clarence went to
the Chancellor and showed him Gus's marriage lines, to see if
anything could be done to help the case, but it didn't help at all
because Old Loughborough ran to the King immediately and
told everything. The Queen is in SUCH a fury for you know
she won't have anything upset the King and he is VASTLY
UPSET. The marriage is to be declared void and Goosy is to be
put away in Devonshire. Imagine! Gouly says there are no roads
there, only muddy tracks and wild moors, so we will never get to
be aunts. The baby is named Augustus which our own Augusta
says adds up to too many Gustuses by far and she wishes they
had called him Harry but as we shall NEVER see him I don't
see that it matters. Now Dolly's wounds are mended and he is
gone back to Flanders so we are all in a slough of boredom and
CHILBLAINS. I hope I may see you soon.*

In fact she didn't see me until the summer. Jack Buzzard
kept me too busy to go on what he called 'a jaunt' to Windsor.
It became my job to wait on the pleasure of a locksmith, who
promised for Monday morning and appeared on Thursday
afternoon, and on the sign-writer who swore he would be
with us by Friday but never appeared at all. Sometimes I
thought I'd have been wiser to go to Hammersmith and

commune with Papi's cow, but working for Jack brought some advantages. It was left to me to go out and about, to buy string and sealing wax and linen straining cloths, and then, there were the accounts to be kept. A confectioner required a great quantity of costly items: balancing pans, brass basins, marble slabs, cocoa beans, sugar, nuts and spices. And a scribbler's notebook was easily concealed beneath a pile of receipts.

The first thing we sold was a tray of Naples biscuits to Lady Abbot. They were flavoured with orange-flower water and she liked them so well she ordered more, but we couldn't make a living on a tray of biscuits. Jack wasn't idle for a minute, putting up cordials and marmalades in case, as he said, we had a rush, but the people who had sworn to follow him from Gunter's didn't come. They were the kind of customers who went out as much to be seen and have their new hat admired as to enjoy a water ice. The Green Pineapple wasn't that kind of establishment.

Jack said, 'I won't let you down, Nellie. Whatever I have to do, we'll have a house. Somewhere fit to raise young Buzzards.'

I said, 'There's plenty of time.'

How I prayed for time. I had my story well sketched out. I'd go to Windsor, or to Weymouth with the Royalties. Tom Garth would be there and find an occasion to speak to me alone. 'Nellie,' he'd say, 'I hear you're engaged to be married. Am I too late to declare myself? Dare this old man hope?' I'd be wearing a particularly flattering gown and a very simple necklace. The fact that I owned neither cornflower blue lawn nor a string of pearls in no way spoiled my enjoyment of the scene. Garth and I ended in each other's arms. Papi's anger was soon extinguished by the sheer superiority of my new lover, Jack nobly released me from my promise and was soon enough married to a suitably bovine girl, and we all lived happily ever after.

Jack said, 'Better to have babies while you're young though. And two or three's enough. I won't see you worn down like my mam. We'll have a girl first, then the boys. Boys are steadier if they have a sister's example.'

That was how he was. Everything according to a plan. When he was making a confection he had each thing laid out in order on the table top: white of eggs, powder sugar, almonds, wafer paper. I suppose that's why he took things so hard if his plans went awry. Jack thought in ounces and gills and degrees of heat. He had no notion of luck or whimsy.

The pink lemons were my idea. We wrapped them in muslin and steeped them in cochineal syrup until they'd taken the colour, then we put them in the window, piled high on a looking glass. Everyone who passed came in to ask what they were and no one left without buying something. Then an enquiry was made from Lady Dummer's residence for a grand dessert, sufficient for twenty guests and appropriate for an Easter luncheon. Jack was on his way.

He made candied jonquils and marzipan cakes pressed with the Dummer heraldic device, and cornucopia wafers to hold the ices which were a sorbet of violets and a cream ice of coffee, all to be set around a crystal bowl of sherry trifle on ratafia biscuits. While he worked I was left to mind the shop. I told him he had better think of getting an apprentice for I couldn't always be there, but he didn't answer me. When Jack was in his kitchen the house could have fallen down around him.

Three days before Easter he came to Miss Tod's house, hammering on the door well after ten o'clock. Miss Tod had just gone to bed but she came down in her nightgown, I think more to know Jack's business than to watch over my virtue.

He said, 'I've had an idea. Two ideas.'

He brought out two sugar-paste eggs, white, about the size of a plover's, and gave one to me and one to Miss Tod.

I said, 'They'd look prettier if they were mottled. Blue and green.'

'They will be. Spinach water and indigo stone. Leave me to know my business. But crack them open.'

They were hollow, and inside each one there was a piece of paper, rolled up.

I said, 'It's blank.'

'That's where you come in. You reckon to be the writer, Nellie. I'll need twenty mottoes, Saturday morning at the latest.'

Miss Tod said she loved a motto and between us we'd think them up in no time. But I knew I'd have them done before I slept that night.

I said, 'What was the second idea?'

'I was thinking,' he said. 'Seeing how things have turned

131

out, instead of the Green Pineapple we should be called At the Sign of the Pink Lemon.'

And as the sign-writer still hadn't deigned to appear, that's what we did.

Morphew came to Meard Street to drive me to Windsor in time for the summer exodus to Weymouth. The Royalties were to call first at Portsmouth, for a review to mark the Battle of the First of June. Our army in Flanders seemed to make little progress so a victory at sea was a great cause for celebration.

Morphew was in a morose mood. Though he was born a country boy he had left Norfolk when he was twelve years old and lived ever since in the city. Hammersmith didn't suit him.

'I can't sleep, Miss Nellie,' he said. 'And I'll quote you the reason. Unhooly noises. Foxes screeching. And howls hooting. Then there's another thing. Sarah Twyvil. She's getting above herself.'

His life had changed greatly since the move. Papi had retired from his daily attendance at the Prince of Wales's household so Morphew had less driving to do and more duties indoors. But Twyvil treated indoors as her own kingdom. She had even insisted on his getting a new wig for she said the old one was so full of animal life she could make stock from it and Mother, ever fearful of losing her cook, had a short tie wig brought in for him. But Twyvil's victory was illusory because Morphew kept his old yellow coiffure in the coach house and the very moment he was out of sight of Seagreens he'd put it on.

I said, 'I think Twyvil is fond of you.'

He chuckled.

I said, 'I think nagging is her way of showing it. Did you ever think of marrying her?'

'I did not,' he said. 'She's been too long without a saddle on her, that one. But I believe you're right, Miss Nellie. I believe she do carry a torch for me. I think Sarah Twyvil has had her disappointments.'

He was a disappointed man himself. The Revolution hadn't come, though he still kept a liberty cap and a cockade in the inside pocket of his greatcoat, just in case. But no gentlemen had been hanged from lamp posts in St James's and the Prince of Wales, who was every week predicted to be ruined, just grew fatter than ever.

Portsmouth was in full fig for the returning fleet. Admiral Howe had engaged a convoy guarding grain ships bound for France. The French had lost seven ships of the line in the battle but, as we learned later, the grain ships had still reached France, so both sides claimed to have won the day. But the King understood that his Navy would like to see him, no matter how diluted the victory. He was their father and they were his lads that had braved the deep Atlantic.

June 27th 1794
   The Majesties and the Princess Royal went aboard Admiral

Howe's flagship, the Queen Charlotte. *Then we all processed to church for a service of thanksgiving. Rolfe and Bulstrode are the equerries, both too ancient to see anything of this war. Sofy mistook my enquiry about Garth for interest in his stable-groom.*

The Portsmouth review was a trying occasion and I thought the strain of it showed on the King's face, for though he was cheered loudly wherever he walked there was no escaping the sight of maimed men. Some were regular serving sailors, some were soldiers who'd been drafted to the marine, but many of them were pressed men, farm hands and labourers who had never in their lives thought of going to sea, still less of leaving a leg or an arm at the bottom of it.

Amelia said, 'Don't look at them, if it offends you.'

I said, 'It doesn't offend me. I know what it is for people to look away. But what will become of those poor men?'

Sofy said, 'I expect provision is made for them. I'm sure places are found for them.'

But what places? What work could a man do if he had no limbs?

I said, 'I wish you would ask the King, Sofy. I should like to know what's done for them.'

'Oh, but I couldn't,' she said. 'The King is not at all well, Nellie. He's not to be troubled. We hope the sea bathing will set him up.'

And Minny said, 'Yes, if we can only get through tomorrow without a squall.'

By which she meant, that the Prince of Wales should come

to Spithead at the appointed hour, launch the ship that was being named for him and go away again without disturbing the Majesties' peace. And so it transpired. He arrived only half an hour late, with a companion who had brought to bear his own soldierly insistence on punctuality.

The King and Queen and Royal and Augusta had lodged overnight at the Governor's House but we were in Portsmouth town with the rest of the suite, in whatever rooms could be found for us. Elizabeth and Minny and Amelia had been watching all morning for the Prince of Wales's carriage. There was a commotion in the street and Minny said, 'He's here. So far so good.'

Then Amelia said, 'Who's that with him?'

Sofy and I joined them at the window. The Prince looked up at once and waved. His face was pink and shiny, as though it had been polished, and he seemed so squeezed into his blue coat I wondered he could breathe. The man beside him was taller and much leaner. He had a patch over his left eye and a scarlet dolman coat slung around his shoulders because his arm was in a sling.

Elizabeth cried, 'It's Ernie! Ernie is home!'

And that was the first time I ever saw Prince Ernest.

13

Prince Ernie had been winged by a cannon ball at the Battle of Tourcoing but was expected to recover the use of his arm. It was, as Minny said, just the right kind of injury: not life-threatening, but visible enough to allow the Royalties their own little bit of glory. His eye, well, that depended on who you asked. Ernest said it was a sabre wound, sustained in close combat, but Mrs Chevely said he had always had a bad eye as long as she could remember.

Whatever the truth, he was quite the war hero, with his sisters falling over themselves to minister to him. He came on with us to Weymouth and the King seemed to relish his company. They rode together every morning after the sea-bathing, and in the evenings Ernie would sit with him and listen to Mr Handel's music. The Princesses were grateful for that. Every day he stayed was one recital less for them to endure and when there was a ball he always accompanied us to the Assembly Rooms and danced with every one of them. He was the perfect partner. A lightly wounded soldier with a pedigree the Majesties couldn't possibly object to.

His hair was tawny, his face was gaunt and his bearing very military, with his chest puffed out. He made me think of a bird I'd seen in a picture book, a golden eagle presiding over his eyrie of sisterly chicks. I disliked him from the first. He was sharp with the servants and made me nervous that I might receive the same treatment from him, but he chose to ignore me instead. I'd have enjoyed Weymouth a deal better without him in the party but I was glad enough to be out of the heat of London and the confines of Jack's shop. As people left the city to spend the summer in their country houses there was little trade but Jack would never think to close his door. Work was all he knew.

We made many excursions from Weymouth that summer. We went to Durdle Door, and to Sandsfoot to see the ruins of the castle, and to Chesil Beach to collect pretty pebbles. Then one day, at Ernest's instigation, it was proposed to drive out to Ilsington House.

Minny said, 'But surely Old Garth is away from home?'

'Makes no difference,' he said. 'They'll put on a good luncheon for us anyway, I dare say.'

Sofy said, 'Oh yes, do let's go, then Nellie may see her ardent admirer. The Major's groom was very taken with her last year.'

'Nellie?' he said. 'An admirer?'

'And she has a suitor, too. Nellie's going to marry Jack Buzzard.'

He snorted.

'Buzzard, eh?' he said. 'What is he, a blind buzzard?'

Prince Ernie thought himself quite a wit.'

So we set off for Piddletown and descended on poor Mrs Chaffey, a party of eight expecting to be fed and watered. Tom Garth was not at home, neither was he a Major any more. He was promoted Colonel and was on manoeuvres with the Sussex Fencibles and then was going back to Flanders directly. I was both sorry and glad. I would have liked to see him but was afraid my feelings would make me tongue-tied in his company. Bashful silence may add to a beautiful girl's attractions but it would have been a calamity for me.

Sofy, who had entirely misread the situation, conspired with Ernie to have me sent to the stables on a needless errand. She said she believed her horse might have sustained a stone bruise. The turning points in life rarely come announced by a fanfare. Little chance events are what set us on one path instead of another. For King Louis and his queen you might say it was a face glimpsed by a rush light, and then a broken carriage wheel. For me it was an empty tack room and my peculiar way of remembering people, not by their face or their voice, but by their smell.

A worn wool coat hung from a peg, full-skirted, deep-cuffed, old-fashioned. I knew it was Tom Garth's and I, pathetic creature that I was, buried my face in it to try and catch the essence of him. It was wood smoke and bay rum. Then I heard a low laugh and I thought my heart would leap out of my chest. Enoch Heppenstall had been watching me.

'Wiping your snout?' he said. 'Colonel won't like that. He's right particular.'

I said, 'I was only smelling it. The coat reminded me of someone.'

He laughed again.

'Smelling it? What are you then, a hunting dog? I remember you. You're not quite right in the head, are you? You're not quite all there.'

His insult didn't bother me. All I cared about was that Garth shouldn't hear of what I'd done.

He said, 'Never worry, I won't let on. You let me see what you've got under your petticoats and we'll say no more.'

I fled before he could touch me. Well, I thought, be calm. He's only a stable hand, and after this moment I need never see him again. But I didn't allow for Sofy who was eager for me to have a romance and whispered most insistently in Ernie's ear.

He said, 'That was speedily done. Did the lad look at the horse?'

'He will.'

'But you didn't *see* him do it? Damnation, I was clear enough. Now go and see to it, and don't come back until you're satisfied.'

He winked at Sofy.

I said, 'I'd rather not.'

'Rather not!' he said. 'Rather not!'

I said, 'I feel a little faint.'

Sofy said, 'She does look very pale, Ernie.'

She rubbed my hands between hers.

I said, 'If it's so important I'm sure one of the Major's maids would go.'

He said, 'Do you think Garth keeps servants to fetch and carry for you, Miss? Now do as I tell you or you'll be sorry.'

No one spoke up to defend me. They all feared Ernie's famous temper.

Enoch Heppenstall was watching for me. 'I reckoned you'd be back,' he said. 'Come to see what I've got for you?'

I said, 'You'll please to put Her Royal Highness's mare to the trot directly.'

'When I'm good and ready. Only I'm good and ready for something else just now.'

He was so close I could see every particular of his mouth: a crooked tooth and bristles he'd missed when he'd shaved that morning, and a string of spit between his parted lips.

I said, 'Don't touch me. My beau'll kill anyone who touches me.'

He sniggered.

'Your beau? Face like your'n, I don't reckon you've got no beau. And if you have, well, I like a slice off a buttered loaf. Now up you go.'

He twisted my arm till I thought I should faint, then he pushed me up the ladder and into the hayloft. I thought to fight him off at first but that seemed to please him so I lay perfectly still instead. Let him make his own pleasure, I thought, and I hoped he'd choke on it. Indeed I thought he might, he looked so angry as he spent himself. There was a sweet smell of wheat straw and the horses below made soft, shifting noises. It was soon over.

He had to help me down from the loft. My legs wouldn't carry me. It was an unavoidable act of gentleness after the violence he'd done me and I hated him all the more for it.

He said, 'You're not bad, you. Apart from your face you're like a normal lass.'

I couldn't look at him.

He said, 'And you can tell the Duke there's nowt wrong with that mare. She's as right as ninepence.'

I found a kitchen maid and asked for a glass of water but my appearance alarmed her so much she ran for Mrs Chaffey. She took me to her pantry and sat me in her high-backed chair.

'You sit here, nice and quiet, my dear,' she said. 'You'll have been thrown about too much in that gig. Bumpeting around the countryside, all unnecessary. I don't know what the Royal Highnesses are thinking of.'

I closed my eyes. I don't know how long I sat there, only that I came back to consciousness with a jolt and was quite certain I wasn't alone. On a shelf, beside the jars of pickled quinces, Garth's parrot was watching me with one black eye.

'Oh dear,' she said, in that unearthly voice of hers. 'Oh dear.'

Sofy insisted on sitting with me in the carriage instead of hacking back to Weymouth on her cursed horse.

'Poor Nellie,' she said. 'I expect it was the pie they served us. I didn't care for the look of it at all.'

Amelia said, 'I ate the pie and I'm quite well. I don't think Nellie's sick at all. I think she's sulking because Ernie put her in her place. He was rather fierce.'

Sofy said, 'Is that it? I do wish you'd say.'

Minny said, 'Leave her in peace. Whatever it is it won't be helped by pestering.'

At Gloucester Lodge I conducted myself very carefully. I answered when spoken to, took nothing but a little egg custard for my dinner, and accepted Mrs Che's suggestion to go to bed early. Sofy crept in to see me.

She said, 'We are still friends?'

'Of course, but Sofy I shall never go to Ilsington House again so please don't ask me.'

'Lord,' she said, 'how very dramatic. But actually, I agree with you. It was too boring. In future, if Ernie wants to go he can go alone.'

We began our last week in Weymouth and word came that the Prince of Wales intended to pay us a visit. He was in Hampshire and expected to be with us by dinner time the next day. This caused great excitement. The arrival of any visitor brought relief from our routine and with the Prince of Wales there was also the likelihood that he would bring his sisters gifts.

Only Elizabeth demurred. She said, 'I wish he wouldn't come. He'll discompose the King and then the Queen will get headaches and we shall all pay for it.'

Minny said there had to be a very good reason for him to leave his jolly friends and come to what would assuredly be a cool reception from the Majesties, and she was right. The Prince of Wales had the soundest possible reason for interrupting the King's summer. He had chosen a bride: Caroline, daughter of the Duke of Brunswick.

Princess Caroline was also a first cousin and for that reason it was possible that the King wouldn't allow the match. He believed removal by one or two degrees was a much sounder principle of husbandry. Also, it was well known that at least half the Brunswicks were mad. But the King didn't reject the idea. In fact he seemed so amenable that the Prince of Wales sent Ernie off to Brighton immediately, to break the news to Mrs Fitz. It was the Queen who raised objections to the marriage.

Sofy said, 'Why must she always spoil everything? I should so like to have a sister-in-law.'

Of course, Sofy already had sisters-in-law but they didn't count. Freddie York's wife divided her time between her bed and the card table and was never seen at Windsor or in town. Goosy Murray was banished, and Billy Clarence's household arrangements were too shameful to be spoken of. Royal and Augusta tried to explain the Queen's reservations.

'Her Majesty feels,' Augusta said, 'that Caroline may not be fitted to the life she'd have to lead.'

Amelia said, 'How can she not be fitted? She is a princess.'

'Let's say she may be accustomed to a *busier* life than a princess of Wales might expect.'

Sofy said, 'But surely no busier than we're kept? I never have a moment to myself.'

Royal said, 'A life can be busy, Sofy, without being industrious. It can be filled from morning to night with silliness.'

'Yes,' Augusta said. 'And that's the point. The Queen feels that Caroline may have been left to run too free.'

'Well,' Sofy said, 'I'm sure all she'll need is our help and guidance. I certainly intend to be her friend.'

The Queen was overruled, the King gave his consent to the marriage and Lord Malmesbury was dispatched to Brunswick with a necklace and a length of very fine Brussels lace. We were at war and many battlefields lay between Germany and England, but the Prince of Wales was in a hurry. He had creditors baying for his blood and marrying meant money. Caroline would bring a dowry and Parliament would vote him a more generous allowance.

We travelled back to Windsor in the first week of September. Morphew was to take me on to London the next morning.

Sofy said, 'I wish you wouldn't go.'

I said, 'I'll come for your birthday.'

She whispered, 'But that's weeks and weeks away, and you know I depend on you.'

She meant her eyes. They never had been strong and the Royalties were so miserly with tapers she had over-strained them. When I was with her I threaded her needle if she found it too difficult and now, with a wedding promised, they were all in a flurry of sewing. Sofy needed spectacles but she refused to admit it.

Minny said, 'I know she struggles, and I have spoken to the Queen about it. But Sofy is a little vain, you know. She's quite convinced she'll never get a husband if she has spectacles on her nose.'

It was too silly. A princess may get a husband without even being inspected.

I said, 'But she knows *I* found a husband and I have something unsightly that can't be taken off and folded away in a case.'

Minny said, 'You're made of stronger stuff, Nellie. When you live twenty years with a mark I suppose it tempers you. Besides, Sofy's such a noodle. She must know by now that none of us will ever be allowed a husband.'

In town the talk was all of Princess Caroline, who would be Princess of Wales and then our next queen – as long as Prinnie didn't eat a beefsteak too many and burst before he came to the throne. Miss Tod said Caroline of Brunswick was reported to have as great an appetite as her future husband, and not only for food. 'Ungovernable passions of the flesh' were the words being put about. Lovers were hinted at, and that was a serious charge indeed. If she was accustomed to encouraging admirers it was a habit that would have to be abandoned for ever. A Princess of Wales was untouchable. She had to be a sacred vessel of the succession, whatever liberties her prince might take. And on that point there remained the question of Mrs Fitz, and also of the new queen bee in the Prince's hive, Lady Jersey.

According to Papi Mrs Fitzherbert had settled amicably. He said she must be glad not to have the Prince coming to her door with noisy friends just as she was going to bed. She was nearly forty and had no patience with rowdy young men who had dined too well. As for Lady Jersey, who was even older than Mrs Fitz and I suppose in even greater need of her sleep, it was *she* who had proposed the Brunswick match. She knew the gravity of the Prince's situation and that nothing short of a marriage allowance would dig him out of it. Furthermore, if he married he would have less time for the boudoir and more money for buying little tokens of gratitude for a helpful, sympathetic friend, so altogether Lady Jersey had managed things very well.

First the wedding was expected to be in October, but Lord Malmesbury sent word from Brunswick that the bride's preparations weren't far enough advanced. Then November was mooted but heavy seas delayed her sailing, and in December a fearful cold blew in from the north and froze the ships in the Hamburg harbour. The marrying had to wait until the spring thaw.

I missed Sofy's birthday that year. It was her seventeenth. I was not well enough to travel. At night the memory of Enoch Heppenstall kept me awake and in the day the lack of sleep and the smell of hot sugar made me faint. Jack put it down to a bilious derangement and suggested a nettle tonic.

A letter came from Sofy:

146

Windsor, October 30th 1794

The P of W has been VERY piano. Minny says he is rehearsing for the role of Uxorious Stay-at-Home. We are our usual dull winter selves and spend our days puzzling what our belle-soeur will REALLY look like. We were told she has excellent teeth but later we heard she had at least two pulled since the marriage was agreed. We had better expect her to have three heads and a wart on each nose, then we shall be prepared for anything.

The Illustrious Personage is still GREATLY displeased with the match but tries not to show it for the sake of the King. His health has been so much better since everything is settled. There has been no recurrence of the Agitations in spite of some cross words with Ernie and the worry of what is to be done with Fred.

After the rout of Dunkirk Fred York had been relieved of his command and sent home with his Field-Marshal's tail between his legs. 'Incompetent,' the *Morning Chronicle* said. 'A perfect example,' the *True Briton* said, 'of the folly of giving high command to a man on the strength of his lineage.' Furthermore, York's Duchess wanted no truck with him and so he hung about St James's with loud friends who rose late and drank deeply. Ernest had returned to Flanders, his shoulder mended, but not before he had quarrelled with the King:

Ernie has only a regiment, which hardly seems fair when Dolly has a corps to command and he THREE YEARS younger.

147

Ernie threatened if he was to be so humiliated he would enlist as a private and let it be the talk of the town, but the King still wouldn't do anything for him, so now he is gone away in a FEARFUL stew. Lady Harcourt says he has BROUGHT IT ON HIMSELF by his unruly temperament. I think it was not her place to say it and I feel VERY sorry for him because I'm sure he's a splendid soldier.

Dearest Nellie, I miss you greatly and pray that you will soon be recovered from your complaint. What do you take for it?

I had gone as far as St Giles's to consult an apothecary. The powder he recommended cost ten shillings. I hadn't seen my monthly indisposition since September and knew I must act quickly. But the powder didn't work though it gave me powerful cramps. Jack noticed nothing. He was swamped with orders – a meringue island set in a lake of elderflower jelly with sugar paste swans for Lady Haddon, flummery and comfits for Viscount Trimm, cinnamon bonbons in baskets of silvered spun sugar for Mrs Garr-Lonsdale – and I was expected to run between the shop and the stillroom. I couldn't face Christmas at Hammersmith with Papi fussing about sending for Dr Mayersbach and Aunt Hanne giving me a searching look. My aunt had always been quick to sense when a woman was carrying a child. I threw myself on the mercy of Miss Tod.

'That's long engagements for you,' she said. 'Men can never contain themselves and it's the girl who must bear the consequences. Why don't you marry him and be done? You can both live with me.'

I said, 'It's not Jack's child.'

'Ah,' she said. 'Well then.'

She loaned me four guineas out of her burying money to pay a certain Mrs Dacey for removal of an internal obstruction and for a chairman to bring me back from Hosier Street. And that dear woman, who you would think had never kept a confidence in her life, took my story with her to the grave.

Mrs Dacey's place of business was her own bedroom. The tools of her trade were a loop of wire, a basin, and a pot of pennyroyal tea. I have never known such pain. But it passed, and when she told me my obstruction was gone and I could be on my way, I felt so light and free.

'Women's troubles,' Miss Tod had told Jack. 'She'll be as good as new tomorrow.'

But that night I took such a fever it was two weeks before I could leave my bed.

'No need to trouble your mother,' I remember Miss Tod saying. 'She's never been the same since she lost Eliza. We'll call it a winter chill, shall we, dear?'

She must have been in a terror of me dying but she never showed it. I burned hot, then cold shivers gripped me till the bed shook. I saw my dead sister. I saw demons unbuttoned in haylofts. Jack closed up the Pink Lemon and sat beside me, white with fear.

'Don't die, Nellie,' he kept whispering. 'I know I've worked you too hard. I'll take care of you. Only don't die.'

I believe I came close to it. Then, as the fever passed and I grew stronger, I thought over my situation. Enoch Heppenstall had done me a great wrong but it was my own foolish fancy that had put me at his mercy, and since God had been good enough to spare me I would turn over a new leaf. I would forget about Tom Garth and try to love Jack Buzzard.

14

I was in the presence of Princess Caroline only once and that was in the summer of 1795. She had come to England in April, when the seas were safer for travel, and of all the people Wales might have sent to meet her at Greenwich he chose Lady Jersey, or at least, he allowed Lady Jersey to choose herself. It was an unkind act, and insult was added to injury by Lady Jersey's coming late and straightway finding fault with the Princess's gown.

No public notice was given of Caroline's arrival. If there had been I'm sure a great crowd would have turned out to greet our future queen. Miss Tod said she wouldn't have missed it for the world. But instead Lady Jersey bundled her into a closed carriage and hurried her to St James's to meet her prince. By Sofy's account he didn't like what he saw. Well, perhaps Caroline wasn't so happy either, once she'd taken a look, for the Prince of Wales had taken to wearing a lilac wig and he had grown fatter than ever. But she was far from home and she had cast her die. Sofy wrote:

Everyone said that Caroline was over rouged which Minnie believes was the handiwork of Lady Jersey, but Lady Jersey is appointed a Lady of the Bedchamber, you know, so I cannot think she would do anything so NAUGHTY. The Prince complained that Malmesbury had dissembled about the excellence of her figure, and that she smelled of yesterday's fish. Altogether he found nothing to praise in her.

We did not see her until the evening of the wedding and therefore by candlelight, but I thought she looked well enough. Our dear Wales looked magnificent but I regret to say he had been drinking, which Billy Clarence said was to deaden the pain of what he must go through. But all went off well, the King beamed with delight throughout and our Illustrious Personage wore her PLEASANT face. There was no wedding breakfast. The Waleses retired to Carlton House, we returned to the Queen's House for bread and milk, and Billy set off for Brighton with a letter for A CERTAIN PERSON, but we are not supposed to know anything of that. Now they are making their honeymoon and are soon to come to Windsor so we shall become properly acquainted with our new sister. I hope you are now well enough that I may see you VERY SOON.

And so I went to Windsor though Jack tried to dissuade me. He said he feared I was not sufficiently recovered from my winter fever, but it seemed to me if I was well enough for making two hundred sweetmeat papers and walking to Holborn to buy gold leaf I was well enough to visit my friend. He didn't have dominion over me yet. Jack wouldn't marry while he had debts, and he had ovens still to pay for. At the time of our betrothal Papi had seemed to promise an investment in Jack's business but times had changed. Every month more of our soldiers were shipped to Flanders and our fleet chased the French about the Mediterranean, but an end to the fighting seemed no closer and war creates new opportunities for a man's money. Much of Papi's had gone into army blankets and ship's biscuits and oakum.

The Prince and Princess of Wales went to Kempshott in Hampshire for their honeymoon and a strange affair it must have been because the Prince had invited quite a party of his friends to join them. Viscount Petersham and Lord Ballantyne and heaven knows what other coxcombs, and Lady Jersey too, for a princess can't be without her bedchamber ladies, no matter who they may be. Then they continued to Windsor as promised and lodged in the Prince's apartments in the Castle. On their second day, while the King and Wales and Fred York went out with the buckhounds, we walked with the new Princess to Frogmore for one of the Queen's rustic tea parties.

Princess Caroline talked a great deal. I suppose she was all nerves. As amiable as the Royal Highnesses were they were still strangers to her. She spoke good English, better than my mother or my father who had been so many years in England, and sometimes she lapsed into French, which always helps to give a refined gloss. But there the elegance ended. She was florid, with a very jutting bosom which her gown did nothing to flatter and her stockings were dirty. Mrs Che had it from Lady Herbert that the Princess of Wales had no objection to washing and changing her linen, only that in Brunswick she hadn't been accustomed to the practice and so would have to be reminded to do it.

She was very jolly, and free with her opinions, roaring with laughter and never hesitating to take a second slice of cake while everyone fixed their smiles and studied the floor. It was so obvious she would not do. I longed for the party to be over. I felt I was watching a fly that was caught in a spider's web but didn't yet realize it.

At supper her flaws were dissected.

Amelia's chief complaint was that her eyelashes were pale and colourless.

'Also,' she said, 'Wales is right, she *does* wear too much rouge.'

Sofy said, 'I think she has a naturally high colour.'

Minny said, 'Her colour doesn't matter and neither do her eyelashes. What matters is she hasn't an ounce of circum-spection. Imagine rattling on like that, and in Her Majesty's presence.'

The question was, who should correct her? Not the Queen, who had never wanted her in the first place, and seemingly not the Prince of Wales who was already finding reasons to be away from her as much as possible. Amelia thought Lady Jersey should take her in hand.'

I said, 'But Lady Jersey will do nothing but mischief. Surely it suits her very well for the Prince to dislike his wife?'

Amelia said, 'What can you mean?'

Minny rushed in. She said, 'Nellie means that Lady Jersey loves a project. She's never happier than when she's being useful. But this isn't her affair. Wales must help Caroline to be more to his liking. He must just try a little harder. After all, the King can't always have enjoyed Her Majesty's particular little ways but he's made the best of things.'

For all the talk of the Prince loathing his wife it transpired that he could endure at least a little of her company. Before my visit ended exciting news was whispered around Lower Lodge. The Princess of Wales had missed her monthly show and was believed to have conceived a child.

Sofy said, 'I do pray it's true. Now we shall *really* be aunts.'

Of course Billy Clarence already had two sons of his actress paramour, Dora Jordan, but, like Prince Gus's child who had been sent to Devonshire, they did not exist.

Sofy begged me to go with them to Weymouth. She said I looked in need of sea air, she said the summer would be dull without me, but I had no wish to go anywhere near Dorset.

I said, 'I can't. I have obligations in London now.'

'Of course,' she said. 'Jack Buzzard. Do you really mean to marry him? You don't seem very eager.'

'We have no money. Perhaps next year.'

'If I had a sweetheart I'd marry him instantly and live on bread and butter. But if Jack Buzzard hasn't named the day why can't you come to Weymouth?'

'Because Jack needs my help and you don't, now you have your spectacles. Isn't it good to be able to thread your own needles again?'

'I suppose so. Even though I look a fright.'

I said, 'You know you don't.'

'Not that it matters,' she said. 'As we're all to be kept walled up like nuns no man will ever have to look at me, spectacles or no. Royal will be twenty-nine in September, you know. It's all too hopeless.'

But Royal's wait was nearly over. Fritz, Prince of Württemburg, had her in his sights. Sofy wrote:

Gloucester House, Weymouth, August 3rd
My dearest Nellie,

The Waleses ARE going to have a baby. Isn't it thrilling? It will be born after Christmas, and now we have another cause for excitement. We may soon be sewing Royal's trousseau! Fritz Württemburg has made her an offer and it is being SERIOUSLY CONSIDERED. Minny says the portcullis has been raised an inch but will need to go a good deal higher for any Württemburg to squeeze under it as they are quite famous for their rotundity. Royal seems well disposed towards the match and the Queen thinks it very suitable, but the King delays and delays and makes endless investigations into Fritz's character. There have been RUMOURS. I wish you were here to help me fathom them.

Miss Tod had never heard of Duke Fritz but she made urgent enquiries. In Soho you could always find someone to guide you through the thicket of European royalty. Here is what she discovered.

Royal's suitor was a widower, with three children. His deceased wife, Zelmira, was the older sister of Caroline, our Princess of Wales. Those were the facts. The rest was conjecture, shrouded in a cold Russian mist. Fritz had married Zelmira when she was fifteen and they had gone to Russia to reap the bounty of his sister's marriage to the Tsarevich. He was given a governorship and they lived there very well, perhaps more comfortably than they would have done in Württemburg. But when it was time for Fritz to return to his Duchy, to prepare for the day when he would be its king, Zelmira had refused to go with him. She said he was a beast and a brute and she would endure no more of it. So Fritz went home without her and took the children with him, and she stayed in Russia where she soon died, some said of a broken heart, some said from an excess of ecstasy while being ravished by a Cossack, and some said from having a pillow put over her inconvenient face.

Duke Fritz was tried before the Meard Street Kitchen Table Court and found guilty of 'something unnatural at the very least'. As Miss Tod said in her summing up, 'What woman would abandon three children, except she has been abominably used?'

Poor Royal. Her first – perhaps her only – chance of a husband, and for the suitor to have such a troubling history. But then, perhaps Royal wouldn't have known how to live with a kindly husband. The Queen had accustomed her to criticism by discovering some fault in her every day. If Duke

Fritz turned out to be all benevolence she might miss her daily scolding.

The Royalties seemed anyway to court bad luck in marriage. York and his duchess lived as strangers, Prince Gus was kept a thousand miles from his true love, Clarence's wife wasn't even to be spoken of and Wales, who had married for money, was as hard-pressed as ever. The great improvement he had expected had been eaten away. Parliament said his vast debts couldn't simply be wiped from the books and therefore monies must be set aside from his new allowance every year until the debt was cleared. We were at war and it wasn't seemly for a Royal Highness to live so free and easy. But the Prince of Wales never did mend his ways. He couldn't buy *one* morning robe or *one* sabre but must order half a dozen. Furthermore, he was stuck with a wife he disliked.

Morphew drove me to Hammersmith for Papi's birthday and gave me his assessment of the Hanovers.

'Bad breeding,' he said. 'All this marrying kin is contrary to nature and I'll quote you a forhinstance. Dogs. If you don't keep them apart before you know it you'll have sisters whelping off brothers and all sorts. Then what do you get? I'll tell you. Temperment, that's what, and runts, with addled brains. Now I never heard of this Fritz Wartyburg but I'll lay you a wager now, no good'll come of it. Boil it down, he's kin. No, if the Princess Royal is getting skittish they should find her an honest Englishman. And you can tell 'em I said so.'

Mother said, 'How vass der jorney, Herzchen? I heff told Morvew he moss not drive so fast und he moss not spit.

Now ve are in Hemmersmit, you know, he sometimes iss not nice.'

I said, 'He didn't spit.'

'Gut,' she said. 'I sink, Nellie, venn you marry Jack ve vill giff you Morvew. Like vedding gift.'

15

On January 7th, 1796 the Princess of Wales was delivered of an enormous, healthy girl. She was given the names Charlotte Augusta. As Sofy wrote:

> *You may imagine that our Augusta is far from pleased. We already have more than enough Augustas and Augustuses and now we begin to have too many Charlottes. She says she prays the next addition to the family will have four paws so it can be named Spot. The King though is GREATLY DELIGHTED with the child and so is the Prince of Wales whom we hope will now be more civil towards his wife.*

But the war between the Waleses was only just beginning. The Prince was more in Brighton than he was in town, though my father had still not been paid for Marine Pavilion, nor ever was, and the Princess lived at Carlton House, ringed about by courtiers of Lady Jersey's choosing. The word from Brighton was that the Prince stayed away from his wife because he couldn't bear to look at her or smell her or listen to her silly chatter, but this last criticism won him little sympathy. He had surrounded himself all his life with silly chattering friends. The word from the back stairs at Carlton House was different: that the *true* reason the Prince declined to share his wife's bed was that he lacked the vigour expected of a young husband and was embarrassed to be found wanting.

Miss Tod said, 'It doesn't matter. He's got an heir, may God protect her, so let them live apart. There's plenty of husbands and wives who'd choose to do the same if they only had houses enough.'

It was a subject close to my heart. Through Jack's hard work and our strict limit to the size of 'brought forwards', especially those of the grander addresses, the Pink Lemon was turning a profit. There was talk that we would soon be in a position to marry.

I didn't quite love Jack but I had grown to appreciate his steadiness and his quiet ways. But I liked my life too, my little room at Miss Tod's, and my freedom. If Jack said, 'Come at nine' and I wanted time to write, I could say Miss Tod needed me till ten. If Miss Tod said she was depending on me to make up a four for whist I could plead ices to be stirred for a ball supper. I knew, though, we couldn't continue that way for ever and I took some comfort that marrying had not prevented Miss Burney from publishing a new novel. It was the promise of seeing her that made me determined to go to Windsor that summer.

Jack said, 'I wish you'd give them notice, Nellie. Tell them you're soon to be wed and you can't be spared. It was a bad day's work when your father put you up for that position.'

I said, 'Some day Sofy will marry. She'll be carried off to some little kingdom on the Rhine and I'll never see her again. But as long as she's kept at home I can't deny her my company. You don't know how dull her life is.'

'My heart bleeds for her,' he said, but still, he accepted my going. For all his growling about Sofy he was in a happy frame of mind on two counts. First, the tenants in the rooms above the shop talked of quitting. Secondly, he'd found a boy to be his apprentice and learn the sugar work. Ambrose Kersie. He was to sleep on a truckle bed in the dry store until we moved upstairs.

Ambrose was an orphan boy. He'd been left at the Foundling Hospital in January of '84, a month old as near as they could say, and they'd named him for the strip of grey kersie his mother had pinned to his nightshirt in case she should come to claim him. But she never did. He was small for thirteen, very quiet and cautious but in good health. He didn't show any great enthusiasm or gratitude for being apprenticed to a master confectioner of Oxford Street. He just followed Jack's orders and kept his thoughts to himself. In a way they were all he had. He came to us without even a locking box.

I asked him if he could read.

'Some,' he said.

I said, 'Would you like to learn?'

'Don't mind,' he said.

That was Ambrose. You'd have thought he was being charged by the word.

I travelled to Windsor on the Oxford coach, and as the weather was set fair I rode on the rumble to save money. I see from my diary that I found the Royalties in a state of discreet civil war:

May 14th 1796

Wales and his princess have given up all pretence of living together and the battle lines are drawn. The King refuses to take sides and Lady Jersey has retired to the country so the Prince has lost his deadliest weapon, but when the troops are counted he still has the advantage. Princess Caroline is apparently such an incurable flirt and such an irremediable slattern that only Billy Clarence and Sofy speak up in her defence.

The prevailing view was that everyone had done their best with Caroline, that all she had needed to do was follow the example of the Queen but she defiantly would not. The fact that the Prince of Wales hadn't followed the example of the King was held to be of no account. Sofy's chief concern was for the baby.

'What if Caroline takes her away?' she said. 'What if she feels so unwelcome here she goes back to Brunswick and takes the little darling with her?'

Minny said, 'Don't be a goose. Charlotte isn't hers to take

163

away. Charlotte belongs to England. And if Caroline doesn't mend her ways I shouldn't wonder if the King doesn't take the baby from her and bring her to us, to be properly raised.'

I said, 'But surely, a child should be with its mother?'

Amelia said, 'No, Nellie. That may be the way with *your* kind of people but for us it's not at all the case.'

And Minny said, 'It's true. The Duke of Württemburg's children have grown up without their mother and Royal hears that they do very well.'

The Princess Royal's betrothal to Fritz was all but sealed. The only impediment to an early wedding was the war. The King wouldn't allow her to travel until she was guaranteed a safe passage. She seemed not to mind the wait. She was fatter than ever and a martyr to her liver but she had landed a husband and so had cleared the way for her sisters to do the same.

Miss Burney, who was now Madame D'Arblay, came to tea at Frogmore and we all attended. She was quite unchanged but I think she would not have known me, had it not been for my mark.

'Cornelia Welche,' she said, 'you're all grown up. I forget how time passes.'

I had bought a copy of *Camilla* for her to sign.

She said, 'And you still write? Of course you do. How could you not when there is so much to observe?'

One eyebrow discreetly raised in the direction of the Royalties.

I said, 'Your husband doesn't mind the time your writing takes?'

'He doesn't. He's a sensible man and not over careful of his dignity. *Camilla* has bought us a house. And are you married too?'

'Soon. Jack's in business and I have to help him. I do write, but every time the shop bell rings I have to leave off.'

'Ah yes,' she said. 'And then there will be children. I have a son now, you know. And I must say he's a greatly superior creation to any of my books.'

She signed my book *To Cornelia, a fellow scribbler.* Then she appended the words, *between each clanging of the shop bell.* I wanted to ask her more. Did she rework what she wrote, over and over until it was a mess or did she play with it in her mind first so it came from her pen clean and perfect? Did she throw away more than she kept? But I lost my chance. Princess Elizabeth interrupted us, very full of herself because she'd had some of her designs engraved and published, to illustrate a little book of verse. They were pretty enough, but un-remarkable. I'm sure it had only been published to flatter her because she was royalty.

Amelia said, 'Poor Burney. She looked quite strained.'

I said, 'I thought she looked very well. And she's certainly very happy.'

Sofy said, 'Nellie was always very thick with her so we must allow her to judge.'

Amelia said, 'But Sofy, they say she has to live on practi-cally nothing a year.'

I said, 'Many people do, Amelia.'

165

She gave me one of her Royal Highness looks that they were all capable of pulling from their sleeve.

Sofy said, 'Well I think it's very romantic. An old maid who must have given up all hope of a husband. D'Arblay's a soldier, you know, and an exile, and Burney's father so disapproved he wouldn't attend the wedding, but she married anyway. Imagine.'

It was the day before I was due to return to London and we were walking in the Great Park, all the Princesses except Royal who was required by the Queen. It was an unsatisfactory outing because Elizabeth liked to stop and examine every twig and leaf and Augusta preferred to stride out briskly. There was still a mist hanging low over the grass and we were all wrapped in our wool cloaks. I imagine we looked like a slow moving herd of sheep.

Amelia stopped suddenly and cried, 'Lord, look who's coming! It's the hobgoblin.'

Tom Garth was riding towards us, the first time I had seen him in four years. I felt composed. The business of Enoch Heppenstall had cured me of a deal of nonsense. 'Well,' I thought, 'this will go easily enough. He has five princesses to attend. He may not even remember my name.'

But he did remember me. He dismounted and walked ahead with Augusta, which I found I minded more than I should. But then he paused while the rest of us caught up, and because Amelia clung to Sofy and made her weave this way and that so as not to have to talk to Garth, he saw I was alone. He fell in beside me and stayed there until we reached Lower Lodge.

He was just back from Corsica.

'Blockading the French,' he said. 'Keep 'em out of Corsica, we keep 'em out of ships' timber. Extraordinary island. Impossible to subdue. But we had excellent boar-hunting. I'm very glad to see you, Nellie. I suppose you are married by now?'

'No, not married.'

He said, 'Then I can apply to you without fear of crossing an irate husband. Concerning my parrot. You remember Milady?'

He said it had been very much on his mind that he should make provision for her, that he was a serving soldier with no close family and death might come at any moment. He had been told by those who knew about parrots that she was young and might live another forty years.

'I have a niece and a nephew,' he said, 'but the one has never seen Milady and the other is terrified of her. And as you showed an interest . . . I realize it is a considerable thing to ask.'

'But a compliment too.'

'Then when I revise my will I should like to name you as Milady's next guardian, if you are willing. You'll need time to consider.'

I said, 'No, I don't need time. I'm willing. But God keep you safe for many years anyway.'

It was as warm as I dared to be.

He said, 'And you'll visit Dorset often, I'm sure, with the Royal Highnesses. With time your ward will come to know you well.'

A silent smile sufficed. My horror at the thought of Ilsington House was more than matched by pleasure at the honour he had done me. Sofy quizzed me endlessly to know the reason for my sudden lightness of mood.

'Then don't tell me,' she said. 'I have already guessed it anyway. Your ardent admirer sent a message with Old Garth.'

16

I did not see Sofy again for a full year. Jack took a lease on the apartments above the Pink Lemon and we were married on January 10th 1797, during the lull in trade that always comes after Twelfth Night. The marrying was at Hammersmith, at the church where my sister lay buried, so Mother remained at home to help Twyvil prepare the wedding breakfast for she could never bring herself to see Eliza's grave.

Miss Tod trimmed my bonnet with Honiton lace; Sofy sent me six silver spoons; Papi showed me the bond he had invested for me in the three percents, and Mother gave us Morphew, just as she had threatened.

I said, 'But what shall we do with him? We have Ambrose to drive the cart.'

Mother said, 'Papi vill giff him liddle pension. Take him, Nellie. I kennot heff him here. He makes big commotions viz Twyvil.'

Morphew had proposed marriage to Twyvil but Twyvil wouldn't have him. She said he only wanted her for a chamber nurse in his dotage but I'm sure that wasn't true. I had certainly heard him remark that she had very handsome quarters and it was only a pity her first husband hadn't trained her to the bit.

Jack said, 'Don't fuss. Let him come to us. I won't see a man put out of his place in the middle of winter. He can paint the cart for a start.'

So it was agreed that Morphew would drive us to Chelsea where we were to spend our wedding night at The Man in the Moon. Then he would continue on to Oxford Street and we would make our own way next day by hackney.

'Just think,' Jack said, 'he can light the stove for us. We can go home to a warm house.'

Which was more than they kept at The Man in the Moon. The wind blew so hard that bed was the warmest place to be, and there we burrowed from ten that night till nine the next morning, the longest time I ever knew Jack to keep his head on a pillow.

He said, 'I'm no good at speeches, Nellie, but I do love you.'

I said, 'I know it.'

I couldn't fault him as a lover. He was neat and quiet, just as he was at his work, and when he was done he seemed contented. If there was still a small part of my heart I couldn't let him have he didn't know it so no harm was done.

I said, 'We should send a letter to your people. Tell them we're married.'

Jack was from Croxton Kerrial in Leicestershire. He was the middle child of nine, with four girls either side of him.

His father had worked in the kitchens at Belvoir Castle and his father before him, and Jack and all his sisters had found work there too, except for the one called Beatie who had a harelip and so had made away with herself, only twelve years old.

'She walked to Knipton,' he told me, 'to find water deep enough to drown in. Here you see all sorts but Croxton Kerrial's not London, Nellie. And Beatie hadn't the strength for bearing such a cross. She wasn't like you.'

I said, 'Is that why you were kind to me? For Beatie's sake?'

'No, you daft woman,' he said. 'I did it to get my hands on your money.'

We laughed, but the tears still stood in his eyes from telling me about Beatie.

'We'll send a letter to your family tomorrow. I'll write it and you can sign it.'

'If you like,' he said. 'You're the scribbler. Only don't make it too high blown. They're not big readers.'

We were well set up in our new home. Jack went to an inch-of-candle sale at Garroway's auction house and bid for a bedstead with a good hair mattress and chairs, two carvers and two ladies, all with hide seats. The trestle table was his too, and four cane rout chairs, also a number of skillets and tinned stewpans, a service of creamware plates, an eight-day clock and a brass fender. I brought with me a mahogany bookcase, a secretary, two silver-plated candlesticks, three pairs of sheets stitched by my sister, a cotton counterpane, four goose-feather pillows, a Wilton carpet, a japanned tea kitchen with a spirit stove, six bone-handled knives, a pewter standish with writing quills, raven and goose, and four quire of cut foolscap paper.

On the matter of the box room, Morphew and Ambrose couldn't agree. Each hoped the other would take it. Morphew said he abhorred an attic room for it suffocated him. Ambrose said he'd count it an honour to continue sleeping in the dry store, to guard the sugar from mice, and so they rearranged such space as there was in there and lodged together peaceably, with Morphew snoring like an old bear and Ambrose falling into such a dead sleep every night he heard nothing.

Some weeks after we were married a small package was delivered to the shop. It was addressed to Mrs John Buzzard and the carriage was paid by Lieutenant-Colonel T. Garth, but the card inside was signed *Milady*. I didn't show it to Jack till evening, till I could trust myself to pass it off as nothing of consequence.

'One of the King's equerries,' I told Jack. 'He's an old gentleman, and he has the very same mark on his face that I have. Milady's his parrot. He means to leave her to me.'

He looked at the bracelet.

'Pretty,' he said. 'Lieutenant-Colonel, eh? Best keep in with him. He might leave you more than a parrot.'

It was a delicate thing, of garnets and seed pearls with a gold clasp. I kept it in my treasure box and often took it out to look at it but I never wore it, not as long as Jack lived.

*

The Princess Royal and Duke Fritz were married in May. I had it all from Sofy:

June 6th 1797

The deed is done, Royal is married. When Fritz arrived she was almost DEAD with fear and had to run three times to the close-stool before she could go in to meet him. Fritz was all composure but I suppose the import of it was different for him, having already had a wife (Minny is whispering for me to write 'a wife that he had k....d!') He is the largest man I ever saw. I would swear his girth is the same as his height and he is exceedingly tall. Royal looked very well on her wedding day.

That was what she wrote, but when I eventually saw her she told it differently. Royal had gone to her fate looking like a boiled suet pudding:

Elizabeth says the Queen spoke to Royal privately about WHAT A WIFE MUST EXPECT but as Fritz left for Württemburg immediately after the ceremony, to prepare for Royal's arrival, I suppose nothing has been EXPECTED of her yet. Then we had to endure the torture of packing her trunks and this week we have had to part with her altogether. The King steeled himself not to weep but at the last he could not help himself. Only the Illustrious Personage remained dry-eyed. She said Royal was doing no more THAN SHE HERSELF HAD DONE AND AT A MORE TENDER AGE. The Prince of Wales promised to come to the leave-taking but did not. Royal pretended not to mind but I'm sure she did and I minded very much. Sometimes I think he considers no one but himself. Well, now he has missed his chance and who knows when we will ever see poor Royal again.

Dolly is to meet her at Hamburg and escort her to Württemburg and Fritz's embrace. Minny says that with Fritz's circumference and Royal's embonpoint they had better both grow longer arms.

Say you will visit us at Weymouth, Nellie, even though you are now a married woman. I must have you here as there are two delightful people you must meet. Our niece, Charlotte Augusta, who is the most delicious, dimpled angel and VERY advanced for her age, and Miss Fanny Garth who is appointed as her under-governess. Miss Garth is the niece of the hobgoblin and a sweet creature. We like her very much but she doesn't write stories so you are still required to entertain a new generation and can never be allowed to retire. Please tell your husband he must spare you. Her Royal Highness COMMANDS!!!

I did not go. I didn't even broach it with Jack. The Pink Lemon was quite the fashion for its ices that summer and he needed whatever help I could give him. There was Ambrose to think of too. He read well enough though it seemed to give him little pleasure, but with figures he was quick and he liked seeing how the accounting was done. I tried to teach him a little every day, when Jack could spare him and when I wasn't indisposed. Before that year was over I had conceived twice and lost both babies before they had even quickened.

Mother said, 'You are young, Herzchen. You heff plenty time.'

But Mother didn't know about my commerce with Mrs Dacey in Hosier Street and the fever which had been added to the bill of sale. Only Miss Tod looked at me searchingly each time we met as though to say, 'Will it all come right?'

I told Sofy nothing of my losses, nor of Tom Garth's bracelet.

Windsor, May 18th 1798
My dear Nellie,

I hope this finds you well. I shall continue your faithful friend and write to you though you have apparently ABANDONED me. Did you hear the sad news that Royal lost her child? It was a girl, stillborn. Royal was fearfully ill after the birth and Fritz kept the news from her till she was strong enough to bear it, but the King received reports almost every day so I suppose we knew the child was dead before poor Royal did.

The Prince of Wales is unwell too. He has had a stoppage of his b…l and is UTTERLY MISERABLE. He begs the King to release him from P. Caroline and I'm sure she would welcome it (she is gone into the country and keeps a very merry house at Blackheath) but the King will not oblige them. He cannot understand their difficulty. After all, it's not unusual for a husband to tire of the marriage bed and there's no need at all for scandal and disruption. The custom is well enough established that he should look for discreet consolation elsewhere.

I am not in good spirits. My spasms have returned and my

joints are so stiff I feel obliged to go to Weymouth to be dipped. We shall be VERY DULL there without your sotto voce sketches of the company at Stacie's Rooms. Does Jack Buzzard keep you PRISONER? Are you locked in a tower?

Will you at least attend me on my birthday, PLEASE, PRETTY PLEASE?

Sofy

I did go to Windsor, in time for an ox-roast and fireworks in the Great Park. After weeks of rumour, one minute optimistic, the next gloomy, it had been confirmed that our Navy had won a great battle, far away at the mouth of the River Nile and the architect of the victory was Horatio Nelson, Rear Admiral of the Blue. He was promoted Rear Admiral of the Red and raised to the peerage. Everyone wanted to see him. People dredged up faint recollections of him and burnished them up into close acquaintance and the longer he stayed away, nursing a head wound and too weak to travel, the more he was adored.

I stayed for Sofy's birthday and the victory celebrations infected even Lower Lodge. Princess Minny and I performed a new Morphew and Twyvil skit I had written, in which Morphew prepared Twyvil for a French invasion using such kitchen implements as came to hand. Jack kindly sent Sofy a pyramid cake set about with marchpane camels. By the time the confection reached Windsor most of them had lost their legs but we pretended they were kneeling, as camels often do, and they were soon enough eaten anyway. We were gay and happy and for once I was truly sorry to leave and go back to my shop counter.

What a difference a year can make. By Sofy's next birthday the old oppressive atmosphere had returned. Amelia was recovering from a severe inflammation of the knee and could barely walk. The King wasn't speaking to Wales because he was rumoured to be dining every night with Mr Fox and planning, like as not, to bring down the government, and Wales wasn't speaking to Fred York who had been kicked upstairs and made Commander-in-Chief of the Army. I'm sure the Prince of Wales had no desire to risk a bullet in his heart nor to go campaigning and sleep in an army cot so I can only think he was envious of York's splendid uniform. Prince Ernie certainly was, even though he'd been created Duke of Cumberland. As for Sofy, she was just plain peevish.

She said, 'I suppose these few days are as much as I can expect now you have your own establishment. I suppose I had better get used to solitude.'

'You have five sisters, and four of them you see every day. I have none.'

'You have a husband.'

'So will you some day. And what about Miss Garth? I thought she had become your great friend.'

'Ah,' she said. 'So that's the reason you stay away. You're jealous of Fanny Garth.'

That was the kind of silly mischief empty hours worked on her mind. I went for a walk and resolved to send word next morning that Morphew should come for me as soon as possible. Better that I should make my excuses and leave before more hurtful words were said. I went as far as the stable yard of Upper Lodge and there I came upon an extraordinary sight. The King was trotting about with Princess Charlotte Augusta balanced on his shoulders and the dedicated Miss Garth running anxiously beside him.

He stopped when he saw me and the child pounded his head with her fat little hands, squealing for him to continue. She was three, nearly four, not the pink and gold angel her aunts made her out to be but a solid girl and slightly scarred, for she'd taken quite badly after her inoculation. She was our future queen though, which was something to contemplate, unless a brother was born and under the circumstances of the Waleses' marriage that seemed unlikely.

His Majesty said, 'Now, Lottie, your poor old horse is tired. You must let him rest and say good day to Nellie Welche.'

I loved old King George. I was never afraid of him, except of seeing him out of his wits again.

I said, 'I'm married now, sir. I'm Nellie Buzzard.'

'Quite so,' he said. 'Good thing. Married. Honourable estate. Time flies. Well here you see your king, Nellie, ridden into the ground by a younger generation.'

I said, 'But it makes a pretty picture, sir.'

I meant it sincerely. He seemed to find more joy in life than any of his children. When I got back to Lower Lodge Sofy had withdrawn to her room, declaring she had the start of the worst head cold ever. Mrs Chevely, was preparing a basin of balsam.

I said, 'Shall I take it in?'

'Not yet,' she said. 'Ernie's with her, not to be disturbed. If he cheers her up we may find her recovered without it.'

Ernie Cumberland was living at Windsor while his apartments at St James's were being refurbished and he hung about Lower Lodge more than I liked.

I said, 'Ernie tête-à-tête again? What can he want? Has he found Sofy a husband?'

Mrs Chevely said, 'I hope so. I hope he's found a brigade of husbands. They're all so mad for anything in breeches. If they were cats you'd have them cut.'

When Ernie came out from Sofy's room he pretended not to see me. It was his usual way and suited me.

He said, 'Don't hover, Che. She has everything she needs.'

Mrs Chevely said, 'Is she sleeping?'

'She's resting,' he said. 'Leave her in peace.'

And off he strode.

I surmised that they'd quarrelled and he didn't want it known but Sofy seemed happy enough. Mrs Chevely though detected a feverish flush. She took away the steaming balsam and brought in cold towels and iced water instead.

I said, 'What did Ernie want so mysteriously?'

'Only to keep me company,' she said, 'when my friends go for long, selfish walks and leave me all alone.'

I said, 'I'll leave tomorrow. You're not well and if I stay we'll only quarrel.'

'Yes,' she said. 'You may go. I really don't need you. I have my brother. At least I know *he'll* never desert me.'

17

No letters came from Sofy and she received none from me. When I thought of her it was with a stab of hurt, to have been cast off like a servant who'd failed to give satisfaction, but my days were too filled to dwell on it often. The Pink Lemon was prospering and Jack and I had leased a house on Seymour Street. More rooms, in anticipation of the babies that still didn't come.

'Don't fret, Nellie,' Jack would say. 'Summer's a better time anyway.'

Then, as another season turned, 'Don't grieve. They say winter babies are hardier.'

I couldn't dash his hopes, but in my heart I was resigned. I had Ambrose at least, to fatten up and chaff with.

It was my mother's birthday. Papi was bringing her to town to dine with us, Jack was busy making almond creams for Lady Mulholland, and I was casting up the month's accounts. A letter came, express, delivered to the shop. It was from Mrs Chevely at Weymouth, dated July 26th. 'Dear Nellie,' she wrote, 'HRH Sofy is v. much afflicted with her old spasms & suffocations. She asks for you often. I wish you wd attend her and oblige, Louisa Chevely.'

I thought I should go.

Jack said, 'Why? What is it to you?'

I said, 'Mrs Che says Sofy struggles to breathe.'

He said, 'What, are you a surgeon now?'

Papi's private opinion was that it would be no great sacrifice for Jack to spare me for a week, but he would not interfere. He suggested I should allow my husband to know best. Mother thought I had been rather ill-used by the Royalties of late but then again, Her Majesty might be gratified by my attendance on Sofy and who could say where a queen's gratitude might lead? I guarantee the kitchen cat would have had an opinion on the subject too, if I'd asked her for it. For two days Jack thumped about the house declaring it would do all Royal Highnesses good to work a day in their life, and then he softened and paid two guineas for an inside seat on the mail passing through Dorchester. From there I was to travel post.

He walked me to the White Bear on Piccadilly.

He said, 'Don't linger, Nellie. Soon as you've satisfied yourself she's not a-dying, you come back where you belong.'

If I'd known what I was going to, that I'd be away from my own hearth four long weeks and caught in such a tangle of secrets, I'd never have climbed into that coach.

It began well enough. When I was set down at Dorchester Tom Garth was waiting to convey me to Weymouth in his

181

gig. My heart leapt to see him. He was the same as ever, smart and polished as a soldier should be, but still sporting that old-fashioned pigtail. I'm sure he found me changed. I was an old married woman of twenty-five.

He could give me no particulars of Sofy's illness, only that she was staying, not at Gloucester Lodge, but in a better appointed residence close by, for greater comfort and convenience. Also that a Dr Milman was attending her and there was no reason to think her life was in danger.

I said, 'Does she go out?'

'This week not at all,' he said. 'Last week, a drive along the Esplanade at most. But the Duke of Cumberland arrives tomorrow so Stacie's Rooms will soon get that dash of royal seasoning they pine for.'

I could have said that I didn't like Ernie Cumberland and had a mind to go straight home if he was expected, but I knew a faithful equerry like Tom Garth wouldn't be drawn. So we talked of other things instead, of the brandy-runners at Chesil Beach, and the French victory at Marengo. Garth said the Austrians had been routed and Boney seemed to carry all before him. There would be no king restored to the throne of France any time soon.

Mrs Chevely was at a window watching for us. I thought how strained she looked.

I said, 'Is she worse?'

'No,' she said. 'Much the same.'

She took me up directly to the sick room. Sofy was on a day bed with the covers pulled up under her chin, and the curtains were closed, but it was plain to see how dropsical she was. She gripped my hand and kissed it and we made our peace and pledged never to quarrel again, though of course we did.

Her troubles had begun in March, she told me, with nervous palpitations and a terrible weakness and fatigue which she attributed to her increased girth. Then through May and June her spasms had returned, much more convulsive than usual, and now it required such an effort to get her breath she didn't know where to put herself. Dr Milman though declined to bleed her or blister her or drain the water from her swollen ankles.

I said, 'Then what does he recommend?'

'Sal ammoniac,' Mrs Chevely said.

I said, 'And does it give you relief?'

'Not yet. But with time it will.'

'Has any other physician given an opinion?'

Sofy caught my hand again.

'Don't worry, Nellie,' she said. 'Now you're here I feel so much better. In a few days I'm sure I shall be well again.'

I dined with Mrs Che.

I said, 'Garth tells me Prince Ernie will be here tomorrow. I thought he didn't care for Weymouth?'

'He's coming for the sea-bathing,' she said. 'And Sofy will be so cheered to see him. He always makes such a pet of her.'

'Then I think I'm not needed.'

'Oh no, Nellie,' she said. 'You are most certainly needed.'

183

She said the other Royalties were not expected until the middle of August at the very earliest.

'Then who has direction of Sofy's care?'

'I do,' she said. 'Well, I've nursed her since the day she was born. Dr Milman visits every day, and Garth keeps the Majesties informed as to how she gets on.'

'Still, it would be better if Minny were here or Elizabeth. Sofy hates to be alone and I'm sure they have nothing to prevent them coming.'

But Mrs Che was like Garth. Her beloved Royalties were above criticism.

She said, 'It's not for the likes of us to decide what the Royal Highnesses may do. The Queen has need of them. Her nerves are still quite jangled, you know, since the affair at Drury Lane. It comforts her to keep them close.'

She meant the incident in which a gun had been fired at the King. It had happened some months earlier. His Majesty had just entered his box at the Theatre Royal when a deranged man fired a pistol from the pit. No harm was done, nothing damaged except a piece of gilded stucco, and the King had come out directly afterwards, quite composed, and showed himself to the people. But it appeared Her Majesty had decided to squeeze the drama to its last drop.

I said, 'Well I think someone should come. I never saw Sofy so bad.'

'They'll come,' she said, 'when it's convenient to them. And Dr Milman believes Sofy's trouble will soon be resolved. I have every confidence in him.'

I was tired and aching from my journey and had no patience with her cipher face and bland assurances. I went to my bed while the sky was still light.

Next morning I read to Sofy from *Robinson Crusoe*. Dr Milman came at eleven o'clock, prescribed slippery elm and left immediately. I took a turn in the sunshine while Sofy slept. It was six years since I had been in Weymouth and I found it changed. A sea wall was being built and a great number of new houses, so the Esplanade was a muddle of dust and stone and shouting, sweating, labouring men. I called at Harvey's Library and bought a copy of *The Mysteries of Udolfo* and by the time I returned to the house Ernie had arrived.

'Nellie Buzzard!' he said. 'How very good you were to come.'

I'd never known him so civil. Ernie Cumberland, who had never given me the time of day, enquiring after my health and thanking me for my kindness to Sofy. I can only think the surprise of it knocked my wits out of me. I should have seen what game he was playing.

I said, 'Have you been up to her? How do you find her?'

'Quite well,' he said. 'Che tells me she's much brighter today.'

I couldn't see it myself. Only that she rallied enough to try the Kashmir shawl Ernie had brought her, and towards evening her breathing seemed to ease and her spasms subsided. We saw nothing of Ernie next day. He was dipped in the morning and then rode with Tom Garth to the Nine Stones at Winterbourne Abbas. But Sofy was contented, knowing he would look in on her after dinner.

She said, 'Nellie, if I should die…'

I said, 'You won't die. You've gone a whole day without a crisis.'

'But if I should,' she said, 'please cut off a lock of my hair, one each for my brothers and sisters. Royal's will have to be sent. Then one for the King and Queen and one for yourself, if you'd like it.'

She'd have gone to her grave completely shorn by the time we got to the end of that list. I instructed her to live long instead and to think of leaving her bed the next day, to put on a day dress and take a little walk in the gardens of Gloucester Lodge, before she forgot what legs were for.

'Not tomorrow,' she said. 'Soon, but not tomorrow.'

I was in a deep sleep when Mrs Che woke me.

'Get up, Nellie,' she whispered. 'You're needed most urgent.'

It was almost midnight. Extra candles had been brought to Sofy's room. Dr Milman was there in his shirt sleeves, and an apothecary called Beevor. The bed was stripped down to one coarse sheet with Sofy stretched upon it in an old, mended chemise. An hour before the sun came up she was delivered of a baby boy.

I thought he was dead he was so blue and silent but I had never seen a child born before. Mrs Che rubbed him with a rag and he mewed, very softly and threw up his little arms.

She said, 'Go to my room, Nellie. You'll find a cloak on a hook behind the door. Put it on and look sharp.'

The baby was swaddled and Sofy was sleeping a laudanum sleep.

I said, 'Where am I going?'

'Garth knows what to do,' she said. 'Mr Beevor has gone to wake him.'

The house was quiet. Dr Milman lit me down the stairs and waited with me until the apothecary returned with Tom Garth. I stepped out into the dark street with Sofy's son held tight in my arms and we walked north along the Esplanade in silence till he stopped suddenly and said, 'Do I go too fast for you, Nellie? I was forgetting your arms are full.'

'Tell me where we're taking him.'

'Not far,' he said.

'To be nursed?'

'Yes.'

'Or to be given up?'

'I really cannot say.'

Our destination was Sharland's Bespoke Tailoring. There was a lantern burning at the back of the shop. Mr Sharland came to the door himself, then his wife appeared behind him.

Garth followed Sharland into his cutting room and they did their business in low voices. Mrs Sharland took the baby from me.

'Small,' she said. 'Boy or girl?

It was only then I realized he didn't have a name.

The sky was getting lighter as we walked back.

I said, 'You knew? When you met me at Dorchester, you knew why I'd been sent for?'

He said nothing.

I stood still, to force him to stop and face me.

I said, 'You knew what Sofy's indisposition was. Why didn't you tell me?'

'It wasn't my place.'

'Whose child is it?'

'You know I cannot answer that.'

We walked on in silence and he handed me in at our door.

The things I might have said . . . *I love you, Tom Garth . . . take me away from this madhouse . . . take me away from this family.*

'Nellie,' he said gently, 'I'm His Majesty's equerry. I do as I'm asked, no more and no less. Whatever I see, whatever I hear, I forget, and you would do well to do the same.'

I said, 'And have you done all you were asked to do?'

'Yes,' he said. 'For now. I shall go home and see to my own business. Bid you good day, Nellie.'

Mrs Chevely was on the stairs. She'd made a caudle of eggs and brandy and was carrying it up to Sofy.

I said, 'Who chose the Sharlands?'

She put her finger to her lips. There were maids about. The house was starting to wake up.

'They're good people,' she said. 'To be relied upon. And they'll be paid well enough.'

Then Ernie Cumberland came slithering out of his hole,

dressed but unshaven. He had left off his eye patch. His bad eye was sunken and silvery. Many people thought him handsome in spite of it but he made my skin crawl.

'All done?' he said. 'All squared?'

I said, 'So that's why you came, to see everything tidied away.'

'Had to be done. Couldn't keep the thing here. You weren't seen, I hope? And Sharland got his money?'

'All I did was hand the baby to Mrs Sharland. Garth saw to everything else.'

'Damned well think so too,' he said. 'In the circumstances it was the very least the old goat could do.'

I said, 'What do you mean? Why should Garth have any obligation?'

He laughed.

He said, 'Sofy didn't tell you, then? Give the girl her due, she can keep a secret. But you're a woman of the world. You can put two and two together.'

Garth. *My* Garth, not Sofy's. Ernie's words hit me so hard I felt I couldn't breathe and he saw it.

'But don't you go gossiping,' he said. 'If it gets about I'll know who's to blame. What's done is done and the best kindness you can do Sofy is to forget.'

Well, I didn't see it that way. I knew how unhappy secrets can devour a person, how I'd longed to tell someone what Enoch Heppenstall had done to me and how I loved Tom Garth. Anyway, I owed Ernie Cumberland nothing. I was determined to hear the truth however much it hurt. Mrs

189

Chevely hardly left Sofy's side that day. When I did catch her alone, when I cornered her in the upper stair hall and asked if Garth was the boy's father she simply held up her hand and shook her head.

'And don't dare ask Her Royal Highness,' she said. 'She's too weak to be troubled with distressing questions.'

But Sofy wasn't weak at all. She was rested and greatly reduced and Dr Milman predicted she would be well enough to sit out of bed in a day or two. When Mrs Che left me to read to her for a while I seized my opportunity.

I said, 'Why didn't you tell me? I thought I was your friend.'

'You are, you are,' she said. 'And I did want to write to you but you were cross with me and then, after my situation was discovered, I was forbidden to write to anyone. You do see?'

She had turned to Minny first, then Minny confided in Elizabeth and Elizabeth went to the Queen. The Queen had asked only that the matter be dealt with in silence and far away from Windsor and the King.

I said, 'You know I have to hear it from you. Whose child is it?'

She would not look at me.

She said, 'I think you know.'

'Ernie hinted at something. It was hard to believe it but I suppose I must, if I hear it from you too.'

'Oh Nellie,' she whispered, 'he told me he loved me. And I know he *does* love me, in his way. But now I'm ruined.'

Then she cried so much she couldn't speak, all the tears

she'd kept pent up even when she was on her childbed, even when her son was taken away. It didn't matter. She had said enough.

I fulfilled the rest of my duties with my heart armoured in steel. On August 14th I went to St Mary's and stood in the shadows to witness the baptism of Thomas Ward, a foundling. Neither Mr Sharland nor the nursemaid appeared to notice me. On August 15th the Royalties arrived from Windsor and took up their summer residence, and on the 16th I was summoned to Gloucester Lodge to admire the spectacle of Princess Charlotte, four years old, being doted upon by her aunts. Only Minny asked how Sofy did.

I said, 'Come and see for yourself. It's no distance.'

'I'd like to,' she said, 'but you see the difficulty? Her Majesty doesn't want the arrangements brought to people's notice.'

Such was the working of the Queen's mind. She believed that whatever she chose not to see must be invisible to everyone else.

I said, 'But you realize the whole town knows?'

'Does it?' she said. 'Yes, I suppose it must. But people don't speak of it, that's the main thing, out of consideration for Their Majesties.'

Out of consideration for their own pockets too, for despite the Royalties bringing their own provisions, their presence was still worth a good deal to Weymouth's tradesmen.

Sofy took her first public airing on the 17th. We walked a short way along the sands. Ernie Cumberland accompanied us and she leaned heavily on his arm. By the 19th she felt strong enough to go a little further.

'Just with Nellie today,' she said. 'I want to hear all about her husband and her new house. I've quite neglected her lately.'

I suggested we go as far as the harbour but she had other ideas.

'Take me to the tailor's shop,' she said. 'I know that's where he is.'

At first I was afraid to do it. I thought it might set her back and bring on her old spasms, but she was quite resolved, whether I helped her or not, and then it occurred to me that it might put her mind at rest, to see for herself where her son was. Mrs Sharland was in the street, talking to a neighbour. They noticed us approaching and Mrs Sharland ran inside, to close the door, I supposed, and save a painful encounter. But as we drew closer she reappeared and the nursemaid too, with a bundle in her arms. Sofy put on the performance of her life.

'This is a very young baby,' she said. 'What's his name?'

'Tommy,' Mrs Sharland said. 'He's two weeks old, ma'am, as far as we can say. He was left on our step and we've taken him in, so if ever his mother should come looking for him, she'll find him where she left him.'

Sofy said, 'You're very good.'

She took his little fingers in hers for a moment, then we walked on.

'Well,' she said, 'did you ever see such a handsome child?

And strong. Did you see how he gripped my hand? He'll be a soldier, for certain.'

I said, 'You managed very well, Sofy.'

'Did I?' she said. 'Yes, I think I did. And it's all so very convenient. I shall be able to walk this way any time I'm in Weymouth and observe how he grows. Ernie has really arranged things so considerately.'

I was certain it was Garth who'd made the arrangements. Mr Sharland was a steady, family man, known in the town but not too well known, and he was a reserve in the Dorset Yeomanry, the kind of man another soldier might apply to. But Ernie Cumberland got the credit.

I said, 'You were very unlucky, to go with a man just once and catch for a baby.'

'Oh but it wasn't once,' she said. 'It was three times at least, for I found it such a pleasure, but then we agreed we must leave off because, you know, we might be found out. I'm sure Che began to be suspicious.'

'And you knew he cared for you? You knew before?'

'Of course,' she said. 'He has always loved me, Nellie, and always will. And now we have a son. I have to be content with that.'

It was offered that Tom Garth be sent for, to drive me to Dorchester, but I declined. I had no wish to see him. There was a Jersey Mail leaving next morning that would take me as far as Kensington.

'It will get me home sooner,' I told them. 'And with no inconvenience to Garth.'

193

Mrs Che walked with me to the Crown Inn.

She said, 'Your husband will be glad to see you. And the ladies who come through the doors of his shop. They'll all be eager for news of the Royal Highnesses, I'm sure. I need hardly say, Nellie, when they enquire, your visit has been entirely without incident.'

18

'And?' Jack said. That was his greeting.

I said, 'Nothing much.'

He said, 'A month's a long time for nothing much. Did they pay your fare?'

Miss Tod wasn't so easily thrown off. She surmised that Sofy was suffering from the King's complaint and I allowed her to believe it had been something of that kind.

'As long as it doesn't rebound on you, Nellie,' she said. 'For you know, after the King recovered from his derangement there were good men, pages and suchlike, lost their positions, and all because of what they'd seen.'

I said, 'Just as well then that I don't have a position to lose.'

Jack often worked until after ten. Then he'd come home, too tired to speak, and go to bed on nothing more than bread and cheese. We had a pretty dining room at Seymour Street but it was never used. He was still at the shop that night and Ambrose with him, trying out new ices for the winter season, and I was alone with my journal. I poured into it my bitterness at Sofy and Tom Garth, and wrote it so it would seem like a novel in the event anyone should find it and be interested enough to read it. One evening I was deep in a trough of self pity when Morphew came puffing and panting up the scullery stairs, calling for me.

'Oh Miss Nellie,' he cried, 'there's news come just now from Hammersmith and I'd have gave anything not to be the bearer of it. It's Mr Welche, God bless him.'

Papi was dead.

I said, 'Why didn't Jack come? Does he know?'

Morphew said, 'He's got a barrel of cream ice he dussen't stop churning, but never you mind. Do you get your bonnet and wrap up warm, I'll drive you directly. Gig's outside the backhouse door.'

At Seagreens there was no sleep that night. Aunt Hanne sat with Mother who, very contrarily, wouldn't take her usual refuge in bed but paced about. One minute she was desolate, lost without her beloved Ludwig, next minute she was angry, that he should have gone so thoughtlessly, without even saying goodbye.

Papi had been in Fulham, taking tea with Mrs Mayersbach and had fallen stone dead reaching for the cream jug. It was over without a moment of suffering, as quickly as the pinching out of a candle. He was fifty-five. Since the doctor's death Papi had made it his business to console Mrs Mayersbach and assist her in matters like the selling of a house, though as Mother said, Sarah Mayersbach had grown children she could call upon for aid without burdening Papi. But Dr Mayersbach had been his friend, and ensuring his widow got the best price

196

for her property was the least he could do. And if Mrs Mayersbach was still a handsome woman, if she bore her widowing with cheerfulness and served the best leaf tea and good seed cake, little wonder he'd been in no hurry to lay down the burden.

By the time I arrived Twyvil had found a local woman who laid out the dead and Papi was washed, dressed in a starched white shirt and laid in his casket in the second drawing room. Uncle Christoff and I kept the vigil.

He said, 'I don't know how your mother will manage without him, Nellie.'

My heart sank.

I said, 'She must come to Seymour Street. We've room enough.'

'Well,' he said, 'time enough to decide what's best. But she can't stay here alone, that much is certain.'

It was strange to see Papi without his black coat. In life the only time he ever took it off was when he cooked *oliebollen* on New Year's Day. He'd make the dough the night before and speckle it with currants then, next morning, he fashioned the dough into little balls and cooked them in melted lard so hot it seethed. Jack despised *oliebollen* because they were greasy and heavy and the powder sugar they were dipped in made them inelegant to eat. I loved them, and as I sat beside his coffin I wished I'd had Papi teach me how to make them. Too late.

A new plot was purchased, close to where my sister lay and with space in it for Mother when her time came, and Papi was buried on October 27th. A great crowd attended, of London tradesmen he'd done business with and Hammersmith neighbours, but Morphew returned from the graveyard in an ugly mood. The Prince of Wales, who had certainly been informed of Papi's death, had sent neither a carriage nor an equerry.

I said, 'I wouldn't have expected it. Papi was a steward, not a friend, and when you're done with Royalties you're done. The book is closed.'

'Don't signify,' he said. 'He should of condoled. After all Mr Welche done for that perfumed pudding. Got him out of his muddles. Kept the bailiff's men from his door.'

Jack didn't stay for the funeral breakfast. He was in a hurry to get back to Oxford Street. Papi had been so careless as to die in the middle of a hectic season of balls and dinners.

I said, 'There's Mother to think of. I can't leave her yet.'

'She can live with us,' he said. 'Only don't linger here. It's bad enough you go running off any time the Royalties send for you. You'll never catch for a child if you're not at home. Bring her to Seymour Street. Not Twyvil though, Nellie. I'm not spending ten guineas a year for a cook I don't need.'

But Twyvil knew which way the wind was blowing and had already made her plans.

She said, 'I'll be sixty come Christmas, Miss Nellie. I can't do like I used to. I'm going to live at my sister's house in Barking.'

Twyvil's sister was the widow of a cod fisher, lost at sea. She was also a paralytic, so whatever price Twyvil paid for accepting the charity of a roof over her head was offset by the prospect of having dominion over a sister who couldn't walk. It was a satisfactory arrangement. Mother wasn't so easily settled.

All she would say was, 'Vot doss it matter ver I liff? Vizout Ludwig my life iss finish.'

The thought of returning to London and being able to see Miss Tod and Mrs Lavelle and Mrs Romilly every day if she wished wasn't inducement enough. So it was agreed that Mother would give up Seagreens and move in with Uncle Christoff and Aunt Hanne to await death. Morphew drove me home.

He said, 'I've been a-thinking, Miss Nellie. If you ask me, your dear father, God rest his soul, should of been gave a title. When he left Wales's service. Sir Louis Welche. Should of been. If ever a man earned it.'

It was a diverting thought. Papi might have enjoyed a title, Mother certainly would have, and it was the usual way for Royalties to express their gratitude, as I soon had a reminder. Before the year ended, Sofy's discreet Dr Milman was created Baronet Milman of Levaton.

I'd suggested to Sofy that I visit her at Kew in the spring and she'd agreed to the plan, but as Easter approached she wrote to warn me there might be an impediment to my visit:

March 19th 1801

My dearest Nellie,

I am very afraid you had best not come, at least not yet. His Majesty is unwell and must have complete quiet and the Queen

199

cannot lodge close to him because his delirium distresses her, so we are in a perpetual state of moving house, depending on the recommendations of Dr Willis. We are presently in Dolly's house on Kew Green but Dolly is expected home so we shall soon be shifting again.

The King's difficulties are not as grave as we have seen them before. You will remember how we feared for his life. Thirteen years ago, Nellie! How ANCIENT we're growing! This time there is a fever, intermittent, and some hurry in his speech, but he is often well enough to receive his ministers and signs papers. He knows the fate of Hanover hangs in the balance, and that a squadron has sailed for the Baltic. The anxieties of the war can only hinder his recovery, I'm sure.

I shall send word the very moment we are able to see our friends again. If the delay continues, please say you will come to Weymouth instead. You will understand I should like to call on Mr Sharland to see how his family does and I can hardly think of doing that without my dear Nellie at my side.

   Yr Sofy

My visit to Kew was delayed and delayed, then it was full summer and time for the Royalties to take the Weymouth waters. The thought of Sofy visiting her child without an understanding soul at her side was more than I could bear. Each evening I planned to broach it with Jack, but the moment never seemed quite right. Then came the day. I'd kept my house in good order, I'd done my duty at the Pink Lemon and in my marriage bed. 'What am I?' I thought. 'A slave? An infant?'

I said, 'I think I must go to Weymouth, and I hope you won't stand in my way.'

He said nothing.

'Sofy needs my help. Just for a week or two. If you only knew.'

Then he turned to me.

He said, 'I have heard talk.'

Of course he had. I don't know how I'd ever imagined such a secret could be kept. The whispers had begun even before Sofy's lying-in was finished.

I said, 'You guessed then? When I was with her last summer?'

'None of my affair,' he said. 'I'm not one for tittle-tattle. You know that.'

'It's the cruellest thing, Jack. That baby boy. She can see him, but she can't keep him and she can't speak of him, not to her sisters at any rate.'

'Load of nonsense,' he said. 'Why didn't they just marry her off quick and be done? They wouldn't be the first to cuckold the parson. Or is the fellow already wed? Is that it? What's his name?'

'I don't know,' I lied, and I was never so grateful for a darkened room.

'Well,' he said, settling down to sleep, 'you can be a soft-hearted soul, Nellie, and I doubt you're appreciated by any Royalties, but if you must go, you must.'

The news sheets had hardly reported the King's indisposition. Vice-Admiral Nelson's victory at Copenhagen was more newsworthy and stories about the Princess of Wales outsold even that. At the Princess's house in Blackheath an infant girl had appeared, about two years old. Her name was Edwardine. Rumours had it that she was George Canning's child. He often dined with Princess Caroline and was known to be a great darling of hers. Others said Admiral Smith was the father. He was another of Caroline's favourites, admitted to her presence even before she was dressed, and the child was reported to have his dark curls. Sofy would have none of it.

She said, 'Edwardine was a foundling and Caroline has taken in the little lamb. She just longs to fill her house with children, and as my brother swears he'll never share her bed again what else is she to do?'

Sofy's only criticism of what went on at Blackheath concerned the visits the King made.

'His Majesty means well,' she said. 'I see his intention, to be her friend when so many have turned against her. He is her uncle, after all. But the doctors shouldn't allow him to go in person, Nellie, not so soon after his delirium. Caroline is liable to jangle the calmest person's nerves.'

Sofy and I grew closer that summer in Weymouth. I'd put all thoughts of Tom Garth behind me. Though he was oblivious of having done me any hurt I felt he had betrayed me just as much as he had Sofy. The indifference of him that August morning! As I remembered it, he hadn't even looked at his son. And then the counting out of money in the

Sharlands' back room, as though nothing of more consequence than a horse was being traded. He disgusted me. And
Sofy needed a friend more than ever. In her family she was
the only one who took the Princess of Wales's part. In her
sisters' company it was heresy to say the fault lay as much if
not more with Wales himself, but she dared to say it. She had
grown up too. During the month I spent with her we often
walked past Mr Sharland's shop and twice we were rewarded
with the sight of Tommy, just a year old and taking his first
comical steps. Sofy never flinched, never cried. No one would
ever have guessed. And Garth, Mrs Che informed me, was
promoted full general and given command of the First Royal
Dragoons. An extraordinary reward, I thought, for a man
who had ruined the King's daughter. I could only think that
there was a bigger plan afoot, to marry Sofy to him quietly,
when the story of a Weymouth foundling was forgotten.

That summer there was another baby born that was not to
be spoken of. Prince Gus's wife had slipped free of her banishment to Devonshire and gone to live with him in Hanover,
quite openly. But his allowance was insufficient to keep a wife
and child so he had come home to try and improve his
circumstances and Goosy with him, visibly carrying another
child. They stayed at Lower Grosvenor Street, where Goosy's
mother had taken a house, and there a baby girl was born.
Augusta, sister of Augustus, daughter of Augustus and Augusta, and born, very fittingly, in August.

Prince Gus declared nothing would now part him from his
wife and children, that he would live privately in England

with his little family, come what may. It was fine talk. The Queen told him he was a fool if he didn't understand that a winter in England would kill him and leave his so-called wife a widow, and so he caved in and agreed to go to a kinder climate with a royal dukedom and a kick up his hinder parts. By the end of the year Gus, Duke of Sussex, was in Lisbon and his wife and children were consigned to oblivion. His sisters may have styled him a great romantic but the truth is he was ever one for a peaceful life.

19

For a few years Weymouth summers replaced the gloomy Windsor visits I used to make to be with her on her birthday. It suited Jack better. October and November were two of his busiest months but August was dead in London. In Weymouth things were livelier, though the Royalties had the gift of stifling anything that threatened to stimulate them. Their routines were sacred, the wheels of their lives struggled through ever deeper ruts. Princess Augusta grew stout. Her dutiful attendance on the Queen kept her from the active life she would have liked, but there was never any question of rebellion. Princess Elizabeth longed for a husband but as there was no prospect of one she ate cake instead and grew fatter even than Royal had been.

With the Royalties there was always at least one topic that must not be discussed. That year there were several:

August 4th 1802
Another child has appeared at Blackheath, an orphan boy called William. The Princess of Wales says she intends to raise

him as her own. There will be talk as to whether he actually <u>is</u> her own, but not in this house. At Gloucester Lodge he is referred to as Caroline's new ward.

P. Amelia is violently in love with an equerry called Fitzroy. This is not being talked about either but I <u>shall</u> say something, to Mrs Che if not to Sofy.

Louisa Chevely wouldn't be drawn on the subject of Amelia's flirtation. She said she knew of no partiality on either side.

I said, 'But she talks of nothing else. If they ride out she's always at his side. When we go to the theatre he must have the seat beside her.'

'Perhaps he does make a pet of her,' she conceded, 'but who can blame him? She's such a dear child.'

But Amelia wasn't a child. She was only a few days short of nineteen and I had seen her designing how she might embroider Fitzroy's initials entwined with her own.

I said, 'Hasn't there been tragedy enough? Does the Queen know about it? Doesn't she care? Or does she think Sofy's little setback was managed so well it won't matter if history is repeated?'

'Nellie Buzzard!' she said. 'You had better hold your tongue or go away.'

Only Miss Gouly shared my anxiety but she was more concerned for Amelia's feelings than for her virtue.

She said, 'I wish Lord Fitzroy would take care. Amelia so looks up to him and he's very indulgent of her. Of course he

206

has a wife in town and a child too, so there can really be no question . . . and I do worry when I see her building these castles in the air. They'll come crashing down and then she'll suffer. You know she's never been strong.'

Charles Fitzroy was married to Lord Londonderry's daughter but that didn't seem to prevent his encouraging Amelia. He was a soldier. Perhaps he enjoyed flirtations wherever he found them, seeing we know not the hour. There was no reason he should understand the working of a girl's heart. Men in gentler professions than his find women an unfathomable mystery.

I had no great affection for Amelia. We had started on the wrong foot all those years ago and I always found her silly and affected, but I didn't wish Sofy's fate on anyone and I would have said something, offered her a gentle reminder, if the subject hadn't been entombed in Royal silence.

August 6th

Two years ago today Tommy was born. We went this morning to Ryal's to buy a new howling hoop for Princess Charlotte. Sofy also bought a horse on wheels and we left it at Sharland's door. The boy wasn't at home but we saw him later playing on the sands. He is tall for his age. Sofy v. quiet afterwards. She asked me why I have no child yet. I told her it's not the getting of them that is my difficulty. Only that my body seems not to know how to keep them. She suggested I take to my bed the minute I know I've caught. Sofy has no notion of my life. Tomorrow we are expected to be sailors.

The *Southampton* stood guard in the bay that summer and the King was rowed out to her as often as the weather allowed. He liked to cruise about off Portland. The Queen didn't go to sea, but if he called for his daughters to accompany him not even a Humble Companion dared refuse him. There was quite a swell that day, I remember, and there were moments when I wished myself on dry land, but then a wonderful thing happened. A convoy was sighted, of victualling boats and transports bound for Guernsey with an escort of frigates and cutters. The *Southampton* signalled that she had His Majesty aboard and as they sailed past us their men stood out along the yardarms and cheered 'God Save the King'. It was something to be there and hear it. I found I had a tear in my eye, though it may have been brought on by the wind for it was blowing very fresh.

We came back to Gloucester Lodge in time for dinner and were met by the sound of laughter coming from the equerries' room. I recognised one of the voices and so did the Royal Highnesses. Minny flung open the door and there sat Wales, unwigged and as fat as a brewery pig, drinking with the equerries Gwynn and Price. What a welcome he had, even from Sofy who was always whispering to me about how cruelly he treated his wife. She loved him nonetheless. All his sisters did. Perhaps even then they had shifted their hopes of freedom to the unmentionable future date when their father would die, Wales would be King and there might be husbands for them all.

He squinted at me.

Sofy said, 'You remember, Nellie?'

'Yes,' he said. 'Nellie. Nellie Welche, how do you do? And your father?'

I said, 'My father died, sir, nearly two years ago.'

'Ah, yes,' he said. 'Of course. Fine steward, Welche. Damned fine.'

I went home to an unhappy house. Jack often grew quarrelsome when I was away with the Royalties, and with every year that passed Ambrose was more inclined to stand up to him. I was to blame, of course, whatever the quarrel.

Jack said, 'You've ruined him with all your teaching. He didn't need it and now he's growing too big for his boots.'

Ambrose was trying his muscles. Eighteen, it was only natural. But there was more than that gnawing at Jack. The war was over, or so we thought. An accord had been signed, the Treaty of Amiens, that everyone believed was a Godsend until they woke up to Boney's wiles and realized it was a five-minute wonder. With peace breaking out Jack expected business to grow livelier, but the opposite had happened. People who had grown bored with giving balls and dinners in London went off in great flocks to Paris and the bell over the door of the Pink Lemon fell very quiet. We lived carefully and we were managing well enough but the question of money came between us that winter and after that it never really went away. Jack thought I was holding out on him.

Since Papi's death I had a small income of my own and I

wasn't willing to throw all of it into the Pink Lemon. Jack often enough made his plans and decisions without consulting me so I felt entitled to do likewise. Some of my money was invested in the Surrey Iron Railway. It was for my old age. I was twenty-seven and childless and, unlike my mother, I'd have no kindly brother-in-law to take me in when the time came. Then there was my book. I was almost done writing, but for want of a patron I knew I'd have to meet the cost of printing it. Money wasted, Jack thought.

He said, 'I'm damned if I know where you get your giddy ideas. You ought to be helping me through a bad patch, not throwing brass away on story books. And you ought to set your mind to giving me a little lad of my own.'

I said, 'Set my mind to it? Is that where you think the deficiency lies? That my babies come off unfinished because I don't apply myself? Don't you know anything?'

He said, 'I know it's not me that's lacking. I've done my duty. I work hard and I've put a good roof over your head. You were let run too free before we were wed. I can see it now. You're too wrapped up in your Royalties and your scribbling.'

Oh how I boiled at his words, as much because there was a seed of truth in them as because he didn't know the half of it. That I'd married him to please Papi and now Papi was gone, so what did his wishes signify now? That I'd wasted my dreams on Tom Garth and he'd betrayed me, without ever knowing it, and ruined my dear friend. Worst of all, that I had once carried a child for nearly three months without any

210

sign of losing it and if I wasn't to blame for the conceiving of it I'd certainly been foremost in destroying it, and with it all further hope of being a mother.

I said, 'All those long years we were walking out, it's a pity you didn't notice we weren't suited. I told you from the start I wasn't cut out for a shopkeeper. I told you I was going to be a writer.'

'Yes,' he said, 'you did.'

He picked up my fair copy. Three hundred pages.

He said, 'You wouldn't credit there was that many words in the world.'

I said, 'It's about your sister, Beatie. About what it must have been to live with a broken face and believe no one would ever care enough to see behind it. Only it has a happy ending. I've written her the life she *should* have lived. It's about her, Jack, and it's for her.'

He looked at me. '*For* her?' he said. 'How do you make that out? Putting her in a book for silly, idle women to read about? You've no right.'

Then he threw the bundle of pages into the fire and held it there with the poker even though I cried and begged and screamed until Ambrose and Morphew both came running. There was nothing they could do. What wasn't burned to ash was scorched beyond reading. It was destroyed.

He said, 'Never disturb the dead, Nellie. Beatie's gone to a better place and she don't need strangers tramping over her grave. Now, let's have dinner on the table and no more quarrelling.'

I didn't speak to him for a month entire, not that he minded that.

'Cold tongue again, eh?' He'd smirk when his dinner was put before him, and he'd bolt it down, scrape back his chair and find some reason to walk back to the shop till late. I didn't lie with him either, which he found a greater deprivation, and I only allowed him what he wanted after I had my revenge well in hand. I commenced rewriting my book.

I hid the pages between the second-best sheets in the linen press and took them out one at a time. Some passages came back to me without any effort, like a spinet exercise remembered by my fingers long after I'd left off practising it. Other passages quite eluded me and I was forced to reinvent them. I comforted myself with the thought that they must have needed improvement and Jack's mean act had done me a service he could never imagine.

20

By May of 1803 we were at war again. Treaties were a joke to Boney. The world lived on eggshells while he marched wherever he pleased and only our Navy kept him at arm's length from England. The Liable List was posted on the door of St George's and Jack's and Ambrose's names were both on it, though Jack wasn't likely to be taken for a soldier at forty-one. But he was strong and healthy and he owned a cart so he could have been called for a constable or a pioneer, and he didn't want civic duties interfering with business. He paid the levy and had his name taken off the list. He said it was twenty pounds well spent and was prepared to do the same for the lad, but Ambrose didn't want to be bought off. He took the King's shilling.

Seven years Jack had invested in him. He called him an ungrateful runt that didn't have the brains he was born with, to volunteer when he could have been exempt.

Ambrose said, 'I can't stay here boiling sugar when there's war on. It don't seem right.'

Though it saddened me to see him go I had to give him my

blessing. I knew he wouldn't get one from Jack. They never spoke again. I hoped the Middlesex militia would keep him safe from any battlefield but the next I heard he'd joined the 3rd Regiment of Foot, the Buffs, and when he came back from Kent to show off his red coat Jack found he suddenly had urgent business in Cheapside and made sure it kept him there till the lad had drunk a dish of tea and gone.

The Buffs went to Spain and a lot of boys fell in battle there. Maybe he was one of them. Or perhaps he survived but thought better of ever calling by and risking Jack's anger again. I still look for him. When I see a skinny rabbit of a boy my first thought is always 'there's our Ambrose'. It's foolish of me, I know. He'd be an old man himself by now. I suppose I wouldn't know him even if I did see him.

Jack wouldn't take another apprentice; once bitten he said, but he couldn't manage without help so he hired Henry Topham who was twenty-three and had already learned his craft at Gunter's. Henry was too rickety for the infantry but he was patient enough to sit on a high stool and do the fine-sugar work, and companionable too. He was an enthusiast. Henry could talk about bonbons till the seas ran dry. He suited Jack better than Ambrose ever had.

There was no Weymouth for any of us that summer. It was deemed too risky for the Royal Family to lodge by the coast when we might be invaded at any moment. Sofy bore the dis-appointment well:

214

Windsor,

July 17th 1803

Dearest Nellie,

You are quite right to say we shall enjoy Weymouth all the better next year for missing it this. Confidentially, I'm relieved. The older Tommy gets the more I dread the prospect of suddenly happening upon him in the street. When he was a baby I could go to the Sharlands' door quite composed but now they take him out and about he can be around any corner.

Garth has proposed to adopt him formally and raise him at Ilsington with a governess. It will be much more suitable and private than his remaining with the Sharlands, don't you think?

Things go very bitterly between the Waleses. The Prince has been summoned twice by the King to discuss what's to be done, and twice he sent word that he was too ill to attend. Now the King seems determined to make a project of Caroline and has granted her the Rangership of Greenwich Park which, with the stipend and the rents for grazing and the sale of milk and whey if she chooses to turn out cows of her own, will bring her in a little extra. I'm happy on her account for I think she has been cruelly used but she's an incorrigible flirt, you know, and His Majesty returns from visiting her VERY flushed and all fret and fidget. You'll understand that we fear for his health.

We shift to Kew tomorrow. I shall hope to see you there.

Yr Sofy

So Garth, whom I'd once thought of as *my* Garth, well up in years and never married, took on a three-year-old and gave him his name. At the time I supposed he had done it as a small act of reparation, to give Sofy a private place, far from London and Windsor, where she might at least visit her child. But then, why not marry her and be done? She stood thirteenth in the succession. She could have married a commoner without the least harm to the house of Hanover.

I put it to her.

'Marry Garth?' she said. 'Lord, no. I'm very glad Tommy's gone to him. I know he'll raise him well. But marriage? Nellie, it's unthinkable.'

I said, 'I don't see why. You tell me you'll get no other offers.'

'It's true,' she said. 'The word has gone out. For reasons best not examined Sofy Hanover is no longer quite suitable. So I must remain an old maid. I'm quite resigned to it. And I shall have the consolation of watching my son grow up. I think he'll be a cavalry man, don't you? Garth is getting him a Welsh mountain for his first pony.'

I was three weeks at Kew with Sofy, Minny and Amelia. We had perfect peace. Building of the King's new house had come to a halt – I suppose it was reckoned too costly to continue with it now we were at war again – and the old white house had been left to grow too damp and neglected, so the Majesties remained at Windsor and kept Augusta and Elizabeth there with them. The weather was so delightful we sat out under the trees every day with our books and sewing and every afternoon Sofy and I walked to the menagerie to see the growing tribe of kangaroos.

She said, 'I wish I were a kangaroo. I should bound over the wall and be gone.'

I said, 'There is no wall.'

'Oh but there is,' she said.

In May of 1804 Miss Tod did me the great kindness of delivering my newly copied pages to the offices of Mr Joseph Johnson in Paternoster Row. I impressed upon her the need to keep her errand secret from Jack.

'Don't say another word,' she said. 'What I don't know I can't let slip.'

I'd called my story *The Blessed,* which was the meaning of Beatie's name, and I signed my work C. Welche. Miss Tod came back quite as excited as if she'd penetrated enemy territory and lived to tell the tale.

'Mr Johnson,' she said, 'is now retired from business, on account of asthmatical seizures, but I put your package into the hands of his assistant, Mr Hunter. He said he'd look it over at his very earliest convenience and I made him promise to recommend Lucas's Pure Drops to Mr Johnson too. Mrs Romilly takes them every day, you know, and they bring her great relief.'

She said Mr Hunter was a man of perhaps forty but quite modern seeming. He wore trousers and his hair was cut in a Bedford crop. I pictured the modern Mr Hunter sitting up late with my book and not going to his bed until he'd finished it and written me a letter, eager to purchase the copyright.

But no letter came. July arrived and still no word. I was anxious that an offer might come while I was at Weymouth and Jack would open it and destroy it, so I went to Johnson's publishing house myself, to see if the surprise of meeting the author in person mightn't rouse Mr Hunter to action.

It was close to noon when I got there but Mr Hunter had not yet arrived at his desk. The clerk said he might appear later, or not, there was no telling. The floor and every other surface were piled high with manuscripts. I couldn't recognize mine.

The clerk said, 'When did you say it was left?'

'May 15th. Are they kept in the order they arrive? Is each read in its proper turn?'

'Oh yes,' he said. 'In a manner of speaking.'

'And then what happens?'

'Mr Hunter thinks about it.'

'And then?'

'I'd tell the author to enquire again after a twelvemonth.'

I began to understand how Miss Burney had submitted so graciously to her years of royal service. Publishers had taught her patience. In August I set off for Weymouth.

Jack said, 'If Boney lands you and your Royalties'll be for it.'

I said, 'If Boney lands so will you.'

Weymouth was full of troops. Beacons had been set up at Blackdown and Ridgeway Hill and Sutton to test the town's

218

readiness for an invasion, though we were given warning of it, for the sake of Her Majesty's nerves. At ten o'clock a single shot was fired. We balanced on stools and crowded to our tiny window. We could see lanterns signalling from the rigging of the *Southampton*. There were answering shots from the cannon at the shore battery, and soon after we heard the sound of the Town Militia marching past and then the cavalry of the Light Dragoons. It was rather thrilling. By midnight all was quiet again and Weymouth slept. It was said that many useful lessons had been learned from the alert.

I felt no apprehension and neither did Sofy.

She said, 'If it comes to it and there's fighting you and I will put on aprons, Nellie, and go out to tend the wounded.'

Minny said heaven help the wounded and we had better practise our bandaging. Amelia said Sofy would never be allowed, that if the French landed any Englishwoman found in the street was likely to be ravished and then put to the sword. Sofy said she was willing to consider anything to escape playing basset with the Queen every evening and was quite ready to be put to the sword, as long as she was ravished thoroughly first.

For two weeks our lives ran in their customary grooves. The King bathed and rode, the Queen walked slowly along the Esplanade and we visited shops, examined hats and lengths of cotton and tabby and bought nothing. The change, the crisis, came on suddenly. One evening we went to the play and the King talked through it so loudly we couldn't make out a word. It was no loss – to my recollection we had already seen *The Lying Valet* three times – but the King's behaviour was alarming.

He said he must have congress with a woman or he'd go off like a firecracker and if Her Majesty wouldn't do her duty he'd install Lady Herbert at Windsor and if she wouldn't cure his needs Lady Buckley would do just as well. Wraxhall and Price were the equerries that evening. They tried first to persuade the King to retire and when that failed Wraxhall had the carriages brought round so that the Queen and the Princesses could be spared any further embarrassment. I was the last to leave the box and the King caught at my hand and pulled me towards him. His breath was foul.

He said, 'You see how things are. Look at my breeches. I stand like a crocus and no one will give me relief, relief, relief.'

Major Price broke the King's grip on me and hissed at me to go quickly. In our carriage no one spoke. When we arrived at Gloucester Lodge the Queen had already gone to her rooms and Augusta and Elizabeth to theirs.

Minny said, 'It's beginning again. I knew it. I saw this afternoon that his spirits were running too fast.'

We lived for two days in a state of high nervousness till Dr Willis could come. The Queen stayed in her apartments while the King paced about wherever he pleased. His colour was livid and his belly strained against the buttons of his weskit. Day and night he talked without a break. One minute he must go immediately to Lord Poulett's for he'd promised to ride out with his pack of harriers. But then he remembered Lord Poulett didn't expect him for two more weeks at the earliest and might not be at home. No, indeed Hanover was where he must go, to inspect his beloved city. Major Price was given the thankless job of telling his king that Hanover was lost to the French and had been for more than a year. I quaked at the thought of encountering him – no hiding place was safe and there was no predicting what he might say. His mind leapfrogged from one topic to another. Dancing lessons for his darling granddaughter; the length of yarn that can be spun from a pound of merino wool; the perfection of Lady Yarmouth's breasts.

The opportunity to escape from Gloucester Lodge for a few hours should have been welcome. But our destination was to be Piddletown. Sofy planned to go to Ilsington House to see her son. Then she remembered my reluctance.

She said, 'You're not still cross with me about your ardent admirer? Well I solemnly promise not to send you to the stables this time. I daresay Ebenezer Huddlestone or whatever his name is has forgotten you by now.'

I said, 'Nevertheless I prefer not to go.'

And there I thought it rested. Days passed and no carriage was ordered. The King's fever continued and his daughters were pulled two ways. They didn't want to see him or hear him, but they feared to leave him.

Then one morning Sofy said, 'Nellie, you're going to be so surprised. Garth is bringing Tommy to Weymouth today. I arranged it all myself, to make amends for teasing you about your admirer. Aren't you vastly impressed?'

I did my best to appear so.

'Well,' she said, 'you might praise me a little more for being so considerate.'

I said, 'You're very good. But I wonder how it's to be managed, a small child coming here. What about the Majesties?'

'Oh, but it's all very easily arranged,' she said. 'The King is confined to his rooms and the Queen is going to visit Lady Digby.'

Garth came at noon. Tommy's governess, Miss Wellbeloved, was a slight, nervous woman and Tommy had complete dominion over her. I found I could not like him. He was four years old and far too pleased with himself. The visit was mercifully short, no more than an hour, so I was spared much conversation with Garth. He was as cordial as ever, told me about a plantation of Scotch firs he had made at Ilsington House, about new words Milady had learned, and about Tommy's riding lessons.

'The best seat I've ever seen on a child so young,' he said. 'Remarkable.'

I responded politely. I couldn't do more.

He said, 'Are you quite well today, Nellie?' He seemed to be searching my face.

'I am, thank you,' I said. 'Very well.'

Before he left he and Sofy circled the garden, deep in conversation. I tried not to watch them but even Tommy's boisterous antics and Miss Wellbeloved's comical attempts at correcting him couldn't distract me. It was the briefest visit but I felt it would never end.

Sofy said, 'Garth fears he's offended you in some way.'

I said, 'How could that possibly be?'

'Exactly what I said. I told him you might be pensive, seeing Tommy, because you have no child of your own.'

She twittered on, about the blueness of Tommy's eyes and the soundness of his teeth.

Then she said, 'Nellie, there's something I must tell you.'

My heart lurches recounting it, even now, knowing what I know.

I said, 'You're going to marry Garth after all.'

'Of course not,' she said. 'Why do you harp on that so? No, this concerns you. It concerns your admirer. He's not in Garth's service any more. He volunteered for a trooper in the Light Dragoons.'

I said, 'Good. Then he did the right thing.'

'They were sent to Egypt,' she said. 'And Mrs Chaffey's nephew – you remember Garth's housekeeper Mrs Chaffey? – he went too and when he came back he told Garth that his groom had been killed in a skirmish and wouldn't be resuming his position. So he's gone, do you see? I'm sorry.'

'He was never anything to me. It was you who made a romance of it, but there was none. It was all of your imagining. How did Garth happen to speak of it?'

'It came out quite naturally,' she said. 'He'd remarked you were very cool with him today so I told him how you hadn't wanted to go to Piddletown, because of my silly meddling. Did I do wrong?'

'It doesn't matter. None of it matters.'

'And you're not heartbroken about the groom?'

223

'No. I'm sorry for him and for all those other young men who won't come home. They're each of them someone's son, someone's sister. But I'm certainly not heartbroken.'

'Good,' she said. 'Then you'll come with me to Ryal's. I want to buy a drum and fife for my darling little soldier.'

Gradually the King's delirium abated. He slept more, talked less, and took a little gruel. His doctors believed he'd soon be well enough to shift to Windsor, and on the day I left to return to London a train of wagons was being loaded with trunks and coffers. The royal household moved like an elderly tortoise.

Sofy said, 'I hate to let you go. I hope I may see you before our next Weymouth season.'

But I was done with Weymouth seasons, though I didn't realize it at the time. It was a crystal-clear morning. There were two frigates at anchor in the bay and ships under sail in the offing – to my eye large enough to be third or second raters though I was no great student of the Navy – and on the Esplanade a picket of infantrymen stood guard. That was my last view of Weymouth.

21

Coming home from the royal hen house was always a shock. At Seymour Street I was the only female. The laundress came three times in a month and we shared a housemaid with the Cutlers who lived next door. Esther lived with them but she came in to us every morning at 5.30 to light the fires and bring Jack's shaving water. I did my own cooking and Morphew and Henry Topham did everything else, running between the house and the shop.

I told Jack my plan. I wanted to take in a foundling girl, the way he had taken in Ambrose.

He said, 'What for? If it's for the sewing get a day woman, or put it out to Miss Tod.'

I said, 'I don't mean a girl to be a servant. It would be someone to help me, but only in the way a daughter would.'

He didn't like that.

He said, 'She'll be no daughter of mine. Some gin-souse's bastard.'

I said, 'But we won't get a child of our own now, Jack. Nearly eight years married. You know it's not going to happen.'

'You give up too easy.'

'How have I given up? Don't I lie with you whenever you ask it?'

It was the truth but Jack had grown bitter.

'When you're not off on your royal jaunts, he said. 'Well if you're set on doing it nothing I say'll stop you. I don't know why you pretend to consult me, Nellie, you always please yourself. But you must do it on your own account. Don't look to me for money. I'm finished with raising ingrates.'

So Sally Blacklock came to live with us. She was fourteen years old. Sally had been left at the Foundling Hospital, just as Ambrose had, but unlike Ambrose there had been nothing pinned to her nightshirt, no name, no message, nothing to suggest that her mother might some day claim her back. So they had named her for her thick black curls. She could read tolerably well, had a cheerful, open way about her and was a good seamstress. When you added her smiles to the excellent repairs she made to Jack's shirts he couldn't resent her for long. He agreed she was a welcome addition to our household. Morphew adored her. 'Whoever could of gave away a treasure like that?' he'd say, and he used to sing to her:

> When she is by, I leave my work,
> I love her so sincerely.
> My master comes like any Turk
> And bangs me most severely.
> But let him bang his bellyful,
> I'll bear it all for Sally.

She is the darling of my heart
And she lives in our alley.

Jack said, 'Only don't ruin her, Nellie. You must keep her active. I don't want to see her with her head in a book, nor scribbling.'

But Sally wasn't interested in books. She liked to sew and put up pickles and hear my stories about the Royalties. At least, those I dared tell.

The King's health settled into a fragile calm. There were only occasional eruptions into mania. At Windsor he ordered Upper Lodge to be closed up and the Majesties moved into the castle, but in separate ranges of rooms. And as the Queen claimed Augusta and Elizabeth as her companions, so His Majesty claimed Sofy and Minny and Amelia for himself. Talk of the need for a regency had subsided again, not least because the Prince of Wales was indisposed himself. Nevertheless Sofy was uneasy:

Windsor, April 4th 1805
My dearest Nellie,

I must begin with sad news. Our darling Mrs Che has passed away. Whatever shall we do without her? I feel I have lost a mother.

Here we are braced for a quarrelsome Easter. The King says the Princess of Wales must be made welcome. The Queen says if that is his pleasure she will have an incurable headache and keep to her rooms. Augusta and Elizabeth appear to take her

side, then go for stomping walks to vent their crossness. Young
Charlotte is our only mutual consolation.

On His Majesty's side we take turns to dine with him as
follows: Minny twice a week, Amelia twice a week and there-
fore this obedient daughter THRICE a week. It is difficult. He
speaks to me more confidentially than I would wish and some-
times his language runs too free. I don't care for it at all, Nellie,
but he has been the best of fathers and so I try to keep my mind
on what he once was.

If things continue in this vein we shall remove to Kew, at least
to be away from the dust and noise of builders. If His Majesty is
well enough to release me a little, please say you'll come. I want
to hear more about yr protégée and I want to read yr book. Have
you heard when it will be published?

Sofy

A sore point. It had been almost a year. Miss Tod went back
to Johnson's offices to enquire after my manuscript and Sally
went with her. They found the premises burned to a shell and
boarded up.

She said, 'I didn't know how I'd tell you. All that writing,
Nellie, gone up in smoke.'

And not for the first time.

She said, 'Perhaps it's not meant to be, dear. Perhaps it's a
sign.'

I even entertained that thought myself, for five minutes.
Then I came to my senses and resolved to try a different publishing house as soon as I could write out another copy.

★

I did visit Sofy but only for an afternoon. She and Minny and Amelia had gone to Kew and were lodged in Dolly Cambridge's house on the Green, an arrangement I found too confining after the freedom of my own house. The King was accommodated in Kew Palace with his doctors. His recent crisis had been the most distressing yet, Sofy said, swinging between madness and lucidity but with no discernible rhythm. He had begun one day very quiet and mild, then had suddenly struck one of his pages across the head, and soon after, coming to realize what he'd done, he'd cried and begged forgiveness of the man. On another day he had walked in the park and talked to Mr Warren about a new chicken coop but when the time came to return to the house he had lain down and screamed and kicked and refused to move. Dr Willis had had him carried to his room on a hurdle and strapped to a correction chair until he came to his senses enough to know he had done wrong and apologized.

Dr Willis's methods seemed to succeed where others had failed. The periods of calm grew longer than the fits of mania and he was allowed to walk about again. Sir Joseph Banks had visited him and they had walked for a full hour discussing the merits of different breeds of sheep. Sofy and Minny had been allowed to read to him too, while he soaked his feet in hot water. This was believed to draw mad humours down from the head. If he continued to improve they were to go to Weymouth for their usual stay. Sofy looked forward to it.

'Even without my Humble Companion,' she said. 'To be anywhere away from the noise and grit of stonemasons.'

The King clearly needed tranquillity and the Queen said she must have complete rest or die, and yet the Royalties lived in a constant turmoil of building and renovations and jangling carriage rides from one inconvenient house to another.

As usual I was at Windsor for Sofy's birthday, her twenty-eighth, but I had promised Jack to be back in town by November 8th at the latest. His order book was full and he couldn't spare Henry for the shop. When Morphew came for me on the morning of the 7th he was wearing a solemn face and a crêpe armband. The French fleet had been vanquished off the Spanish coast at Cape Trafalgar but Admiral Nelson was dead and that took the shine off a considerable victory.

All the newspapers printed extra editions. Our Navy had taken on the French and the Spanish fleets, outnumbered and outgunned, but by Admiral Nelson's audacity we had taken twenty of their ships and lost none of our own. Morphew claimed him as no ordinary hero. He was a *Norfolk* hero. The Admiral was from Burnham Thorpe, Morphew was from Wiggenhall, many miles to the west. But Nelson's mother was a Suckling and Morphew's great-aunt Pru had been a kitchen maid in some Suckling household and that was connection enough. By the time we reached Seymour Street Morphew's handkerchief was sodden and he and Nelson were practically cousins. He caught the mood of England exactly. Trafalgar was a great triumph, so much so that people dared to think the war might soon be over, but England had lost a treasured son and a favourite brother.

The battle had been fought in October but it was nearly

Christmas before Nelson's corpse reached England. They had brought him home in a leaguer filled with brandy, then he lay at Greenwich till everything had been made ready for his funeral. He was carried up the Thames on the King's barge with an escort of River Fencibles firing a salute every minute. Sally and I went with Morphew to Westminster Bridge hoping to watch him taken off at Whitehall Steps, but the crowd was so great we saw nothing. His casket was gilded oak but within it he lay in an inner coffin, made from the main mast of a French ship he'd sunk at the Battle of the Nile. It was said that he'd kept it in his cabin, as you might keep a chair or a bookshelf, so he should always be reminded that a war-time admiral might not live to see old age.

Morphew was determined to get a better vantage point to see the funeral procession and laid out money for places in a stand on Ludgate Hill. Jack had intended to keep the shop open but I persuaded him to close up and come with us. I knew Henry would like to see it but he'd never have dared ask Jack for time off. We'd a good four miles to walk so we set out before first light, bundled against the bitter cold but very jolly. I suppose we must have looked like a regular family. It struck me then that Jack and I never walked out together. He just worked and worked, afraid of failing if he stopped.

As Henry put it, 'we're only ever as good as our last box of bonbons'.

Reluctant as he'd been, even Jack was caught up by the magnificence of that day, the banners and the muffled drums of the dead march and the casket on its ship-shaped carriage

231

flanked by officers from his flagship. Then the Royalties came, walking behind: the Prince of Wales and Fred York, both in Field Marshal's uniform, Billy Clarence got up as an Admiral, Dolly Cambridge and Gus Sussex in Major-General full dress, and two faces I didn't know but guessed to be Kent and their cousin Gloucester. Sally was very impressed that I could name so many. God knows, I could have done more than name them. Mr Pitt was there too, very pale and not long for the world himself, and Greenwich pensioners in their blue coats and tricorns, and the crew of Nelson's flagship, their faces stained with tears.

Around midday the sun put in a brief appearance, then disappeared. Our feet were numb and our bellies were empty and still the procession went on. We were fighting our way through the crowds towards Fetter Lane when someone called out 'Nellie! Mrs Buzzard!' and I turned to see Tom Garth. He was carrying young Tommy, though he was a tall, strong boy by then and I'm sure in little danger of being crushed, unlike delicate Miss Wellbeloved who struggled along at his side. They had come all the way from Dorset.

Garth said, 'The crowds are fearsome, but it couldn't be missed. It's a day the boy will remember all his life. Nellie, I wonder if you recall the story of how I came by my parrot?'

I said, 'Of course. It was in Jamaica, and you were in an infirmary.'

'I was,' he said. 'Put there by a young hothead who didn't know his limits. That was Horace Nelson. And here I am, a hundred miles from home, come to eat my words and pay my respects to him. Well, well.'

Jack offered to carry Tommy a while, 'to spare the old gentleman's arms' as he said later, but our paths lay in different directions.

He said, 'The little lad? That'd be his grandchild, I suppose?'

'No,' I said. 'A foundling he took in.'

Sally said she was glad he hadn't chosen her when he was looking for a ward. She said it wasn't the mark on his face she minded for she'd grown accustomed to mine and thought nothing of it, but the General was so old and severe looking, she was sure he must frighten the little boy half to death. I think she was wrong. I don't believe Tommy Garth ever feared anyone.

Jack took my arm. 'You were right to make me come today, Nellie,' he said. 'It was a sight to see and no mistake. And I venture to say I'd have done no trade anyway.'

We were going against the flow of the crowd and it was dusk before we reached Seymour Street but Morphew kept us merry, singing *Heart of Oak* over and over until Henry and Sally had learned the words well enough to join in.

22

The victory might have been ours at Trafalgar but on dry land Boney carried all before him. In Württemburg he put Royal's compliant husband on the throne, so Royal was now a Queen.

Amelia said, 'But only because Fritz bowed his knee to the French. What a coward!'

'Actually,' Sofy said, 'I don't suppose he really bowed his knee, for if he did how would he ever get upright again? But you know Nellie, Royal is getting quite above herself. In her letters she now addresses the Queen as "Sister". Our Illustrious Personage regards it as a huge impertinence.'

Royal's sudden loftiness gave them something to smile about in the midst of a gathering storm. It concerned the Princess of Wales. That she was unruly, that she omitted to wear her stays, told coarse jokes and received men in private, all this was regretted – but accepted as being beyond correction. As long as she lived in the country a pretence could be made not to notice her. But the story that Edwardine and Willy were her own natural children and not foundlings at all had changed from a wisp of smoke to a raging fire. Lady

Douglas was one of those fanning the flames. The Douglases were neighbours of the Princess at Blackheath and had been her greatest friends, in and out of each others' houses every day until they had quarrelled. Then the sweet gush of affection turned to a drip of poison. Lady Douglas said the Princess of Wales had lovers, and children born the wrong side of the blanket.

Information was brought to the Prince of Wales. He took it to the Prime Minister who advised that it must be laid before the King, for if the Princess of Wales lived so promiscuously how certain was the succession? The whole world knew that Wales had lain with his wife very rarely and that under duress. What if he were not even Princess Charlotte's true father? Well, I could have settled that for them. All they had to do was use their eyes. Charlotte was Wales to her fingertips. But I wasn't consulted. A Commission of Enquiry was set up to investigate.

Testimony was heard from a great many people. Loyal friends and lost friends, servants and former servants. A person's story was one thing when it was bandied about and different when it was examined under oath. Sofy was very uneasy.

She said, 'I'm sure I've always tried to be Caroline's friend, but now she begins to say that if the commission goes against her she'll broadcast secrets about our family and you know what I fear, Nellie. I don't think she means to be vicious but she's silly enough to say harmful things without a care for the consequences. What if Dr Milman is questioned?'

I said, 'I imagine that baronetcy sealed Milman's lips. But if there's any doubt about him I'm sure being raised to viscount would make him forgetful.'

'Don't jest, Nellie,' she said. 'Then there's the Sharlands. What if they talk? Dear Che has gone where she can't be quizzed, that's a comfort. Not that she would ever have been disloyal. But there was an apothecary. Do you remember his name? What if he's hunted out?'

It didn't occur to Sofy that it was common knowledge she'd had a child and, furthermore, that no one cared about ancient scandals when they could enjoy fresh ones.

The investigation was completed and the evidence against the Princess of Wales was found to be ambiguous, but she had survived by a whisker. The King ruled that in future she had better keep her distance from his daughters, wear her necklines higher and her hemlines lower, and leave off politicking against her husband.

My Aunt Hanne, who was the enemy of anyone who tried to bring down the Prince of Wales, said it was a pity Brunswick had fallen to the French, otherwise we might have sent her back where she came from and good riddance. But the Princess of Wales had no desire to leave England. Banishment from court was no hardship to her when she could find a hundred enjoyable ways to be a thorn in her husband's side.

Princess Charlotte was lodged at Warwick House, to be kept away from her mother and under the closer supervision of her father. Riding was her great enthusiasm and Sofy and Augusta loved to keep her company. They doted on her and so began to come much more often to town. There was little else for them, except to play cards with the Queen. The Royal Highnesses were old maids, more or less. Augusta was forty, Elizabeth was thirty-eight. Amelia was the only one who still had any claim to youth but she seemed to damn herself to spinsterhood too, believing that she was engaged to Lord Fitzroy despite the stubborn existence of his wife and four children.

Sofy still hoped to see Princess Elizabeth married, to clear the way, as she saw it, to Minny getting a husband too:

Augusta is quite content with her riding and her gardening. I don't know that she ever wished very much for a husband. I, of course, have NO PROSPECTS and Amelia is a hopeless case. She half believes herself already married to Fitzroy. But Minny would love to have a child and she really should be allowed to marry while she still has her looks, if only Elizabeth could be settled. Louis–Philippe Orleans did offer and I believe she would have had him but he refused to give up his Church. She is also rather smitten with Alleyne St Helens (did you ever see him, I wonder? He was Lord of the Bedchamber to the King). She spoke to the Prince of Wales to see if he could further her cause with the Majesties but he said he couldn't recommend the match because St Helens enjoys shockingly poor health and anyway is not the marrying kind. What can he mean? Surely men only

remain bachelors when fate denies them a suitable wife and here
sits Elizabeth, plump and pink and ready to be asked.
　Yr Sofy

In fact Elizabeth had a long wait yet for a husband, and
Minny too. Amelia still talked fancifully of eloping. She
grew thinner every time I saw her and she had never had the
heavy build of the Hanovers. I took it to be a bad case of
lovesickness, but then she became so weak she couldn't ride
and if she didn't ride she practically never saw her beloved
Lord Fitzroy. That was when I realized how ill she was. She
began to cough. She had pains in her side which calomel did
nothing to ease. Minny went with her to Weymouth but the
waters did nothing for her either. The Majesties seemed
unconcerned.

The King did visit Amelia, but his poor sight prevented
his seeing how frail she'd become. The Queen was more ex-
ercised over the Duke of York's personal difficulties. Absent
the embrace of a loving wife he found consolation wherever
he could, and two of his lady friends were discovered to be
trafficking in army preferments, £300 for a captaincy, £700
for a major. One of them, a Mrs Carey, had actually set up
shop in Threadneedle Street until she was threatened with
prosecution. Another, Mrs Clarke, who conducted business
from her sofa, was questioned in Parliament. Well, she said,
what else was she supposed to do? The annuity York had
settled on her wasn't enough to live on and keep an
establishment suitable for entertaining a Royal Highness.

Everyone does it, she said. Everything is for sale. Why pick on me? However much the news sheets painted her as a greedy trollop she emerged from the affair looking better than Fred York. He'd have done better to make do with a thruppenny upright when the urge came upon him and then go home to his duchess.

In April Uncle Christoff wrote to say I had better go to Hammersmith. Mother's dropsy grew worse by the day and her physician said she could not survive long. In fact she lived another three months, struggling for every breath. She was lifted out of bed and put in a chair, which seemed to me only to prolong her agony, but Aunt Hanne insisted on it. Tapping did little to relieve her.

'Help me, Nellie,' she used to gasp, when Aunt Hanne had left the room. '*Bitte, bitte*, put pillow on my face.'

And I did think of it. Perhaps if it hadn't been in my uncle's house. Every morning I thought 'Well, if the end doesn't come today…' I wouldn't have allowed a cat to suffer as my mother did. In the final hours she mistook me for my sister, Eliza, and hers wasn't the only confusion. My aunt began to call her Ursel but Mother's name was Margret. Ursel was Aunt Hanne's own long-dead mother.

Uncle Christoff said, 'A slip of the tongue. It's the lack of sleep.'

But it wasn't. It was the first sign that Aunt Hanne was turning planet-struck.

239

Mother died at the beginning of July. She was buried in the same grave as Papi, reunited with him after six years of dogged grieving. It had never occurred to her to turn back to life, to visit her friends, to ask after anyone else's health and happiness. No one ever squeezed the pips of widowhood harder than my mother.

23

On the last day of May, 1810, Jack brought home a late edition of *The Times*.

'This'll be of interest to you,' he said.

An attempt had been made on the life of Ernie Cumberland.

He had been asleep, at St James's Palace. A man had appeared at his bedside and attacked him with his own regimental sword. Ernie had fought him off and the assailant had fled. The alarm was raised, the outer gates were locked to prevent escape, and then Ernie's valet was found with his throat cut from ear to ear. It was clear enough what had happened. A deranged servant had tried to assassinate his royal master, failed in the attempt and had then chosen to end his own life. The case was no sooner opened that it was closed.

The next day people began applying to view the scene of the crime. The valet's body still lay there in a great quantity of congealed blood so it was reckoned well worth a visit. Miss Tod was very eager to go.

She said, 'Come with me, Nellie. They'll certainly let us in with your connections.'

But I had no wish to see a man with his throat cut nor to go anywhere near Ernie Cumberland's apartments. Then it was circulated that the dead man, Joseph Sellis, was to be buried at the three-went way at Charing Cross with a stake through his heart so she went to see that instead. Sally wanted to go with her but I wouldn't allow it. She was a good girl, Sally. I'd never had trouble with her, but she sulked and stamped her foot over that. She was going on twenty but she still lived under my roof and I put it to her that it wasn't right to gloat over a man's burying, whoever he was, whatever he'd done. God would judge him, and the rest of us should spare a thought for his poor wife and children.

So Miss Tod went with Mrs Romilly and Mrs Lavelle for company. There was quite a crowd, she said, very jolly, and hawkers came selling pork scratchings and hot pippin pies. They had waited a good few hours but nothing happened so they went home, thwarted but still as merry as if they'd been to a carnival. Mr Sellis was buried at dead of night, behind Scotland Yard, and his wife and children were put out of St James's and thrown upon the parish. Then the whispering started up. That Sellis was the gentlest, most loyal servant that ever was, with fourteen years of faultless service to his name. That he had unmasked another valet, Cornelius Neale, as a cheat and a thief and had made a mortal enemy of him. Also, that the Duke of Cumberland, far from being gravely wounded, had been seen walking quite spry in the grounds of Carlton House, and what good fortune for him that he'd been attacked by an assailant so half-hearted that he'd done no more than scratch his sleeping victim. With a sabre! And in a room where a night lamp was kept burning!

Sofy saw things differently:

I visit Ernie every day. Augusta and Minnie and Elizabeth remain at Windsor to sit with Amelia. He is such a rock and bears up very bravely, even with my scolding for you know he is a LITTLE to blame for what happened. He should never have employed the man. A SARDINIAN, Nellie! It's well known they are all BRIGANDS. Ernie was far too trusting. But I thank God he is safe.

Amelia slowly slipped away. Her ailment consumed her with pains and coughing and then, as though she hadn't suffered enough, with an attack of the Holy Fire.

She couldn't bear to be touched, nor to have noise. Brandy, laudanum, drainings, cauteries ... Nothing helped her except to see Fitzroy one last time. This was arranged very kindly and discreetly by Augusta. I was at Windsor. After a tormented night Amelia was reported to be sleeping peacefully. Minny and Augusta were sitting with her, Sofy was attending the Queen and I was writing my journal. I heard a maid crying, then another:

November 2nd 1810

P. Amelia died an hour ago. Her suffering is over. She was twenty-seven but she remains fixed for me as the golden, silly child I first saw at Kew. P. Minny hardly left her side these past two days and is close to collapse. Sofy is too stunned to move or speak. She had convinced herself that it was just an episode and Amelia would recover. Augusta and Elizabeth are all practicalities. The Queen is closeted with her ladies. The King has been told but is too deranged to understand. Wales has just arrived with Fred York and Billy Clarence. Ernie Cumberland and Dolly Cambridge are expected soon. Another dreadful anniversary to blight Sofy's birthday.

I stayed until after the funeral. The day had been cold and misty and after dark the fog thickened and deadened the tolling of the chapel bell.

'Just as well,' Sofy said. 'It would be a dangerous thing if the King heard it and came to a realization that they're taking his angel to the vault.'

All we could make out through the window were the torches of the linkmen as the casket was carried in to St George's.

Sofy said, 'No more birthdays for me, Nellie. They're nothing but a curse. I'm thirty-three, blind as a mole and spoiled for any suitable husband. Bring a blunderbuss next time you visit and put me out of my misery.'

There was news awaiting me at home. Henry Topham had

proposed marriage to Sally and she had accepted him. Jack was dead against it.

He said, 'They've lived like brother and sister.'

I said, 'But they're not brother and sister.'

He said, 'It's still unnatural.'

I had my reservations too, but for a different reason. Henry was such a dry stick. He could bore a cat out of a tree. Sal was a livelier spark. She loved company.

I said, 'You'll never see him. He'll never take you to the Pleasure Gardens. He'll be in those kitchens from dawn till night and when he comes home he'll be fit for nothing but sleep.'

But she wouldn't be dissuaded. She'd spent her first fourteen years belonging to nobody and all she wanted was a husband who'd never leave her, never let her down. And as they were determined to marry, blessing or no, as soon as Sally was twenty-one, Jack said they had better do it at his convenience, in the January lull. They were married at Hanover Square on January 10th 1811. Morphew gave Sal away and blew his nose through all the vows and Jack stood up for Henry, and after we'd had ham and eggs they caught the Piccadilly Flier to Brighton, to see the sea and discover if they had anything to say to each other.

The marriage even had royal approval. Sofy sent Sally a good dress-length of grey silk tabby:

I know she is as dear to you as a daughter, she wrote, *and though I have never met her I think of her as a kind of niece. I*

also disagree with Mr Buzzard's objection. As you rightly say,
they are NOT brother and sister, and frankly Nellie, what if
they were? I have never understood the prohibition. Much is
made of knowing a person before marriage, of avoiding the dis-
covery of unpleasant histories after the contract is sealed, so what
could be more sensible than marrying a man one has known all
one's life? I'm sure I'd have been happy to marry ANY of my
brothers. Well, perhaps not Billy Clarence!

As the year turned the King had begun to recover his wits a
little. The Prince of Wales, on the other hand, was a mess of
prostrations and nervous tremblings and couldn't get through
a morning without nipping at the curaçao. It seemed that
whoever reigned over us was liable to wear a straitcoat sooner
or later so the regency was declared. The King didn't oppose
it. He said it was time he retired anyway. The Queen though
was furious. Bad enough that a daughter now addressed her as
'Sister', worse still that Wales was no longer obliged to defer
to her. But the regency was limited, to be reviewed after one
year, and anyway the Prince Regent, as we were now to call
him, proceeded very tentatively. He kept the Tories in
government, to the great annoyance of his Whiggish friends
who thought their day had dawned. Even his enemies allowed
that he had begun creditably and showed consideration for
the opinions of His Majesty. Little by little the King's delirium was abating and Wales was careful not to do anything
that might bring on a reversal.

I was twice at Windsor that year. I went in April because Sofy had been sick, feverish and full of aches and pains. By the time I got there the worst of that was over and she had a new affliction: she had fallen in love with her physician. Sir Henry Halford had been recommended by the Prince Regent. He was a kind, comfortable man who did what he could to reassure the invalid while Nature cured her in its own good time. When he went home to Lady Halford and his children I doubt it crossed his mind that he left behind a love-struck patient.

'Don't look at me so, Nellie,' she said. 'What else am I to do but dream?'

After a week she was sufficiently recovered to ride out and the King was reckoned to be well enough to go with her. The equerry General Spencer accompanied them. Also Augusta, who never missed an opportunity to be in Spencer's company, and young Princess Charlotte, rising fifteen and no shy violet. Minny and I watched them go off from the stable yard. She wiped a tear from her eye.

She said, 'I never thought to see His Majesty go out in the park again. At this rate perhaps we shan't need the regency next year.'

But the King sat his horse like a feeble old man and as the summer came on he relapsed into mania. By the time I visited again in September he was entirely mad. He believed Amelia was still alive and talked to Octavius and Alfred, his two little sons who had died, as though they were playing at his feet. And even though the Prince Regent was almost as demented as his father there was no longer any talk of dispensing with the regency.

Sofy wanted me with her in September for a particular reason. Tommy was due to start at Harrow School and Garth had suggested bringing him to Windsor. They would put up at an inn for a few days so she might see how Tommy had grown and have some time with him. She was very nervous.

Everything was managed from a careful distance. Garth and the boy hacked up from Windsor town. Augusta, Sofy and Princess Charlotte hacked out from the castle with Spencer in attendance, and Minny and I followed in a donkey cart. We couldn't hear what was said but it has been my experience that a great deal can be learned about people by observing their deportment and gestures. In that pretty tableau it was clear that Tommy had no interest in Sofy and regarded himself as superior to everyone else present, that Princess Charlotte knew him to be sadly mistaken in the matter, and that Augusta was in love with General Spencer.

Sofy came in very pleased with what she'd seen.

I said, 'What do you feel, when you look at Tommy?'

'Sheer delight,' she said. 'I couldn't be more pleased.'

'Do you feel love for him?'

'With all my heart.'

'And will he ever be allowed to know you're his mother?'

'I don't know,' she said. 'Perhaps when he's very much older. I suppose it's rather for Garth to decide.'

I said, 'And what do you feel towards him?'

I could never quite leave it alone, like a tongue that will

248

seek out a rotten tooth and not stop until it's caused a twinge of pain.

'Towards Garth?' she said. 'Well, immense gratitude, of course. I think he is doing a fine job, don't you?'

I stayed two weeks at Windsor and while I was there Billy Clarence dined with the Queen no fewer than five times. Her Majesty, who grew shorter and wider and yellower every time I saw her reminded me very much of a toad.

'Our Illustrious Personage,' Sofy said, 'has a new project. She means to separate Billy from his wife and I think it very mean of her. They seem perfectly contented and no trouble to any of us. I don't see why the Queen must interfere.'

But I could see why. With seven sons living and still only one grandchild, the Queen was thinking of the succession. It was time to remind the royal dukes of their duty, and as Fred York had a wife he could neither breed from nor get rid of, she proposed to start with Billy Clarence.

Poor Dora Jordan stood no chance. She was offered £1500 a year and a house for herself and her daughters. Clarence would keep and maintain the sons. All this was on condition that she gave up acting in plays and promised never to write a memoir. It was grossly unfair, to deprive her at one stroke of her husband *and* her public. Heaven knows, Clarence had been glad enough in the past for her to drag herself from theatre to theatre – Hull, Glasgow, Manchester – playing Widow Cheerly six nights out of seven because he had only £18,000 a year and twelve hungry mouths to feed.

It was a spineless thing Clarence did to give in to the Queen and he should have had the sense to know that Dora Jordan couldn't afford to keep her side of the bargain. But Royalties never did understand the cost of a pair of boots.

24

Windsor looked very different the next time I saw it. By the spring of 1812 a full regency had been declared and everything now devolved to Carlton House. Servants had been let go, horses sold. There were fewer guards, no bustle and clatter of comings and goings, no bands playing. It was dead. There was talk of moving the King to Kew, his needs were so modest and the chief of them being quiet and privacy, but Her Majesty wouldn't hear of it. She didn't see why she should reduce her household and threw up objections to every economy that was proposed. She was the Queen of England and she intended living as such. A person could see her point. No one else was being asked to retrench. Wales was still ordering gloves by the dozen pair. Indeed one of his first acts as regent was to raise his sisters' allowances. Sofy now had £10,000 a year.

I said, 'You could set up in your own house.'

'I could,' she said. 'But the Queen says it would be improper as long as we're at war, and unfeeling towards His Majesty too. And she's right, Nellie. What if the King

251

recovered all at once and discovered I'd abandoned him?'

She knew as well as I did that the King wouldn't recover. He had slipped too deep into madness. But he served as her excuse for not living her life. She discovered new pains and spasms every day, seldom rode, and rarely bought a gown or a bonnet with her new wealth.

'Why would I?' she said. 'Who is there to admire it? My sun has set, Nellie. They might as well put me in a sack and drown me. I'd be less of an expense to the nation.'

Her only pleasure was to buy things for her niece. Sofy indulged Princess Charlotte. Over-indulged, according to Minny. She said, 'Charlotte needs to learn self-control. If she isn't reined in she'll go the way of her mother. The Queen should do it or the Prince Regent, but no one listens to me.'

The Prince Regent did try to minimize his wife's influence on Charlotte. She could only meet her when he gave his permission, and Charlotte was kept in close orbit of the Queen and the Royal Highnesses. But her nature was to be loud and headstrong, and she was all too aware of her important position. Her grandfather was too frail to reign and too mad. Her father was half-destroyed with food and drink and sleeping drops. Some day she would be queen, and perhaps not so very far in the future. She knew too that the public took an interest in her, in where she went and what she wore. She was no beauty, being rather heavy-set and inelegant, but she loved to display herself, riding about, nodding and waving, and every curl and dimple got written up.

I have many reasons for remembering the month of May in

1812. On the 4th, Mr Crosby of Exeter Street wrote to offer me forty pounds for the publication of *The Blessed*, on commission. The title would have to be changed and fifty pages cut, at the publisher's discretion. The author to receive twenty copies, sewed, not bound. I accepted but told no one. I wanted to save my moment of triumph for when I held a copy in my hand.

Early in the morning of the 5th Sally and Henry's first child was born, in the rooms above the Pink Lemon. A girl, very small but sound and healthy. They named her Cornelia, for me, and Ann, but she was soon called Annie, Cornelia being such a mouthful.

Jack said to Henry, 'She'll do, for a start. Your next one'll be a lad.'

On the evening of the 11th, as I walked back from my daily inspection of little Annie, I saw my neighbour Mrs Cutler in a cluster of excited people on the corner of Portman Street. They had it from a watchman who'd heard it from a constable who'd had it on good authority from a Bow Street horse patrol that Mr Perceval, the Prime Minister, had been shot and killed and in the very Houses of Parliament themselves. I ran back to the shop to tell Jack.

'Damnation,' he said. 'We've twenty custard tarts finished and ready to go to Lady Radnor's. She'll cancel, for sure. Well, she'll be billed for them whether she eats them or not.'

Morphew said, 'Is he took? The assassin?'

The word was that the killer had given himself up without a struggle.

Morphew said, 'Then I'll give notice now, I shall expect a day off for the hanging.'

It was a terrible business. Mr Perceval was a mild man, and as politicians go quite honourable. There were plenty of candidates more deserving of John Bellingham's bullet, I'm sure, but Bellingham was more interested in the principle than the particulars. He said His Majesty's government had done him a great wrong and left him to moulder for some years in a Russian gaol, that his patience was all used up, and though he was sorry to deprive Mrs Perceval of a husband and their thirteen children of a father, nevertheless it was a fair outcome because his own family was ruined too. He was tried at the Bailey. More than one person testified that he was as crazed as a sack of ferrets and had been so for many years. He was convicted of wilful murder and sentenced to be hanged.

A seat could be secured for half a crown but a guaranteed view cost a guinea. Morphew said he preferred to stand for an execution. More respectful, he said. He left the house before six to be sure of getting a good position and was home by noon, quite subdued.

'I've seen better hangings,' he said. 'I'll quote you Harry Jacques, who snivelled and begged for his life. That was years ago, at the Tyburn Tree. And I'll quote you Ida Parkin, the poisoner. She went off at Newgate, singing and laughing. This morning though, there was something wanting. When you think what he did, this Bellingham, you'd have expected him to put on a better show. They brung him out and he seemed to say he didn't want the hood but they told him he

254

had to have it and he let them put it on him, very polite. He was dropped on the seventh stroke of eight and I tell you, Miss Nellie, all my years I never heard such quiet. They left him swinging about an hour, then they put him on a cart to take him up to Smithfield to be anatomized. So then I come back here. And that's the top and bottom of it.'

Lord Liverpool was sworn in as the new Prime Minister, John Bellingham was forgotten and through the thundery summer months, while the milk soured and fish turned before it could be cooked, the news sheets grubbed about for a story. Any story. Princess Charlotte was rising sixteen so there began to be speculation about who she would marry, but there wasn't yet fuel enough to make that topic catch fire. It was the old story of Ernie Cumberland and the valet Sellis that broke out again. How had Sellis failed to kill his sleeping master? How had the Duke failed to identify his attacker when the room was lit? And what could have been Sellis's motive, employed fourteen years in the royal household, well-regarded, treated with such kind condescension that the Queen had even sent his child a christening gift? Dark secrets, blackmail and unnatural relations were hinted at, Miss Tod said when she applied to me to know what was meant by 'Italian orgies'. I was unable to help her.

Sofy was outraged:

Poor Ernie. Why do they pick on him so? He truly has nothing but bad luck. All he wishes for is a corps to command but he's been refused even that. He says there's nothing for it but to go

255

overseas and try his luck and as sad as I shall be to see him go I believe he's right.

Cumberland did go abroad. He offered himself to Bernadotte in Sweden and to the Russian Tsar but neither of them wanted him. Then he went to Hanover, expecting he'd be given the governorship, but he didn't even get that. It was given to Dolly Cambridge instead. Ernie's luck did turn though. He found a wife, or at least someone else's wife. Frederica was one of his Mecklenburg cousins and was very conveniently about to be divorced. The Queen was appalled. Even when Frederica's husband was obliging enough to die, rendering a divorce unnecessary, the prospect still laid Her Majesty so low with catchings of her breath and swimmings of her head that she bowed to medical opinion and went to Brighton to take the waters.

Sofy was chosen to go with her, an honour she would have been happy to cede to one of her sisters but they insisted that Sofy was in need of a cure herself. It was true she'd never entirely thrown off the slow fever and she had grown so thin that her gowns hung loose. Now, when a royal pebble drops into a pond the ripples travel far. Billy Clarence's discarded wife was supposed to open in *The Beaux Stratagem* at Brighton the very week the Queen wished to go there. Clearly something had to be done, and quickly. Dora Jordan found her engagement suddenly postponed and she was obliged to go to the Isle of Wight to play Mrs Sullen instead. How she must have fumed, for the Queen tried the Brighton waters for two days, declared she felt no improvement and hurried back to Windsor. Sofy stayed on and wrote immediately, begging me to keep her company. As London was so stifling and we were caught, if there was a breeze at all, between the smell of the Guards' stables and the flies from Copley's slaughterhouse, I took Sal and baby Annie with me, and we lodged a week at the Old Ship.

It was the first time I'd been there in twenty-three years, since I'd visited with Aunt Hanne in 1790. I should hardly have known the place. Where Papi's accommodations had stood there was now a garden and a conservatory, and curved wings had been added either side of the oval drawing room with bedchambers and wardrobes and toilettes for Princess Caroline and her Ladies, who had never occupied them. The old breakfast room had been made a library, and where the old library had been a wall had been removed and a yellow room created, all paradise birds and bamboo chairs and Chinese wallpaper. The ceiling of the drawing room was painted like a summer sky and its gas lights were housed in immense tassled Chinese lanterns. And the work was by no means finished. I believe Wales enjoyed dreaming up new schemes for his houses far more than he enjoyed living in them. Plans were already underway for a great banqueting hall, and a music room that would be even more fantastical with serpents and dragons and painted scenes that tricked the eye. Only the stillroom, where I tasted my first water ice and Jack Buzzard had decided I'd do for a wife, remained unchanged.

Sally's great hope was that she'd be presented to the Prince Regent so that when she was grown up Annie would be able to say, 'King George? I met him, when I was a babe in arms', but we saw him only from a distance, lumbering about like a caparisoned old elephant.

Sofy said, 'His hands shake, Nellie. I believe he takes too much laudanum.'

She may have been right. Too much laudanum, too much cherry brandy, too many roasted chickens and candied chestnuts. His great project that summer was to find a husband for Princess Charlotte. The Duke of Gloucester was available, but he was a first cousin, a closeness some people advised against, and anyway he was no sprig.

Sofy said, 'I think Gloucester would do very well. He may not have the most brilliant mind but he's not completely ancient and he seems not to have any vices. I believe Charlotte might agree to him. But the Prince Regent, you know, is pressing for her to make a foreign match. He's very keen on Dutch William. I see his stratagem. He wants her out of the country. She begins to put him too much in the shade.'

On that point she was certainly right. Our Prince Regent was getting up in years, fifty-two, and still the King omitted to die and vacate the throne. The country had had years enough of the Prince's debts and his dramas. It was avid for something new, like a young Princess it might take to its heart. Wales was no fool. He understood that a daughter can eclipse her father without even trying. And then, what if she conspired with her mother to bring him down? What if they wore him out with their lies and their plotting and he never gained the throne he'd waited for all his life? No, marriage to Prince William of Orange was the thing. Pack her off to the Low Countries and the sooner the better.

25

We had a hard, hard winter of it. The Thames froze, the last time I remember it happening. That was 1814. The first week of February we went down to the Frost Fair, Sally and I and Morphew, who carried little Annie on his shoulders. He could still out-skate me. There was a skittle alley set up at Hungerford Stairs and two book stalls. Sal told the man at Nicol's stall that Thomas Crosby was going to publish my book.

'Oh yes?' he said. 'Well I hope you live to see it.'

He didn't even trouble to look at me. I suppose to a bookseller writers are like waves on the sea. They rise up all roar and bubble, but before you know it there's nothing to see but a patch of wet sand, and it doesn't matter because there'll be ten more along directly.

We had hot mutton, a shilling a slice, and glasses of porter, and I took Annie to ride on a merry-go-round, which is as close to being on a horse's back as I ever wished to be. It was a splendid, sparkling day.

'All right for some,' Jack said, but he was happy enough. He had a full order book. We'd defeated Old Boney at Leipzig and we had him on the run. People were in the mood to give dinners.

By dusk the sky was full of snow again and it fell without a pause until the next morning. In Hammersmith, while Uncle Christoff slept Aunt Hanne walked out into the drifts. She wasn't found until the thaw came in March.

Uncle Christoff said, 'She couldn't rest, you see? She was always on the move. It was the brain fever caused it. She didn't know what she was doing, Nellie.'

I've often wondered. My aunt had gradually slipped into a world of ghosts, searching for my mother, mistaking Uncle Christoff for her own father, but occasionally she would return to the land of the living. I'd seen her take my uncle's poor, tired face in her hands and kiss it with such tenderness. So perhaps that last walk in the snow was intended, to spare him any more heartache. We'll never know. What was clear was that Uncle Christoff couldn't remain alone in that big house. Jack told him he must move and live with us at Seymour Street and he gave us no argument. With Aunt Hanne gone he shrunk and withered like a pricked pig's bladder and Morphew, who had always made a mystery of his age but could surely have given my uncle ten years, made it his business to push him out every day in a wheeled chair, whatever the weather.

All through that year the Prince Regent and his wife tussled over the future of Princess Charlotte. He wanted her to marry

Dutch William. Caroline opposed him. She said William was insipid and would not do. Minny had seen him with her own eyes and said that apart from his rabbit teeth and spindly legs he was a fine figure. Charlotte had grown quite florid and she had sturdy Brunswick legs so it seemed to me a passable child might have come out of the mix, but no one asked for my opinion. Anyway, Caroline's real objection was that the marriage would remove Charlotte from England. The English people would forget they loved her, Wales would force a divorce and try to get a son by some new wife and Charlotte's importance to the succession would be reduced. It was the bark Caroline clung to, that whatever was said against her, however much she was investigated and deplored, some day her daughter would be queen. Then people would treat her with more respect.

In any event William of Orange was suddenly in a crowded field of suitors. With Napoleon confined to his little empire on Elba, London began to fill up with foreign Royalties eager to travel and see old friends. We had Bourbons and Hohenzollerns and Saxe-Coburgs and Romanovs. Royal's Württemburg stepsons were in town too, staggering from one drunken rout to the next. All summer there were levees and balls. Princess Caroline was quite excluded from every occasion at court, and though she had her loyal clique she must have known that nothing she did in Blackheath could compare with the splendour of Carlton House. In August she flounced off to Italy and took her wards, Edwardine and Willy, with her.

Minny said, 'Good riddance. I hope her ship goes to the bottom.'

Sofy said, 'She shouldn't have gone away. Charlotte needs her.'

But Charlotte managed very well without her mother. Her eye had been caught by Prince Leopold, a Saxe-Coburg and a major-general in the Russian cavalry. Sofy approved and, far more importantly, so did the Queen.

'A rare thing indeed,' Sofy whispered to me, 'for me to agree with our Illustrious Personage, but if Leopold is amenable I truly think Charlotte should be allowed to marry him.'

Prince Leopold *was* amenable but the Prince Regent, reluctant to give up his own preference for William of Orange, took such an age pondering and dithering that Leopold gave up hope and went back to his regiment.

'No matter,' Sofy said. 'They're both young. Better they wait than rush into something that turns to misery. I'm sure we've seen enough of that in our family.'

Those summer celebrations of Bonaparte's abdication turned out to be premature. In Vienna they were drawing a new map of Europe, but the war had been long and the grievances and claims were many. Every little duke and princeling wanted his slice of the cake, and every new dispute gave Boney fresh hope that his old enemies were far from united and that France would welcome him back. He escaped from Elba. Slipped away at night, they said.

'Slipped away, my foot,' Jack said. 'He was let go.'

And Jack wasn't the only one of that opinion. Miss Tod believed Napoleon had diabolical powers and had escaped in the form of a cat. Uncle Christoff said it was clear enough he'd been allowed to escape so we'd have a sound reason to put him away for ever, in a deep dungeon at the ends of the earth.

Morphew had another theory: that with Louis XVIII as the alternative, Bonaparte seemed like a better choice. 'Old Bumblehead on the throne?' he said. 'The Frenchies don't want it and no more do we. That's why the powers as be let Boney get away. Where was his guards? And how did he happen to get a brig all at the ready to sail away? No, Miss Nellie, that was a put-up job and you heard it here.'

We had had nine months of peace. Now we were at war again.

It had rained all day so when the sky cleared in the evening Morphew took my uncle out for a late airing. They came home very excited. They had been crossing Grosvenor Square when a chaise and four passed them at great speed and stopped outside Lord Bathurst's house. It was the Duke of Wellington's adjutant, they'd learned, and he was looking for the War Minister to give him news of a great victory in Flanders.

Morphew said, 'He was a sight, weren't he, Master Christoff? Covered in mud. You couldn't make out his rank nor his regiment, but he bounded up them steps so lively. Well, that's old Boney beat and I'll quote you why. We've got his flags. The coachman told us. He said that soldier was Major Percy, come directly from the battlefield without sleeping, and he had Boney's standards rolled up under his arm, one for the Minister and one for the King – well, for the Regent. He'll be on his way to Carlton House with it now. And all I can say is, Boney brung it on hisself. He bit off more than he could chew.'

That was how we heard of Waterloo. The news spread and the church bells started up and by the next morning there was quite a crowd gathered outside Major Percy's house, just around the corner from us on Portman Square. People wanted to see the man who had brought the news of victory. There was dancing in the streets and two nights running there were firecrackers let off in the park. But I'll tell you something else I remember: within a week there wasn't a yard of black crêpe to be had. This really was the end, they said. This time we really would have peace. But how many widows had it taken to pay for it? How many mothers' sons?

None of our royal dukes fought at Waterloo though, as the years passed, the Prince Regent managed to convince himself that he had been there. He always did love a good story and drink and the befuddlement of age did the rest. Ernie Cumberland would have fought; Sofy said he had begged for a command. But if he won no battle honours, he at least brought home a wife. In spite of the bride's hectic marriage history and the complete disapproval of the Queen, he married Frederica in Mecklenburg and sent word that they would be in London before the end of the summer.

Sofy talked more of Ernie's marriage than she did of Waterloo.

'I'm glad for him, Nellie,' she said. 'I truly, truly am.'

I said, 'Of course. Why would you not be?'

'People think so ill of him. I know you did. That much was clear when his valet was found dead. I remember the faults you found in Ernie's account of what had happened, but you don't know him as I do.'

I assured her I was glad to hear of any happy marriage. Even better, I thought to myself, if Ernie decided to settle in Germany and spare us all his swaggering.

I said, 'And perhaps his duchess will make a more satisfactory sister-in-law. You haven't had much luck so far.'

'If the Illustrious One ever allows us to meet her,' she said, 'which I very much doubt.'

She was right. Frederica arrived and the Queen refused to receive her. For the Prince of Wales it was a different matter. The regency had loosened the Queen's hold on him. He came back to London in the middle of his Brighton season and opened up Carlton House to make a wedding for the Cumberlands. They were married according to the rites of the Church of England on August 29th 1815. Fred York was present, and Billy Clarence and Eddie Kent, back from long years overseas. The Archbishop of Canterbury officiated.

Sofy was quite resigned to not meeting Frederica. She said, 'At least we have dear Ernie back where he belongs, and you know, the Queen may relent with time. Perhaps when she sees it's a good marriage. Billy Clarence says he never saw such a devoted pair.'

Then Princess Minny said a very odd thing.

'That may be so,' she said, 'but I still won't be left alone with Ernie. Not for one minute.'

Sofy's aches and pains never left her entirely and she'd been advised to try the Brighton waters again, but in the event she went to Weymouth instead and Sir Henry Halford, quite unaware that he was the cause of his patient's racing heart, agreed to attend her there.

She said, 'I don't care for Brighton, Nellie. The Prince Regent keeps his rooms far too hot. And anyway I must go to Dorset. I should like to see Tommy before he goes away.'

Tommy Garth was fifteen. He'd left Harrow School and was going to Paris to improve his French.

'Then to Hanover, for his German,' Sofy told me. 'And then he'll return to England. Garth has purchased him a cornetcy in the Dragoons. Isn't it splendid? My son a cavalry man, just like his father!'

26

I had wondered if the flood of dukes and princes into London after the peace might carry with it a suitable husband or two for the Royal Highnesses. Many of those who came were of mature years, and some too flawed even for the most desperate spinster, but some were widowers who might have been acceptable – perhaps the Princesses' last hope of settling. Augusta was forty-eight and far too old for any man who needed an heir, but she never seemed unhappy about her situation. She was gay whenever General Spencer was in her vicinity, and when he wasn't she filled her days with worthy activities and dutiful attendance on the Queen.

Sofy said, 'Gusta is our draught horse. She hauls us all behind her. She walks and gardens and plays faro until she's too exhausted to feel cross.'

Elizabeth and Minny clung to their dreams of marriage though, and if Sofy had none for herself I still hoped she'd find a husband willing to overlook one unfortunate piece of history. Compared to her brothers she seemed to me to have lived a blameless life.

'No,' she said. 'I'll never be a bride now. But I do the best I can as an aunt, and I hope I may be a great-aunt too. And don't forget, Nellie, I have the consolation of a son. I doubt my sisters will ever have that.'

In fact there were two weddings that year. First Princess Charlotte. She knew her mind and had worn her father down. His hopes of despatching her to the Netherlands were extinguished anyway, for Dutch William had tired of waiting and married a Russian Grand Duchess instead. So Charlotte won her father's blessing to marry Prince Leopold of Saxe-Coburg and Gotha. I had it, chapter and verse, from Sofy, and other news too:

Windsor, May 10th 1816
My dearest Nellie,

Charlotte and Leopold were married at Carlton House last Thursday week and now they are in Surrey making their honeymoon at Fred York's house. Heaven knows why they chose Oatlands when they might have gone to any number of more agreeable houses. Minny was there last summer and she said the furniture is crusted with bird lime and everything smells of wet dogs.

The wedding went off very well though no amount of schooling succeeded in getting Charlotte to lighten her tread. She's not an elegant girl, as you know, and the floor quite shook when she came in. The marrying was done in the red state room because an altar was still set up there from Ernie's wedding, a reminder that did NOT please Her Majesty, as you may imagine. Charlotte was in silver and white, quite glowing with happiness. Leopold wore his regimentals. I like him VERY much. I think she has chosen well. What a sad thing though for her not to have her mama there.

They are to live in Esher when they're not in town and plan to have a nursery full of babies. How old it makes me feel, Nellie. My little niece is now a married woman! My other news will make you smile. Minny is to be married too. Silly Billy Gloucester made her an offer and she accepted him. Can you believe it? He has no looks — did you ever see him? No chin and his eyes positively BULGE — and no wits either. Our dear Prince Regent hates him with a passion but he's too fond of Minny to prevent the marriage if it's what she wants. There's also the delicate matter of Gloucester's background, of course, but we don't speak of it, to spare the Queen. She'll be inconvenienced enough by Minny's selfishly abandoning her without rubbing more salt on the wound.

Do come to Kew in August. I LONG to see you and have a great number of questions to ask about The Outcast, *which I have read and passed around and bragged of my acquaintance with the author.*

Yr Sofy

The Outcast was the new title of my novel, insisted upon by Mr Crosby who said *The Blessed* sounded like a theological work, and anyway it was his experience that the public bought books that promised drama.

'Injustices done, revenge, triumph, you know the kind of thing,' he said.

Miss Tod was the first to read it and declared it a masterpiece. Morphew read it slowly and in secret. He knew Jack's opinion of my scribbling and he wanted to keep a roof over his head.

When he was done he said, 'That's a miracle, Miss Nellie, and I'll quote you why. All them words, strung together so perfeck, and after Mr Jack firebacked it that time too. I don't know how you done it. Mr Welche would have been proud of you. He'd have danced a jig and that's a fact. And as for Mr Jack he oughter be proud of you too but he's stubborn as a molly mule.'

Jack didn't trouble me. I had my published book in my hand and my mind was on what I'd write next. But anyway, I was telling about Princess Minny's husband.

Silly Billy, the Duke of Gloucester, was Minny's cousin, but no ordinary cousin. He was of regrettable descent. His mother had been someone's natural daughter, his grandmother had been a milliner. He couldn't be denied his title, but the distinction had always been made and he and his sisters were kept at arm's length from the Royal Highnesses. Perhaps that was the reason he had such an inflated opinion of himself. He kept state like a Crown Prince.

The wedding took place in the Chapel Royal at St James's Palace. Sofy said, 'Minny was very quiet at dinner. I think she began to have some doubts though she never admitted to them. She said she was far too old for quantities of lace so her

271

gown was very plain, but she carried it off. She looked quite beautiful. But it wasn't the gayest of days, thanks to certain brothers. Did you ever know such a quarrelsome family?'

Ernie Cumberland had stayed away from Minny's wedding. He refused to go where his wife wouldn't be received, and anyway he loathed Gloucester. The Prince Regent had attended, but begrudgingly. Being an outsider himself Gloucester had naturally sided with Caroline in the war of the Waleses. This unforgivable offence prevented the Regent from graciously walking his sister to the altar so Minny had gone to her voluntary fate with Dolly Cambridge on one side of her and Billy Clarence on the other.

Sofy said, 'Clarence was very tearful. His Mrs Jordan died, you know. He's taken it very hard.'

Crocodile tears. He was the one who had cast her into exile. We didn't know it then but Dora Jordan had died, all alone in the world, and been buried by kindly neighbours. She'd beggared herself supporting all those children she had of Billy Clarence, and not one of them was at her side when she died.

I'd say Gloucester did well to get Minny. She was still handsome at forty. How well she had done was open to argument. True, she'd broken free of Windsor and would be mistress of her own establishment at Bagshot Park, but at a price. Her husband was dull and conceited and his only interest in life was shooting.

'And the house!' Sofy said. 'You can't imagine. It should be pulled down. The roofs leak and there really isn't one good

272

drawing room. Gloucester might do less preening in other people's houses and put his own in better order. I predict Minny will come to town as often as she can, to get away from him and away from those shabby apartments.'

The honeymoon was very soon over. Minny and Gloucester became like the man and woman in the weather house. When he was at Bagshot she was in London, when he had business in town she hurried back to Surrey, or visited her sisters. Marriage had put Windsor in a different light. Now she was free to come and go, now she was no longer absolutely bound to sit with the Queen, she was surprised that those who were obliged found it so wearisome. Such sudden failures of memory and imagination are not unheard of.

Minny wasn't the only one with a short memory and a sudden surfeit of opinions. In far away Württemburg Royal's husband died. The cause of his death wasn't made clear and we could only surmise: sat on a pin and burst. But Royal began to fill her widowed days composing letters of advice. 'Augusta and Elizabeth should take on some of the Queen's drawing rooms,' she wrote. 'I'm greatly surprised Her Majesty's physician hasn't recommended it, and you might think of taking a turn yourself, Sofy, as soon as your spasms recede. Inactivity is the friend of ill-health, you know.'

Sofy was furious. She said, 'All very well for her, sitting in her dower house giving orders. Let *her* come and do the drawing rooms. I can't think she has anything to keep her in Württemburg.'

The word 'inactivity' goaded her though. So when I told her about the new bazaar John Trotter had opened on Soho Square and when Minny said she would like to see it, Sofy rose from her day bed and declared she'd a mind to go with us. We had been friends for twenty-eight years and it was the first time she had agreed to step into my world.

I knew Mr Trotter from my childhood. He had been a neighbour and a man after Papi's heart, indeed they had had some business together in the matter of army stockings and laundry soap. When Papi and Mother moved to Hammersmith Trotter had taken our house as his residence and used his old accommodations as a warehouse. The rooms had been filled with army greatcoats and haversacks and water canteens and harness leather. Those long years of war had made Trotter a rich man. Now, he said, he intended to give back a little of what he'd received. He opened up his old warehouse for small traders to sell their goods. War widows, he said, could rent a stall 'very reasonable' and sell items they made at home – baked goods, embroidery, beadwork. It would give them independence, he said, and dignity.

'And put rent in his pocket,' Morphew sniffed. 'Do he mean to help war widows he oughter give them a bit of jingle and be done.'

But Trotter had plenty of takers for his stalls. Not all were poor widows by any means and those that tried their hand at shopkeeping found they liked it. The bazaar was a busy, friendly place and there was money to be made. Miss Tod was one of the first to secure a small stand.

Sofy was all a-tremble at the prospect of walking about the streets of London.

She said, 'What if we're recognized?'

Minny said, 'Two old dames, shopping for notions? Believe me, Sofy, no one will look at us.'

Anyway, they both wore such deep coal-scuttle bonnets their faces were quite hidden. Only Miss Tod guessed who my companions were and she tied herself in knots to keep the secret, casting her eyes down and pinching herself not to curtsey. Minny bought an Indian shawl, a pair of mother-of-pearl hair combs and a beaded sovereign purse. Sofy bought a paste brooch for herself, a child's gingham parasol for my little Annie and an embroidered cap for the baby Princess Charlotte was expecting. Minny was against buying the baby bonnet. She said it was one thing to sew garments at home but it tempted fate to buy clothes for an unborn child. And indeed Charlotte miscarried and then again, later in the year.

Sofy was so enjoying herself she forgot to be an invalid. We walked from Soho Square to the Pink Lemon, where Minny bought cinnamon jumbals, Sofy bought chocolate drops and Henry wrapped them in two perfect tissue paper packages. Morphew peered open-mouthed through the curtain behind the shop counter.

Only Jack stayed stubbornly out of sight, 'loading a drying cabinet with candied-orange flowers', Henry said. A delicate operation that couldn't be hurried and served my husband very well in his determination not to bow his head to any Royalties.

Minny's carriage followed us to Seymour Street. Sal made tea, Annie paraded up and down with her new parasol and Sofy declared she had seen and done so much she was sure she wouldn't sleep that night. As soon as Morphew had done his deliveries he hurried home to tell Uncle Christoff about the royal patronage of our shop, only to discover that my uncle could trump him. *He* had taken tea and cake with the Princesses. *He* had reminisced with Princess Minny about the time he'd worked in the old Duke of Gloucester's establishment, a young man not long out of Hanover and still learning to speak English.

When Jack came home he said nothing.

Uncle Christoff said, 'Royal Highnesses eh, Jack? That'll help trade, when word gets around.'

Jack said, 'My trade doesn't need any help.'

I said, 'Why must you be so stiff-necked? Why wouldn't you come out and be presented?'

'I was busy,' he said. 'And anyway, enough we've got one in the family dancing to their tune.'

Henry said, 'Still, Jack, it'd be a nice thing for us if they came in regular. Very pleasant ladies. And they paid on the nail. They never asked for credit.'

Jack said, 'Don't be fooled, lad. Some folk lull you with cash a time or two. Then they start taking liberties.'

Morphew said, 'They didn't look like Highnesses at all. Plain wool coats. You never would of thought. And when they was taking their leave one of them, the one with the barnacle bins on her nose, she gave me such a sweet smile.'

I said, 'That was Princess Sophia.'

'Princess Sophia,' he said. 'Well, that'll be something to treasure.'

I said, 'But never forget, Morphew, they're only hooman.'

27

After two infants had miscarried, Princess Charlotte's third pregnancy went well. The baby quickened, Charlotte was active and healthy and the Princess of Wales threatened to return to England before December to be with her daughter for the lying-in. On the afternoon of November 7th I received a letter, express from Sofy. The child, a boy, had been stillborn and Charlotte had survived him by only a few hours. She was twenty-one years old.

We hardly know what to do with ourselves. It is difficult to understand how things went so badly wrong. You know Leopold is the most considerate of husbands and I'm sure would have made no demands on Charlotte. She was purged every day, as recommended, and had blood taken every two weeks. Her pains began on Monday after dinner and by Tuesday morning the Lord Chancellor and the Archbishop had been sent for, so we believed the birth must be imminent. But then her pains lessened and Dr Croft and Dr Baillie consulted another accoucheur, to have his opinion of the case. The baby boy wasn't delivered until

Wednesday evening. He never breathed. Dr Baillie says Charlotte bore up very cheerfully, under the circumstances. She took some tea and slept a little but was light-headed when she woke and then became very restless. I don't know what was given her except camphor and then some laudanum. Every account we hear is different. The only certain thing is that she suffered a great convulsion and died at about two of the morning. Augusta woke me with the news. She, poor dear, hadn't slept. She said she had the strongest premonition of something bad.

The Queen was away at Bath with Billy Clarence and Elizabeth. We expect them at Windsor tonight. Leopold is apparently very calm, as though he is sleepwalking. Our Prince Regent though is prostrate. He was in Suffolk when he received word that Charlotte's pains were well advanced and set out for London immediately. They had stopped at Ipswich for fresh horses when the messenger delivered Dr Baillie's note, that the child was dead but Charlotte was quite well. He continued on to Carlton House and went to bed, little thinking. York was sent in to tell him. Fred said he let out such a terrible cry he quite thought he would die on the spot. Now he keeps to his bed and puts off writing to Caroline to break the news to her, though pen and paper have been put in his hands. What ever shall we do, Nellie?

Sofy

The news was already spreading on the streets as I read Sofy's letter. The Exchange suspended business, the assizes were postponed, shops closed their doors. Even Jack Buzzard knew better than to resist. Though he carried on working in the stillroom he pulled down the shop blinds as a mark of respect. There would be no parties. The country was plunged into sadness, as though people had known Charlotte personally.

On November 18th the bodies of Charlotte and her son were brought from Esher to Windsor. They rested one night at Lower Lodge and were buried the next evening in the vault of St George's, where Amelia already lay. Caroline was still on her way from Italy, the Prince Regent was too ill to attend and the old King was too mad.

After the first weeks of mourning had passed, here's how things stood: King George had fathered fifteen children. Three were dead, and now his only grandchild recognized in law was dead too. The rest was nothing but scandals and bastards. And so began the headlong gallop to produce an heir and secure the succession, a cavalcade of ageing princes who had sowed their oats and now found it advisable to marry appropriately and breed. The runners in this tragi-comical race were Billy Clarence, Eddie Kent, and Dolly Cambridge. Ernie Cumberland, already married, had a start on them, and hints that his duchess might already be with child concentrated the minds of his brothers with even greater urgency.

In the following year there were four royal weddings and the first of them was the most surprising. Princess Elizabeth received an offer from Prince Frederick of Hesse Homburg and, seeing a gap open up in the Windsor wall, she squeezed her ample body through it and accepted. The match had just about enough to recommend it. Elizabeth could provide money and Humbug, as they called him, could provide a little kingdom where she would be her own mistress. And as he was over fifty and so corpulent he moved about with difficulty, if he turned out to be a beast of depravity she wouldn't have long to endure him. The Queen's doctors feared the loss of Elizabeth would kill her but Sofy knew differently.

'Not at all,' she said. 'Nothing revives Her Majesty so well as a grievance and she is EXCEEDINGLY angry with Elizabeth. Her pulse was quite feeble before, but this engagement has made it race along merrily.'

Elizabeth was married in April at the Queen's House:

Eliza v. pink and beaming. She wore white, a nod to her undoubted virginity, though the effect was of a frigate under full sail. Fred York handed her in because the Prince Regent sent word that he was very bad with gout and could not come. I think he does not care for weddings any more. They remind him too much of our dear Charlotte. I, on the other hand, am GENUINELY gouty. Her Majesty graciously allowed me to remain seated with my leg on a stool.

Humbug had tobacco on his waistcoat and traces of his dinner. He seems to adore Elizabeth and she told me the prospect of being a wife held no fears for her. However I noticed she lost her usual glow when the time came for them to leave us. The wedding night was spent at Windsor. Humbug rarely leaves off sucking on his pipe, you know. Minny and I surmise he may have kept it to hand, even in the BRIDAL BED.

Now they are gone to Homburg and the good Lord knows if we shall ever see Elizabeth again. The Queen suffered a great reversal after the wedding, as I knew she would with no bride to peck at. She is at Kew now with Augusta, I am at Windsor with our poor darling King and Minny spends a great deal of time in her carriage, travelling between us and so avoiding her husband.

I told the King Elizabeth was married. He seemed to understand and showed no distress. He just sits and sits, Nellie. I can't imagine what his thoughts are.

Sofy

In May Dolly Cambridge brought home a German princess, Augusta of Hesse Kassel, and they were married in London.

'Yet another Augusta!' Sofy said. 'But I like her. And she's young and healthy. I'm sure we can depend on her to give us babies.'

Meanwhile Billy Clarence was feverishly searching for a wife and the Duke of Kent was putting his own affairs in order with surprising haste. I had never met Eddie Kent and Sofy hardly knew him. He had been overseas since she was a girl of eight and had lived many years in Canada. By 1818 he was in Brussels and his wife with him, though as there was no evidence of a marrying, Julie St Laurent wasn't the kind of wife any Royalties would recognize. There was talk that they had children too, though if they existed they certainly didn't live in his household.

'I really cannot comment,' was all Sofy would say. 'He's a stranger to me, Nellie, and the little I do know of him I don't care for. He seems always on the verge of a terrible rage. And of course we can never receive Madame St Laurent.'

It didn't matter. Madame St Laurent's days were numbered. Perhaps Kent consulted Billy Clarence on the best way to shake off an inconvenient wife of twenty years' standing. By the end of May he had courted and married Victoire Saxe-Coburg. She was a widow with a son and a daughter, so in the important matter of child-bearing she had already established her credentials.

Clarence had found himself a German bride too: Adelaide Saxe-Meiningen – 'dear, cheerful Adelaide' as Sofy called her. She had no looks and little money and seemed grateful to get any husband. A double wedding was made at Kew that summer to save the Queen the discomfort of travelling. Billy Clarence to Adelaide and Eddie Kent to Victoire. A cannon was fired in Hyde Park in salute to the royal couples, but it seemed to me more like a signal that the race for the throne had begun.

No suitable house had been offered to the Kents so they went back to Germany to address the urgent business of getting a baby. Ernie Cumberland's wife was regularly rumoured to be pregnant but just as regularly failed to produce the evidence, so the matter of who would succeed when the old King and the Prince Regent were dead was as pressing as ever.

At Kew, after the last of the carriages had driven away and the marriage chapel had been dismantled, the Queen entered her final slow decline. I was at Windsor in early November, in time for Sofy's birthday, and the news then was that Her Majesty slept in a chair to ease her breathing, and was to have her legs drained again the next day.

Sofy said, 'I hope death comes soon. Minny says she suffers terribly.'

A horse was kept saddled night and day, ready to take the news to London.

I said, 'Will you go to Kew, to see her one last time?'

'No,' she said. 'My place is here with His Majesty.'

I said, 'But the King doesn't know you're here.'

'Nevertheless,' she said, 'I will not leave him.'

Queen Charlotte died on November 17th. The Prince Regent was with her at the end, and Augusta and Minny. Then her body was brought to Windsor with a cavalry escort and buried in the vault of St George's Chapel next to three generations who had gone before her: Amelia and Charlotte, and Charlotte's little son who had no name. She went to her grave not knowing that three of her sons were to be fathers. Adelaide Clarence had miscarried but Gusta Cambridge, Vicky Kent and Frederica Cumberland were all with child and blossoming. The country had gone from no heirs to a sudden superfluity.

Kew was closed up for that winter of 1818 and Augusta moved to Windsor. The Queen had bequeathed her the Frogmore house but for the time being she chose to live with

Sofy within the castle walls. The King might not have known she was there but Sofy was very glad of her company. The Queen's bequest to Sofy was Lower Lodge.

She said, 'Such a cold, gloomy old place. I shan't keep it. I can't think why she gave it to me.'

I said, 'I suppose she wanted you to have a house to call your own.'

'But I have money,' she said. 'When I'm not needed at Windsor any more I can buy a dear little cottage.'

She never did, though. The Prince Regent took on Lower Lodge and Sofy's money was spent on other things. The first claim on her generosity was made that winter. She asked me to go with her to Drummond's bank to arrange for money to be sent to Tommy Garth. He was in Melton Mowbray for the hunting season and living well beyond his means.

She said, 'I'm sure Garth does what he can for him, but I should like to help him too. He's been very sick of a marsh fever, you know.'

Though not too sick to chase foxes across Leicestershire.

I said, 'Did Tommy apply to you for money?'

'Yes.'

'Then he knows you're his mother?'

'Yes.'

'And he thinks he can play the prince even if he lacks the title.'

'Well, Nellie,' she said, 'you must agree, his position is difficult. I'm sure many in his situation would become quite resentful, but Tommy is such a sweet-natured boy.'

I couldn't properly say. I'd seen him for no more than a few minutes since he was grown up, but I'd always feared he would grow up ungovernable. Garth had been too old to raise a child and Miss Wellbeloved too nervous. They had both indulged him and now Tommy saw himself as quite the dasher, buying horses and ordering hunting coats and all on a lieutenant's half pay. Furthermore, he had a hold over Sofy and knew he could always apply to her for funds. It might have been better for everyone if he'd been left with the Sharlands and had never been told his parentage.

28

The royal babies were all expected in May. The Ernie Cumberlands were in Berlin and the Dolly Cambridges were in Hanover. The Eddie Kents decided to return to England for Vicky's confinement.

Sofy said, 'It's too silly. There's nowhere for them to live.'

I said, 'What about Lower Lodge?'

'Not at all suitable,' she said. 'Don't you recall how small the nursery was?'

'Or Frogmore, if Augusta doesn't mean to live there?'

'No furniture,' she said. 'Everything was sold.'

That had become Sofy's way of thinking. She was stuck in her ways, always finding reasons things couldn't be done, always discovering obstacles to her comfort and happiness. I grew very impatient with her.

I said, 'Why do you stay at Windsor? It's so miserable.'

'Because the King is there. It's my duty and Augusta's.'

'But you could live in some cosy lodge across the park and be just as dutiful.'

'No. You don't understand.'

Letters were her chief pleasure, especially from Elizabeth. She was refurbishing Humbug's little kingdom so her letters were filled with sketches and plans. On days when no mails came Sofy grew quite crotchety.

'You'd think,' she'd say, 'it wouldn't be beyond a sister's means to write a few lines each day.'

'You'd think,' I'd say, 'that a Royal Highness, with money and time and no ties of marriage, would find some project to occupy her.'

And she'd say, 'You and your projects. You have no idea. Your life is very different to mine.'

Indeed.

Eddie Kent was in high spirits and not at all deterred by the lack of accommodation in London. He wanted his child to be born in England though it made not a jot of difference to the succession. Billy Clarence was the older brother and therefore Clarences would always take precedence over Kents, wherever any of them were born.

Sofy said, 'Eddie asks after poor Adelaide Clarence in every letter he sends. Well, I see through him. He has his eye on the throne, Nellie, and I'm sure his wife is urging him on. They mean to set out their stall, in case Adelaide continues to miscarry. They mean to have the news sheets writing them up and the people doting on them.'

The Kents set off for England at the end of March with a muddle of old carriages and borrowed carts, all overloaded in the name of economy. They were on the road when Dolly and Gusta Cambridge's son was born and didn't hear the news till they reached London. In Hanover, on March 26th 1819, George William Frederick Charles.

Sofy said, 'Do you know what Eddie said when he heard? He said, "Dolly's child doesn't signify. He won't be needed here. *My* son is the one the country's looking to." Imagine! I was so cross with him. I'd have reminded him about poor Charlotte, reminded him not to count unhatched chickens, but I couldn't, not with Vicky standing there like a mare with hay belly.'

Temporary apartments were found for the Kents at Kensington Palace. A terrible suite of rooms, according to Sofy, where you couldn't hear yourself think for the noise of the vermin in the walls. On closer acquaintance with Vicky Kent she had decided to like her and to take her part.

She said, 'It's not right, Nellie. The paper is peeling from the walls and there's not a comfortable place to sit. I've had two sleeping chairs sent up from Kew. A woman in Vicky's condition must have somewhere to rest. And I've ordered a bed from Gillow's warehouse for Feodora. Sweet child. The dear has been sleeping on a broken truckle cot and hadn't liked to complain.'

Feodora was Vicky Kent's daughter from her first marriage. There was a son too, but he had remained in Leiningen to finish his education and prepare to rule his principality. Feodora was eleven years old and had been uprooted from everything she'd ever known, obliged to fall in with her mama's new life. She was expected to speak English at all times and to look forward to the arrival of a brother or sister whose birth would perforce push her into the shade. I was glad to think she'd found an ally in Sofy.

On May 24th Vicky Kent was delivered of a girl. A few days later, in Hanover, the Cumberlands had a son, another George. The Kents had intended to name their daughter Georgiana but the Prince Regent absolutely forbade it. I suppose he didn't care for the idea of a new generation of Georges flowering while he waited and waited for the throne. I could have felt sorry for him, his only child dead, his looks gone and his health, and still no crown on his head. I saw him at Windsor that summer, walking with a cane and breathless after two steps. He would powder his face with Pears' Imperial, but what with all his perspiring and dabbing the effect was so mottled it was no improvement, and his new Waterloo teeth moved about when he spoke. He was a pitiful sight, and bad-tempered too.

'Name her anything but Georgiana,' he said. Though I imagine he wouldn't have liked them to choose 'Caroline' either.

In the event she was named Alexandrina Victoire and for years the only name I ever heard her called was Drina. That only ceased when it became clear that some day she would be our queen. But I'm getting ahead of myself. Drina and the two baby Georges were heirs enough for the time being and Eddie Kent was cock of the walk, quite intending to add sons to the nursery and remove any doubts about the succession.

He took Vicky and Drina and Feodora off to Devonshire and leased a house by the sea. Sofy was disappointed.

She said, 'Such a great distance away but Eddie says he can't afford to live in London. Now I shall never see those little girls. Of course if the Prince Regent would only do something for them it wouldn't be necessary for them to go so far into the country, but he will not. I have to console myself with the thought that the sea air will be beneficial for the children.'

Beneficial for the children, perhaps, but not for Eddie Kent. Before January was out he was dead of a pneumonic fever and Fred York had to send an equerry through the snow and ice to pay for a casket. The undertaker wouldn't allow the body to be carried off to Windsor until his account had been settled. The Kents' credit wasn't good in Sidmouth.

There was little mourning for the Duke of Kent. That news soon dropped from sight because a week later the King was dead. The abbey bell tolled first, then every other church took up the sad note. Sofy wrote:

Our darling is gone. Augusta and I had both sat with him during the afternoon. He called out for Amelia once but otherwise he seemed at peace. He was so terribly frail, Nellie. It was hard to remember what a fine, vigorous figure he used to cut. He passed away just after eight o'clock. Fred York was with him at the end.

All those years the King had seemed not to know how to die, it was a relief to think he'd gone to his rest. The mad-doctors had stopped trying to cure him long since and his lamps had gone out. He just sat in his chamber, bundled in a baby napkin and gazing into God knows what hell, waiting for death to remember him. But, wrote Sofy:

Now our new Majesty lies gravely ill. He has an inflammation of the lungs and his physicians are most anxious. We must pray, Nellie, that we shan't bury two kings in the same week. It's sad enough that Drina will never know her papa.

I took young Annie to hear the proclamation at Charing Cross. Nearly eight years old, it was something she'd re-member all her life. When I told her that our new king was the person who had put me forward to be a companion to his sister she said she wished she had a brother to do her such a kindness. But Annie wasn't meant to have brothers or sisters. Sal had had three babies after her and every one of them was buried in its chrisom cloth.

She said, 'I expect he picked you out because of your harlequin face.'

Annie thought my mark was something very special, perhaps the only one in the world, so I told her about Tom Garth, whose face was a mirror-image of mine.

She said, 'Then I'm right, Grandma Nellie. The old King had a harlequin so the Princess's kind brother got her one too.'

I shouldn't have spoken of Garth. After all those years his name still opened my old wound. But I would do it.

When the trumpets sounded for the proclamation Annie clung to my arm. It was a sound to make your hair stand on end. But she paid such close attention to what was said that when we went back to the Pink Lemon she performed it for Jack and Henry – nearly word perfect!

'George Gustus Frederick, Prince of Wales, by the death of the late sovereign, of happy memory, is now become our only lawful and rightful leaf lord, George IV, King of Great Britain and Ireland, Defender of the Face.'

The funerals of Eddie Kent and the old King were delayed until our new Majesty was well enough to rise from his sick bed, and in the hiatus it was decided to move the coffins of little Prince Alfred and Prince Octavius from where they lay in Westminster Abbey to Windsor, to be reunited with their parents in the family vault. Sofy wrote:

The King, I mean the OLD King, often asked for Alfred and Tavy in recent times. Sometimes he imagined they were alive and playing in his room. I hardly remember those little boys, you know. How long ago it all seems. But I'm glad to think they'll all be together again.

Now my boxes are packed and so are Augusta's. She will go to Frogmore directly after the funeral and I shall come to town. I'm to have rooms at Kensington Palace and Vicky Kent will bring the children back from Devonshire and live there too but not until the place is made fit to live in. In the meanwhile I shall lodge at Minny's house on Piccadilly while the renovations are done and will expect to see my Humble Companion VERY OFTEN. There's no place for me at Windsor now, Nellie. Our new Majesty must have it, to do with as he chooses. He is still v. weak but his doctors' bulletin struck a brighter note this morning.

Old King George was buried on February 16th 1820, and our new King George rallied and lived to reign. Then the question was, did he have a queen or did he not?

29

In April Sofy left off her black bombazine and began wearing grey. In May she put on lavender and ventured out with me to buy bed linens and new spectacles, fashionable ones with side pieces so as – she said – to look a little less like an old owl. Her company was more enjoyable than I ever remembered it. With the old Majesties gone a weight had been lifted from her. She had money to spend and when the mourning period ended she was free to go wherever she pleased. She bloomed, a little. And on the subject of the King she grew very outspoken.

One of his first acts had been to have Caroline's name omitted from prayers for the royal family. Caroline, *Queen* Caroline as many now called her, asked that a ship be sent to bring her back to England in fitting style.

Sofy said, 'And do you know His Majesty's reply? Not only will he not send a ship, he's also demanded the return of a particular tea service. As if he doesn't have cups and saucers enough.'

At first the King seemed not to grasp the mood of his

people. Caroline's absence had made their hearts grow fonder. Wasn't she the mother of Charlotte, flower and hope of the nation, whom we had lost? And whatever was said about her, could she be any less regal a figure than her husband?

'That painted lump,' Morphew called him. 'He's afeared she'll come and bump his fat cheeks off the throne. Well there's plenty wouldn't mind to see her do it.'

Caroline took her time, assembling her suite to travel north, and the delay played on the King's nerves. He began to lose his appetite for a fight and sent her an offer: a pension for life if she would renounce her claim to a crown and stay permanently out of the country. On the other hand, if she persisted in coming to England all the stories of her bedfellows and her irregular household would be examined and she risked being tried for high treason.

Sofy hoped and believed that Caroline wouldn't come.

'She must know the King means to break her,' she said. 'The mother of his child. It would be too awful if he dragged her through a trial. Minny says he truly means to do it and of course she eggs him on, though I don't see what Caroline ever did to offend her. I'll tell you frankly, Nellie, I think Minny only does it to annoy her husband. Gloucester always took Caroline's side, you know?'

Caroline was neither interested in a pension nor intimidated by the threat of a trial. She had decided to come to England and be crowned alongside her detested husband and come she did, by the Calais packet. She landed at Dover at the beginning of June and made her way to London, slowly and in an open carriage, to make sure the populace had a good view of their new queen. I saw her myself. Sally and I were returning from Voss's consulting rooms where I had just had two teeth pulled and there was such a press of people we couldn't get through to Park Street. They said Queen Caroline was expected at any moment, on her way to a house in South Audley Street where she was to spend her first night. My jaw was throbbing but Sal so wanted to see her we waited an hour, and in the end I was glad we'd persevered for I was able to give Sofy every detail.

She was all in black, long-sleeved, high-collared and very proper, and wore a splendid hat, with a jewel and three high feathers. Her coach was a poor shabby thing but I thought her deportment was altogether very queenly. She had an escort of gentlemen on horseback, and seated with her in the carriage was a lady and a swarthy young man looking most uncomfortable in a top hat and a grey cutaway coat. An Italian friend, I thought.

'No,' Sofy said. 'Not Italian. That was Willy Austin. She's brought that orphan boy with her. Minny is delighted. She says Caroline couldn't have played a worse hand if she'd tried. Now the old gossip about will be raked over and that can only improve the King's stock.'

But Minny and Sofy didn't go about as I did, hearing what was said on the street, and both misjudged the country. Men who had come home from Waterloo expecting to be heroes were still without work and yet the new King was as profligate as ever. Therefore, any enemy of His Majesty was the people's friend, or so the reasoning went. Uncle Christoff told me Morphew fully expected royal heads would roll and had searched out his old liberty cap, to be ready when the call to revolution came.

Queen Caroline took a house on St James's Square and kept indoors. Society was waiting to see how the cards were dealt so no one risked inviting her to dinner and the only callers she had were lawyers. In July a Private Bill was placed before the House of Lords accusing Caroline of adulterous knowledge of her Chamberlain, Mr Pergami. The Bill asked that the royal marriage be dissolved and that Caroline forfeit her title and privileges as Queen Consort. The King shut himself away at Windsor while the Bill was under consideration, to escape the sound of stones being thrown at his London windows.

Both sides engaged lawyers and, according to Sofy, no effort was spared to bring the parties to an agreement – though I was never sure I believed that, for what does a lawyer enjoy more than a famous trial? It was unlikely anyway that either the King or his Queen would give any ground. Sofy dreaded a trial.

She said, 'Who can say what may come out, what may be said in anger? And yet they both carry on as though they *want* a trial. I despair of them, Nellie, both of them. I'm only glad Charlotte didn't live to see it.'

The trial was set for August 17th and Caroline had every reason to feel confident. If she went about she was cheered in the street, and every day more people wore the white cockade to show they were of the Queen's party. The King's friends boarded up their windows and hurried away to their country estates, and Lady Haddon told Henry she had been twice to Drury Lane to see Mr Kean's *Othello* and the orchestra had omitted to play *God Save the King* on both occasions for fear of being attacked by the audience.

In the royal family Sofy was almost alone in her support for Caroline. Only Minny's husband, Gloucester, sided with her. Augusta, Minny, Fred York and Billy Clarence were all firmly behind the King. Gus Sussex too, in spirit, though he found it conveniently necessary to go to Bath for a water cure and so was spared the unpleasantness of going to Westminster for the trial. Sofy found it so uncomfortable, lodging at Gloucester House where husband and wife were at loggerheads on the subject of the Queen, that she moved to a house in Connaught Place until her new apartments were ready and so became my even closer neighbour. We saw each other almost every day.

She said, 'Augusta told me the King's nerves are so bad he's liable to die, and the way she looked at me as she said it you would have thought *I* was to blame for his situation. Well, I will not be bullied, Nellie. I'm sure I wish His Majesty no ill, but I will not say he's in the right when I believe he's in the wrong. He has supporters enough to do that.'

I'd never seen her so fiery. I encouraged her to stand firm and she did, even when one of the King's pillars threatened to crumble. The Duchess of York died and Fred York, the brother on whom the King leaned more than any other, collapsed with unaccountable grief. Contrary to all appearances it had apparently been the happiest of marriages, conducted in separate houses and never fewer than fifteen miles apart. There were no children. This may have been due to some deficiency in the Duchess, but by all accounts her bed was a heaving mass of dogs and cats so making access to her person difficult for the nimblest of husbands; and Fred York was a lumbering man, cursed with the Hanover belly.

The days before the trial began were unpleasant. Mobs formed, shouted threats against the King, then dispersed as suddenly as they had gathered. Rocks were thrown, fires were set, slogans appeared on walls. Jack and Henry slept at the shop, to keep watch. Morphew thought it should be his job but Jack didn't trust him.

He said, 'For one thing, he's too old. He's liable to fall asleep, and for another thing, he doesn't know if he's a hare or a hound.'

I said, 'And where do you and Henry stand, for king or queen?'

He said, 'We stand for trade, Nellie. Good order on the streets so decent people can keep their houses open and give dinners. That's what we stand for. You're to keep Morphew at home. He knows he's needed there anyway to help your uncle go to the necessary.'

Morphew grumbled quietly, but obeyed. He was always careful not to make Uncle Christoff feel a nuisance.

★

The day before the enquiry began dragoons appeared on the streets. By the next morning there were Foot Guards all the way down Whitehall to Parliament Square and two yawls were at anchor in the river, with cannon in their bows. *The Times* said the whole business was a travesty, a trial in which the Lords were both prosecutors and judges. And how could the Queen be accused of impurity without the King's conduct in the marriage also being inquired into?

That first day seemed endless. I sat with Sofy all afternoon, wondering what might be happening at Westminster. Her hope was that the Bill would be dismissed immediately and the King would have to find a way to accommodate his queen. At six o'clock, as I was about to leave, Mrs Denman came in to tell us that the Lords had voted in great numbers to proceed with the Bill and that the Attorney General and Mr Brougham had given their opening speeches. Mr Brougham was Caroline's attorney and Mr Denman was his second.

Mrs Denman said the Queen had worn full mourning for the Duchess of York and had remained in the chamber all day, listening to what was said. Mr Brougham, she said, had made an excellent beginning. He wasn't a strong man, was given to sudden collapses and prostrations, but he had spoken very eloquently of the fundamental wrongness of the Bill. If the Queen was guilty of such a long list of offences and over such a long span of years, why had she never been impeached?

Mrs Denman said, 'Of course, Mr Brougham was most careful not to name the King.'

He'd said he wouldn't for one minute suggest that

spitefulness lay behind this sudden inquiry into the Queen's character and then, having trailed the coat tails of the idea, he'd prayed he would never be obliged to make such a suggestion. The House of Lords had adjourned at five and the Queen had retired to Hammersmith. She had taken a house there, to be away from the noise and crowds of town.

Two nights in the country refreshed her sufficiently that she felt well enough by Sunday afternoon to drive all about London and test whether her popularity had cooled. It had not. The news sheets made such mouth-watering reading she was cheered everywhere she went. As Sal said, it was better than going to a play because every day some new scene was added. The Queen cast out, without the consolation of a husband and expected to live like a nun. The Queen, seen jiggling on the lap of her *valet-de-chambre* and wearing no stockings.

On the third day witnesses were brought in from Caroline's own household, Italian servants who had been kept in a secret place until they were called, to prevent any London mob from hanging them. The Queen, Mrs Denman reported, had risen from her seat and cried out in alarm when she saw one of her manservants brought in.

'So now,' she said, 'Mr Brougham has advised her to stay away while such disagreeable testimony is heard.'

But the Queen didn't stay away. She recovered her composure and listened to everything.

'All filth and depravity,' Miss Tod said, and she studied every report, to make sure.

Sofy began to waver in her support for Caroline. She said, 'It's far, far worse than I expected. How can she bear to have everything picked over? Even the state of her bed sheets, Nellie. It's too shaming.'

My feelings ran the other way. The more I heard the more I pitied the Queen. If the King could take women to his bed; why was a different standard applied to Caroline? She was beyond the age of child-bearing. The succession wasn't in jeopardy. She was indelicate, certainly, and indiscreet, but those were weaknesses, not crimes. It seemed to me her greatest error was marrying into such a nest of hypocrites.

The prosecution continued for three weeks, then a recess was called. Sofy thought this detrimental to the Queen's case, to interrupt the enquiry when the sympathy of the country was so strongly for her, but of course the Lords knew little and cared less for the views of the people. Besides, Mr Denman had suffered an eructation of the liver and Mr Brougham was exhausted. Both needed to rest if they were to give of their best in the Queen's defence. The trial continued at the beginning of October and Mrs Denman resumed her daily reports.

'Mr Brougham has been on his feet all day,' she said. 'Mr Denman says he never heard him so persuasive.'

One of Brougham's themes was that the witnesses for the prosecution were all foreigners, famous for being unreliable, and that no two of them had agreed on anything. And where were the English servants, supposedly too scandalized to have remained in the Queen's service? Not one of them had been brought forward.

All through October Caroline's following grew. Wasn't she a simple, vulnerable woman, far from home, with no brother or father to protect her? Didn't her only child lie in a tomb at the very heart of her enemy's castle? She was every wronged wife, she was a most particular tragedy, and if she kept pistols in her house was it any wonder when the Royalties were clearly plotting to do away with her? At Hammersmith there was a constant traffic of supporters, sporting white ribbands and feathers and carrying declarations of her innocence. Sometimes the road was so crowded with well-wishers she was obliged to travel to Westminster by barge. No sensible man in the street, the *Morning Chronicle* wrote, could fail to be convinced that the Queen was the object of a vicious persecution by a person who could not be named. But the Bill wasn't being considered by sensible men in the street. It had to be decided by men like Fred York and Billy Clarence.

By the beginning of November I was perfectly bored with the Queen's case. It was Sofy's birthday but I knew how the afternoon would go if I sat with her in her drawing room. The clock would tick, she'd pick over what she'd heard from Mrs Denman, and my eyes would grow heavy.

I said, 'Let's go out.'

'I can't,' she said. 'I must stay in. What if there's news?'

'There won't be any news. They haven't even begun the closing speeches.'

'But Nellie, it may not be safe while this dreadful business goes on. York had mud flung at him, you know. What if I'm noticed?'

'You won't be noticed. Don't you know that a lady becomes invisible at forty? And anyway, if the Duke of Clarence dares to be seen drinking in Brooks' Club I'm sure his sister may visit the Exeter Exchange.'

We took a hackney carriage to Piddock's Menagerie to see the elephant and the rhinoceros, then to Mivart's for a pot of chocolate and a slice of cake and back to Connaught Place before dark. No news had come, no mud had been flung and Sofy had a little colour in her cheeks.

30

The Bill was put to the vote on Monday afternoon and approved by a narrow majority. Then the horse-trading began. The divorce clause should be dropped. The divorce clause must by no means be dropped. There was a great fear that if the Bill proceeded to the House of Commons the Queen would unleash stories against the King that would certainly bring him down. The Lords voted twice more and at each vote the majority was reduced. The Bishop of London thundered, Lord Liverpool raged and at the end of another long day the Bill was abandoned. The Lords had effectively declared the Queen guilty but the country believed her innocent, or innocent enough, and therefore no one dared to take the matter any further.

Mrs Denman said the Prime Minister had gone to St James's to break the news to the King. It was the worst possible outcome, a partial, paper victory that left him as married as ever, as encumbered with the Queen as ever, and now universally despised by the people.

Sofy cried a little. She said, 'If only he had not begun it. I think it will be the end of him, Nellie. I think he may retire to Brighton and leave Fred York to reign.'

As word spread, the King hurried away to Windsor with his carriage blinds closed and the Queen made her triumphal torch-lit way to Hammersmith. Bonfires were lit in Hyde Park, every boat on the river had its lanterns hoisted, and Jack kept the night watch again. As he said, when the man in the street gets what he's agitated for he's still liable to break a few windows, by way of celebration.

After a week of jubilation the people began to discover little reasons to deprecate the Queen: for sure she'd soon be pocketing a handsome pension; what had she ever done for them? And why must she guy herself up with so much lace and rouge? No, perhaps they didn't love her so much after all. A few days more and the King had recovered his spirits well enough to enjoy planning a coronation for himself and himself alone. Another week, and Sofy found something new to fret about. Adelaide Clarence had reached her eighth month and happy though Sofy was to think that her sister-in-law would be blessed with a child at last, she had rather pinned her hopes on Drina Kent for the succession. I noted the sad rivalry in my journal:

December 14th 1820

The Clarences have a daughter. She will be called Princess Elizabeth. Everyone is delighted except the Duchess of Kent, now reduced in rank to Mother of a Spare and Sofy who regrets whatever Vicky Kent regrets. At least the famine of heirs is at an end.

The Duchess of Kent came back to London and moved into Kensington Palace, though the builders still weren't finished, and Sofy decided to follow suit. She said it was for the pleasure of seeing little Drina and Feodora every day but there was undoubtedly another attraction. Vicky Kent had retained Eddie Kent's equerry, Captain Conroy, to have charge of her household, and the very mention of his name made Sofy blush. She was in love again.

John Conroy was ten years Sofy's junior, with a wife and five children at home in Shooters Hill, but that detail didn't signify. The affair took place entirely inside her head. A prince might live like a tomcat but she had learned the hard way that a princess could not. But she wore new shawls and laughed gaily whenever Conroy was close by, and in the spring she bought a horse and kept it at Fozard's livery so she could join the party whenever the Duchess and her chamberlain rode out.

For a while I hardly saw her. Jack laughed about it. 'Out of favour are we?' he said. 'You'll end up in the Tower yet, Nellie.'

It didn't grieve me. I loved Sofy but I couldn't sit five minutes with Vicky Kent. She was a silly, vain woman. I was glad of time to myself too. A person can waste a great deal of precious writing time while a Royal Highness dithers over which gloves to wear.

★

308

In March the Clarences' baby girl died, only three months old, and the Kents' star began to rise again. Drina was third in line, after her uncles Fred York and Billy Clarence. 'I'm very sorry for Billy and Adelaide's loss of course,' Sofy said, 'but you know the child never did thrive. Drina will make an altogether better heir, so sound and healthy and it's clear she's going to be such a beauty.'

Well, there spoke a blind and doting aunt. Drina was a stolid Hanover child, her father all over. Feodora was the one who had the good looks and a blighted blessing that must have been. Bad enough to outshine any half-sister, but to put a little Crown Princess in the shade was unthinkable. I predicted an early marriage for Feodora, to some faraway duke. From then on all efforts were bent to turning Drina into a future queen and the first step was a more queenly name.

Captain Conroy says... three words that I saw with ever greater frequency in Sofy's letters:

Captain Conroy says we had better call her Victoria, and she must be guarded NIGHT AND DAY. He has secret information that there may be an attempt on her life. Imagine! Vicky believes the threat comes from the Cumberlands. She thinks Ernie will stop at nothing to put his own boy on the throne but she doesn't know Ernie as I do. He's quite contented in Hanover and you know Drina, VICTORIA as I must now remember to call her, can never be Queen of Hanover. Their law prevents a female succeeding. So Ernie's son can have Hanover and

VICTORIA can have England and there will be no need at all for any unpleasantness. Nevertheless I do agree with Captain Conroy that we must take the greatest care of our angel child.

Our new King's coronation was fixed for July 19th and preparations were well in hand. It was a vast project. The robing before the ceremony and the banquet after it were to take place in Westminster Hall and its stone floor had been overlaid with wood and carpet. The path between the hall and the abbey was canopied and carpeted, and inside the abbey boxes were built to seat the Royalties. But of the King's sisters only Minny Gloucester and Augusta planned to attend.

Sofy said, 'It would be too long a day for me. I'd have to be in my carriage by five. And then those hateful, heavy robes, and in July. I'd die.'

Elizabeth said she couldn't come. She'd poured all her money into Humbug's bottomless pit so she had nothing left to pay for jaunts. Royal pleaded poor health and said she wouldn't come.

Sofy said, 'It really doesn't matter. I'm sure none of us will be missed.'

It was true, the only question that interested people was whether Caroline would be crowned too. She had applied to the Privy Council to know what arrangements had been made for her procession and crowning. The answer came back that no arrangements had been made. There would be only one crown and one throne and the Queen had better stay at home and keep the peace.

Sofy said, 'But I'm certain she'll go to the abbey, Nellie. You know how she is. Nothing will keep her away.'

All the signs were there. Caroline rode about town every day to keep herself in view, and she made sure to have her gig pulled along by broken-down horses and always to have a hole in her stocking so people might think how ill she was treated. It came to two days before the coronation and the question was still being debated: did common usage give a queen the right to be crowned whatever the King might say, or was a coronation in the King's gift and therefore his to withhold? The lawyers argued the case back as far as King Canute but the material point was this: Caroline had better have her crown or windows and heads would be broken.

Sofy said, 'I'm sure she's given the King every opportunity to climb down. You know, she offered to be crowned on a different occasion, perhaps next week, if another throne can't be brought in by Thursday. One can't say she's being unreasonable, but His Majesty won't have it. Minny says his insides are in knots. Well, the remedy is in his hands. He should make peace with his wife.'

On Wednesday morning foot soldiers appeared on the streets around St James's and by evening the abbey was surrounded by guards. Sal had planned to take Annie down to Horse Guards to see the new King ride by but Henry wouldn't allow it. He thought blood would be shed before the day was over and he didn't want any of it to be Topham blood. Uncle Christoff declined too. He preferred to sleep late. But Morphew minded neither early mornings nor the danger of a riot; in fact I believe he was hoping for a little mayhem at the very least.

I went with Sally and Annie to see the boat races on the Serpentine. It was a perfect, sunny day, not too hot, unless you were the King, sweating under your wig and cap of state. I'd given Jack instructions that Henry was to be let go no later than six o'clock so he could take Sal to the burletta at the Adelphi. There was to be free admittance, in honour of the day, until the theatre was filled up.

Annie and I stayed in Hyde Park until they lit the Chinese lanterns. Every tree, every booth, every boat on the water had lights.

'Like fairyland,' Annie said.

She might not have seen King George in his crown but she'd seen a parade of elephants dressed up in pink and gold and she'd seen a hot-air balloon that carried two men in its basket high over the rooftops.

Jack was asleep in a chair when we got back to Seymour Street, worn out from a day of sugar-boiling, and Morphew was in the summer kitchen giving Uncle Christoff a report of the day's events.

'What a day, Miss Nellie,' he said. 'I've seen things today I never would of thought.' He had managed to get as close to the abbey as Broad Sanctuary, and what he hadn't seen with his own eyes he had heard passed through the crowd and improved on with each telling.

Queen Caroline had arrived in a coach and six, and with Willy Austin at her side.

Morphew said, 'She had a lady attending on her of course, a long drink of water she was, and then that lad the Queen keeps, all tricked out, waving and carrying on like a Prince of the Blood. Ask me, he isn't hooly right in the head.'

It occurred to me then that Caroline had had just one aim that day: to make a spectacle, whatever the cost to her own dignity. If she couldn't be crowned she could at least steal the show from the King. She had gone first to the west entrance, then to the north, but both doors were barred. At the last she had left her coach and walked round to the eastern cloister but there too the guards wouldn't let her in. Morphew had witnessed her retreat.

He said, 'We could hear folk a-shouting. They said she beat on every door. "Let in your queen," she cried, but they gave her the same answer everywhere she knocked. No ticket, no entry. Then they reckoned somebody took pity on her and gave her a ticket that was meant for their own selves but she wouldn't take it. She wouldn't go on in without her suite, see, and the ticket said Admit One. Well, fair dues, a queen don't go anywhere on her own. So then back they all come in the landau and I seen her myself. She held her head high but you could see she was shooken up and I'll quote you why. There was more laughing at her than there was cheering and she hadn't bargained for that. I felt sorry for her, Miss Nellie, and that's the truth. I harn't got a lot of time for Royalties but I don't care to see a lady made a mockery. Then off she

313

went and soon as she was gone out they come, like rats at midnight. All the Highnesses, in a procession. I suppose somebody told them the coast was clear. York come waddling along, looked like he'd tip over if you gave him a nudge, he's got such a belly on him. Clarence isn't much better. And the scar-faced one was there too. Cumberland. And the King… well, I'll tell you something and I don't care who hears it. I can't ever think of that great wobbling lummox as king. Know what he looked like? He looked like one of Mr Jack's almond flummeries, been left out in the sun.'

The news sheets said the coronation had provided a welcome lift to trade. For the banquet, three hundred and fifty bottles of sherry wine and a hundred dozen of hock. One thousand yards of best damask table covering. The embroidery of the King's velvet train alone had given employment to a dozen needlewomen, and its ermine trim was estimated at a worth of eight hundred pounds. Then there was the new diadem commissioned by the King, said to be decorated with twelve thousand diamonds, but the diamonds were rented and, as Jack said, bottles of hock and new crowns are only good for trade if they're paid for. He'd lived in dread of being asked to furnish ices for the banquet. An honour like that could ruin a man.

Sofy said, 'I suffered all day, Nellie. My heart pounded and my insides griped. I felt certain something bad would happen, and I was right. It was altogether badly done. Minny said the King nearly fainted with anxiety of what Caroline might do, and then the heat and the weight of his robes. Twice he had to be given vinegar. And then did you hear what happened at the end? Dear Ernie came in to see me in the evening and told me such a terrifying story. A coach overturned in St Margaret's and two horses had to be shot and dragged away, so the procession was quite blocked. They had to take another route, through the most terrible, dangerous streets.'

It had been a grimy end after the splendour of the day. The King's procession had been forced to drive through Devil's Acre. His Majesty will have been glad of his perfumed handkerchief.

I said, 'But I think it very fitting for a new-crowned King to show himself to the people of Pye Street. They're all his subjects, after all.'

'Oh no, Nellie,' she said. 'If they hadn't had an escort of guards I'm sure they might all have been set upon and killed. Ernie said the King was so frightened he had to be lifted down from the coach when they reached Carlton House. His legs wouldn't support him.'

The Queen had driven back to Hammersmith and shut herself away. It was predicted she'd soon be gone, back to Brunswick or to Italy, where no one would find fault with the way she carried on. I know Sofy would have liked to visit her but she didn't quite dare.

'Poor dear,' she said, every time I saw her. 'I wonder if she sees anyone. I wonder if I should write to her?'

After a week of dithering she sent a letter and heard by return that Caroline was unwell. 'Mine Dear Sister,' Caroline wrote, 'I thank you for your Kind Missage. I am very bad with Stomick Colicks since my Ordeal. Dr Rollins have give me magnesia. Dr Woodford have give me calomel and Purges of salt water but still I am costiff. I try to bear up cheerful for sakes off My People. Yr Queen and Sister, Caroline.'

On August 3rd Sofy asked me to have a box of Jack's chocolate-dipped figs sent to Hammersmith. That was Friday. On the Monday Lady Anne, one of the Bedchamber Ladies, wrote to convey the Queen's gratitude. The figs were much appreciated and she was feeling a little better. On Wednesday morning Jack woke me before it was light.

He said, 'Something's up, Nell. The abbey bells are ringing. I reckon the King must have passed.'

But it was Caroline who was dead. She was fifty-three. Some said a contortion of the bowels had killed her, some said poison. Lady Anne told Sofy she had suffered two days of agony but the last hour had been peaceful. There was to be no viewing. The Queen had expressly forbidden it.

Sofy said, 'And do you know what her words were? "Those who cared for me came to see me while I lived." Oh Nellie, now I feel so badly that I didn't go to visit her at Hammersmith.'

She had the least reason to reproach herself. Minny Gloucester could have paid a call, or Augusta. Men may act pigheaded but women should know better how to treat a sister.

The King was on his way to Ireland and heard the news when his ship put in at Holyhead. He made a face of being sorry and then gave orders she was to be put in her coffin and dispatched to Brunswick as soon as possible. I thought it the meanest thing. She was the mother of his child and she'd done him the greatest favour, dying and leaving him to reign un-encumbered. He could at least have been civil to her in death, but no. He commanded that her casket be brought quietly, with a small escort, from Hammersmith to Kensington, then taken north and east to reach the Romford turnpike and avoid the heart of the city and any troublesome crowds that might gather. This took no account of what the people expected. They'd laughed to see her humiliated on Coronation Day, and now she was dead they wanted their money's worth of weeping. His Majesty should have understood that. He was fond of theatricals himself.

It was a filthy day, mild and wet, with a lowering sky, but people were still out on the streets and there was a plan afoot. When the procession reached the Kensington gravel pits the way north was blocked by wagons. For an hour everything came to a halt and as the crowd was growing bigger and uglier it was decided to take the coffin along Kensington Gore and then turn north along Park Lane. But at Cumberland Gate the crowd tried to force the procession to turn onto Oxford Street and a great fight broke out. Brick ends were thrown, shots were fired and two men were killed.

Jack had opened for business but when he heard what was coming his way he closed the shutters and stayed inside, with his cudgel at the ready, long after the military had prevailed and the hearse had crawled on along the Edgware Road. It wasn't the unremarked departure the King had hoped for and the battle still wasn't over. When the procession reached Tottenham Court Road the people had their way again, forcing it south. Francis Street had been dug up and carts blocked Great Russell Street to prevent any further detour from the route the people wanted: along the Strand to Temple Bar and through the heart of the City. The escort of foot guards grew tired of being pelted with mud and threw in their lot with the crowd. London had its procession for dead Caroline after all.

Sofy said, 'Everything of Caroline's goes to the boy Willy, you know, when he reaches his majority. Well, I suppose she had no one else. I just hope he'll have someone to advise him. Money can easily go to a young man's head.'

She pretended concern for Willy Austin but it was her own Tommy she had in mind. He was only a half-pay captain but he kept ten hunters at livery in Leicestershire.

I said, 'How does he manage it?'

'Very badly. But he'll have more funds now he's of age.'

'From Garth?'

'Of course not from Garth,' she said. 'I imagine Garth has very little to spare. No, from me. I made Tommy an allowance. Caroline died on his birthday, did you realize? Is a thousand a year too much, Nellie? Or too little?'

What did I know? It was a handsome amount but Sofy could afford it. One thousand pounds a year though was the only commerce between her and her son. Her banker must have understood the nature of the arrangement and all of Weymouth had long guessed whose child it was the Sharlands had taken in. Tommy was a grown man, quite capable of discretion and consideration, yet I never knew him to visit her. That was my only sad observation.

31

My Jack was never sick. He was never a lie-a-bed. If he took a head cold he'd still be at his work, croaking orders to Henry. It all started with one of his eye teeth, which should have been pulled but he wouldn't spend the money. He sent Sally to borrow pincers from the farrier in Park Street and told Henry to do the deed but Henry didn't have the stomach for it and I didn't have the strength. So the job fell to Morphew who had been itching to do it anyway. He went at it like a terrier clamped on a rat and the tooth was so rotted it soon came away but its root was left behind.

Morphew said, 'That won't harm you. Do you take a good swig of brandy you'll be as right as rain.'

Which Jack did and was back at work within the hour, making a sugar beehive and gum-paste bees for Mrs Garr-Lonsdale's midsummer ball. He was feverish that night though, turning and tossing and talking nonsense. He wanted the window open because he couldn't breathe, then he wanted the window closed because he swore the street was full of bees. I got up at six, when I heard Esther come in with the milk, but Jack didn't move.

He said, 'Nellie, are you there? Light the lamp.'

But the sun was up and the room was bright. Only Jack was in darkness. His eyes bulged out like coddled eggs and they saw nothing. I sent Esther to fetch Dr Jebb as fast as she could and Morphew to fetch Henry and while we waited I sat with Jack and told him some things I'd neglected to say in twenty-five years of marriage.

I said, 'You've been a good husband, Jack.'

He laughed. 'Been? What, am I finished? Light the lamp, Nellie. It's time I was up.'

He didn't move though.

'Where's Henry?' he asked. 'We need alum bringing in, and gum dragon.'

I told him to rest, not to fret about business. He touched my hair.

He said, 'No need for doctors. When did I ever need a doctor? All these folks crowding in on me. I've got to get up, get shaved and dressed.'

Dr Jebb said it was a brain fever, caused by the piece of cotton and oil of cloves and recommended Keeley's Bromide and poppy tea until the sight was restored. Five minutes after he had left Jack said, 'Well I'll be jiggered, now here's our Beatie come to see me,' which was his sister, long dead, and he sank into a deep sleep.

He lay two days without waking and then expired.

What can I say? I had never much wanted him for a

321

husband and there had been many times I'd thought him narrow and unfeeling, but as soon as he was gone I wished him back. If we'd chafed each other it had done me no harm. In fact I believe it made me all the more determined to find quiet ways of doing as I pleased. I'd held out on him, keeping my secrets, and secrets can be powerful things. And when all was said and done, he was the only man who'd ever taken me in his arms and told me I was bonny enough for him. I slept in a fireside chair, after he first passed, for to lie in bed and hear the silence beside me always brought me to tears.

Sally felt the loss too. Jack had argued against my taking her in but he'd been a father to her, in spite of himself, and he'd loved young Annie like she was his very own. Morphew was undone.

He said, 'That ain't right, Miss Nellie. He's gone and I'm still here. And now what's to become of the shop?'

The Pink Lemon was the least of my problems. It had been Jack's intention that Henry should have it some day and that day had come. Sal knew how to run the shop and people liked her. She had an open manner the ladies liked, respectful but willing to appear interested in what people should serve at their tables. She was more of an asset to the place than I had ever been. All Henry had to do was find a suitable boy to learn the sugar craft. My difficulty was myself. I'd longed to be my own mistress and now I was I yawed about like a ship whose rudder doesn't answer.

★

Sofy was a true friend to me in those grey days. Every day I walked through the park to Kensington Palace and she'd ring for tea and listen while I talked in circles. She said it was a matter of time and I must be patient, that when the old King died and she was free to leave Windsor she had fallen into a terrible melancholy and not been able to decide the simplest thing.

'And look at me now,' she'd say. 'Did you ever see such a gay old trout?'

It was the Conroy Effect. Vicky Kent's steward was in and out of their apartments constantly. Sofy could depend on seeing him several times a day, or rather *not* seeing him, for she always snatched her spectacles off her nose the instant she heard his voice. She never hid the pleasure his company gave her.

She said, 'I know you think I'm silly, but what harm does it do? I think I'm allowed a little fancy in my old age. Remember, I never had a husband.'

I said, 'You may yet. Princess Elizabeth was older than you when she married.'

'True,' she said, 'but look what she settled for. You don't suppose Humbug ever causes her any raptures?'

I said, 'If it's raptures you want you'll do just as well without a husband. Husbands are for a different kind of comfort.'

She was silent for a while. Then she said, 'But Nellie, perhaps that's why you never caught properly for a baby, if Jack gave you no pleasure, for you know I'm convinced it was my rapture that brought on Tommy.'

I remember smiling at her imperfect understanding of things, great woman of the world that I was.

I said, 'Sofy, it wasn't *your* rapture that caused Tommy. It was Garth's.'

She spilled her tea. 'Garth's?' she said. '*Garth's?* What is he to do with anything?'

I wasn't smiling then. My first thought was to retract, but I couldn't. The ground for retreat was cut away the instant I'd said Garth's name.

I said, 'Garth is Tommy's father. You told me so.'

'I certainly did not!' she said. 'Garth! That ugly old man! How could you imagine such a thing?'

Then we stared at each other, both dumbstruck. She was affronted. That was simple enough. But it was nothing to my embarrassment and confusion and the first pang of something else. My old feelings for Tom Garth, shut away for so long. Sofy broke the silence.

She said, 'I cannot believe it, Nellie. Where did you get such an idea? Garth was always very helpful, admittedly. It was his suggestion to take Tommy into his own household when those Sharlands grew indiscreet. I'm sure I shall always be obliged to him for that. And he quite adores Tommy. But that I lay with him? You cannot have believed it. I know he always made a great pet of you but even you must admit the idea is repulsive.'

Then I couldn't think of Garth at all. I began to see what was coming, what had always been under my nose. Nevertheless I had to ask.

'Then who is Tommy's father?'

She laughed and blushed, like a young girl again.

'Why Ernie, of course,' she said. 'That's why Tommy has turned out so handsome. You must surely see that?'

Ernie Cumberland, who had lurked about Gloucester Lodge that dreadful August, pretending brotherly concern. Who had stayed out of sight until that tiny baby had been hurried out of the house and then had laid the blame at Tom Garth's door.

I said, 'He forced himself upon you.'

'No,' she said. 'Well, perhaps at first. But I found I enjoyed it. It wasn't at all what I'd expected. The Queen, you know, when Royal married Fritz, warned her it was a most disagreeable duty, but that wasn't my experience. Now your face says all. You disapprove.'

I said, '*Disapprove* hardly meets the case. Do you realize what you're saying? Ernie is your brother.'

She picked at a loose thread on the arm of her chair.

She said, 'I know it isn't usual.'

Usual!

I said, 'It's contrary to nature, Sofy. It's contrary to God's word.'

'Oh,' she said, 'And when did you grow so pious? A man may not *marry* his sister, that's what my prayer book says. Well there was no marrying. I love my brother and he gave me something wonderful.'

'What kind of gift is it that you're not allowed to keep? You never held your child in your arms. Not once. Do you remember what you said to me after Tommy was born? You said "I'm ruined". And so you were.'

'You never liked Ernie,' she said.

She reminded me of Amelia when she said that, petulant and silly. There was grey in her hair but she was pouting like a little girl.

I said, 'And now I have particular reason, though I'm too shaken yet to quite believe it.'

'Well,' she said, 'don't imagine you're the only one who's affronted. That you could think Old Garth was my lover! It's too awful. I'm sure I shall have nightmares about it.'

I said, 'He would have been a worthier one than Cumberland. Hasn't Garth done everything a good husband would do? He's protected your character. He's raised your son and given him a name.'

She said, 'I don't deny it. Don't lecture me. Garth knows I'm grateful and he did well enough out of it. He was promoted full general, you know, which he had no reason to expect. Ernie arranged that, of course. Ernie saw to everything.'

I stood up.

She said, 'Anyway, what is it to you? If anyone has suffered it's me. I'm the one left an old maid. Though Ernie always visits me when he comes to England. He never misses. I'm one of the very first calls he makes. And I have my consolation. I have Tommy.'

She saw I intended to leave. Usually she would find a dozen little reasons to make me stay another hour but that day she was too fired by the romance inside her head, too determined to defend it from any criticism.

She said, 'I know what it is, Nellie. You're jealous, because I have a son and you don't.'

It was the Duchess of Kent who saved me from myself. She came in to the room, with John Conroy padding at her heels, and began talking at once. Vicky Kent believed the world was a series of theatres, with scenes set and actors frozen on their spot, waiting for her to make her entrance and bring the play to life. She failed to notice Sofy's cross, flushed face so a Humble Companion with tears in her eyes was certainly invisible.

I didn't take my usual path home. It would have taken me through Cumberland Gate and that was a name I preferred not to be reminded of. I walked along the Serpentine to Stanhope Gate and then up Park Street and as I sifted through the day's revelations one thought began to overweigh all others. For twenty-three years I'd believed Tom Garth to be a seducer and a scoundrel. I'd been curt with him. I'd put away his garnet bracelet and never worn it since. And now I knew he was innocent. Doubly so, for he'd endured the gossip and raised Sofy's son in dignified silence.

32

Nearly three years passed before I saw Sofy again. For me they were three years of change, most of it slow and inevitable, but some of it exciting. I began a new story and, spared Jack's disparagement and Sofy's demands on my time, I wrote freer and faster than I ever had before. Mr Crosby paid me £50 for the copyright of *The False Construction*. He said it was a much more saleable work than *The Outcast*, containing as it did the suspense of a conspiracy, the tragedy of unrequited love, a light peppering of wit and, above all, a happy ending. It was published in June 1825 and reprinted after only seven months.

My Uncle Christoff died in his sleep on Christmas Eve. As near as we could say he was seventy-five. He had outlived Papi by a quarter of a century and no two brothers could have been less alike. Papi had thrived in company and being a mere steward to society didn't trouble him. At Carlton House he'd been at the gilded, sparkling heart of dull old Hanover and to Papi it was a world of opportunities. My uncle preferred the quiet, domestic life. He had that same Weltje nose for turning a profit but he'd conducted business from his country retreat and, unlike Papi who'd been a shameless murderer of the language, he did it in almost perfect English.

Without my uncle to push about in his invalid chair Morphew found he had no purpose in life. By Twelfth Night he followed him to the grave. I felt his loss more even than Papi's, perhaps more even than my Jack's. Morphew had been a presence for every one of my fifty years – trusty coachman, begrudging footman, kitchen-table revolutionary, Mrs Twyvil's spurned lover, a kindly, sentimental man and a sniffing, scratching snub to my mother's genteel ambitions.

He had caught a head cold and though he kept to the fire-side and took nothing but brandy and milk the inflammation invaded his lungs.

He said, 'I ain't too fierce today, Miss Nellie, but do you bring me the tin of dubbin and my brushes I'll shine up the boots.'

The next time I looked in on him the boots were polished and Morphew was gone. He looked like a man sleeping peace-fully. It was only when he had passed away I realized how little I knew about him. That he was Norfolk Fenman, that he must be closer to eighty than seventy and that I had once heard Twyvil call him Dick. Sal and I opened his locking box and we put together the pieces of his life. According to his last will and testament his name was Nehemiah Richard Murview born, *best as I can calkerlate it, 1737.*

This made him the grand age of eighty-eight. He left a gold spade guinea to Sally, his bone skates to Annie, and a much-thumbed copy of Mr Defoe's *Captain Singleton* 'to Miss Nellie, as I've known from a babe and has gave roof and family to this poor batchyller'.

Suddenly I was alone and Seymour Street was too big for me, full of rooms I never entered from one week's end to the next. Sal and Henry said I must go to them and live above the Pink Lemon, and I did begin to think of it, what I could take with me, what I should have to sell. It would have been easier for them to come to me but Henry wouldn't. He liked living over the shop. Jack had been the same, twitching all night about the next day's work, jumping up before first light to run to his beloved drying cabinets. Then just as I'd braced myself to give up my house and be reduced to the rank of elderly widow, I found I was needed again.

Annie was nearly fourteen. It was time for her to leave the parish school in South Street and learn the confectionery trade from her father but she had no heart for it. She said, 'I know I must do it, Grandma Nellie, but the smell of the sugar makes me sick to my stomach.'

Annie's a good girl, dutiful and hard-working, but she was always too sharp and enquiring to be wasted on making bonbons. I went with her to every school from Park Street to Soho and she got taken on at the National School in Rose Street, to help with the elementary class, two shillings a week and six hot dinners.

'Father won't be pleased,' she said. But I knew how to deal with Henry Topham.

We walked round to Trotter's Bazaar to say good day to Miss Tod but she wasn't there. She hadn't been seen for months. We went to her house in Meard Street but a stranger came to the door.

'Gone,' she said. 'Ask for her at Poland Street.'

Miss Tod, my mother's oldest friend and quidnunc, had gone quietly to the poorhouse, too proud to ask for help.

I said, 'Why didn't you come to me?'

She said, 'I'm well enough here, Nellie. I keep busy. They put me to knitting stockings, while my eyes last.'

'But you have to sleep in a room full of cots while I'm rattling around my house with bedchambers to spare.'

She hated to be beholden, she said. It really wasn't so very bad to live in a dormitory, she said, and besides she had always expected to end in the workhouse, not having any family to turn to.

I said, 'You have me to turn to, just as I turned to you all those years ago when I needed a friend.'

'Did you?' she said. 'I don't remember. I don't recall things as well as I used to.'

God love her. There was nothing wrong with her memory.

At the Pink Lemon Annie's news received a mixed hearing. Sally was secretly pleased. She knew Annie was better suited to teaching than she was to spinning sugar, but Henry was put out and whatever discommoded him discommoded her.

He said, 'You'd no place interfering, Nellie. What am I to do now? You can see I'm stretched with Jack gone.'

I said, 'Then do what Jack did. Take on a lad. You turned out well enough.'

'I was no lad. I knew my craft. Take on a boy, you never know what you're getting. Look what happened with the first one Jack took on.'

'There was nothing wrong with Ambrose Kersie. He just wasn't suited to it, and neither is Annie. She's got a brain in her head.'

'I know,' he said. 'And that's what I'm afraid of. I worked long enough with Jack to see the damage books can do to married life.'

Annie cried. She said she'd do as her father wished and give up her place at Rose Street and once Henry had seen her shed a few tears he was satisfied. He said no one should ever work for him against their will because their resentfulness would show in the quality of their work and if she didn't mind appearing too bookish ever to get a husband he wouldn't stand in her way. He could be a very cussed man, Henry Topham.

So that was settled, and then Annie came with me, with a handcart from the shop, to bring Miss Tod and her few bits from the poorhouse to Seymour Street.

She said, 'Grandma Nellie, what did Miss Tod do, when you needed a friend?'

She was old enough to be told.

I said, 'When I was a girl, when I was walking out with your Grandpa Jack, another man forced his attentions on me and I caught for a baby. Miss Tod helped me. She told me a house to go to and loaned me the money to get the baby fetched away, and when I got sick afterwards, very sick, Miss Tod cared for me and kept my secret.'

Annie was quiet for a while. It must have conjured up a shocking scene, a man forcing himself on stain-faced old Grandma Nellie.

She said, 'Was it a girl baby or a boy baby?'

I said, 'I don't know. You can't tell when it's so small. But listen to me, Annie Topham. Don't you be such a chicken heart as I was. If a man ever comes at you when you haven't encouraged him, you kick and scream and make him think better of it. I don't want you going to any Mrs Dacey, getting your insides all ruined.'

She wanted to know, who was the man?

I said, 'He was a stable groom at a big house I used to go to, and now he's dead and I'm old and none of it matters.'

'And anyway,' she said, 'you married Grandpa Jack and lived happily ever after.'

'Yes,' I said.

That's what they call a white lie.

I hadn't expected to hear from Sofy ever again. In those first weeks I'd thought she might send a note but nothing came. The heat had gone out of our quarrel but as time passes the embers of a friendship may grow too cold to be rekindled. The attempt, when it came, was from Princess Minny.

★

Gloucester House, May 2nd 1826
Dear Nellie Buzzard,

    I do not know, nor wish to know, the nature of the quarrel between you and Sofy. Only that she feels your absence greatly and is perhaps too obstinate to say so. The Duchess of Kent and I are her sole company and nothing we do succeeds in lifting her mood. You were ever a dear and loyal friend to her. I wonder can you find it in your kind heart to call on her?

    Minny Gloucester

For a week I did nothing. I had missed Sofy but I wasn't sure I had the patience for Royalties again. They dilly and dally and change their clothes too often and before you know it the day is wasted. There was also this conundrum to unknot: Sofy's secret and Ernie Cumberland's lie had caused me years of pain, but Sofy didn't know that. She had no idea, yet her innocence didn't lessen my need for recompense. And then, what could that recompense be? She couldn't turn back the clock.

Eventually I wrote to Kensington Palace, and received a reply by return:

Dearest, dearest Nellie,
    Forgive a silly old woman. I long to see you.
Yr Sofy

33

I believe I found Sofy more changed than she found me.
Instead of getting stronger eye glasses she had taken to peering closer at her sewing and her books and so had grown quite
stooped. She had also developed a type of deafness, not un-
common, in which the clarity of hearing comes and goes
according to the agreeableness of what is being said. There
were but two topics of conversation: dear Conroy, now
promoted to major, who was everything considerate, and
naughty Tommy Garth who was not.

Tommy had made love to another man's wife and a great
scandal was about to erupt. He had met Lady Astley in Leicestershire, riding out with the Quorn Hunt, then followed her
back to London. Sir Jacob Astley, careless of his property, had
gone to the North Country to see a promising chaser put
through its paces and while he was away Tommy Garth was
continuing his flirtation – and in broad daylight. Sofy was
afraid that the talk would grow too loud for Sir Jacob to
ignore, that he would call Tommy out, a duel would be
fought and Tommy would be killed. She drafted a letter to

Old Garth, begging him to remove Tommy from London and the temptation of Lady Astley, but then she hesitated to send it.

She said, 'Garth is so ancient now. I don't suppose he can do anything. And as you once reminded me rather sharply, he's done so much over the years. I shouldn't ask any more of him.'

I said, 'What about Ernie Cumberland?'

'Oh I couldn't trouble Ernie,' she said. 'Besides, he's in Hanover. What could he do?'

The subject was dropped for the rest of the afternoon while we debated the relative merits of Campden Hill and Vicarage Gate as places where Major Conroy might live. Sofy said Shooter's Hill was a vast distance for him to travel when he was needed so frequently and so urgently at Kensington Palace. Something had to be done to make his life more comfortable. What I failed to understand, perhaps because my attention had wandered, playing with an idea of far greater interest to me, was that Conroy's new residence was to be paid for by Sofy.

My little idea kept me awake that night. I could call on Garth and discuss with him Sofy's worries about Tommy. I might be able to carry back to her some words of comfort. It would be my perfect cover for seeing him and perhaps putting the record straight. For a week the idea grew and possessed me. I said nothing to Sofy but I did try it out on Miss Tod. An old gentleman, I said. And a misunderstanding I should like to put right.

'Why, for heaven's sakes,' she said, 'of course you must call on him. I can't think of any reason against it.'

Twice I set off for Grosvenor Place and then turned aside when my nerve failed me. The third time I rang the bell. The maid who came to the door gaped at my face.

She was gone for an age. The house was silent and there was no sign of the parrot in the front hall. As I waited it became clearer and clearer to me that it was one of the most foolish projects I had ever embarked on. Then the maid returned, wearing a faint smile.

She said, 'General's in the morning room, madam. He don't get many callers.'

I saw little change in Tom Garth. He was as neat and poised as ever, and very pleased to see me.

'Dear Nellie Buzzard,' he said. 'It's been far too long.'

Milady, perched on the back of a chair, was not so welcoming. She began weaving from side to side and clicking her bill in an alarming fashion.

Garth said, 'Perhaps a walk? I have a small garden. I'm afraid Milady regards this room as hers. She's forgotten her manners. We get so few visitors.'

I said, 'I imagined you were in Dorset. Princess Sofy and I, we had a falling out. It's only since we made up I discovered you were in town.'

He said, 'My movements no longer merit mention in the Court Circular. I live very quiet.'

We talked generally. He condoled with me on the loss of Jack and wondered could it really be twenty years since

337

we'd met on the day of Admiral Nelson's funeral procession.

I said, 'You were carrying Tommy in your arms, because of the crush of people. He was still a little boy. *That's* how long ago it was. There are two reasons I came today and both of them concern Tommy.'

'Ah,' he said.

He said he was sorry to see Her Royal Highness put to such torment but he was at a loss to know what he could do. Tommy had grown arrogant and wouldn't listen to advice. He lived recklessly, as though the laws and rules of civilized society didn't apply to him, as though he were untouchable.

I said, 'Is it because he knows his parentage?'

Garth said he feared it was.

I said, 'But does he know it fully? Sofy makes provision for him, I realize, and that never was the closest of secrets. But has he been told who his father is?'

He busied himself, plucking dead leaves from a currant bush.

I said, 'The day Tommy was born, after we had carried him to the Sharlands and you had left Weymouth, I was led to understand, to *misunderstand,* that you were his father. I knew no different until three years ago and then I learned the truth, quite by chance. It was the cause of my quarrel with Sofy. All those years I blamed you for her ruin.'

There was a little arbor with a seat.

He said, 'You weren't the only one. Even those who knew the truth found it was better to forget it. It was a clever stratagem, to give people a bone to gnaw on. Old Garth and a

338

lovely young princess? *La belle et la bête*? How could such a thing be? Don't worry, Nellie. I guessed the reason you became so prim with me.'

We sat and talked and talked. Of poor Queen Caroline, and of Willy Austin, who'd come back to claim his inheritance but was kept out of it on the grounds that he wasn't right in the head. Of the King, who'd gone to Waterloo field to pay homage to Lord Anglesey's leg and come away quite convinced that he'd been present on that glorious day and had led a great cavalry charge himself. The only name Garth wouldn't be drawn on was Ernie Cumberland's.

'Bad business,' was all he'd say. And he pressed his lips together and shook his head.

I ventured another look at Milady before I left. 'As she's taken against me,' I said, 'perhaps you should think of another guardian for her?'

'Oh, but Nellie,' he said. 'All she needs is time to get accustomed to you and now I'm absolved of being a scoundrel, I hope you may call again.'

I had achieved nothing for Sofy. Tommy was apparently an incorrigible rake and we could only pray that he tired of Lady Astley before her husband came home and counted the spoons. But on my own account I was deliriously happy. I believe it was the most joyful I had felt since the summer of 1792 when we had attended the Weymouth Assembly Rooms and Princess Augusta had obliged Garth to dance with me.

The first thing I did when I returned home was take out his bracelet and put it on my wrist, and the second thing I did was rest for an hour with a towel across my brow.

Miss Tod said, 'It'll take more than a wetted cloth to put out the twinkle in your eyes.'

Not much got past Miss Tod.

I said, 'It's a very strange thing. When I was seventeen he was far too old for me, but now I'm fifty he's not. How can that be?'

'I'll tell you how,' she said. 'A bachelor enjoys a most restful life. But think of all that's befallen you. You've done a good deal more living. You've used up more road than he has and caught up to him.'

I said, 'You make me sound like an old cart wheel.'

'Not at all,' she said. 'You're better off now, Nellie, than those that were great beauties. You never had that and you're the better for it. And if it should come about that things go further with this bachelor gentleman, if he should make you an offer, don't let me hold you back. I'm sure they'd have me again at Poland Street.'

From that day on I saw Garth every week. If the sun shone we walked in Green Park, if it rained we sat in his drawing room. Once he went with me to Kensington to call on Sofy but it was a difficult hour, full of awkwardness and things unsaid, and Sofy's apartments were so stifling hot I thought I should faint. John Conroy lurked and so did the shadow of Ernie Cumberland. Then Gus Sussex came in, old cloth slippers on his feet and a copy of *The Mechanism of the Dead-*

beat Escapement in his hand. He'd taken neighbouring apartments and quite often called by with some exciting horological discovery he wished to share. It was a relief when Vicky Kent brought in her daughters and we were free to leave.

Garth said, 'It was a mistake. I shan't go again. I think I discharged my duties some time ago.'

I said, 'She insists Cumberland is blameless in the affair. She adores him, you know.'

He shook his head. 'I'm thankful she has your friendship, Nellie. Heaven knows, she has little else.'

In July Lady Georgiana Astley abandoned her children and eloped with Tommy Garth. They went first into the country, then to France, and finally back to London, to Jermyn Street, where they took up residence in Batt's Hotel. Sir Jacob had gone to law immediately and sued Tommy for criminal conversation with his wife. She was Sir Jacob's marital property. Tommy had trespassed upon it and was liable to pay compensation. And when Sir Jacob instructed King's Counsel, Tommy had to go one better and instruct a Serjeant-at-Law. Garth feared it would be his ruin, but it was Sofy I worried for. Tommy conducted himself with such swagger. He cannot have cared much for Lady Astley's feelings, nor for her poor children. The more I observed him the plainer it was he was Ernie's boy. He was every inch his father. And the caricature-makers loved him. They fed off him for weeks, gradually slipping in more and more sly references to his royal connection.

Sofy was pulled this way and that. Tommy pestered her for

money and John Conroy did his best to protect her from Tommy's supplications but he did it out of self-interest. He had found a house in Campden Hill and Sofy had promised to pay for it.

I said, 'They both take advantage of you.'

'No,' she said. 'I do it gladly. What do I need money for? Better that it's put to use by those who need it.'

There was soon another burden on her too. Fred York was dying. His dropsy was no longer eased by tapping and he knew he couldn't survive much longer. He asked Sofy if she would execute certain delicate aspects of his will, to pay legacies and to fend off possible false claims.

The New Year came in and the Duke of York went out. He'd come to town to die and Sofy was at his side at Rutland House when the end came.

'Poor dear,' she said, 'he so hoped the King would visit him, to be assured no ill-feeling remained between them, for you know there was always a little rivalry there. When the old King was alive Fred was always his favourite.'

His Majesty had failed to visit his brother, pleading a head cold, but York was nearly the death of him anyway. The funeral was at Windsor on the coldest night of the year and they all caught such chills – Sussex, Clarence, Gloucester, and the King himself – we thought we'd be burying the lot of them. Sofy huddled by her Kensington hearth, with John Conroy at her side, and picked at the tangle of her brother's legatees. He acknowledged a Mr Frederick Vandiest and a Mrs Louisa Crockatt as his natural children; also Captain John

Gibbes of Fulham Lodge, and a son, John Molloy, by Countess Tyrconnel. A third John, by housemaid Emma Stilwell, had fallen at Waterloo and died without issue. There were bequests too for two particular friends: Mrs Clarke, now residing in Boulogne, and Mrs Sinclair Sutherland of Portman Street.

Sofy said, 'Disbanding Fred's troops has quite exhausted me. I pray Billy Clarence won't ask me to do the same for him. I dread to think how many there would be, leaving aside all those Fitzclarences. He probably had a family in every port. Well let him ask Augusta to do it.'

34

The case of Astley versus Garth was heard in the Court of Common Pleas in February 1827. Sir Jacob's counsel painted him as the most devoted of husbands in the happiest of marriages. Tommy's counsel posed the question, why would a wife leave such domestic felicity? Then swiftly answered it themselves by bringing into court a number of doxies willing to testify that they had entertained Sir Jacob.

My own dear Garth was very distressed by the proceedings.

He said, 'I raised Tommy to be a gentleman, but it's all too clear what he intends.'

What he meant was that the evidence Tommy's lawyer had brought, that Jacob Astley was known to every drab in Leicestershire, might prevent his being allowed to divorce her and cast her off. And if Sir Jacob's petition for divorce was dismissed it would be very convenient for Tommy for then he wouldn't be obliged to marry Lady Astley.

Garth said, 'He stole a jewel and paraded it about, and now he's dulled its lustre I fear he'll throw it back to its rightful owner. He'll be the ruin of that poor woman.'

I said, 'Then like father, like son.'

He pressed his lips together. It was his habit whenever I mentioned or even hinted at Ernie Cumberland's name.

The judge seemed not to care one way or the other about Lady Georgiana's fate. He instructed the jury that whilst Lady Astley had failed in her wifely duty to correct her husband's weaknesses, and that a wife's adultery was always more fatal to a marriage than the husband's, Astley had nevertheless thrown away his entitlement to compensation through his own debauchery. Sir Jacob was awarded compensation of one shilling and sentenced to remain married to Georgiana till death did them part.

Georgiana applied to her husband for funds, for Tommy lived far beyond the means of a captain's half pay and his allowance from Sofy was soon swallowed up. Sir Jacob granted her a very modest sum, but it was nothing like sufficient for them to live on and satisfy Tommy's creditors. It was inevitable he would turn to Sofy again, and that he would let drop the faint suggestion of using the secret of his parentage to strike an advantageous bargain.

I said, 'Tell him you won't be intimidated. Tell him you'll cut him off without a penny if he ever threatens you again.'

Wasted breath.

Sofy's first thought, as with everything, was to put the matter entirely in John Conroy's hands. Then Minny Gloucester intervened. She spoke to the King and the King said Sir Herbert Taylor was the man to deal with it. Sir Herbert had been Fred York's adjutant, then the old King's secretary and after that Queen Charlotte's treasurer. There was no man more loyal to the Hanovers and I was relieved to think Sofy had him to protect her feelings and her bank deposits.

Garth knew Sir Herbert and was worried about the appointment.

He said, 'Now Tommy has met his match. He had better go very carefully. Taylor may seem anodyne but he's a clever man and he'll use every trick he knows to protect Her Royal Highness.'

Poor Garth. His instinct was to protect any lady, even one who sometimes forgot the gratitude she owed him, but he loved Tommy too, like a true father. As for Ernie Cumberland, he was everywhere and nowhere in all this, living untroubled – or so I believed – in Hanover, and a picture of married contentment.

That summer, while Sir Herbert calculated and Tommy ran up still more debts, Sofy had a distraction. Royal came to visit, hoping to find a cure for her dropsy. It was the first time she had returned to England since her marriage. Augusta had visited her in Württemberg and so had Elizabeth, but Minny and Sofy had not seen her in thirty years. Augusta went to Greenwich to meet her and took her first to St James's to see the King and then on to Frogmore, which is where I saw her when I accompanied Sofy to Windsor.

Royal, Dowager Queen of Württemburg, was enormous:

a vast bombazine-wrapped egg of a woman, without a neck or waist or ankles. She couldn't walk and could only sit if her back was well supported. That she had made the journey at all was a miracle. And what changes she must have observed. The old Queen's House, now renamed Buckingham Palace, doubled in size and left in a mess of stone and timber while the next stage of its renovations was agreed. Upper Lodge demolished, our new King bloated and tearful, Augusta gouty and walking with a cane, and Sofy, bent and half-blind.

But Royal held court, pink and smiling, doling out gifts and talking endlessly of the rising generation of Württemburgs. There were a great number of Fritz's grandchildren for her to run through.

Sofy said, 'Why does she go on so about them? Why should we care? I'm sure I was in complete muddle with all their names.'

Tedious as it had been to hear about someone else's faraway relatives, I believe it was something else that had put Sofy out of sorts: Royal's talk of nearer relatives, Dolly Cambridge's children whom she saw quite often and — more particularly — the Cumberlands' son, George.

'Such a darling,' Royal said. 'Ernie is besotted with him. But he has that same weakness in his eyes that Ernie had. I do pray something can be done for him.'

I watched Sofy as Royal talked of the Cumberlands. She showed nothing of what she must surely have felt, hearing of Ernie's happy circumstances, of his devoted duchess and his angelic son. What had happened between them had cost Sofy

347

everything and Ernie nothing. I noticed a difference too in the way Royal condescended to Augusta and Sofy. She had had a husband and a throne while they remained spinsters. Towards Minny, who had married, she was far more respectful.

At the beginning of October Royal began her slow homeward journey. Augusta and Sussex saw her off. The King, who had promised to say goodbye, stayed away at the last minute, indisposed again.

Sofy said, 'Gusta is in such a fury. She says her gout is every bit as bad as his, he just makes heavier weather of it. And you know, I quite agree with her. He should have said farewell to Royal. After all, none of us shall ever see her again.'

I said, 'That's a sad thought.'

'Not at all,' she said. 'She's grown insufferably smug. If I had heard another word on the glories of Ludwigsburg I should have screamed.'

As the days shortened Garth and I left off our walks in the park and stayed by his fireside. He seemed aged suddenly. What self-discipline and a sober life had kept at bay had been undone by Tommy's reckless goings-on. Creditors left unsatisfied, Sofy's name mentioned in caricatures, and Georgiana Astley consigned to limbo, for her husband had been refused the divorce he'd sought and her lover couldn't afford to keep her.

Sir Herbert Taylor had prepared an offer. Tommy might

have twelve hundred pounds a year, for life, if he signed a pledge never again to apply to Sofy for funds, never to communicate with her and never to speak to others of their connection.

'Too harsh,' Sofy said. 'A boy can't be asked to cut himself off from his mother or starve.'

But John Conroy's advice prevailed and for once I agreed with him. Tommy was no poor, motherless boy. He was a grown man who would stop at nothing to have his own way.

'Besides,' I said to Sofy, 'when does he ever visit you, except when his pockets are empty?'

'Well,' she said, 'he is so often in Leicestershire, Nellie, and that's a great distance away, you know.'

Such nonsense. Anyway, Tommy put his signature to the document without agonizing too long over the sacrifice. Then, almost immediately, he thought better of it. He said Sir Herbert had placed him under unfair pressure to sign at once or the offer would be void. Day after day he wrote, arguing his case and seeking another interview with Sir Herbert. He received no reply.

I saw the toll this took on Garth.

He said, 'I must see him settled. I can't be long for this world and I must know Tommy is provided for. This house will be his when I'm gone, but there'll be little else.'

I said, 'Perhaps he should work for his bread instead of begging it? How does he think others live?'

He looked at me, perplexed. It was a reminder of what different worlds we came from.

I said, 'He could go to India. I've heard that's one way young men solve their difficulties.'

'But Nellie,' he said, 'he does have a claim, as you well know. And then, there's Lady Astley. She may have acted rashly, leaving her home, but a lady cannot be blamed for being seduced. We must think of her. What if a child were to be conceived?'

It was the closest I ever came to quarrelling with Garth. Wearing himself to a shadow over that thankless rip. I had little sympathy for Tommy and I raged against Ernie Cumberland who came out of it all too lightly. I raged on behalf of Sofy who could not condemn him and Garth who would not.

One afternoon when I arrived at Grosvenor Place I found Garth in a kind of fever.

He said, 'I've made a decision, Nellie. I've sent for Tommy.'

He had papers, bundled on his table and tied with a string. Over the next hour we sorted through them and put them in some kind of order. Singly they were just letters, jottings, a few receipts, but together they told a story: that Tommy's father was the Duke of Cumberland. When Tommy came the next day Garth put the papers in his hands. He believed they would help bring Sir Herbert to heel and persuade him to tear up the promise Tommy had signed in haste.

He said, 'I should have done it sooner, Nellie. Those papers have hung about me like a millstone. I'm relieved to be rid of them.'

I said, 'But what about Sofy? Tommy doesn't have your niceness. If he allows everything to be generally known it will be terrible for her.'

He said, 'I wish Her Royal Highness no ill, but she has ever protected Cumberland's name. So let them sink or swim together. Herbert Taylor's a cunning fellow, though. If he settles reasonably it need never come out. Tommy can use those papers to secure his future. Indeed I hope he writes to Taylor this very evening. The sooner this is tidied away the sounder we'll all sleep.'

But Tommy didn't apply directly to Sir Herbert. He went instead to Mr Westmacott, the proprietor, editor and chief gossip merchant of Miss Tod's Sunday extravagance, a news sheet called *The Age*. And upon hearing this Sir Herbert Taylor became suddenly available to meet Tommy or his counsel and to reconsider the bargain that had been struck.

35

From April until September I hardly saw Sofy. Ernie Cumberland was in town and a frequent caller at Kensington Palace. I had no wish to be in his company. The reason put about for his return to England after so long an absence was the Catholic question. Ireland was boiling with rebellion and it was said Catholics must have the vote or there would be war but the King, who had seemed sympathetic to the idea, began to waver. The Duke of Cumberland had come to put some spine into him, to warn him that if the Catholics were indulged the shade of old King George would surely rise from its Windsor vault to haunt him. So Ernie divided his time between Windsor, where he urged the King to grind Ireland under his heel and save us all from Popery, and St James's, where he could keep a discreet eye on the case of Tommy Garth.

Sir Herbert put a fresh offer to Tommy: his debts cleared and three thousand pounds a year for life in exchange for surrendering the documents Garth had given him. An agreement was reached but before the capital fund was set up Sir Herbert insisted that the papers be sealed and lodged in a safe place. Garth suggested the chambers of Tommy's counsel in Lincoln's Inn but Tommy, put too much at his ease by the thought that his money troubles would soon be over, preferred to deposit them at Mr Westmacott's bank. He was given no receipt.

Through the summer of '28 I was Garth's daily companion.

'Nellie!' he'd call, when he heard me at the door. 'Come in and divert an old fool.'

To be with him was as easy as slipping into a pair of old shoes. But I could see that his anxiety over Tommy was robbing him of his health. First, Tommy was called out by Lady Astley's aggrieved husband. When Garth heard about it he reported the challenge, hoping to have Tommy arrested before a shot was fired, but by the time the meeting place was discovered and the constables had arrived Tommy and Sir Jacob had kept their appointment, shot wide and managed not to kill each other, and had both left the scene. There was worse to come. Sir Herbert Taylor seized on a providential opportunity.

The Age was known to be solid in its opposition to the Catholic vote. So was Ernie Cumberland. This was important common ground between adversaries, and when a matter of great national importance is at stake the influence of a royal duke is far more important than passing loyalty to a royal bastard. Charlie Westmacott, owner of *The Age* and custodian of Tommy's vital papers, was bought.

The King and Parliament battled all through that year.

Whenever the Catholic question was raised he'd threaten to leave England to the priests and go to Hanover, but it was an idle threat. He could never have travelled so far. There were many days when he didn't leave his couch. Breathlessness deprived him of the pleasure of racing at Brighton, kidney pain kept him from watching the chases at Goodwood, and when Vicky Kent's daughter, Feodora, was married at Kensington Palace dyspepsia prevented him from leading her in, as he had promised to do.

Feodora's husband was Prince Ernst, a Hohenlohe relative of Billy Clarence's wife, Adelaide. It was reckoned to be a good match. Prince Ernst was apparently free of the worst vices and his estates were in Langenburg, which removed Feo from the English stage. She was a very pretty girl and there had been a growing concern that she would out-dazzle Victoria. I couldn't see the difficulty, myself. Victoria had other qualities, far more useful in a future queen. She was strong and healthy and she had just the right endowment of wit; enough to deal with politicians but not so much that she'd find court life unendurable. In any event Feodora was apparently happy to marry Prince Ernst and Victoria's champions were relieved to see her go. She was to be a neighbour of Royal, though not for long. Royal died in October, drowned by her own dropsical waters. She was buried in the vault at Ludwigsburg.

As Sofy said, 'And then there were four. Royal and Amelia. Our bookends are gone, Nellie.'

She didn't mourn. Actually, she seemed quite gay, for she

believed Sir Herbert had tidied away the problem of Tommy, and John Conroy could be depended on to find diverting new projects for whatever was left of her money. Rather I was the one touched by death. I came home from Kensington one afternoon and found Miss Tod, composed but lifeless in a fireside chair. She was a very great age, for she had remembered the old King's grandfather, who was George II.

Sally said, 'Now you must come to us. This house is too big for one.'

I said, 'Then you move in with me.'

'Henry won't,' she said. 'He likes to be over the shop and Annie's closer to her work. It's easier for one to move than three.'

She was right, but I had no appetite for any more changes. My mind was entirely on Garth. I knew I wouldn't have him much longer. First our walks ceased, then our conversations dwindled. Often he would doze while I sat beside him and read, but if I got up from my seat and tried to slip away without waking him he would sense it and catch my hand to keep me there. I took him beef tea, I had Henry make him egg custards, but nothing tempted him.

'Waste of rations,' he'd joke. 'Broken down old nag. I don't merit my oats, Nellie.'

He seemed tired of life and yet did not know to quit it. I believe he clung on hoping to see an end to Tommy's difficulties, but Tommy was in a worse state than ever. He had received none of the funds Sir Herbert had promised and the papers, his great bargaining weapon, were in the hands of a turncoat. Westmacott held the receipt and the key to the safebox and would not surrender them. There could be no clearer sign of Tommy's desperation than that he had applied to Chancery for relief. The Court of Chancery was and is a graveyard for litigants and a screw press for filling lawyers' pockets.

Spring arrived and with it returned Ernie Cumberland, twirling his moustachios. He said he had come to dissuade the King from caving in to the Catholic faction, but he had other business. When he wasn't at Windsor browbeating the King, he was in town conspiring to silence Tommy Garth. Everywhere there was talk of the action Tommy had begun in Chancery, and whispers about a scandalous secret he threatened to reveal. Sofy's name wasn't spoken but the hints were heavy. In *The Age* Westmacott wrote in defence of his new master. Gossip about the Duke of Cumberland, he claimed, was a vile falsehood put about by those who feared defeat of the Catholic Bill. The *Standard* asked, 'Who is this Captain Garth? The Duke of Cumberland knows nothing of him.' *The Times* published the figure of £3000 a year, promised by Sir Herbert in exchange for the contents of a certain box.

As Henry Topham said, 'Three thousand a year. I wish I had such a secret to sell.'

I feared Garth would be dragged into the affair and called to give evidence and I said as much when Tommy came to Grosvenor Place one afternoon.

He said, 'He won't be troubled. I have such damning letters. York knew the whole business. The Queen knew.

And it wasn't just my mother, you know? Princess Amelia made allegations too.'

I said, 'But York is dead, and so is the Queen and so is Amelia. Who does that leave? Sofy mustn't be shamed to get you your annuity. And Garth mustn't be questioned. It would kill him.'

'What's that to you?' he said. 'He can't live for ever.'

He wanted me dismissed while he talked to Garth but Garth wouldn't have it. He said, 'You can speak freely before Nellie. She is my dearest friend. We have no secrets.'

Tommy said Herbert Taylor and Westmacott had tricked him out of his documents, therefore he had no choice but to speak publicly of the claim he had.

Garth said, 'You know I gave you those papers on condition that you'd never use them in any way to harm a certain lady's reputation.'

Tommy said, 'I surrendered them on condition I was given a fitting income. An agreement was made but I haven't seen a penny. That certain lady has it in her gift to help me but she does nothing. And what about Georgiana? She's a lady too. Why should she suffer?'

Garth said, 'Lady Astley had a husband. If she's thrown away the protection of marriage it's hardly Her Royal Highness's fault. This is a bad business, Tommy. I can't tell you how your mismanagement grieves me.'

'You might judge me less harshly,' Tommy said, 'if you knew what Taylor begins to say about *you*. He says you

357

tricked my mother out of her papers, then doctored them, out of malice, to destroy the Duke of Cumberland.'

Tommy was like a thwarted child. But at the end of the interview he took Garth's hand and promised to be careful of Sofy's good name. I confess I felt a twinge of pity for him. He did have a claim, of sorts, but compared to him Herbert Taylor and Ernie Cumberland were a pair of Goliaths. He seemed doomed to fail.

Garth was silent for a long time after Tommy had gone.

Eventually he said, 'Nellie, I believe I've made a great mistake. I should have claimed Tommy as mine from the start. I could do it now. Is it too late, do you think? Half the newspapers already have me as his father, and what does it matter? I'll be gone soon enough.'

I said, 'I think it is too late, and besides, why should you sully your own good name to save Cumberland's? You know, the outcome of this may be that he scuttles back to Hanover and never shows his face here again. The country might thank you for that. And changing your story wouldn't help Sofy. Nothing can do that.'

'No,' he said. 'That's true. And no one in their senses would believe it anyway. An ugly old devil like me? Who would ever have had me for a husband?'

So there it was, in an innocent little remark, in a closing note of self-mockery, the invitation I'd longed for and imagined. It hung between us in the twilight of Garth's drawing room but only I was aware of it. Garth was already thinking of tea. And for all the years I'd had to rehearse my lines when my moment came all I managed were tears. Men hate a woman to commence crying, I know. A weeping woman is a puzzle they've no appetite for solving. They'd rather have doors slammed and dishes thrown and be done with it.

I tried to master myself. Garth sat frozen.

All he said at last was, 'My dear.'

Then he said, 'It was an unpleasant conversation. I shouldn't have asked you to be witness to it. Forgive me.'

Now, I thought, go cautiously, Nellie Buzzard. Don't alarm a dying old man.

I said, 'Not at all. There was nothing said I hadn't heard before. It just saddened me to hear you speak of yourself that way. You're one of the kindest men I ever knew. I'm sure you would have been the best of husbands to Princess Sofy. Or to any other woman lucky enough to win your heart.'

He took my hand and raised it to his lips.

'Dearest Nellie,' he said.

Had I been twenty years younger I fear I'd have said more, grown bold and perhaps struck out for deeper waters, but it was enough. I felt at peace.

36

Whatever Ernie Cumberland did to oppose it, however many troops he mustered in Parliament and the press, the Catholic Relief Bill progressed slowly towards victory. The Duke of Sussex supported it, Billy Clarence was indifferent towards it. The King, wavering, feared it but recognized the inevitable and lay down and waited for its wheels to roll over him. Sofy pitied his situation.

'Poor King,' she said. 'It goes contrary to his Coronation Oath, you know, but Wellington means to wear him down and His Majesty is too sick to resist him. If he'd just listen to Ernie. He has all the arguments at the tip of his tongue. He should leave it to Ernie.'

Parliament passed the Catholic Relief Act in March 1829 and in April the King gave it his assent. I expected, hoped, that Cumberland would leave immediately, that he would want to put many miles between himself and the defeat of his campaign, not to say the matter of Tommy Garth's suit in Chancery. But Cumberland stayed on and, furthermore, sent for his duchess and his son to join him at Kew. He hoped to make a match between his son and Princess Victoria and so reinforce the crumbling walls of the House of Hanover, but Vicky Kent wouldn't countenance it. She loathed Ernie and anyway, George Cumberland and Victoria were still children, barely ten years old.

Sofy said, 'Little George is such a sad stripling. He's pale and thin and blind in one eye. The measles, you know? Major Conroy says he will never amount to anything.'

So that was the end of that. But Ernie's wife was very pleased with the outcome of her visit. Where she had once been ostracized by the old Queen, she was now welcomed warmly, by order of the King. She dined at Frogmore with Augusta and at Bagshot with Minny Gloucester and eventually took tea with Sofy at Kensington Palace. Sofy played her cards close.

Was the Duchess beautiful?

'I couldn't say. My eyes were very bad yesterday.'

Was she amusing?

'Her English is limited. My German is rusty. It would be difficult to judge.'

I was never in Frederica Cumberland's company, but I saw her being handed in to her landau one day and had an impression of loftiness. She was like a woman got up to play the part of a royal duchess.

Fritz Homburg died that spring and Elizabeth was left a widow. For years she had promised to visit England and Sofy quite expected she would now come, and stay for good. But with every letter she found some new reason to delay.

Humbug's brother had succeeded to the title so Elizabeth's rank was reduced to dowager, but she found she was by no means discarded. 'I find I'm as much needed here as I was when dear Fritz was alive,' she wrote to Sofy. 'Louis won't hear of my leaving.'

As Minny Gloucester observed, it wasn't Elizabeth that Louis Humbug feared to lose, it was her money.

Tommy Garth was still out of funds and Sir Herbert Taylor wriggled on the hook of the offer he had made. He said he had never actually read these famous documents. Nevertheless, without putting himself to the trouble of reading them, it was his learned opinion that they would have no value in a court of law and he had only offered to buy them to secure their destruction and protect the feelings of certain individuals whose names might be muddied by their mischievous publication. But Tommy Garth, he said, had now devalued his treasure by speaking of its contents to every one of his hunting friends. Therefore the offer was withdrawn.

It was a wretched, cold summer. I went to Grosvenor Place every day to sit with Garth and eat my commons with him, though all he took was boiled sago or a little rice pudding. He liked to talk about Dorset, the loveliest county in England, he believed, and I had no grounds to disagree. It was the furthest I had ever travelled out of London, and still is.

He had a fund of stories about the Dorset smugglers, 'owlers' he called them, and there was no romance to his tales. Garth was firmly on the side of the Excise and the Preventy Men.

'Armies must be paid for,' he'd say, 'and how's that to be done if tobacco goes untaxed, and brandy and tea? They call themselves free traders, but they wouldn't be free anything if law-abiding people hadn't paid their dues. They'd be under Boney's heel and speaking French. And they're savage men, Nellie, and their womenfolk too. They'll murder anyone who crosses them, even one of their own.'

That was how the seed was sowed for *The Owler's Daughter*, though a year passed before I began working at it. My writing life was something Garth and I never talked about. Caesar's *Gallic Wars* were his only reading and C. Welche was my secret refuge.

Sofy was a little jealous of my attention to Garth.

She said, 'Great heavens, how good you are. Old Garth has really done very well. He's had the joy of Tommy and now he's gained a devoted daughter without ever having the inconvenience of a wife.'

Sofy was feeling lonely. Billy Gloucester was away shooting grouse so Minny was making the most of her husband's absence and had gone to her country house. Ernie Cumberland no longer called at Kensington Palace quite so frequently either. While Frederica played the duchess at Kew he had a new interest. Her name was Lady Graves and she was no girlish sprig. She was in her middle years and had brought a vast number of children into the world. Her husband was one of the fattest men in England and one of the most pitied, for it was said that others had already been where Cumberland now trespassed and, so to speak, warmed the sheets.

The *Morning Chronicle* reported that a lady related to Lord Anglesey – Lady Graves was his sister – had been discovered by her husband, surprised in the arms of a person of the very highest lineage and no stranger to scandal. I was afraid the story would revive the embers of interest in Ernie's connection with Tommy Garth but it had the opposite effect. Tommy was forgotten and the Graveses were talked about everywhere. The public will always choose fresh meat over yesterday's fish.

At the end of September Garth's nephew and his wife called on him, to see how he did. He was quite his sharp old self after they had left.

'Well, Nellie,' he said. 'I suppose I had better be measured for my box. When relations drive fifty miles to take a glass of sherry wine with an old man, it's an infallible sign.'

The snow began in October. I didn't remember it ever having come so early. Sally left off begging me to move in with them over the Pink Lemon and nagged me instead not to walk about while the streets were so treacherous. But I did walk about for I couldn't be away from my Garth, and that was how I came to fall and crack my wrist, and I thank God every day I live that it was my right I injured and not my left, for people were tumbling like skittles and there wasn't a surgeon or a blacksmith to be hired. The best we could get was Jane Bunney, who had had a good reputation for her bonesetting before she went into retirement with her gin bottle. By the time she came my arm was red and swelled and she put me through an hour of torment, returning the broken part to its correct place and fixing it there with a piece of flour sack stiffened with egg-white and the end boards of Mrs Turner Smith's *Marchmont*. I never cared for the book.

All this was how it came about that my right wrist is now so twisted and useless and how I had only one good arm to wrap around my darling Garth as he died. It was a Monday. Tommy had been with him all night and was overcome with grief when he realized the end was truly near. There was no sign of his usual bluster. Garth kept asking was it morning yet. He seemed to want to see the sun rise, but even when the day broke the sky was dull and yellow with more snow. Tommy told him he was heartily sorry for any distress he had caused and Garth scrabbled about on the coverlet, searching for his hand. I should have liked one last moment alone with him but Tommy wouldn't leave his side.

I told him that I loved him with all my heart and I wished he would not leave me.

'Nellie,' he whispered. Then, 'Milady,' reminding me of the promise I'd made all those years before. Then he closed his eyes and never opened them again.

He was buried, Friday sennight, in the new vaults at St-Martin's-in-the-Fields. They hadn't yet been consecrated and I'd have preferred to see him taken to Bayswater Road where Jack Buzzard and my uncle and Morphew all lay, but it was for Tommy to decide, not me. And as it had to be St Martin's I was only glad he hadn't died sooner. They were clearing away the old burying ground for a grand new square to honour the victory at Trafalgar. He'd have been no sooner buried than dug up again.

No Royalties attended Garth's funeral. Sussex had a shaking fever, Ernie Cumberland had a head cold and His Majesty was too indisposed even to think to send an equerry.

Sofy said, 'To tell you the truth, the King is quite deranged. Minny says he keeps to his bed in a greasy old nightshirt and cannot do without his Bateman's Drops. He flies into a rage if he finds his bottle empty and no fresh one put in its place. And he's telling everyone how he rode Zinganee to win the Gold Cup. He gives them every particular of the race, furlong by furlong, but you know he didn't win any such race. He didn't even go to Ascot last summer. I'm terribly afraid for him, Nellie. What if he ends like our poor darling Majesty?'

That was a sad prospect. I'd seen enough over the years to dilute my affection for the King but I could never forget what he had been when I first knew him, how warm and kind, in spite of his splendour. Sofy was too worried for her brother to notice my grief.

'Well,' she said, 'Garth was a great age. He was "Old Garth" for as long as I can remember. But I'm glad Tommy was with him. It must have been a comfort to them both. And now I suppose Tommy won't be in such straits. I'm sure Garth will have left him something.'

In fact Tommy inherited the London house and fifteen hundred a year from consol bonds. Such furniture as remained at Piddletown was his too, though the house itself was rented, and also the contents of Grosvenor Place, after I had taken any pieces I especially wished to have. I chose Garth's leather lug-chair that bore the impression of his head, and a woollen greatcoat – not the one that had been my undoing with Enoch Heppenstall, but his favourite one, that had been with him in every campaign he fought. It had a faint smell of Hungary water.

But my principal legacy, a parrot that had never done more than tolerate me begrudgingly, was short-lived. She refused her food and plucked out her neck feathers and then, on the very day she was to come to live with me at Seymour Street, she disappeared.

The men had come from Bonhams to take away furniture for auction and the door was open for hours while the carts were loaded. I can only think she saw her opportunity and hopped out into the snow to die. May God and Garth forgive me, I was relieved not to have the care of her.

37

In the New Year, in that dull grey time when ballrooms fall silent and spring still seems a distant prospect, the news sheets returned to the topic of Lady Graves and her royal lover. The Duke of Cumberland had been seen leaving her Hampton Court apartments at an hour when ladies don't receive. But Sofy still wouldn't have it.

She said, 'Ernie only visits her to relieve her loneliness, I'm sure, for she never sees her husband. They say he's a horrid man.'

I said, 'Then Ernie would do better to send his duchess to see Lady Graves. You can't really be surprised if there's talk.'

She said, 'Those newspapers are determined to dislike Ernie. Whatever he does they'll always find fault with him.'

Even Minny Gloucester grew impatient with her.

'Nellie's right,' she said. 'Ernie invites scandal. He should at least install this person in town. To keep her so close to Kew is quite flagrant. A lover should be lodged at least seven miles distant from a wife. Everyone knows that. Well, Frederica has endured enough. She means to go back to Hanover as soon as the roads are fit for travel.'

But before Frederica Cumberland could escape the talk in London there was worse. Lady Graves's horrid husband was found dead. His throat was cut and his dressing room awash with gore. An inquest was convened, a verdict was reached that he had picked up the razor in an inexplicable moment of insanity, and he was buried, all in a single day. No Lord was ever so swiftly rubbed out. But the story was too tasty for the news sheets to cease picking over it. Had Lord Graves left any letter, any message for his many children? Why wasn't Lady Graves called to the inquest to give an account of how things stood between her and her husband? And what an unfortunate coincidence it was that yet again a royal duke was associated, albeit glancingly, with a death by razor.

No one went so far as to suggest Ernie Cumberland had wielded the razor, indeed Ernie was never named, but what other royal duke could it have been? Dolly Cambridge was in Hanover and neither Gus Sussex nor Billy Clarence had ever been connected with any violent death. And the speed and manner with which Lord Graves had been tidied away didn't go unnoticed. Unlike Mr Sellis, he wasn't buried at night at a three-went way. He was committed like a good Christian to the vault of the Hanover chapel-of-ease, just as surely as if he had died quietly in his sleep.

At Kensington Palace Ernie was held to be blameless.

Vicky Kent said, 'Ziss iss nonsense story. I can tell you, Frederica never did hear off ziss Lady Grave. Und who vill be loffer off Ernie? He iss ugly old man.'

Sofy said, 'He is *not* an ugly old man. He's still very

dashing. But anyway, all men have their needs and they have their ways of settling differences too. Why couldn't Graves have called him out? No blood need have been shed. They could both have mis-aimed. Taking his own life seems to me very mischievous of Lord Graves and quite unnecessary.'

I said, 'Perhaps Lord Graves loved his wife. Perhaps he despaired of winning her back from a royal duke.'

She said, 'Despair is a weak, unmanly thing, Nellie. Lord Graves should have had more spine. Now Ernie is blamed for everything and threatened and I don't know what. I hope he doesn't go away on account of this but I shall understand perfectly if he does.'

'You mean if Ernie doesn't show some manly spine?'

'That isn't at all what I mean,' she said. 'Ernie has the succession to consider. His life is precious.'

Which jolted Vicky Kent back to life.

She said, 'For succession ve heff Clarence und den ve heff my Victoria. For sure Ernie can go avay, bye-bye.'

But Ernie didn't go avay, bye-bye. Lady Graves moved back into town and after a few weeks he began calling on her again, to take tea, as Sofy interpreted it, with a lonely widow. Sofy was a little lonely herself and made great claims on me now that, as she put it, Old Garth didn't have me on a string. Even Gus Sussex didn't look in on her as often. Goosy, his long-abandoned wife, had finally given up the ghost so he now felt free to look about for a companion for his dotage. There was something dog-like about Sussex. When he'd married Goosy, contrary to law, the old Queen had beaten him with her scowls and threats and cowed him into giving up his wife and children, yet I think he'd never quite ceased dreaming of digging up his treasured bone. Why else did he not marry again until he was an old man and Goosy was in her grave?

In May Sofy talked of going to see the King and of my accompanying her.

'He never comes to town,' she said, 'and I should so like to see him. If only it were any other place but Windsor.'

His Majesty had been sounded and discovered to have a stone in his bladder. He had been leeched but without any relief, and laudanum didn't help him either. Perhaps he had grown too accustomed to it. So he avoided the jolting of a carriage ride and remained where he was. His ministers went out to Windsor almost every day and so did Ernie Cumberland, to whisper in his ear and warn him against any more reforming ideas, for what the Catholics had won others began to agitate for: a vote for every working man.

I was sorry for the King's pains and wished him long life, but I had no more desire to go to Windsor than Sofy did, and far less reason. In the event she didn't go. He had his sister Augusta close by at Frogmore and Minny, who often stayed with her, and a dozen doctors and apothecaries to care for him. I think we didn't understand how sick he was. He'd cried wolf so often we didn't pay much attention until Minny came to Kensington to give Sofy her report. The bladder stone, she said, was the least of it. He was bloated, like a dead sheep, and suffered terrible spasms that left him blue in the face. He was tapped every day.

371

'Pints and pints,' she said, 'but it doesn't help. He sleeps in his chair now and he's so big it takes three men to sit him on his night-stool. I fear for his life, Sofy, I really do. Billy had best prepare himself.'

If Billy Clarence was readying himself to reign he didn't show it. He was a regular sight around town, purple-faced, white-haired, swaying along the pavement as though he was still on the quarterdeck. Henry Topham knew one of the waiting men from Brooks's Club. He said Clarence made the windows rattle with his booming laugh and often he seemed to laugh at nothing, though of course his friends were always kind enough to laugh with him.

Henry said, 'I reckon he'll wear a straitcoat, that one, before ever he wears the crown.'

But less than a month later George was dead and Clarence was King. The Abbey bells began tolling at six. It was a fresh summer morning, full of promise. It didn't seem right that anyone should die on such a day and I must confess I shed a tear for my king. I'd been privileged to see the very best of him, when he was a young buck but kind, and yes, a little silly. It grieved me to think of what he had become. How he'd ruined himself with drink and gluttony, how spitefully he'd treated his wife, and how his people despised him to the point of no return. In the end there was no love for him, even when he lost his child.

I went to Sofy as soon as I was dressed. People were on the

streets already, making for St James's, hoping to catch sight of their new king. Kensington Palace was all a-buzz too. Vicky Kent and John Conroy were closeted in a state of high excitement for Princess Victoria was now the next heir and only eleven years old. Major Conroy was laying his plans for when Vicky might be called upon to be regent and he would be her indispensable chamberlain.

Minny was already with Sofy, more angry with the Kent carryings-on next door than she was grief-stricken for the King.

'Insufferable,' she said. 'Our darling has hardly been laid in his casket and that Irish fox is scheming.'

King George had died at three of the morning and had suffered very little at the end. Sofy wept, regretful that she hadn't gone to Windsor to see him, but Minny had no patience for that.

She said, 'Don't maudle. You could easily enough have visited him but I'm sure he thought none the less of you when you didn't. He didn't ask for you. He didn't ask for any of us.'

Cumberland, Sussex and Gloucester had gone to the palace ready for the proclamation and the King and Adelaide were on their way from their country house at Bushey. What a thing to wake up to. They had gone to bed the Clarences and risen king and queen. We heard the cannon salute at ten. King William IV was proclaimed at St James's, then at Charing Cross and Temple Bar and the Royal Exchange. That was June 26th 1830.

Sofy said, 'I wonder where they'll settle? Adelaide likes to live very plain, you know. I can't believe they'll go to the Queen's House.'

She never did learn to call the old Queen's house Buckingham Palace. King George had made a project of enlarging it, thinking Carlton House wasn't splendid enough for a king and St James's Palace was too gloomy but, as often happened with his renovations, he seemed not to know when to stop. Sofy was right. King William and his queen chose to keep Clarence House as their London home. And while the old King lay in state at Windsor the new King looked through the account books and planned how he would reduce his brother's establishment.

On the day of the funeral all places of business were closed, and from Gravesend to Windsor a chain of minute guns were fired from early morning until the hour of the burying. Sofy was in a peppery mood.

'I hate change,' was all she could say to explain it, and there was plenty of change to put her out of sorts. Billy Clarence, or His Majesty as I now had to remember to call him, had his faults but extravagance wasn't one of them. Secretaries and chaplains were sent away. Cooks and bandsmen and pages and stable grooms were thrown out of work. The menageries were broken up and the animals were sent to the new Zoological Gardens. Contracts with architects and builders were cancelled, horses were sold and great quantities of clothes, ordered by King George but never worn and certainly never paid for, were bundled up and returned to the tailors and linen drapers. And with a new King came a new government. The reformers saw their opportunity. King William was a man of the people. He'd served as a midshipman and had his royal corners smoothed. He would understand the country's mood. For how could it be right for the pocket boroughs to be represented in government when great cities like Manchester were not?

I tried to explain the reasonableness of it to Sofy. That those who add to the wealth of the nation should have the vote and be able to send their chosen man to Westminster.

'Oh dear,' she said. 'It sounds rather dangerous to me. I wish people would leave things as they are and not meddle. And do you know His Majesty's latest notion? He says he won't have a coronation. He says the Archbishop can just as well anoint him privately in the Chapel Royal without going to the expense of processions and robes and banquets. But how can he expect the people to respect him if they haven't seen him with the crown on his head? I just hope Adelaide can make him see reason.'

And Adelaide did. She was a dear, sensible soul, and never seemed to take offence if Vicky Kent mocked her plain looks, nor to resent the great tribe of children her husband had of Dora Jordan, though they hung about, full of expectations now their father was king. So at Queen Adelaide's insistence a modest coronation was fixed for September of the next year and His Majesty began to plan what he could do for his numerous Fitzclarences.

38

Tommy Garth was still in great difficulties. Herbert Taylor delayed in making him any payment on the grounds that he was by no means satisfied that all the disputed and sensitive documents were accounted for. What if copies existed? What if they fell into unscrupulous hands? For a man who discounted the truth of the story the documents told, for a man who claimed he hadn't even troubled to read them, Sir Herbert made a mighty meal of dragging out a settlement. And nearly a year after Old Garth's passing the will was still not proved.

In October the bailiffs found Tommy where he and Lady Astley were hiding from their creditors and he was arrested. I heard of it in the most unpleasant way: hammering at my street door late in the evening and a greasy messenger on my step, asking for money. Tommy had been taken to a sponging house in Clerkenwell and he needed funds to pay for his bed and board. 'Only assist me,' he wrote, 'until I can apply tomorrow to one on whom I have a true claim. Please do it for my dear departed guardian.'

I wasn't willing to put coins in the hands of the messenger. He looked the kind of varmint who'd spend it on drink and go back to the bailiff empty-handed, but I gave three guineas to the outdoors boy I shared with my neighbours and a shilling for his trouble, and he took it to the address in Skinner Street. I did it for Garth and I did it for Sofy, but mainly I did it because whatever Tommy has become, however wrong-headed he is, I can never forget holding him in my arms, only an hour old, and carrying him off in the dark to live with strangers. I never had a son of my own. Ambrose Kersie was the nearest I came, and Jack Buzzard saw him off. But I've seen enough of life to know any child can go to the bad, even the most wisely raised. So what chances then for one reared on whispers and hints and over-indulgence?

When I went to Kensington the next morning, the news had already reached Sofy.

'Don't worry, Nellie,' she said. 'Major Conroy and Sir Herbert have everything in hand.'

I said, 'Then I hope Sir Herbert moves faster than his usual snail's pace. Tommy only has a few days, you know. After that it'll be the King's Bench for him.'

She said, 'I'm sure it won't come to that. And anyway, I believe Old Garth left him quite well set up.'

Sofy had no idea of money, nor of the amount of credit allowed to a young man with connections, or the games lawyers play, always to their own advantage. It suited Sir Herbert and Ernie Cumberland very well for Tommy to go to gaol, and it suited John Conroy even better, for he had other uses for Sofy's money. On her birthday, though we didn't know it at the time, while we drank tea and ate the macaroons Henry Topham had made for her, Tommy was rowed across to Borough and incarcerated in Banco Regis. Lady Astley followed him there. She had sunk from a grand house on Grosvenor Street and a fine country mansion in Norfolk to a furnished room on Lant Street. She may have done it out of true love. I fear she did it because she found all other doors were closed to her.

Tommy must have imagined he wouldn't be in prison for long, that Sofy would soon have Sir Herbert rescue him. He settled for the cheapest accommodations and boiled up his own rations in the snuggery, the better to conserve what little money he had. If he'd been master of some trade he could have helped himself. If he'd known how to sew a seam or mend a boot he'd have been much better placed. Plenty of those locked up with him managed to live quite well on what they earned but Tommy was at a disadvantage. His only talent was for spending money and his only skill was obtaining credit.

The amount he owed was more than eight thousand pounds, a considerable amount of it due for horses and harness and livery. There were also lawyers bills, and there was the bind: the attorney acting to prove Garth's will wouldn't lift his pen until he was paid what he was already owed and without his inheritance Tommy couldn't pay him. Sofy was his only hope and that was no hope at all.

'Major Conroy is seeing to it,' was always her answer.

★

The thought of Tommy's predicament troubled me. Garth wouldn't have allowed it to continue, for Georgiana Astley's sake if nothing else. It was none of my business yet I felt I should do something, in his memory at least. I had no one to talk to about it. I knew what Henry Topham would say. 'Let the fool rot. Spare your tears for the tradesmen kept waiting for their money.' He was a man after Jack Buzzard's heart. And whatever Henry said, Sally agreed with. Miss Tod could have advised me, or even Morphew, but they were gone, and I was surely old enough to know my own mind. Still I dithered.

I turned to Annie. She was going on nineteen and risen to a full-pay teacher. I'd found too that she often thought along the same lines as me, and when we want advice we generally go to those who'll tell us what we want to hear.

'Grandma Nellie,' she said, 'I think you should take this man a little money but not too much. Then you'll feel better and so will he. And I think a prison would be something to see, for a person who writes stories, don't you? I think it would be very interesting. But you shouldn't go alone. I'll come with you and we'd better have a man with us, to protect us. I'll ask Mr Clearwell.'

I said, 'And who's Mr Clearwell?'

She said, 'He's the new master at Rose Street. He has brown eyes.'

Robert Clearwell did indeed have brown eyes, and a fine, sharp mind, but he didn't have a lot to offer as a bodyguard. I've seen more flesh on a sparrow. We went to King's Bench on Saturday morning, the first time I had ever set foot in Southwark, still less in a place of correction. We asked at the gatehouse and were directed across a crowded yard. We found Tommy Garth lounging against a wall with two other gentlemen in threadbare coats and frayed cuffs. He was thinner but he hadn't lost the old bluster.

'In expectation of relief any day,' he said, adding, 'a man couldn't ask for better company while he waited for his just dues.'

To hear him talk you might have thought he'd been admitted to Boodle's Club.

It wasn't easy to draw him away from his companions. He was so determined to appear at ease, as though we'd bumped into him on Berkeley Square and thought of joining him at Gunter's for an ice. I'd taken him fifty pounds, but I didn't want the whole yard to know about it. Robert and Annie understood my wish to speak to Tommy privately. They expressed an interest in seeing the prison workshops and tap rooms and so lured Tommy's friends away and left us alone for a while.

He asked after Sofy. I made excuses for her, that she was unwell and still quite undone by the King's death. That money matters were different for Royalties, especially princesses, who relied on their stewards to settle their accounts. The delay was regrettable, but not unusual.

'Yes,' he said. 'Of course.'

I said, 'What I don't understand is why you still don't have Garth's bequest. I know he left everything in good order. What does the lawyer say?'

'Sacked him,' he said. 'The man was a damned scoundrel. I shall hire another, as soon as my annuity is paid.'

He told me that what I'd given him would be enough to discharge what he owed his shirt-maker, and to buy coal for Lady Astley and decent dinners for himself for a month. His voice grew thick when he thanked me.

He said, 'The old man always said you were the best of women.'

Robert Clearwell was full of what he'd seen. Stinking privies and inescapable noise. Men three to a room unless you were a person of such consequence that the Marshal knew he could squeeze you for the rent of superior quarters of the State House. Annie harped on just one thing: a woman she'd seen, with a baby at her breast.

'Not her own child,' she said. 'Imagine, Grandma Nellie, sending your little one to be nursed in such a terrible place.'

I said, 'Well, mother's milk is mother's milk, even in King's Bench, and I suppose prisoners come cheaper than country nurses.'

Robert said, 'Yes. And if it puts a few coins in the woman's pocket. Better that than her plying the other trade. How else is she ever to get out of there?'

Annie said, 'If you ask me, creditors shouldn't allow people to get in so deep. There should be a law to prevent it.'

I could see at once that Annie and Robert were made for one another. Between them they knew how to put the world to rights. An education, the means of earning a living, a fair wage, and laws to regulate every occasion. Well, Tommy

Garth had had an education and none finer, if you rate schooling by the guinea per term. He had a profession too, if ever
we had another war. But it was the worst day's work ever
done when he was given to Garth and allowed to know his
origins. He should have been left in ignorance and raised by
the Sharlands to be a Dorset tailor.

First I'd hesitated to visit Tommy, then when I had done it
I hesitated to tell Sofy, but one thing I knew for certain. I'd
visit him again. I'd go for Garth's sake, I'd go to damn Ernie
Cumberland and all his works, and yes, I'd go because the
place was full of stories. We fell into a routine, Annie, Robert
and I, to go to King's Bench the first Saturday of the month.
Sometimes I took money, sometimes a piece of bacon or a
fowl, and shirts and stockings that had been Jack's and still
had wear in them. The second time we went Georgiana Astley appeared and what a sad, reduced creature she was, only
thirty years old but faded and gaunt with a great deal of silver coming into her black curls. That was what prompted me
to tell Sofy I'd been to see her boy.

I said, 'Herbert Taylor must release some money. Enough
for Tommy to pay the attorney and get his Garth inheritance,
if nothing else. As things stand, his situation is impossible.
And if you could see Lady Astley, cut off from her children,
cast out by her family.'

Sofy said, 'But Nellie, if only she hadn't been so impetu-
ous. I wonder if her husband could be persuaded to take her
back?'

'Too late for that, and anyway, I think she means to stick
by Tommy, whatever happens. I suppose she loves him.'

'Is she a beauty?'

I said, 'I believe she was, before she lost her teeth.'

She sighed, then changed the subject.

She said, 'Gus Sussex is to be married next week, you know. To Lady Buggin. I'm so glad for him. He's been alone far too long. I just wish he'd do it *properly*. He says he doesn't care a damn about Acts of Parliament, but he should consider his bride. I'm sure she'd rather like to be a duchess.'

Cissie Buggin lived not far from me in Great Cumberland Place. She was a fat, jolly little widow, fond of giving parties and a good paying customer of the Pink Lemon. To make her his Duchess Sussex needed the King's permission for the marriage and the King would undoubtedly have given it, but Sussex wouldn't ask. Perhaps the prospect brought back painful memories, of another king's refusal and poor abandoned Goosy and her children. Or perhaps it was an indignity too far, a man of fifty-seven obliged to apply to his brother. It seemed to me it was Sussex and Lady Buggin's private affair. Sofy's business was Tommy Garth.

I said, 'Just a little money, Sofy. It would make all the difference.'

'Yes,' she said. 'You keep telling me so, but things are difficult at present. Major Conroy says I'm over-extended.'

'But how can you be?' I asked her. 'You never buy anything.'

And at that moment her hearing failed her, as it did more and more frequently whenever a disagreeable question was asked.

★

383

Eighteen thirty-one was a strange unsettled year. Times were changing and I began to feel old. All the talk was of voting reform, and more than once the House of Commons approved the Bill only to have the Lords reject it, and at every reversal windows and heads got broken. Agitators were hanged and rioters were transported and not only in London. Every city seemed to be coming to the boil. The papers said the only thing for it was for His Majesty to create a great number of new peers, forward-thinking men who could be relied upon to vote the Bill in before the country burst into flames.

The King hesitated to do it, though he wasn't averse to ennobling Dora Jordan's children. His oldest boy became the Earl of Munster and was summoned to be an aide-de-camp. The middle boy was given command of the royal yacht, the youngest was promoted colonel in the Foot Guards, and the daughters, who had all made advantageous marriages, were raised to the rank of a marquess's daughter. The coronation, when it eventually took place, was a sober affair. There were no newly woven carpets, no cloth of gold or borrowed jewels, and no banquet. This was good for business at the Pink Lemon, for while the King and Queen went back to Clarence House for a plain roasted chicken every hostess in London gave a seated dinner in honour of the occasion.

Sofy was out of town. Elizabeth's long-threatened visit from Homburg had finally begun. She was staying with Augusta and Sofy had gone to Frogmore to see her so I was free of any obligations on Coronation Day. I went with Annie and Robert and their Rose Street pupils to Whitehall to see the King and Queen ride by on their way to the abbey.

'This is Mrs Buzzard,' Robert told the children. 'In her lifetime Mrs Buzzard has seen three kings. Who can name the two who came before King William?'

They all could. They knew their Georges. But they gazed at me like I was Methuselah.

I said, 'Not only that, Mr Clearwell. I've been in the presence of every one of their Majesties and their Queens and spoken with them too.'

Those children looked at me as though I was one of the wonders of the world.

I said, 'And who will reign over us next, after King William? Who knows that?'

That had them thinking. One little lad ventured, 'The King's boy?'

Annie said, 'The King doesn't have a son, nor a daughter. No, it will be Princess Victoria. When her uncle King William dies we shall have a queen.'

It was comical to listen to them chewing over that. The boys thought the King had better get himself a son and quickly, the girls thought a queen was an excellent idea. The procession, such as it was, left me feeling flat. I'm no lover of extravagance but I wished the Majesties had put on a little more show for those children. A fat old man in an admiral's uniform, a lady in a plain white gown and grubby diamonds. Where was the majesty in that?

Sofy returned from Windsor scandalized at the size of Elizabeth.

'Every bit as fat as Royal,' she said. 'She puffs and wheezes.

How do they allow themselves to grow so big? She's as sweet-natured as ever, but what do we have to say after all this time? Nothing at all. Augusta will soon find her too confining. You know how Gusta loves to go for vigorous walks and Elizabeth can't take a step without her cane. I suppose we shall all be expected to take our turn at entertaining her. Well, let her go to Minny first. Perhaps by then she'll be homesick for Homburg.'

But Elizabeth stayed on and on, into the spring of '32. Then events in London made her long for the peace of her little German kingdom. The House of Lords rejected the Reform Bill yet again and there was rioting such as we hadn't seen since the days of poor Queen Caroline. Many people closed up their town houses and went into the country and there was a week when the banks ran out of ready money. Ernie Cumberland was pelted with mud when he came to town to vote and Cumberlands made of straw and rags were burned on a few street fires too, or so I heard, and Wellington and any other Lord who opposed manhood suffrage. Annie, who attended meetings and read pamphlets put out by Mrs Wheeler, had become a very advanced thinker and believed that the Bill went nothing like far enough, that women should have the vote too. Her father used to laugh at her.

He'd say, 'And dogs and horses. Why should they be left out? Then the kitchen cat'll start agitating.'

Sally despaired of her. She said, 'She'll end an old maid. What man is going to want her, spouting off her silly ideas?'

But I never worried about Annie. For one thing, Robert

Clearwell encouraged her in her thinking and he loved the ground she walked on, and for another, there are worse fates in life than being an old maid. Minny Gloucester could have attested to that, rattling back and forth between Bagshot and Piccadilly to make sure of always just missing her husband.

In June the Reform Bill was passed, by a squeak, and perhaps more out of the Lords' fear of the alternative than of their being convinced of its rightness. So anyone in possession of a male member and property worth ten pounds had the vote and the country was pulled from the brink. The danger then was that women and other lowly beasts might commence agitating for the same. My Annie is convinced the day will come and though I shan't live to see it, I hope she's right. Women have run behind men with a bucket and broom long enough. It seems only fair they should have their turn at making a mess of the world.

39

As Sofy's eyes grew cloudier and sewing became impossible she decided she would embark on a programme of intellectual improvement, and that I should join her. She had Mrs de la Motte come in twice a week to read to her from Marivaux but as I hadn't a word of French I made it my business always to be occupied on Tuesdays and Thursdays. On Wednesdays Herr Krause was asked to come in to improve our German and I decided I would take up that challenge, though Sofy and I were starting from very different places. She knew a little of the *Hochdeutsch* her mother had spoken and her brothers had been obliged to learn; I remembered only my parents' mix of Low Saxon and Brabant Dutch. Still, Herr Krause did the best he could with us, and what we lacked in grammatical correctness we made up for with merciless impersonations of my papi and the Illustrious Personage. Gus Sussex's wife, Cissie, heard our laughter and said she had half a mind to join us, we seemed to have so much fun.

I went to Kensington one afternoon and found Herr Krause leaving, our lesson cancelled, and John Conroy barring my way.

'Her Royal Highness,' he said, 'is with the eye doctor.'

Sofy had woken that morning completely blind in one eye. I said I would wait. Conroy said in all likelihood the surgeon would couch the eye there and then and Sofy wouldn't be well enough to receive anyone.

I said, 'Nevertheless I shall wait. I've been with Princess Sofy through every infirmity since she was eleven years old. *Every* infirmity.'

He took my meaning well enough.

He said, 'If you insist. Though I can't be answerable for how long that wait may be.'

I said, 'Of course. I understand your position perfectly, Major. What you are answerable for and what you are not. I wonder though, with your great influence, that you can't ensure something is done for Captain Garth.'

'I believe Herbert Taylor deals with that person,' he said.

'He does. Except nothing is ever done. The Captain's situation is very bad. I've seen it for myself. A sum of money was agreed that has never been paid, and as you seem to hold the key to the coffers you must surely be answerable for that. Her Royal Highness tells me she's out of funds and yet I can't remember the last time she ordered a new gown. She did mention properties she thought of buying, but I think it was a passing fancy. She has no need of houses. She rarely stirs from this apartment. And anyway, I never saw her put her name to anything. Well, you would know. So I think she must certainly have sufficient to help Captain Garth in his distress. Unless some unscrupulous rogue has robbed her. But of course that could never be, when she has you guarding her affairs so carefully.'

There was nothing to be read in his face, though he had a ruddy Irish flush on his cheeks. I had made my point but we both knew I was powerless. He was in thick with Vicky Kent and Sofy, and Cissy Sussex was half in love with him too. Well, every dog has his day and John Conroy didn't waste a moment of his.

Sofy's eye wasn't couched. The surgeon said it was a perilous procedure with a far from certain outcome and he couldn't recommend it. He advised her only to preserve the sight in her remaining eye by leaving off all reading. The damage done to women's health by novels, he said, was greatly underestimated. They overtaxed the eyes, aroused the appetites and wasted valuable time. He said he wouldn't have them in his house. He had a wife and daughters to protect.

She said, 'Pompous old humbug. I shall still be read to, Nellie. I rather like to have my appetites aroused and as for time, I have vast amounts of it to waste. I wish you would write me stories, like you used to when we were girls.'

But I was writing Tommy Garth's story and I had no intention of sharing that with her.

Tommy gained some relief later that year. With a little help from me and from those few friends who pitied Lady Astley, he was able to pay the attorney and receive part of his inheritance from Old Garth. He discharged what he owed his

London tailor and a horse veterinarian in Leicestershire, and was able to move out of the room where he'd chummed with two others and move into the Select. You might think it an extravagance that he should have used the extra shilling a week to reduce his debts, but I believe he made a wise choice. The same week that Tommy moved to the State House there was a death on the stinking staircase he had just quit: a case of cholera, and it wasn't the last.

Sally had a terror of infection. She begged me to cease going to Southwark.

She said, 'If you stop going Annie will stop too.'

I doubted that. Annie and Robert liked to look into all the worst stews and shambles and discuss what must be done about them. It was their pleasure, their Vauxhall Gardens.

Then there began to be talk of cholera in other parts of the city. They said it came in with men from the North Sea colliers, and by Christmas there were fever boats on the river at Wapping. Sal and I had words.

She said, 'You must stop going to that dreadful place. What is it to you if that old man's boy is in there? He brought it on himself, spending what he didn't have.'

I said, 'I know that, but the way he was raised is the cause of much of it. He was encouraged to have expectations, then nothing came of them. I go there because his guardian's dead and gone, and it would break the old General's heart to think Tommy had been forgotten.'

'You and that old man,' she said. 'I swear you showed him more consideration than you ever did Jack.'

And of course the truth of that stung me so hard I hit back. I called her an ignorant, ungrateful wretch and told her Jack's words, that if I wanted to bring her from the Foundling Hospital I must pay for her food and keep myself and not expect anything from him. That brought tears to her eyes, for she'd loved Jack and oftentimes called him pa, and he'd loved her in his funny, begrudging way. So we parted on bad terms and I had cause to regret it because the next day she took ill.

Annie came to Seymour Street, to find out why Sally and I had quarrelled.

I said, 'It's the prison visiting. Your mother thinks it'll be the death of you and I'm to blame for putting the idea in your head.'

'Mother forgets I'm a grown woman,' she said. 'But I hate you to quarrel, especially when she's feeling so low. Go and see her, Grandma Nellie. Make your peace.'

Sal had a stiff neck, Annie said, and her throat was sore. I went to the Pink Lemon next morning and took her a bottle of Lucas's Drops and a piece of red flannel for the stiffness. Henry was in a fine old mood. He had an order from Lady Haddon for candied chestnuts and a great sugar-work candelabra and he needed Sally to mind the shop.

He said, 'I suppose we've you to thank for this. You're the one who's in and out of prisons. She was all right before she called on you.'

I said, 'And how can I be to blame? I'm not sick. I'll help in the shop till Sally's right again.'

'You will not,' he said. 'There's no telling what pestilence you're carrying.'

Sal's throat was swollen. I went down to the ice pit and brought her chipped ice to suck on.

I said, 'We shouldn't fight.'

And though it pained her too much to talk she smiled. It was clear she was glad I was there. I sat with her till Annie came home from her work.

'Ah,' she said. 'Peace has broken out. Good.'

It was Peter, Henry's apprentice boy, who came to fetch me. The watch was crying three o'clock as we crossed Oxford Street, not a soul about and there was a fine rain falling.

The wind was gone out of Henry's sails. He said, 'She's worse, Nellie. Her breathing's very laboured.'

Robert Clearwell had gone to fetch a doctor. I said, 'Why didn't you send for him sooner?' But I knew the reason. Money. Just like my Jack, Henry Topham wouldn't spend it until he had no choice. They weren't kin, but by God they could have been.

Annie said, 'Father thinks it's cholera. He's worried word will get round.'

He said, 'Don't look at me like that, Nellie. I've a business to think of. Something like that could ruin a man.'

Well, any fool could have told him it wasn't cholera, nothing like. With the cholera everything runs through you like water. I went in to Sally. She was red hot to the touch. Her breath was putrid and she struggled for every breath. I held her in my arms while Henry paced the floor and Annie waited on the doorstep, keeping watch for Robert. It was after four when he returned, with a surgeon he'd roused from his bed on Audley Street, a dithering old wreck who should have taken down his brass plate long since. He said it was as bad a case of quinsy as he had ever seen and while he fumbled about, preparing camphor vapour and laying out his lancets, my darling girl turned blue about the lips and expired.

I call her mine. She wasn't mine by blood, and she had never called me 'Mother', only 'Aunt Nellie'. But Jack and I were all the family she ever had and she'd never showed the least resentment of her lot, never wondered who her mother had been or why she had left her at the Foundlings. Whether I did for her all that a natural mother would I cannot say. I think I did well enough, but it seems the memory of that last silly quarrel will never leave me. Just when I think I've conquered it I turn a corner or open a door and it springs out at me: 'You and that old man. I swear you showed him more consideration than you ever did Jack.'

We buried her at Brompton Road, in the grave where her sons lay, feeble little souls who'd had no interest in breathing. Henry opened up the Pink Lemon the next day and took his grief into the kitchen. Annie did her best to be rational, as recommended by Robert Clearwell. We are born to die and if we don't the world will soon be so crowded we shall have to stand on each other's shoulders. Sometimes, though, she came to me in the evening and we enjoyed a good irrational weep together.

★

394

It was quite expected that Annie and Robert would marry. They were together every working hour and many evenings too, and they never seemed to quarrel. They were an earnest pair, fond of reading and debating, which I do commend, but I wondered never to see any little touches of longing between them. Those late years with Garth had made me regretful of what I'd missed. And then there was the case of Sofy, primed and brought to a fever of passion by Ernie Cumberland, then cast aside, ruined, without any hope of being loved again. I wanted everything to be right for Annie. They waited six months after Sally's passing.

Annie said, 'Grandma Nellie, I have something to tell you.'

I'd guessed it, of course, but not what followed. The marrying was to take place in a meeting hall. There'd be no wedding gown, no flowers, no clergyman. Robert had joined the Society of Friends, Annie intended to follow him, and they were to take up posts as teachers in a Quaker school in Stoke Newington.

I said, 'I shall never see you.'

She said, 'You would if you lived with us.'

In Stoke Newington! The very idea! It must be eight miles out of town if it's an inch.

I said, 'You know I'm not suited to country living.'

'Well,' she said, 'you might if you tried it again. Better than staying here alone.'

I did think of that, of course. This is a big house. I'd offered rooms to Georgiana Astley but she preferred to stay at Lant Street, to be close to Tommy she said. And not to run the risk of turning on to Portman Street and seeing people she used to count as friends.

I promised Annie I would go to Stoke Newington when her babies came, to help her with her lying-in.

'Oh,' she said, 'that won't be any time soon. We have work to do. Robert uses an assurance cap. He buys them at the barber's shop, so there won't be any babies until we're ready for them.'

I thought, well, if there's to be no clergy and no babies I wonder they're bothering to marry at all, but I said nothing, at least, not to Annie. I picked it over with Sofy instead.

She said, 'A wedding without a vicar? I can't believe it's lawful. And wherever Stoke Newington is, you mustn't go there. How would you ever come to Kensington?'

Chiefly though she was interested in the preventing of babies. She had never heard of Dr Newman's prophylactic sheaths. She declared that if she'd known of such a thing she'd have taken a dozen lovers, and still would. She had no idea what a comical sight she made, dry and shrunken, peering out from her lace cap and talking of taking lovers. As her sight failed we'd grown closer in one respect. She was too blind to see her reflection and I still avoided looking-glasses as I had done all my life. We both knew we must be growing old and lined and whiskery but between us we either couldn't or wouldn't see it.

Robert and Annie named the day. May 5th 1834, which was her twenty-second birthday. The marrying was to take place in Finsbury, at a meeting room in Bunhill Fields, after a period of silent contemplation. I asked Henry his opinion.

He said, 'They're a queer pair and no mistake, but if it's what they want. I'm not one for a lot of churchifying, as you know. And we don't have to be there till five o'clock so I shall only have to close up for half a day.'

Annie wore her blue sarsnet gown and her everyday mantle. No bonnet. But she did carry Sal's old kid-skin gloves and she humoured me by borrowing the garnet bracelet given to me by Garth. There was no procession, no giving away. We sat for an age, with no sound but the creaking of chairs and Henry Topham cracking his knuckles. Then suddenly – I suppose the spirit must have moved them – Annie and Robert got to their feet and married themselves.

'Friends,' he said, 'I take this my friend, Cornelia Ann, to be my wife, promising to be a faithful and loving husband to her until it shall please the Lord by death to separate us.'

'Friends,' she said, 'I take this my friend Robert to be my husband, promising, with divine assistance, to be a faithful and loving wife to him as long as we both shall live.'

Then they shook hands.

As Henry said, 'All the way to Bunhill Fields for that.'

And for once I agreed with him. We rode back into town together, as silent as a Quaker wedding, then as we got to St Giles's he said, 'Nellie, you may as well know. I'm going to marry Grace Messenger. She's a butcher's widow from Woodstock Street.'

Well, I knew Grace Messenger. I knew her when she was married to Bardwell who kept two rag and bottle shops. She seemed to turn a good profit marrying tired men with thriving businesses.

He said, 'It's been more than a year, since Sally. I'm not cut out for being on my own.'

I said, 'Yes. I see that.'

'Grace is a good woman. She's clean and cheerful and she's careful with money.'

'Does she have children?'

'None living,' he said, 'but she's only thirty-six so I have every hope. Not to find any fault in Sal, but you know I always wished for a lad to carry on the business.'

If Grace Messenger was only thirty-six I was the King of Spain's daughter.

I said, 'You're an old man, Henry, to be starting again with babies. I'd leave it to Annie and Robert. They might give you a boy to learn the sugar work.'

He said, 'I wouldn't depend on that. They'll be too busy setting the world to rights. Anyway, I'm not so old. There's life in this dog yet.'

I didn't want to hear any more about that. I could see what would transpire. He'd marry Grace Bardwell Messenger, she'd ride the lovesick fool to death and the Pink Lemon, that Jack and I had struggled and worked for, would be hers for the price of a few midnight tumbles.

I began to think I had lived too long, but here I am still.

40

A memoir is doomed to end with a recital of death and decay, unless the writer believes the history of her life to be so compelling she plans for it to run to several volumes. I have one last story to tell and only set down this list of the departed to clear the stage for it.

Billy Gloucester died, which was a loss for his gamekeeper and his ghillie but a triumph of survival for Minny. Mrs Fitzherbert died, and no one noticed. Henry Topham died, not from an excess of love as I'd predicted but from the bullying and badgering of his new wife and the two grown men who appeared directly after the wedding and identified themselves as her previously unmentioned sons. The business and the rooms above it were sold before the earth had settled on Henry's grave. It's a poulterer's now, with cockerels and pigeons hung up where the sign of the Pink Lemon used to swing.

I never really cared for the place. I disliked its sweet smell and I had unhappy memories of being chained to its front counter in the early days, liable to be jerked out of my thoughts at any moment by the jangle of the shop door opening. Nevertheless, I cried a little when I heard it was sold and even now I take care not to walk that way, if I can at all avoid it.

So much for those who passed unmourned. Then there were those who went before their time. By 1834 Tommy Garth was near enough solvent to be allowed to live outside the confinement of the King's Bench gate but 'within the rules' as they call it, on Lant Street. Nature took its course and before the year was out Lady Astley was carrying a child, a daughter. She was born in the summer of 1835 and named for the mother she would never know, for within a week Georgiana Astley was dead. It was given out in the news sheets that she'd succumbed to scarlatina but it was childbed fever that killed her, in a mean house in Southwark, and in the arms of a man who wasn't her husband. The Astleys and Georgiana's own family were powerful enough to make sure such embarrassing facts weren't broadcast in *The Times*.

In this sad way Sofy became a grandmother, though she never saw little Georgiana nor even asked about her. Fate, on the other hand, brought me closer to my granddaughter. Robert Clearwell was lost in the great snow storm of '35, walking home from a meeting of the Anti-Slavery Society. It was the same death that had claimed my Aunt Hanne and they say it's a gentle way to go. Robert was a young man, though, with his busy life before him. For a time my Annie was quite unhinged by her loss. In these cases the Quaker way is to give thanks for a joy received, to trust in providence, and then continue along life's path without faltering. But Annie wanted to put on mourning clothes and rage against God, and so did I. I brought her from Stoke Newington to be with me at Seymour Street.

There are others, more illustrious, whom time has gathered in: Elizabeth Homburg, Frederica Cumberland, Gus Sussex, and of course, the King. But I'm running ahead of my story. In 1837, or perhaps it was '38, I met a man called Ernest Jones. It was after King Billy had died, that much I know for sure, because Victoria was on the throne and John Conroy, understanding that his Kent goose was cooked, had become even more attentive to Sofy. He hardly left her side. And it was Conroy who foisted young Jones upon me one afternoon, to get him out of Sofy's drawing room.

'I believe Mrs Buzzard is something of a scribbler,' he said. 'You should ask her advice.'

It was at Vicarage Place. Sofy had gone there after a hole in the roof had finally brought down the ceiling plasterwork in her apartments and obliged her to leave Kensington Palace. The Royalties and their suite were all on the move anyway, as happens whenever a sovereign dies. Our new young Queen had gone to live in Buckingham Palace and had taken Vicky Kent with her. Victoria was still very young, but she understood only too well that her mother had better be kept on a short tether. John Conroy had been kicked upstairs to a baronetcy and told to stay away. With King William dead, Adelaide moved out of Clarence House and became a wandering, childless dowager, visiting friends in their great houses, a month in this county, a month in that, but never grand or demanding, always easy to satisfy. Princess Augusta, who had begun to find Frogmore cold and lonely, took over Clarence House, and Dolly Cambridge, who hadn't been in England for twenty years, brought his family home and opened up his house in Piccadilly. He was no longer needed as viceroy in Hanover. Its ancient laws prevented Victoria from reigning as its queen which, as far as I was concerned, was as much our gain as their loss. It meant that Ernie Cumberland had succeeded as their king and would trouble us no more. So that was how things stood.

Ernest Jones was Ernie Cumberland's godson. His father was Major Charles Jones, who had served beside Ernie many years in the Hussars and then in his household in Hanover. The Major was now in poor health and living in Marylebone. It was a fine afternoon so after we left Sofy's house Mr Jones and I walked together across the park. He was a pleasant young man, I suppose no more than twenty years old. He had already had a number of his poems published in Hamburg and now wished to try his hand at novelizing. My advice was to learn a useful trade first, like the pulling of teeth, something that could always be depended on to provide an income, and then to turn to writing.

I said, 'I'm the last person you should apply to. Each book I write sinks faster than the one before. No publisher will deal with me now except I agree to pay their losses. But it may help to be a new name. That's the most encouraging thing I can say to you. The reading public soon grows bored and books aren't like great monuments, you know. They're soon pulled off the shelf to make room for something new. Pulp to paper and back to pulp.'

'Oh,' he said, 'but what about Miss Austen? What about Sir Walter Scott?'

Well, Walter Scott wrote himself to death and still left his bills unpaid, and as for Miss Austen, I could have disliked her for the way the public had taken up her books so avidly, but she was fifteen years in her grave before they did it and it would be a pitiful thing indeed to envy the dead.

I supposed he had gone to Vicarage Place looking for a patroness.

I said, 'If it's funds you're seeking I can tell you Her Royal Highness won't help you. Everything she has is spoken for.'

He said, 'I didn't go there to beg. Not exactly. I went to ask her to intercede. It's my father, you see. His investments have failed and he finds himself in great need. He applied to the Duke of Cumberland more than once, but the Duke, well, I must remember to call him King Ernest now, but King Ernest doesn't reply. And my father said of all the Royal Highnesses still living Princess Sophia has the most influence with the Duke, with King Ernest.'

I said, 'I don't know that she has any influence there. Rather the opposite. She dislikes any criticism of her brother.'

We passed the Powder Magazine and out of habit I turned to take the path to Stanhope Gate.

He said, 'You don't go the most direct way?'

I said, 'I like to walk. But you mustn't feel obliged to accompany me. Young men are always in a hurry and old ladies are not.'

And then I said, 'To tell the truth, Mr Jones, I avoid Cumberland Gate. I dislike any place or person with that name attached.'

'Ah,' he said. 'That *is* interesting.'

He saw me to my door.

He said, 'My father doesn't go about much. His health is quite broken down these days. But I wonder though if you would think of calling on him? He has a story, concerning the Duke, concerning King Ernest. In the right hands I believe it might help him get the pension he deserves.'

'You've been in Hanover, so you've no reason to know the story is common knowledge here. I'm afraid it wouldn't be worth a farthing.'

His face fell.

He said, 'You mean he's been named?'

'As good as. The child, Cumberland's natural son, or some might say his *unnatural* son, began an action in Chancery to be recognized and paid an allowance. Let me tell you, all it brought him was ruin.'

'A natural child?' he said. 'But all the Royalties have those. My father's story isn't about a child. It's about a crime that has gone unpunished.'

I took his card. Then I lay awake for many nights arguing with myself about what to do. Extortion is a dirty business.

It demeans those who practise it and it doesn't always succeed. Whatever mud was flung at Ernie Cumberland (I still cannot bring myself to call him King Ernie) slid off him. If all those caricatures about him – hinting at Sofy, mocking Lady Graves – if they hadn't shamed him when he was riding about London, why should any revelations trouble him now he was installed on a throne in Hanover? Could a sick old adjutant fleece a king?

There was Sofy to consider too, who could never, ever think ill of him. She had decided, back in 1800, to redraw Ernie, to make him her valiant cavalier, only prevented from being her husband by a pettifogging canon law. Making a hero of Ernie was her way of accommodating the sad facts of her life and I had given up disturbing whatever peace she'd found. And then there was Tommy. Fatherhood appeared to have made a man of him at last. He'd taken a modest house in Brompton and employed a nurse for little Georgiana, but I foresaw the risk that any new scandal about Cumberland might reignite his own hopeless claim for money.

Put together, these points were a strong argument against hearing what Major Jones had to say. But then, listening can be a neutral thing, done out of politeness, or to relieve the teller of the torment of secrecy. Repeating what's been heard, using it maliciously, inciting others to use it, *that* would be a wholly different matter. And so, partly suspecting Major Jones was a lonely old man who just wanted someone to talk to, and partly because I could never resist the promise of a good story, I set off one afternoon for Montagu Street.

41

A weakness of the heart had robbed Major Jones of any soldierly bearing or vitality but he wasn't so very old. I could
have given him ten years at least. He had fought in the cam-
paigns in Flanders and Corunna and at Waterloo. Then, after
the peace, he'd been summoned to Hanover to be Ernie
Cumberland's personal aide. There seemed to have been a
manly bond of affection between them, as is commonly the
case with army men. Garth had often spoken lovingly of men
who'd served under him.

Several times Jones paused from what he was telling me to
say, 'You understand, Mrs Buzzard, I have always tried to do
my duty. You understand, only need has brought me to the
point where this burden is too heavy for me to bear. My wife...'

His wife was a delicate, gentle person. She knew little of
the wicked ways of the world and was inclined to see everyone in the best possible light. This quality had allowed her to
ignore the gossip and become quite dedicated to Frederica
Cumberland. It was therefore unthinkable for the Major to
share with his wife what he was about to tell me.

Major Jones had arrived at Herrenhausen Castle in the winter of 1815 and found Ernie in a brooding, bitter mood. He'd been kept away from Waterloo and so deprived of glory in battle. He had been passed over for the vice-royalty of Hanover in favour of Dolly Cambridge. And, to heap insult upon injury, our new Queen Victoria had ruled that his dear duchess should never be received by herself or any of the Royal Highnesses. Ernie had nothing to do all day except fume and rant and find himself cruelly used.

The Major said, 'The Duke came to me one evening, very agitated. I thought he might have a fever but he wouldn't have a doctor sent for. He said he began to wonder if his misfortunes were a kind of judgment on him, that things he had tried to bury kept rising to the forefront of his mind and he had no friend he could confide in. He said he must have relief or go mad. What could I do but offer him my ear? He made me swear not to tell another living soul.'

I said, 'And did you?'

'Never,' he said. 'My boy knows a little of it. He believes I should profit from it, but as a last resort, you understand? I'd hoped His Majesty would remember my loyal service and help me in my difficulties. But Mrs Buzzard, more than that, I feel the need to share what I know, to dilute the hold it has on me.'

I said, 'I've known the Royalties since I was a girl. Nothing you tell me about Ernie Cumberland will surprise me.'

'Very well,' he said.

Then he sat in silence for an age, gazing into his cup. I

think he had to put up one last struggle before he surrendered his secret.

Eventually he said, 'It concerns an unlawful death. That evening His Royal Highness said to me, "Jones, I once killed a man, and now he haunts me." I replied that we were soldiers and it was our business to kill. "In war, yes," he said. "But not in the bed chamber." Then he gave me a full account.'

I knew at once what name I was going to hear. Joseph Sellis.

He said, 'It was many years ago. The Duke was a young man. In youth the appetites often outrun prudence. Is there a man alive who hasn't something foolish in his past?'

Well, when Sellis died Ernie Cumberland must have been approaching forty, which is stretching the notion of youth even for Royalties, who are famously slow to mature. I said nothing. The next part of his account was what seemed to give Major Jones the most trouble, far more than the slaughter or the covering up.

'His Royal Highness,' he said, 'had been tempted into perversion. I cannot say how it came about. Perhaps in drink. Perhaps an ungovernable urge after a romantic reversal with a lady. Or a bout of playful wrestling that had grown too warm. One can imagine that. The fact remains that he was discovered in a certain act, with a valet. The discoverer was another valet. It was an aberration, admittedly, but it was committed in a private household, not in some common molly house. The matter should have gone no further.'

I have heard that men do such things, though how it's achieved I have never managed to understand.

I said, 'You mean an act of sodomy.'

Poor Jones shuddered.

He said, 'I can only call it an ill-advised shirt dance.'

And so I heard, at second hand, Ernie's confession. Joseph Sellis had witnessed something he should not have seen and had tried to profit from it. He had threatened to go to the press, to the King even. Ernie had had no choice but to silence him.

I tried to recall what had been said about Sellis. That he was a *Sardinian*, yes, as though that alone were a hanging offence. But also that he had been a devoted servant, and a family man. His wife and children shared the advantages of his position. They had a comfortable place to live and perquisites. What more could Sellis have hoped to gain? The Royalties probably take as long to pay their extortioners as they do their tailors. And then, who would have believed him? If there was talk at all about Ernie Cumberland it was that he was a ruthless ladies' man.

Jones said, 'The Duke didn't act alone, you see. The valet Neale assisted him, the same that had been discovered... well... let's say no more about that. Neale arranged the items that were found by the constables: a lantern, a pair of cloth slippers with Sellis's mark on them, and the empty scabbard of His Highness's regimental sword. The wounds the Duke received were inflicted by himself, before or after, I don't know. And when the time came to raise the alarm, Neale played his part, word perfect. The worst of it is this: when His Royal Highness went to despatch Sellis he found he lost all command of himself. He was possessed by a rage he still cannot explain – "not myself, Jones" – those were his words. When the terrible deed was done he found he had attacked Sellis with such force, that he had cut him so deep, from ear to ear, that his head was almost severed.'

I had read something of the sort. It was the reason people had queued to see the body.

I said, 'Where is the valet Neale now?'

'In Kensington,' he said. 'Living quite high. His lips are sealed by a handsome pension.'

Poor Jones. Anyone could sympathize with his position. Neale, who had been an accomplice to murder, lived in comfort and he, who had done neither more nor less than hear a man's confession, had nothing.

He said, 'After the Duke had given me his account he seemed much calmer. He said, "I shall sleep tonight, Jones. Sellis has been haunting me these recent weeks. Every time I closed my eyes I saw his lolling head. But tonight I shall sleep. He's lost his power over me. I can feel it." Then he shook my hand and went very cheerfully to his supper. He came back to me twice before he retired, begging to be assured that I should never tell another person what he had told me. In the end he went off quite happy, and I saw a change in his mood from that day forward. So did the Duchess. He whistled. He was like a boy set free from school. But the torment that had weighed him down seemed shifted to me. In my dreams I saw Sellis with his lolling head, as though I had been there. I still do.'

I said, 'And now I suppose, so will I.'

I wasn't too fearful. I've never allowed dreams to trouble me and since my sister Eliza I'm very firm with phantoms. They may visit me for the first year. After that they must go to their glory. The rule seems to work. Papi I smelled whenever I sat at my desk. Laundry soap and Old Paris snuff. Morphew was on the back stairs, an unmistakeable blend of horse and beer and rancid wig. Sally I saw reflected in the window of the Pink Lemon. Jack Buzzard never manifested himself, perhaps because he didn't believe in such nonsense. And Garth? I neither saw nor smelled Garth, and yet many times that first year I knew he was there beside me, as sure as this pen is in my hand.

Major Jones asked my opinion. My advice was that if he needed financial relief he'd do better to invoke the comradeship of Waterloo and apply to Lord Anglesey or to Wellington himself. The Duke of Cumberland, the King of Hanover if you please, was a man any sensible person would avoid. I wasn't convinced though that Jones was sensible. He looked to me to be on the very brink of madness. I never saw him after that day and his story cost me no sleep. His son did cross my path again, but not for some time. First there is another Royal Highness I must lay to rest.

Our young Queen was married on February 10th 1840, to Prince Albert of Saxe-Coburg. He was a cousin, inevitably, and very young and green, but everyone was happy with the match. The wedding took place in the chapel at St James's Palace. Annie had no interest in seeing the procession, she thought it all bread and circuses. I would have gone down to the Mall if the weather had been kinder but as it was it rained without a break all morning so I took a growler to Kensington instead and sat with Sofy.

At about four o'clock Minny Gloucester and the Dowager Adelaide came in from the wedding breakfast and gave us their report. Victoria had worn white satin, with a veil of Devon lace and a garland of Kew orange blossoms in her hair. Albert was in a Field Marshal's uniform. Both had looked very bonny, everyone had remembered their place and their lines, and the Queen had seemed not in the least nervous about becoming a wife.

Minny said, 'Quite raring for it, I'd say. Not like when Royal married Fritz. Remember Sofy? She was so terrified she could barely walk.'

Sofy said, 'That was because she'd had A Talk from our Illustrious One. I'm sure she was expecting torture by strappado.'

'When in fact,' Minny said, 'in Royal's case, it was torture by being laid on by an elephant.'

Adelaide said, 'But Minnychen, tell about poor Gusta.'

Princess Augusta had shocked them by her appearance. Her face, that had always been round and rosy, was gaunt and grey, her arms were thin, and her belly was swollen.

'Und she eats nussink,' Adelaide said. 'Only liddle trink

off brandy. Oh Sosie, I sink Gusta iss ver bad. I sink ve lose her.'

And lose her they did, though she confounded all her doctors and lived fully two months longer than they said was possible, consumed by a growth in her bowels and whispering for more opium. Sofy and Minny were at her side when she died, and Adelaide and the physicians and Dolly and Gussy Cambridge too. There can hardly have been elbow room.

'A good sort' was the spoken epitaph from her surviving sisters. She had been a private, uncomplaining woman, a passionate gardener, a hearty walker, and an attentive aunt.

Sofy said, 'I think she was a saint. After Royal escaped our Illustrious One fastened on to her like a limpet, and you know, Gusta never complained. I think she just never longed for a husband.'

That wasn't my impression of Augusta. I hardly knew her but I remember very distinctly a late summer's day at Windsor . . . how many years ago? I lose count, but I know Tommy Garth was still a boy. The sun was low but hot and the King was sufficiently restored to health to be allowed to ride in the park. Brent Spencer was the equerry, most attentive to His Majesty, watching for any sign that the excursion was proving too stimulating. Spencer's eyes never left the King and Augusta's eyes never left Spencer.

42

Annie, who likes to investigate every new enthusiasm and anything that promises progress, decided we must try out one of the new railroads, to judge for ourselves whether rail travel has a future. We took a hansom carriage to the London Bridge Railway Station and then were forced to wait behind a closed gate while the first class passengers took their seats. Annie wouldn't hear of our travelling in the superior accommodations. It is her philosophy that if some people must suffer the wooden benches of life, we must all suffer with them. It's my philosophy that those who can afford a padded seat should buy one and those who can't should aspire to.

The gate was eventually opened and we were swept along in a great crush of people fighting for a place to sit. A young man took pity on me, otherwise I should have had to cling to Annie and hope that the sheer press of bodies would prevent me from falling over. At Croydon we changed to a different locomotive and a different line, but not before I had paid five shillings for a first class seat. Annie stuck to her communistic principles and stood all the way to Brighton.

They say the railroads grow more popular by the year but I don't know that I should ever be tempted again. It was faster than travelling post, but surely the point of travel is to see different landscapes, not to hurtle past them at thirty miles to the hour and plunge into suffocating tunnels. Admittedly there are no delays while fresh horses are put in, but we seemed to stop just as often to take on water for the locomotive, and if we didn't end the journey covered in dust we certainly came away from it with a fine coating of soot. I think the public will soon cease being enchanted by it.

It was thirty years since I'd been to Brighton, since Sal and I had taken little Annie there, to get away from the summer stench of London. An esplanade had been built along the water's edge, much like the one at Weymouth, and that was where the crowds now walked up and down. There were very few people on the Steine and the Pavilion was closed up. Tiles had fallen from its walls and the rose beds looked neglected. I was telling Annie how it had grown in my lifetime, from a small villa to a grander house and then to the most fantastical confection of a palace, when who should come strolling by with a young lady on his arm but Mr Ernest Jones. He recognized me at once.

'Mrs Buzzard,' he said, 'do you know this building?'

I said, 'I did know it. My father leased it for King George IV when he was Prince of Wales.'

'Oh, King George!' he said. 'Wasn't he a fat old soak?'

I said, 'The years weren't kind to him, but when I first saw him he was a fine young man. He cut a figure, I can tell you.

415

It was his doing that I was sent to be a friend to Princess Sofy.'

Mr Jones introduced his companion as Miss Atherly. He said they were soon to be married. Miss Atherly looked a good deal more pleased with herself than she did for making our acquaintance.

He said, 'I must tell you, I've recently published my first novel. Messrs Boone took it. Now I think of it I shall send you a copy. You won't find my name on it, mind. I'm going in for the law, you see, so I thought best to bring it out anonymously.'

I said, 'I congratulate you on all counts. You'll have the satisfaction of seeing your words in print without the irritation of people telling you how you might have done it better. And with lawyering you're guaranteed never to starve. How is Major Jones?'

He said, 'My father passed away this past winter. A tragic accident.'

A mishap whilst cleaning his pistols, apparently. I condoled. We parted, he and Miss Atherly in the direction of the seafront, Annie and I towards the tea gardens.

'Major Jones?' she said. 'Another of your old military beaux?'

'Yes,' I said. 'Yet another.'

It was too tangled a story for explanations.

I thought what a very careless way it was for a soldier to die. Cleaning a pistol without emptying its chamber first? More likely I'd been given a version of his death suitable for telling in front of Miss Atherly. And then, a week later, after a signed copy of *The Wood Spirit* had been delivered to my door, I thought, well, God is good. At least the poor, mad soul didn't live long enough to have to read *that*.

When Sofy told me that Ernie was coming to England I had no reason to think I would see him, and yet something urged me to make sure I did. There were two purposes to his visit: a wedding and a christening. Dolly and Gussy Cambridge's daughter was getting married to a Mecklenburg cousin, a grand duke who was as rich as Solomon, and Ernie loved any opportunity to play the king in front of his German neighbours. Also, our queen's new baby was to be christened and Ernie had been chosen as one of her godfathers. Princess Alice was the Queen's third child and she's had three more since, though I don't know why. She doesn't seem to like any of them very much. Perhaps she means to continue until she gets one she can love.

King Ernie duly arrived but within a week there was a quarrel. It was all about the order of seating at a dinner Minny Gloucester gave in Piccadilly. Ernie said he must take precedence over Albert because a King of Hanover certainly outranked a Prince Consort, and the Queen said if Minny gave way to Ernie's demands neither she nor Albert would attend. It was an easy decision for Minny. She loved her Queen and she adored the Queen's babies. She wasn't going to risk her place in their lives just to humour old Ernie. So Minny stood firm and then, seeing the way things tended, Ernie announced he wouldn't go to the dinner and furthermore, he wouldn't go to the christening to be insulted. Dolly Cambridge had to stand proxy.

Sofy said, 'It's so difficult. I'm very fond of Albert but Ernie is a king after all. Albert doesn't even have a dukedom.'

I said, 'Yes he does. He's a Duke of Saxony.'

'Oh but, Nellie,' she said, 'that doesn't count at all.'

In the two weeks between the christening and the Cambridge wedding Ernie seemed to recover his sense of proportion, at least until after the marriage vows had been exchanged. Then a genteel tussle had occurred when Ernie tried to sign the register ahead of Albert, but our little Queen had overmastered him and gripped the pen tightly until she could put it in her husband's hand. But as the wedding party formed up to process to the breakfast, a most unroyal scramble had broken out.

Minny said, 'What do you think! Ernie quite jostled Albert out of the way, and Albert, I will say, stood very firm, but they processed far too quickly and glued shoulder to shoulder, each of them determined not to give way to the other. It was too shaming. Well, actually, it was rather comical.'

Sofy said, 'That was naughty of Ernie. Of course he's perfectly correct. He *should* take precedence over Albert, but sometimes we old ones must be prepared to save the blushes of the younger generation. And you know, Minny, we must make allowance too. Ernie isn't at all himself since Frederica died.'

★

A few days later I saw the King of Hanover for myself when he walked into Sofy's drawing room. His hair was thinner, his face more livid and his eyebrows more prodigious, but in temper he seemed to me to be entirely unchanged.

Sofy said, 'Darling Majesty, you remember Nellie Buzzard.'

He didn't say he did, he didn't say he didn't. I don't know whether Sofy hoped I'd withdraw. She peered for him with her one dim eye and grasped his hand, and I kept my seat and observed him. He was quite the king, even if all he had was Hanover. Of them all, of the seven Princes who lived to manhood, he's the one that has the steel, the bearing. Sooner or later the others all ran to blubber and silliness.

I said, 'I've become acquainted with a godson of yours, Majesty. He was named for you too, I imagine. Ernest Jones. The late Major Jones's son.'

I saw the name hit its mark but I rattled on, just like the railway journey I described in tedious detail and how it had taken me to Brighton where I'd learned of the Major's demise. That registered too.

I said, 'I once met Major Jones. I liked him very much. He was so full of wonderful soldiering stories. Such a sad end, but not unexpected considering the tortures he'd endured, wouldn't you say, sir?'

Sofy said, 'What tortures? And who was Major Jones? Did I know him?'

I reminded her of the day young Ernest Jones had called on her but she couldn't call it to mind.

I said, 'He'd come to ask you to intercede with His Majesty for a pension for his father, but Conroy headed him off, of course. You know how Sir John likes to protect you from supplicants. So I took him out of your way. We walked across Hyde Park together and he told me a little of the Major's story. People do that, you know. When they learn that a person is a writer of fiction they often come out with a splendid tale that deserves to be published, indeed they keep meaning to write it up themselves but somehow they never find the time. Well of course, I couldn't resist. I went to see the Major, to hear the dreadful details from his own lips.'

Sofy took the bait. What 'dreadful details', she wanted to know.

'Damned lunatic,' Ernie muttered. 'Had to send him packing. You don't want to hear Jones's ravings, Sofy. Fine soldier but he went to the bad. Battle fatigue.'

I said, 'But you'll be glad to know he made a kind of recovery. He wasn't raving at all when I saw him. Quite the opposite. He was very composed, but oppressed. And when I heard his story I understood why. A murderer had confessed to him, Sofy, confessed all to relieve his own conscience and then sworn him to eternal secrecy. Well, who could endure that? I lost a little sleep myself, wondering if I should report what I'd heard to a constable, but then, I thought, that was the Major's prerogative, and as long as he lived I should leave it to him.'

Sofy said, 'But Nellie, if the Major's dead I think you *should* tell a constable. After all, the murderer is still free to strike again. If you know his name you must report it, then we can sleep more safely in our beds. Do you know his name?'

I said, 'I do. But he's an old man by now, and settled overseas. I'm sure we're quite safe from him. And I take a deal of comfort from the thought that soon enough he'll stand before his Maker. Better for him to be required to answer to God Almighty than to a mortal officer of the law who might bungle the affair.'

Sofy shivered. I kept my eyes on Ernie and he never once looked at me, but his cheek twitched and the jutting eyebrow above it, like a great rippling silver caterpillar.

He jumped up and said, 'Can't stay, dear one. I promised Dolly I'd call on him. But I'm going to send you Hildegarde Groote for a companion. You'll like her. You can practise your German. It'll be better for you than listening to gossip about murders.'

Sofy said, 'You're very good to think of it, but you know I have my readers, and I can't be without Nellie. She comes here in all weathers and she keeps me very cheerful.'

When I stood up to leave her I found my legs had been turned to water by my pretty little speech to the King of Hanover, and that instead of my customary route across the palace gardens and over the Long Water into Hyde Park I turned onto Kensington Gore and hailed a hackney. I'm not a woman given to nervous imaginings but Ernie's cold-eyed parting had made me think of deserted paths and shrubberies and cut-throat razors.

43

Gus Sussex died in April of '43 so Cissie Buggin, or Her Grace, Cissie Inverness as I must remember to call her, didn't have him for long, but she has borne her widowing with a smile.

'We were very happy,' she said. 'And nothing is for ever. I'm content.'

By rights he should have gone to the vault at Windsor but he knew they'd never allow Cissie to lie beside him so he had left precise directions with Dolly Cambridge that he was to be buried at Kensal Green, with space for Cissie, when her time comes.

Sofy said, 'Nellie, I need your help. I want to rewrite my will.'

I said, 'Tell me what you want and I'll set it down, though I wonder you ask me. I thought Conroy was your man for such things.'

'He is,' she said, 'but I don't know when he'll come back from the country and I'm liable to die at any time.'

Well, which of us is not?

Sofy lived in the dark but her mind was still sharp. She knew by heart all the small bequests she'd made and none of those were to be altered. There was nothing for Tommy, nothing for little Georgiana. She simply wished to stipulate that she should be buried at Kensal Green.

She said, 'I was buried years enough at Windsor. You know, I always dreaded the idea of being taken back there, to be lowered into that charnel house, but until Gus died I didn't realize I was allowed to choose a different resting place.'

That was Sofy. Sixty-six years old and in many ways still like a nervous child. Was this permitted, was that permitted? She'd seen so little of the world it seemed not to occur to her that she'd committed one very great transgression and no thunderbolt had struck her down. So why worry about receiving Gus Sussex's natural daughter or ringing for tea a little earlier than usual?

There was no drawn out suffering for Sofy, I'm glad to say. She escaped the family curse of dropsy or Augusta's costive agony and slowly faded away. Whenever Minny was in town she would take her for a ride in her carriage or bring one of the Queen's little ones to sit on her knee. She longed to be useful, and for a while Cissie Inverness had her filling bags with lavender flowers but more lavender landed on the floor than in the sachets. It was not a great success. Ladies still came to read to her, though she had less and less staying power for a story and often fell asleep. Mainly she liked conversation, and sometimes we would make quite a coterie. Cissy Inverness, Minny Gloucester, Gussy Cambridge. Three duchesses and one humble companion. When we were so many Sofy said very little but she listened intently, leaning forward, not to miss anything.

When it was just we two she loved to talk, chiefly about men. Did I remember a page called Cake? Or a gardener called Blinkhorne? And what about Henry Halford? She asked me one day about Jack Buzzard. Had he been the love of my life?

I said, 'I think you know he wasn't. But he was a good steady husband. I've nothing to complain about.'

She said, 'I believe I know who you'd have preferred.'

I said, 'I doubt it.'

'Oh yes,' she said. 'I do. It was that stable hand from Piddletown. What was his name? Ezekiel? Ephraim? It was something very biblical.'

I said, 'It was Enoch, and you couldn't be more wrong.'

We agreed to toss a sixpence. If it fell to the head I must tell, if it fell to the reverse I could keep my secret.

'I'm trusting you now, Nellie,' she said. She had no choice. She was quite in the dark by then. But when old King George landed face down, I found I was disappointed. I wanted to tell her how I'd loved Old Garth.

She refused to believe it, of course.

'No, no, no,' she said. 'Don't tease me now. You promised to tell the truth.'

And even though I offered to swear it on the Testament I know she never took me seriously.

'But he was old,' she said. 'And *so* ugly. I remember when you thought he had been *my* lover. I had bad dreams for weeks. No, you must come up with someone more plausible. He'd better stand six feet in his stockings and have a firm, manly chin.'

I had no intimation that the end was so near. She had become the kind of desiccated old lady that can last for ever, like a dried fig. On Thursday I sat with her for an hour but she was very tired.

She said, 'I'm an old bore today, Nellie. Come on Monday. I promise to be livelier by then.'

We'd been bottling gooseberries, five pounds of red and ten of white. I don't know why we do so many for there's only me and Annie to eat them, but I still take a kind of comfort in a shelf of preserves. I was standing in the cool of the larder admiring the look of them when a messenger came to the street door. Sofy was dead.

Gussy Cambridge had been with her, and Mrs Corcoran, her dresser, and the chamber nurse. I went directly to Vicarage Place. Doctor Snow had been, confirmed the diagnosis and left. Minny Gloucester was there, and Dolly Cambridge, very teary and blowing his nose. Another sister gone.

Minny said, 'I was with her this morning. It never crossed my mind.'

Gussy said, 'But she vent vair easy, like she vass aslip.'

Dolly said the Queen wished to be informed of the arrangements.

'Windsor, of course,' he said. 'So the only question is when.'

425

I said, 'No, not Windsor. If you find her will you'll see she wanted to go to Kensal Green.'

They didn't like it. Dolly shook his shiny dome of a head. Kensal Green!

I said, 'It's not as though she's the first.'

I helped Mrs Corcoran to wash her and put her in a cambric winding sheet and we sat with her through the night, with eau de cologne on our handkerchiefs and a fly tormenting us. At ten the next morning Minny returned with the Cambridges and the search was begun for Sofy's will. Everything was gone through, though that didn't amount to much: books she'd still liked to have read to her, a few pictures she'd kept though she couldn't see well enough to make them out, and her old sewing table she hadn't used in years. She'd perched in that house like a little bird that was too tired to flutter any further.

It was wrong of Dolly to shout at Mrs Corcoran. A lady's dresser may know a great many things but she couldn't be blamed for not knowing where the will was kept. John Conroy was the man they needed to ask about that, but the very mention of his name brought on one of Gussy's nervous sinkings.

'Oh Dolly,' she whispered. 'I beg you vill not send for him. Zey say if you look in his eyes he kenn bevitch you.'

Minny said, 'What nonsense. Have him come at once.'

I agreed with Minny. I'd looked John Conroy in the eye often enough and all I'd seen was the glitter of other people's money. Some people said he was the Devil incarnate but in my opinion he was just a regular scoundrel. On the subject of Conroy Sofy and I never did agree. Personally I'd no more have trusted him than I would a rat in a coal hole but in all matters financial she deferred to him. He was sure to know where her will was lodged but he couldn't be asked. He was out of town, visiting his estate in Montgomeryshire. Then Mr Drummond came from the bank with the vital document in his hand and the burying at least was settled.

Dolly Cambridge was Sofy's executor, he and Minny her residual legatees.

He said, 'Very simple, very straightforward. Just a few modest bequests.'

Drummond said, 'Just as well, sir. Her Royal Highness spent rather freely these recent years. There's very little left.'

Dolly said, 'Spent on what? I never knew anyone live as modestly as Sofy. Has someone been fleecing the old girl?'

I said, 'I can tell you Tommy Garth got nothing. Conroy and Taylor saw to that.'

Gussy Cambridge said, 'Who iss Tommygart?'

Then a terrible hush descended. I'd said the unmentionable and drawn attention to my strange position. What was I? Not a servant, not family, not a suitably noble attendant. Mrs Corcoran would be dismissed, the doctor would be paid, but what was to be done with Nellie? There were no rules concerning a humble companion. I was something left behind by Sofy, like the felt slippers worn to the shape of her feet, and it was time for me to be disposed of. As I descended the stairs for the last time I heard Dolly say, 'Less than two thousand pounds! Then where has it all gone? There should be three or four *hundred* thousand at least.'

I met Cissie Inverness at the front door. Another encumbrance for the Royalties but not one they can so easily dismiss. Gus Sussex had married her before God but he did it without the King's permission and that made all the difference. Was she a duchess? Sussex certainly thought so. Could she be a *royal* duchess? Never in a month of Sundays.

'Nellie,' she said, 'what a sad day. But I'm glad to hear she'll be buried near my Gus. I shall go there too, of course, in time. We shall be neighbours again.'

So indeed Sofy was buried at Kensal Green. It's a pretty place, with lawns and winding walks and birds singing. These new garden cemeteries are quite the fashion.

As we drove back along the Harrow Road Dr Snow returned to the subject of my connection with Sofy. He thought the idea of a humble companion for a princess was a singular theory.

'King George,' he said, 'must have been more of a thinker than is generally allowed.'

I said, 'Yes, I believe he was, when he had his health. The Queen was too tired to interest herself in how they were raised. Fifteen children, it's no wonder. But the King was quite attentive to a great many things.'

Dr Snow said, 'And did you ever see him?'

I said, 'I saw him as close as I am to you, and conversed

with him, and ran away from him once as well, when he seemed not quite himself and I was afraid of what he might do.'

'Ah yes,' he said, 'his indisposition. An interesting case.'

'An interesting case? Is that what they say about it now? I can tell you the physicians were at their wits' end. They thought whatever it was would kill him and ruin them. Still, they lived to prosper.'

'And the King lived to a good old age.'

I said, 'There was nothing good about his old age, and I'll tell you something else. I knew the two who came after him, George who was the Fourth and then King Billy, and neither of them was right, not in the constitution nor the head. There was a weakness in them all. Well, now we have a queen to reign over us, which I think is a good thing for women are often made of stronger stuff.'

He said, 'And the idea of a companion like yourself was to give the Royal Highnesses an insight into the lives of the humbler classes? A very advanced theory.'

'Well I wasn't so *very* humble a companion. My father kept a house on Soho Square. I'm talking of sixty years ago, when it was a good address. But King George was a husbandman and a horticulturalist, you know. I think he was testing the old saw that if you grow an onion or two in the cabbage patch they'll help to keep the worm away. It's a pity he didn't think of it before Princess Sofy. Some of her brothers might have benefited from it.'

'I see,' he said. 'You were the onion in Princess Sofia's

cabbage patch. Really very interesting. And was the experiment repeated?'

It was not.

I said, 'After Sofy there was only Princess Amelia and by then His Majesty's mind had begun to cloud. It wouldn't have suited Amelia, anyway. She'd have driven any humble companion to distraction. It was a long time before she could be convinced I wasn't going to give them fleas and steal their horses. And I don't know that the plan worked, even for Sofy. There was certainly one worm I failed to keep away. Her Royal Highness never did grow very worldly but I became her friend, which is an entirely different and better thing to be than an onion.'

Epilogue

My grandmother, Nellie Buzzard, wrote this story and left it in my hands. She said it was a true account of her dealings with the Hanovers, who were the biggest tribe of oddities she ever knew and therefore required no author's fanciful embellishments. As to whether it should be published, she was entirely indifferent. She was the author of three novels, brought out without any fuss or fanfare under her maiden name, C (for Cornelia) Welche. It was better that way, she said. My grandfather thought writing was a mischievous waste of time and she never had the slenderest hope of persuading him otherwise.

Grandma Nellie's books gained her complimentary notices and some modest earnings, but in her final years she claimed she had nothing new to say and the world would thank her for sitting quietly by the fire with her tea kettle and her memories.

I'm partial. To me she was a dear and admirable grandmother, so in the interests of accuracy I have consulted others who still remember her, as to her true character. Here is how she has been sketched: forebearing, impatient, retiring, outspoken, a cruel mimic, a kind friend, tough as an almond shell, and soft-hearted enough to give you the cloak off her shoulders. It seems to me to render a good likeness.

She died in her sleep last Whitsun Eve. She was eighty-one and was wearing the treasured garnet bracelet she had lent me for my marriage day.

Annie Topham Clearwell
April 1857

Read on for a note from Laurie Graham
about her research and inspirations for
A Humble Companion

How *A Humble Companion* came to be

I first heard of the strange lives of King George III's daughters long before I thought of writing *A Humble Companion*. Their father, poor mad George, was a figure well known to readers and theatre-goers, and the Prince Regent, one of their many brothers, had been much written about and caricatured. But of the six girls there were only thumbnail sketches and whispers, in particular concerning Princess Sophia.

For years my idea of telling Sophia's story gathered dust. I wasn't sure I could make the leap from writing contemporary comedy to historical fiction, but from time to time I'd take out my notes and wonder if I could do it. Its moment eventually arrived, and with it the need to do far more research than any previous book had required. The 18th century is a different country.

Fanny Burney became my companion, with her delicious diary observations of King George, Queen Charlotte and their enormous family. Then I had to revise long-forgotten history lessons — the story spans the reigns of four monarchs, the French Revolution and the Napoleonic Wars — and explore topics that my schooldays had never touched on: the history of ordinary people's lives, how they lived, what they ate, what they wore.

I had two early decisions to make. First, who was to tell the story? My preference is always for First Person narration. It imposes certain limitations, but for me those are more than made up for by its power to draw you in to the very heart of the action. The question was, who should that narrator be? I needed someone who could be close enough to make a credible witness to a royal story – so not a servant – but independent enough to have a life of her own, so therefore not a royal sister. A companion was the answer, someone who travelled between Sophia's cloistered life and the real world. And so was born Nellie Buzzard.

The second decision I needed to make was about the style of language. I have a horror of books written in fake Olde Englishe. Nellie was anyway a woman with a modern outlook on life, but I needed to beware of using anachronisms. I added the Shorter Oxford English Dictionary to the stack of reference books at my side. It has the very useful feature of saying when a word was first used.

A character needs a back-story. Even if, as in Nellie's case, she's telling the story from the perspective of an elderly woman, you still need to know where she came from and what shaped her. Part of that job was already done for me: the character of Nellie's father was based on someone who really existed and who worked in the royal household. Ludwig Weltje was major domo to the Prince Regent. He even has a street named after him, in Hammersmith, where he retired when his days of royal service were done.

So I knew the kind of milieu Nellie would have grown up in, but I needed a precise location. I spent a few days in London and, after much wandering around, I settled on Soho Square. In the late 18th century it would have had the right cosmopolitan mix of tradesmen, immigrants and professional classes to have appealed to a man like Nellie's father, a German pastry cook made good. Some of the buildings Nellie would have known are still standing and the little park isn't very much altered either. By the end of my location-seeking trip I found I was having to remind myself that Nellie was purely my invention. She was starting to take shape. And it was sitting in Soho Square among the buzz of lunchtime office workers that I first heard Nellie's voice and set down the opening lines of Chapter 1.

The other place I visited on that research trip was Kew and its modest palace that was one of the childhood homes of Princess Sophia and her sisters. It seems like an unlikely royal residence, but is quite in keeping with what we know of King George, a man who kept sheep and liked to wade into the Thames to chat to the basket-weavers gathering rushes.

Kew Palace is open to the public and some of its rooms are untouched by time, especially on its upper floors. I found it very easy to imagine the confined lives of the six princesses, kept on a short tether by a demanding mother and a father who couldn't bear to let them marry and go away from him. Historical Royal Palaces, the organisation that curates Kew, have installed a modern recording that plays in one of the corridors, and gives an impression of servants' footsteps, laughter, doors banging, and brings those empty rooms to life. If Sophia returned today she would recognise it without much difficulty.

The creation of Nellie was easy. I liked her and her company soon dominated my working day. Capturing Princess Sophia was a harder challenge. When there is little record of a historical figure's life and achievements, when they had no public presence, the only way to form an image of them is from the fossil-like impressions they made on those who were around them. The fall-out from her scandal certainly kept the royal lawyers busy.

Princess Sophia, the second youngest of the brood, was a ghostly figure in life, rarely seen, but she left behind her rich pickings for a novelist. Secrets are powerful things, though just how secret Sophia's story was is arguable. At least one caricaturist of the time made reference to it.

Nevertheless I had always to be mindful that in writing this book I was waking the dead. My aim, in Nellie's telling of Sophia's story, was only ever to follow where the evidence pointed. The fact that her cousin, Queen Victoria, eventually paid Tommy Garth an annual pension out of her own purse seems to me to be eloquent testimony to the truth.

It is one of my writing quirks that I like to create a minor character, a bit-player, who amuses me when progress is slow or I've hit a problem of plot. Some people have a desk toy. I have a Morphew. Characters like Dick Morphew are an example of the inexplicable, thrilling things that can happen when you're writing fiction. I have no idea where Morphew came from. He just stepped onto the page, growling and sniffing and scratching underneath his insanitary wig. He cost me no sleepless nights. He arrived perfectly formed and he still makes me laugh.

Towards the end of the process of writing a book I'm contractually obliged to start thinking 'what next?' Sometimes I'm undecided, but when I was wrapping up *A Humble Companion* I had no such doubts. A new voice, a generation younger than Nellie, had already announced herself. Nan McKeever's story, *The Liar's Daughter*, will be published later this year.

Reference Books

Daily Life in the 18th Century by Kirstin Olsen, (Greenwood Press)
Behind Closed Doors: At Home in Georgian England by Amanda Vickery, (Yale University Press)
The Complete Servant by Samuel & Sarah Adams, (Southover Press)

A Writer and Reader's Life

Laurie Graham

Why do you write?
It's an unstoppable habit. As a child who was a duffer at many things I discovered writing was something I could do with ease. Creating an inner world was and still is a seductive pleasure.

How do you write? On a page, or on a screen?
Both. I use A4 pads for planning and for trying to resolve problems. The rest of life tends to intrude and I end up with shopping lists and messages to myself embedded in my longhand writing. But when I'm really writing, when things are really flying, I love the speed and capabilities of my computer.

When do you write?
Always in the morning, sometimes on into the afternoon, but I take a lot of breaks. A morning without achieving something makes me uncomfortable, but the achievement is not necessarily 1000 words added to a novel. It may be 1000 words deleted. I work slowly.

What's a typical writing day?
No two days are alike. I generally have several projects on the go and although the current novel is uppermost in my mind I may have to lay it aside. Journalism jobs arrive out of the blue and are required yesterday. Or I might discover a hole in my research and need to spend a day reading. Life is very varied.

Best part of writing?
Sometimes, when a character's voice comes through loud and clear, or a scene just seems to write itself, I experience a physical, literally visceral sensation, like the flutter of adrenalin. You can't force it. It comes unbidden and disappears all too easily.

Worst part of writing?
The things that can happen after it leaves its mother's tender care. In the case of a book, ill-conceived packaging, or getting ignored by reviewers. In the case of journalism, getting mutilated in a hasty copy-edit. Letting go of control is hard.

What's the best piece of writing advice you've ever received?
The only advice I ever remember receiving was from my mother who told me to sit up straight and get a decent desk lamp before I ruined my eyes. But seriously, I've never sought advice because I believe writing is learned by doing it and by reading the work of masters.

What's the first book you fell in love with?

Delia Daly of Galloping Green by Patricia Lynch. I have it on my shelf here beside me. The descriptions of life in a fishing village were poetry to a girl growing up in the landlocked Midlands, and Delia, a tough little nut growing up in the shadow of a prettier sister, felt like a friend. I borrowed it from the library week after week. And never dreamed that someday I'd be living in Ireland myself.

What's the last book you read?

Another book from my childhood, John Masefield's *Box of Delights*. I'm revisiting a lot of those childhood classics with my grandchildren in mind. I'm now re-reading *The Eagle of the Ninth* by Rosemary Sutcliffe, the first book I ever heard dramatised for radio, back in the Fifties.

Which book do you wish you'd written?

A Handful of Dust by Evelyn Waugh. I think it's simply perfect.